W/D

B

The Omega Expedition

Tor Books by Brian Stableford

The Omega Expedition

BRIAN STABLEFORD

A Tom Doherty Associates Book • New York

This is a work of fiction. All the characters and events portrayed in this novel are either fictitious or are used fictitiously.

THE OMEGA EXPEDITION

Edited by David G. Hartwell

A Tor Book
Published by Tom Doherty Associates, LLC
175 Fifth Avenue
New York, NY 10010

www.tor.com

Tor® is a registered trademark of Tom Doherty Associates, LLC.

Library of Congress Cataloging-in-Publication Data

Stableford, Brian M.
        The Omega expedition / by Brian Stableford.—1st ed.
        p. cm.
        ISBN: 0-765-30169-5
        1. Immortalism—Fiction.   2. Life on other planets—
Fiction.   I. Title.

    PR6069.T17 O43 2002
    823'.914—dc21
                                    2002028577

First Edition: December 2002

Printed in the United States of America

0 9 8 7 6 5 4 3 2 1

For Jane, and all who fully appreciate
the bittersweetness of transience

Acknowledgments

A shorter and substantially different version of the narrative framing the text of this novel was published as "And He Not Busy Being Born . . ." in *Interzone* 16 (1986) and was reprinted in *Sexual Chemistry: Sardonic Tales of the Genetic Revolution* (Simon & Schuster UK, 1991). That story—the first of many recapitulating and recomplicating the future history sketched out in *The Third Millennium: A History of the World, A.D. 2000–3000* (Sidgwick & Jackson, 1985; written in collaboration with David Langford)—was the foundation-stone of the series of novels whose sixth and final volume this is, and of the larger enterprise of which that series is a part. I am grateful to David Pringle for its first publication, to various editors who have reprinted it, including Robyn Sisman, Sylvie Denis and James Gunn, and to Damien Broderick for his complimentary remarks on its composition.

I should also like to thank Jane Stableford, my first and best audience; Al Silverstein, for taking an interest; David Hartwell, for seeing the series through to its end; Ian Braidwood and Nick Gevers, for their altruistic attempts to promote the series; Bill Russell, for his constant support and enthusiasm; and Wolf von Witting, who will approve of the ending for all the wrong reasons.

Introduction

This novel is the final volume in a loosely knit series of six. The other five are all more or less independent, each one carefully constructed as a literary island entire in itself, but this one is different. In order to bring the project to a satisfactory conclusion the major narrative threads running through the series had to be gathered together and integrated into some kind of whole. For that reason, this volume is readable as a direct sequel to any one of four earlier volumes (because it carries forward the stories of characters featured in each of them) and forms a parenthetical pair in association with the other. The purpose of this introduction is to make adequate provision for readers who have not read all—or any—of the earlier volumes in the series, and to enable those who have to refresh their memories.

Volume one of the series, *The Cassandra Complex*, is set in the year 2041. It tells the story of the belated public revelation of an accidental discovery made by a biologist named Morgan Miller while conducting experiments in the genetic engineering of mice. Miller's discovery had allowed him to produce a number of mice whose life spans were much greater than those of mice produced by natural selection. Although he had some reason to suppose that a similar genetic transformation might have a similar effect in humans, the process had certain awkward limitations which discouraged him from reporting his findings, even to his closest friends, while he searched for a means to overcome them.

Having grown old without ever solving the problems associated with his life-extending process, Miller had begun to investigate the possibility of handing his results over to an institution capable of carrying on his work. Unfortunately, an imperfect rumor of his long-kept secret had already leaked out, and this move provoked precipitate action by people intent on claiming the rewards of the research for themselves. (I am being deliberately vague here because the novel is framed as a mystery, and I do not want to spoil it for any reader who may want to go on to read it.)

One of the institutions contacted by Miller was the Ahasuerus Foundation, which had been set up some years earlier by a man named Adam Zimmerman to conduct research in technologies of longevity and suspended animation. Zimmerman had been one of the first people to place himself in cryonic suspension before suffering a natural death in the hope that he might one day be revived into a world which had the technological means to keep him alive indefinitely. The continuing work of the Ahasuerus Foundation is a recurrent element in the subsequent books in the series, whose underlying theme is the gradual evolution of a whole series of longevity technologies, each one of which brings humankind a further step closer to "authentic emortality." Emortality—a term coined by Alvin Silverstein—signifies a state of being in which an organism does not age, and is thus potentially capable of living forever, although it remains permanently vulnerable to death by mortal injury (it is preferable to "immortality" as a specification of the plausible ultimate goal of biotechnology and medical science, because immortality implies an absolute invulnerability to death).

The money that enabled Adam Zimmerman to establish the Ahasuerus Foundation was earned in the service of a powerful consortium of multinational corporations known by a set of more or less derogatory nicknames, including the Secret Masters [of the World] and the Hardinist Cabal. Having benefited from the general tendency of capital to become concentrated in the hands of relatively few very large institutions, and the contrivance of a spectacular stock-market crash in the year 2025, this consortium has become the effective owner of the world. Its members have, however, been careful to provide a philosophical justification for their takeover of the world, in terms of an ideology whose most succinct statement can be found in a classic essay by the economist Garrett Hardin, "The Tragedy of the Commons" (first published in *Science* 162 [1968] pp. 1243–8, but reprinted many times)—hence the appellation "Hardinist Cabal."

Hardin's argument, in brief, is that when land is made generally available for exploitation—as the commons of ancient England were to owners of livestock—it is in the interests of each and every individual to increase the proportion of his own share, with the ultimate result that overexploitation obliterates the resource. Thus have many fertile areas been turned into desert, just as the world's oceans are presently being depopulated of fish. Only when a resource is privately owned, and its exploitation carefully constrained, can it be protected from devastation. In my future history, this argument—applied to the Earth as a whole—is used as a justification by the discreet board of directors who have usurped effective ownership of all its resources. The more cynical characters, however, regard the position as a mere pose, suspecting that the new breed of allegedly benevolent dictators are, like all their predecessors, far more interested in dictatorship than benevolence.

Volume two, *Inherit the Earth*, is set in the year 2193, in a world where the preservative labor of complex sets of nanotechnological devices has extended the attainable human life span to at least 150 years. No one is certain how far this figure might be extended, because its limits cannot be ascertained until the relevant time has actually elapsed, but there is a general optimism that people wealthy enough to have access to the best Internal Technology—IT for short—ought to be able to benefit from an "escalator effect," whereby each new technological advance will give them sufficient additional life span to be around when the next technological breakthrough arrives, and so on.

An ecocatastrophic Crash, complicated by chaotic "plague wars" in which biological weapons were deployed—mostly by unidentifiable aggressors—had earlier culminated in the advent of a number of new diseases whose result, if not their aim, was the universal sterilization of human females. The response to this crisis, securely in place at the beginning of the novel, was the development of artificial wombs in which egg cells stripped from the wombs of as-yet-uninfected females in very large numbers can be safely isolated, fertilized, and brought to term. The biotechnologists credited with the development of this technology were a closely knit team working under the direction of Conrad Helier.

In the world of the novel, therefore, very few children are reared by their biological parents. Although the right to found a family currently recognized by the United Nations Charter of Human Rights is still cherished, it is almost universally accepted that in a world whose citizens have a reasonable expectation of living for a very long time, the right to found a family ought to be exercised posthumously. The novel's central character, Damon Hart, is the biological son of Conrad Helier, who was born not long after his father's death and raised by the surviving members of Helier's research team. When the novel begins, however, he is estranged from his former foster-parents, having rebelled against the expectations they had of the career path he would take.

The plot of the novel describes events following the kidnapping of one of Damon's foster parents, apparently by members of a disorganized movement called Eliminators, whose modus operandi is to publish accusations that certain individuals are "unworthy of immortality" and call for their assassination. Among the allegations made on this occasion is the claim that Conrad Helier is still alive, in hiding because he was not only the architect of the solution to the final plague but of the plague itself. Damon sets out to make his own investigation of these allegations with the aid of Madoc Tamlin, a man only slightly older than he, who fancies himself something of an outlaw. Damon had befriended Tamlin during the most extreme phase of his rebellion against his foster parents and the surrounding society, and their friendship has survived the strain exerted upon it by their mutual close acquaintance with the volatile Diana Caisson.

With Tamlin's aid, and the ambivalent encouragement of interested parties within the Hardinist Cabal, Damon contrives to arrive at the truth of the matter before various rival investigators, who include representatives of the Ahasuerus Foundation as well as the police. He and Tamlin are then faced with awkward decisions regarding the uses to which they might put the information they have gained, and the new career opportunities that have opened up for them.

Another recurrent factor in the series' future history introduced in this volume is a set of technologies gathered under the nickname "gantzing," the reference being to a pioneer of biological cementation named Leon Gantz. At this relatively early stage, gantzing microorganisms do little more than stick formerly unpromising materials together in order to make building blocks, but as the series advances gantzing techniques become fundamental to all construction and demolition processes.

Volume three, *Dark Ararat*, complicates the chronological sequence of the series in being set three years after the arrival of the space Ark *Hope* in orbit around an "Earth-clone" world in a distant solar system (in 2817, according to the ship's calendar). *Hope* had been built as a response to the ecocatastrophic Crash that occurred between volumes one and two; the Ark had been completed in 2153 and had left the solar system in 2178. The central character of the story,

Matthew Fleury, is one of the would-be colonists carried by the Ark in cryonic suspension; from his viewpoint, no time has elapsed since he was frozen down with his two daughters, Michelle and Alice, in 2090.

While the Ark has been en route its crew-members have lived through several generations; during that time they have formed a new view of their mission and destiny that is at odds with the ideas of the Ark's Hardinist builder, Shen Chin Che—whose claim to own the Ark they fervently dispute. As a result of this difference of opinion the colonization project has gone badly awry. Many of the colonists taken down to the surface of the new world have concluded that the world is not a close enough twin to their homeworld to enable them to flourish there. The genetics of the new world's ecosphere are peculiar, the native life-forms having cultivated a kind of natural emortality with the aid of a mechanism that echoes Morgan Miller's ill-fated experiments. Further complications are added to the situation by the knowledge that Earth had not been utterly devastated by the Crash, and that the most recent news from the home planet—which is more than eighty years old—suggests that it is now a burgeoning paradise of near-emortals. (The Ark's passengers are, of course, mere mortals.)

In the great tradition of Ark-staffing, Matthew was recruited to the human cargo as one member of a pair, in his case of ecological geneticists. He has been revived because his counterpart, Bernal Delgado, has been murdered while investigating the ruins of a city whose unexpected—and rather belated—discovery has added more fuel to the debate about the hospitality of the new world. The humanoid aliens who built the city may well be extinct, but if they are not they must have suffered a social and technological regression so extreme as to have given up on the domestication of fire. The city's investigators were about to undertake a trip down the nearby river to a peculiar plain, in the hope of clearing up this mystery, when the murder took place. The weapon used to kill Delgado was a crude nonmetallic blade modeled on those once used by the indigenes, but of recent manufacture.

The plot of the novel follows the process of Matthew's slightly incredulous discovery of *Hope*'s circumstances, and then describes the expedition from the city to the plain in search of further enlightenment as to the fate of the humanoid aliens. Matthew's hope that solving the mystery might also allow him to heal the breach between the various rival factions is further emphasized by the knowledge that the future of his two daughters, who are still in suspended animation, depends on the achievement of a healthy and progressive consensus.

It may be relevant at this point to note that although the series was always intended to run to six volumes it was conceived as two sets of three, although this pattern was disrupted by the fact that the books were not contracted for publication—and therefore not issued—in chronological order. The first three books were designed as earnest and relatively orthodox thrillers, whereas the remainder were designed as flamboyant comedies, whose mystery elements would be more obviously contrived.

The reasoning behind this scheme was born of the fear that as the world depicted in the series came gradually closer to a Utopian condition, stories set there would be robbed of most of the dramatic impetus that worlds far from the ideal provide in abundance. Utopian fiction has a notorious tendency to be boring, and the demands of melodrama have been a key factor in determining the preference which science fiction writers have for dealing in more or less horrible futures. My hope was that I could compensate for the melodramatic drain inherent in mapping an improving situation by switching to an alternative narrative currency. For bridging purposes, however, Volume four of the series, *Architects of Emortality* retains a calculatedly absurd murder-mystery framework in which a genetic engineer specializing in flower design named Oscar Wilde lends his expertise as an aesthetic theorist to the investigation by UN policepersons Charlotte Holmes and Hal Watson of a series of murders signed (pseudonymously) "Rappaccini."

By 2495, when *Architects of Emortality* is set, the limitations of nanotechnological repair as a technology of longevity, even in combination with periodic rejuvenative somatic engineering treatments, have been conclusively shown up. All recent progress has been made in the field of genetically engineered longevity, which had gone through a long period of relative unfashionability as a result of the seemingly insuperable problem of the Miller Effect—although some further progress was made by courtesy of the continued efforts of such diehard adherents as the Ahasuerus Foundation. Another problematic side effect of longevity has also been publicized, although its existence and effects are dubious: the tendency of long-lived individuals to lose their mental adaptability.

The story told in *Architects of Emortality* takes place at a crucial historical juncture, when the last generation of humans who did not receive the longevity-providing Zaman Transformation at the single-cell stage of their development is approaching the limit of their endurance—the oldest of them routinely attaining a life span of 300 years, but not much more—and the first generation ZT beneficiaries are still young. No one knows, as yet, whether the members of the latest New Human Race are in danger of falling prey to robotization. One of the new breed of genetically enhanced emortals, a junior member of the still-thriving Hardinist Cabal named Michael Lowenthal, attaches himself to the Holmes/Watson investigation as an interested observer. He and Wilde become rivals in their attempts to construct hypothetical motives to rationalize Rappaccini's murders. Although Wilde proves, in the end, to be the better interpreter, it is Lowenthal who actually reaps a profit—on behalf of his masters—by following the investigation to its astonishing conclusion.

The seemingly final conquest of death that is visible to the characters of *Architects of Emortality* is fully realized in volume five of the series, *The Fountains of Youth*. Unlike its predecessor and the present volume, *The Fountains of Youth* is a comedy *bildungsroman* rather than a comedic mystery story; it constitutes the autobiography of Mortimer Gray, a member of the New Human Race born in 2520.

When he writes his autobiography, in 3025, Mortimer still expects to live for several more centuries, if not millennia, but he thinks it worth producing a summary record of the first great project of his life's work: the compilation of a definitive history of the role formerly played in human affairs by death, issued in ten volumes over a period of four hundred years.

Mortimer Gray's autobiography records how his determination to write the history of death was actuated by a close encounter of his own, when the cruise ship on which he was taking a holiday was caught up in the Coral Sea Disaster of 2542, when a rift in the Earth's crust split the ocean bed and spilled out massive amounts of hot magma, causing the sea to boil and sending huge tidal waves to devastate the Pacific Rim. In the aftermath of the disaster Mortimer made the acquaintance of the abruptly orphaned Emily Marchant, whose own determination to make the most of her life was similarly hardened by the misfortune. Emily subsequently becomes very rich, by virtue of extrapolating gantzing techniques to solve the problems of construction in extraterrestrial environments. She is heavily involved in the construction of "ice palaces" on the Jovian and Saturnian satellites—edifices which find an earthbound echo in showpieces constructed in Antarctica, where Mortimer resides while researching the middle part of his project.

Being somewhat accident-prone by the standards of his day, Mortimer has several other close encounters with his subject matter during the compilation of his masterpiece, one of which is consequent on his troubled relationship with the Thanaticists, a briefly fashionable cult interested in the aesthetics of death and disease. The last of these near misses results from a fall through the Arctic ice cap while traveling in a snowmobile. The long discussion about life's prospects he once shared with Emily Marchant is eerily echoed in a similarly extended and equally intense discussion about death's significance that he shares with the snowmobile's navigator: a moderately sophisticated silver. (Over the centuries, Artificial Intelligences have been routinely subcategorized as "sloths" and "silvers"; the acronym AI has been redefined to signify "artificial idiot," and ai is the Tupi name for the three-toed sloth, while more advanced machines have been redesignated "artificial geniuses," and Ag is the chemical symbol for silver.)

Toward the end of his labor on the history of death Mortimer has some dealings with the Cyborganizers, a new existential avant garde dedicated to the progressive fusion of humans and inorganic technology. Cyborganization is widely accepted as the emergent norm in extraterrestrial communities, with the exception of faber society—fabers are humans genetically engineered for life in low or zero gravity, whose legs are replaced by an extra set of armlike limbs. On Earth, however, cyborganization is a mere fashion rather than a matter of utilitarian necessity, and it is rivaled there by many other philosophies. These include the ecological mysticism of the Gaean Liberationists, and the ambitions of the Type 2 Movement—followers of the twentieth century prophet Freeman Dyson—whose aim is to extrapolate the technologies employed in continental engineering and terraformation to the construction of vast new macrostructures within the solar system.

I apologize for the fact that this torrent of data is a great deal for the interested reader to bear in mind while following the plot of *The Omega Expedition*, but the future is a big place and one of the few things that we can confidently say is that it will get less like the present the further it goes. If technological and social progress continue—as we must all hope, in spite of our keen Cassandrian awareness of the impending ecocatastrophic Crash—its strangeness will probably increase much faster than my exceedingly modest future history is content to suppose.

One other thing that the reader might care to bear in mind, if it is not asking too much, is that the greatest merit of science fiction as a genre is to demonstrate by its plenitude that the as yet unmade future holds a multitude of possibilities, whose actual outcome will depend on the choices we make in the present day. There are no predictions in this series of novels, or any other work of science fiction that aspires, no matter how feebly, to intellectual seriousness; all anticipations are conditional. The only purpose the series has, beyond that of providing harmless entertainment, is the hope of making a contribution, however minuscule, to the information of the present-day choices that will determine which of the infinite number of possible futures our emortal descendants will eventually inherit and inhabit.

PROLOGUE

The Last Adam: A Myth for the Children of Humankind

by Mortimer Gray

PART ONE

ONE

T his is the way it must have happened.
In September 1983, shortly after returning from his honeymoon in the Dominican Republic, Adam Zimmerman began to read *Sein und Zeit* by Martin Heidegger. He had decided to improve his German, and he did not want to practice by reading novels in that language because he considered all fiction to be a waste of time. He wanted to read something that was serious, difficult, and important, so that he would obtain the maximum reward for the effort he put in.

That was the kind of man he was, in those days. He could not have regarded himself, at the age of twenty-five years and four months, as a *complete* man, but he had put away all childish things with stern determination. He hated to let time go to waste, and he required full recompense from every passing moment.

It is tempting to wonder whether the history of the next thousand years might have been somewhat different if Adam had chosen to read, for example, Friedrich Nietzsche's *Also Sprach Zarathustra* or Arthur Schopenhauer's *Die Welt als Wille und Vorstellung*, but there was no danger of that. Both those books had been published in the nineteenth century, and Adam was very much a twentieth-century man. We, of course, have grown used to thinking of him as *the* twentieth century man, but while he was actually living in that era he was far from typical. He must have been considerably more earnest than the average, although he would probably have gone no further on his own behalf than to judge himself "serious."

Although he was a native of New York in the United States of America, Adam had always been conscious of his European ancestry. He was the grandson of Austrian Jews who had fled Vienna in 1933, when his father Sigmund was still a babe in arms. Sigmund Zimmerman's only sibling—a sister—was born in New York, and he had not a single cousin in the world to lose, but the war of 1939–45 contrived nevertheless to inscribe a deep scar upon his soul. Sigmund frequently declared himself to be a "child of the Holocaust," and sometimes applied the same description to his own son, even though Adam was not born until 13 February 1958.

Neither Sigmund nor Adam ever visited Israel, but Sigmund certainly considered himself a Zionist fellow traveler, and that conviction could not help but color the idealistic spectrum of Adam's adolescent rebellion against the ideas and ideals of his parents. Although that rebellious phase was in the past by the time of his marriage to Sylvia Ruskin (a gentile), its legacy must have played some small part in Adam's decision to try to perfect his German with the aid of a philosopher of whom his father would definitely not have approved.

Perhaps that same awareness assisted, if it did not actually provoke, Adam's powerful reaction to Heidegger's argument. On the other hand, it might have been the fact that he set out to wrestle with the text purely as an exercise in linguistics that left him psychologically naked to its deeper implications. Then again, it does not seem to have been at all unusual for males of his era and cultural background to hold themselves sternly aloof from *schmaltz* while being extravagantly self-indulgent in the matter of *angst*.

For whatever reason, Adam was ready-made for the strange sanctification of self-pity that was the primitive existentialist's red badge of courage. While he read Heidegger, a couple of chapters at a time, on those nights when he elected not to claim his conjugal rights, Adam felt that he was gradually bringing to consciousness precious items of knowledge that had always lain within him, covert and unapprehended. He did not need to be persuaded that *angst* is the fundamental mood of mortal existence, because that knowledge had always nested in his soul, waiting only to be recognised and greeted with all due deference.

Heidegger explained to Adam that human awareness of inevitable death, though unfathomably awful, was normally repressed to a subliminal level in order that the threat of nothingness could be held at bay, but that individuals who found such dishonesty impalatable were perennially catching fugitive glimpses of the appalling truth. Adam felt a surge of tremendous relief when he realized that he must be one of the honest few, and that this was the explanation of his inability to relate meaningfully to the insensitive majority of his fellows. It was as if a truth that had long been captive in some dark cranny of his convoluted brain had been suddenly set free.

When Adam laid the book down on his bedside table for the last time, the silken caress of his expensive sheets seemed to be infused with a new meaning. For twenty-five years he had been a stranger to himself, but now he felt that he had been properly introduced.

He woke Sylvia, his bride of eight weeks, and said: "We're going to die, Syl."

We must presume that although she may have been mildly distressed by being hauled back from gentle sleep in this rude manner, Sylvia would have adopted a tone of loving sympathy.

"No we're not, Adam," she would have said. "We're both perfectly healthy."

Perhaps that was the crucial moment of disconnection which sealed the eventual doom of their marriage.

"Death is the one constant of our existence," Adam told her, calmly. "The awareness that we might be snuffed out of existence at any moment haunts us during every bright moment of our waking lives. Although we try with all our might not to see the specter at the feast of life, it's always there, always seeking us out with eyes whose hollowness insists that we too will one day forsake our *being in the world*. No matter how hard we strive for mental comfort and stability, that fundamental insecurity undermines and weakens the foundations of the human psyche, spoiling its fabric long before the anticipated moment of destruction actually arrives.

"We all try, in our myriad ways, to suppress and defeat it, but we all fail. We invent myths of the immortality of the soul; we hide in the routines of the everyday; we try to dissolve our terror in the acid baths of love and adoration—but none of it works, Syl. It *can't* work. If I read him aright, Heidegger thinks that if we could only face up to the specter we'd be able to exorcise it, liberating ourselves from our servitude to the ordinary and achieving authentic existence, but that's like trying to pull yourself up by your own bootstraps; it's nothing but another philosophical word game. The issue can't be dodged—not, at any rate, by any cheap trick of *that* kind. The *angst* will always win."

In the course of a year-long courtship and eight weeks of happy marriage Sylvia Zimmerman must already have had abundant opportunity to study her loved one's slight penchant for pomposity, but she was prepared to forgive its occasional excesses. She loved Adam. She did not understand him, but she did love him.

"Go to sleep, Adam," she advised. "Things won't seem half so bad in the morning.

As it happened, though, the sheer enormity of Adam's realization denied him escape into the arms of Morpheus. He turned out the bedside lamp and sat in the dark, appalled by the vision of nothingness that had been conjured up before him, languishing in the sensation of having no hope. And when morning came, it found him in exactly the same condition. It is useless to speculate now as to whether sleep might have saved him from further anguish; if he could have slept in such circumstances, he would not have needed saving. In fact, because he was the person he was, Adam Zimmerman became in the course of that insomniac night a man obsessed. Those few roughhewn sentences which had poured out of him as he tried to explain himself to the sleepy Sylvia became the axioms of his continuing life.

Sylvia must have tried other arguments in the days that followed, but none fared any better than her first shallow riposte. This was not her fault; if Martin Heidegger could not succeed in persuading Adam that there was a satisfactory answer to the problem of *angst*, Sylvia Zimmerman had no chance. She was not an unintelligent woman by any means— her academic qualifications were superior to Adam's and she certainly had a broader mind—but she did not have Adam's capacity for obsession. Her cleverness was diffuse and highly adaptable, while his was tightly focused and direly difficult to shift once it had selected an objective.

Sylvia was adept at moving on, and that was the way she coped with all life's intractable problems; if one proved too difficult she simply put it away and redirected her attention to more comfortable and more productive fields of thought and action. However ironic or paradoxical it may seem to us, in the light of subsequent events, *moving on* was the one thing that Adam Zimmerman could not do. Once the crucial fragment of philosophical ice had penetrated the profoundest depths of his conscious mind, his life could no longer flow as the lives of other men and women flowed; from that moment on his inner self was cold, crystalline, and hard as adamant.

For some years, Adam let his wife follow her own advice while he continued to brood privately, but his preoccupation was not a secret that he could keep from her, even if that had been his desire. It could not help but surface repeatedly, each time more insistent than the last. Heidegger's analysis of the human predicament—that all human life is underlaid, limited, subverted, and irredeemably devalued by its own precariousness in the face of death—gnawed at Adam's guts like some monstrous hookworm, and he could not help coughing up the argumentative flux whenever it threatened to over-whelm him.

He consulted many other philosophers in the hope of finding a solution to his predicament, but all the cures they suggested seemed to him to be no more than shifty conjurations based in dishonest sleight-of-mind. He even went so far as to consult the novels of Jean-Paul Sartre, but *Nausea* only confirmed his long-held prejudice against the fallaciousness of fiction. Try as he might, he could attain no age of reason, obtain no reprieve, and discover no iron in the soul. He could not believe that anyone with a clear mind could draw an atom of satisfaction from the prospect of "living on" after death in the pages of authored books, the strokes of a paint-brush, or the notes of a musical composition. Nor could he consider the remembrance of children or the extrapolation of a dynasty to be of the slightest palliative value. The prospect of being a born-again optimist could not tempt him even when everyone alongside whom he worked waxed lyrical about the power of positive thinking, the rewards of "proac-tivity," and the vital necessity of a "can do" attitude. He needed something far more solid than the gospel of self-help in which to invest his commitment.

Adam was tempted for a while to abandon his job as a consultant in corporate finance, on the grounds that there was something absurdly meaningless about the ceaseless jug-gling of figures. He was a very accomplished saltimbanque, to be sure, and he prided himself on the fact that no one could walk the tightrope that separated tax avoidance from tax evasion more surefootedly than he, but even the most cre-ative exercises in bookkeeping seemed to exemplify the des-perate absorption in the trivial that was one of the most obviously hollow of all the false solutions to the problem of being.

Although he had no talent at all for composition, Adam did play the guitar quite well—it was one of the few activities capable of relaxing him—and for a while he contemplated beginning a new career as a spaced-out folksinger. He imagined for a while that he might grow his hair long, wear a beard, and change his name to Adam X in order to symbolize the falseness of family as a conduit of intergenerational continuity. He decided soon enough, however, that such a career would be no less absurd than a career in corporate finance, and a good deal less profitable.

Sylvia applauded this particular decision heartily, but Adam's *angst* became, in Sylvia's eyes, a marital misdemeanor. She was eventually to divorce him on the grounds that he could not provide her with essential emotional support. "The trouble with you," she said, on the day she finally left him, "is that you're incapable of enjoying yourself."

Sylvia never remarried and remained permanently childless, living comfortably on the alimony which Adam paid her until she died in 2019, but whether she escaped the ravages of her own *angst* remains unclear. Adam always claimed, with a hint of residual vindictiveness, that she died an alcohol-sodden wreck; although he was an unusually honest and serious man, all other surviving documents suggest that she lived a rich life, within the constraints of her time, and died as happily as anyone can who accepts the necessity.

ere mortal though he was, by the time Adam Zimmerman was asked to compile a definitive account of his formative experiences he had forgotten many significant details. He could not recall when he had first become aware of the central thesis of Garrett Hardin's essay on "The Tragedy of the Commons" or when he first read *Conquest of Death* by Alvin Silverstein. Given that he was only ten years old when the former item was first published, it seems likely that he must have run across it at a much later date, in one of its many reprintings. It is conceivable that he had read the latter item in 1979, when it first appeared—four years before his close encounter with Heidegger—but had not been in a position to anticipate the significance that its central concept would eventually come to assume within his thinking.

That central concept was, of course, emortality.

The word "emortality" is such a commonplace item of contemporary vocabulary that it is difficult to imagine a time before it was coined, but it was almost unknown in Adam Zimmerman's day. The distinction between "immortality"—which implies an absolute immunity to death—and emortality did not seem worthwhile in an era when both were out of reach. Although a condition in which individuals were immune to disease and aging, and enjoyed a greatly enhanced capacity of bodily self-repair, was *imaginable* in the twentieth century, it was the stuff of fantastic fiction—a medium even more despised by the cultural elite of the day than the determinedly unadventurous naturalistic fiction that Adam

Zimmerman considered futile. Silverstein was among the first mortals to propose, in all seriousness, that the scientific conquest of death might only be decades away, and that a term was therefore urgently required for the state of being in which human life *might* be extended indefinitely, although remaining permanently subject to the possibility of accidental or violent death.

Adam did recall that his interest in Silverstein's thesis was, for a while, confused in his mind by another proposition, popularized by R. C. W. Ettinger, that the advancement of science might one day make it possible to revive some individuals who would be considered clinically dead by twentieth-century standards. Ettinger proposed in the 1960s that people then alive might be able to take advantage of such future progress if only their bodies could be preserved in a state immediately following the moment of death-as-currently-defined. The method of preservation he favored was, of course, freezing. By the time Adam was forty years old, a considerable number of people had made provision for themselves to take advantage of this potential opportunity by arranging to have their bodies frozen after death and maintained indefinitely in a cryogenic facility.

Adam could never convince himself that a death once suffered could actually be reversed, but he did interest himself in the possibility that humans who were frozen down while still alive might be resuscitated at a later date, in order to take advantage of the biotechnologies that would make emortality a reality. Within a year of his divorce, perhaps because Sylvia's defection had cleared way the last obstacle to the focusing of all his mental resources, Adam had decided that the only possible escape from the ravages of *angst* was to place himself in suspended animation, avoiding death until his frozen body could be delivered into a world where the indefinite avoidance of death had become routine.

Adam recalled that when he mentioned this possibility to his ex-wife she laughed contemptuously, having left behind the loving state of mind that would have forbidden such indelicacy. That, for him, was final proof of the fact that she had never really understood him, and it served to harden his resolve implacably. Might that bitter laugh have changed the course of history? Probably not, given that Adam's resolve was already firm enough—but it is heartening to think that good can sometimes be assisted, accelerated and amplified by malice. The world would be a much poorer place if it were not so.

By the time the twentieth century lurched to its inauspicious end, Adam had made his decision and formulated his plan. He was determined to avoid that tax on existence which his peers called death, and the means by which he would contrive the evasion was ice: not the kind of ice which spiced the upstate lakes in the depths of winter and suspended icicles from the ledges of the city, but the kind of ice that comprised comets and encased the satellites of distant planets; the kind of ice which could suspend all animation and preserve organic structure indefinitely.

Adam knew, of course, that neither the technology to accomplish this nor the legal apparatus to enable it was yet available, but he was an accountant by trade and vocation. He understood that the motor of technological progress was money, and that laws were made to control the poor while enabling the rich. There was a problem of timing to be solved, but that was all that was required to bring his ambitions to their consummation. He would need considerable wealth if he were to get the best of care during several centuries of inactivity, but the manipulation and redirection of wealth was his specialism and he was an accomplished practitioner of the economic arts.

It could not have been easy to weigh all these things accurately, but years of devotion to the juggling of figures had honed Adam's calculative skills to near-perfection. He eventually decided that he needed to be frozen down before he reached the age of eighty, and that seventy would be preferable, so he set a preliminary target date for his entry into suspended animation of 2028, extendable to 2038 if all went well enough in the interim.

For safety's sake, he calculated, it would be necessary to leave at least a billion dollars to the organization entrusted with his preservation. It would, however, be convenient if he could raise twice or three times as much in the shorter term, in order to make sure that research in cryogenics was properly funded. It would be helpful, too, to have a couple of billion dollars to spare when the time came, in order to give an appropriate boost to the technologies of emortality that would facilitate his return.

He decided that he needed to make his first billion by 2010, his second by 2020, and however many more he could contrive in the remaining eight to eighteen years of activity. In the meantime, he had to make every effort to remain perfectly healthy.

Adam had never smoked and had always been a very moderate drinker—he indulged in the occasional glass of red wine but never touched spirits—so the only additional effort he required was to exert a greater discipline over his diet and dedicate at least one hour a day to the exercise machines in his private gym. He decided that the only other hazard which stood in the way of achieving his targets was the possibility that he might have to endure another divorce, but that was an easy hurdle to avoid by the simple expedient of refusing to marry again.

He contemplated remaining celibate for the remainder of his days, but having studied Jacques Bertillon's data regarding sexual activity and death-risk he decided that keeping a string of mistresses was a justifiable expenditure. For this role he was careful to select unusually docile and rational young women, whose looks were only slightly better than average and whose appetites were as moderate as his own.

THREE

I f I might be permitted a brief historical interpolation here, it may be worth my pointing out that there were several ways in which an ambitious corporate accountant could plan to make a billion dollars in the early years of the twenty-first century. Global Capitalism was newly entered into its Age of Heroes, and those heroes had already reduced national governments to the status of mere instruments. The only significant ideological opposition to the dominance of capitalism during the twentieth century had been provided by Marxist socialism, but the governments which pretended to operate on that basis had been thinly disguised oligarchies or autocracies, all of which had either collapsed or embarked upon programs of accommodation by 2000.

Ironically, the Marxist economic analyses which had avidly anticipated the collapse and supersession of capitalism had been largely correct in anticipating the phases that the system would pass through as it approached that final crisis. Capital had indeed been concentrated in fewer and fewer hands, while the vast majority of the laborers producing its material goods remained direly impoverished. The inherent revolutionary potential of this situation had, however, been conclusively defused by the clever use of new technologies of production and communication. Mechanical production not only robbed laborers of much of their potential disputative power but also helped to supply the direly impoverished masses with goods that they could never have produced themselves. Mass communication allowed the avarice and envy that had always been the twin motors of human progress to be manipulated in a subtler, cleverer, and more intense fashion than ever before.

With the aid of hindsight, we can now see an apparent inevitability in the fact that the final victory of Global Capitalism took the form of a Cartel of Cosmicorporations, which put an end once and for all to the Era of Competition. We can see, too, that the Universal Cartel did not arrive a day too soon, if it was indeed the only practical solution to the Tragedy of the Commons. Many historians, having taken this for granted, have regretted that some such cartel did not emerge a hundred years earlier, while the big corporations had not yet become entitled to such prefixes as mega- and cosmi-. In another place, or another history, some other solution might have been found which did better service to the glorious traditional ideals of Liberty, Equality, and Fraternity, but in our world no such solution ever succeeded in making itself credible.

The twentieth century was an era of unprecedented economic growth, based on unprecedented population growth. Production and consumption increased hand in hand, and their increase was exponential. This could not continue indefinitely, because the toll that it was taking on the Earth's ecosphere could not be sustained. The twenty-first century was bound to see a qualitative change in the pattern, and the momentum of the system ensured that it would begin with a catastrophic Crash. The only issue in doubt was whether the crisis could be moderated in such a way that the world economy could regain a more-or-less stable and sustainable equilibrium, or whether the Crash would be so destructive that a centuries-long period of recovery would be necessary—after which the problem would inevitably recur, and keep on recurring until a sustainable equilibrium could be reached.

Ecology was an infant discipline in the twentieth century, and its interrelationships with economics were poorly understood by the great majority of practitioners in either field. The fusion of the two disciplines pioneered by Garrett

Hardin had yet to win wide acceptance at the beginning of the twenty-first century, partly because there were few individuals or corporations who had anything substantial to gain from accepting it. Men were mortal then, and few had sufficient imagination even to anticipate the changes and challenges they would have to face within a limited lifetime. From its earliest embryonic days, however, the Universal Cartel had every reason to take aboard the crucial lesson set out in the most significant scientific parable of the twentieth century, "The Tragedy of the Commons." Nobody now remembers who coined the term "Hardinist Cabal"—it was not Adam Zimmerman—but it was a notion whose time had certainly come.

As soon as its formation was begun, the Universal Cartel had no alternative but to accept as its primary purpose and objective the management and control of the inevitable eco-catastrophic Crash, with a view to steering its course to the only imaginable healthy outcome. Among the many advisers and consultants hired to help them organize and discipline the world economy, Adam Zimmerman was one whose understanding of that necessity, and the means to attain it, stood out very conspicuously. He was, therefore, in exactly the right place at exactly the right time to further their strategy and his own, in near-perfect harmony.

FOUR

Adam was not in the least surprised that he became known, in the years before he absented himself from the twenty-first century, as "the man who stole the world." He did not resent the appellation; indeed, he was very proud of it.

"The world had to be stolen," he told me, by way of explanation. "In exactly the same way that the ancient commons of England needed enclosure and usurpation, so the entire surface of the Earth had to be enclosed within tight bonds of ownership, in order that its resources and productivity might be sensibly controlled."

"Was there no other way?" I asked.

"None," he said, adamantly. "The users of the land could not be allowed to continue exploiting it competitively, each to his individual advantage, and they certainly could not be trusted to exercise restraint within the framework of any voluntary agreement. A firm ruling hand was necessary. The long-term needs of the Commonweal had to be substituted for the short-term ambitions of individual greed. Political communism had attempted to do that, but it had failed in spectacular fashion to contain or constrain the urgings of envy and avarice."

"Was there no intermediate course that might have been plotted between the two extremes?"

"No. The objective could only be attained by an approach from a diametrically opposite direction. Consumer demand could only be controlled by its makers and organizers; social and technological progress could only be subjected to managerial control by people who understood management theory as well as scientific theory. Whatever moral reservations the people of my era may have had as to capitalism's disregard for social justice and equality of opportunity, the greater need had to be served.

"Big business already ruled the world—the only question was whether it could get its act together in time to do the job properly. The world's property was distributed far too widely and indiscriminately, but most of the people who had pocketed it were living on the economic edge, waiting negligently to be pushed over. The people who knew what they were doing, and what still needed to be done, already had the lion's share of the wealth *and* control of the markets. They were the people who had to steal the rest, because they were the people who could.

"The people who were destined to own the world were already well on the way to that goal in 2000, but they needed to accelerate the process if they were to complete the grab while the world was still worth stealing. I helped them obtain that extra boost. It was simple enough—the 1929 example was in all the textbooks, offering the definitive model. Engineer a big bubble followed by a big burst, then send the carpetbaggers in; repeat until the process is complete."

Adam was, of course, being unduly modest. The principle might have been simple, but the execution of the series of financial coups that began in 2010 and reached its climax in 2025 was anything but easy. It required an awesomely detailed understanding of the constitution and behavior of the world's markets. Adam's reference to "the 1929 example" was, of course, slightly disingenuous, because the key to the manipulation of twenty-first-century markets was an intimate knowledge of the computer systems that were handling the bulk of trading. Although they would not have qualified as artificial intelligences by today's standards, the systems in question were experts of a sort. They could outperform humans in all the circumstances of which their programmers had taken account, but were also capable, in certain extraordinary and unanticipated circumstances, of almost incredible stupidity.

What Adam Zimmerman contributed to the Universal Cartel's Hardinist property grab was the knowledge of exactly how to bring about the extraordinary circumstances that would cause the computerized trading systems to trash the world's markets, and exactly how to take advantage of the ensuing chaos.

Contrary to popular belief, the Earth was not won on a single day on 20 March 2025, but it *was* lost on that day. When the second day of the new spring dawned, the way was clear and the pattern of acquisitions had become inexorable. The world woke up in the secure grip of an association of megacorporations whose chief executives formed the tightly knit conspiracy that soon became known by such journalistic catchphrases as the Secret Masters, the Inner Circle, and the Invisible Hand. The actual agents of the coup were more than content to remain hidden behind such euphemisms, while allowing their humbler instruments to bear the burden of personal notoriety. Adam Zimmerman was not, in any *literal* sense, "the man who stole the world," but he was certainly in the forefront of the great heist. He organized the shock troops which led the rapid-fire asset-stripping raids that bankrupted whole nations and cornered every significant commodity whose futures were dealt. Like any true hero, he did not act for himself but for the captains of Global Capitalism, and hence for the world as a whole—but he did take a perfectly reasonable commission on every deal he made.

By 2010 Adam had already made his first billion dollars and had laid the groundwork for the Ahasuerus Foundation. By 2020 he had made his second billion, and the Ahasuerus Foundation was becoming a significant force in longevity research and the commercial development of suspended-animation technology. In the spring of 2025 he made five billion dollars more, and the Ahasuerus Foundation became the leading institution in both its fields of sponsorship.

Although his part in these transactions made him one of the wealthiest men in the world, Adam remained scrupulously unassuming in dress and manner. His legion of aides and assistants thought him rather shy, and they were as grateful for his unfailing politeness as they were for his measured generosity. The only slight resentment that his employees harbored was against his habit of lecturing them on the necessity of self-discipline, the virtues of thrift, the dangers of hedonism, and other related topics. They valued the truths that were invariably to be found in these homilies, but were inclined to think the lectures themselves a trifle pompous.

Despite his nickname and the notoriety it reflected, Adam did not like to expose himself to the public gaze, and he became increasingly reclusive as the twenty-first century wore on. One of his favorite sermons, in fact, was a warning against the seductiveness of fame.

"Fame," Adam would sternly advise his closer acquaintances, "is essentially a matter of attracting attention, and attention is always fatal to men who make their living by dipping into other people's pockets. People like ourselves should make every effort to avoid being *interesting*; it not only renders one vulnerable to the iniquities of inquisitiveness, but makes one susceptible to flattery. Flattery is a powerful force, and its attractions can be difficult to resist. One must constantly remind oneself that fame is one of the most awful reminders of one's own mortality. The masses are always hungry for misfortune and disaster, and they love to revel in the tragedy and grief which attend the sufferings of their idols. The public invents celebrities mainly in order to revel in their decay and extinction, and fame always breeds sickness and self-abuse. The unluckiest men in the world are those who have a fame thrust upon them from which they cannot escape."

These were wise words. I could have judged them wise even from my own very limited experience of the fame I gained as the author of the definitive *History of Death* and the pioneer of emortal spiritual autobiography, but Adam

Zimmerman provided a far more telling example himself. While he remained hidden from the world he was able to retain the status of a mere shadow on the page of history, an elusive myth—but the longer he remained in his chrysalis of ice the more certain it became that he would wake to find himself famous, with disastrous effect.

FIVE

A dam Zimmerman's speeches warning against the hazards of fame and sermons on the benefits of thrift were sometimes taken by those who did not know him well as evidence of cynicism. Here was a man, his critics argued, who was notorious throughout the world as the greatest thief in history, who poured the billions of dollars that he stole into esoteric scientific and technological research. In contrast to the great philanthropists of Classical Capitalism, who had endowed universities, art galleries, and museums for the betterment of their humbler fellows, Adam Zimmerman seemed to care for nothing but the preservation of his own self, desiring only to become "immortal" in the crudest imaginable sense of the word.

What fools those mortals were!

"It is difficult for those who can see to imagine the plight of those who are blind," Adam told me, when we discussed his treatment in histories other than my own, "but it ought to be impossible for any reasonable person of *your* day to entertain an atom of sympathy for my critics. It should have been obvious, even to my contemporaries, that I was the ultimate incarnation of the underlying philosophy of capitalism, as first set out in Bernard de Mandeville's *The Fable of the Bees; or, Private Vices, Public Benefits*—but I suppose we ought to be generous and remember that Mandeville's writings were also misconstrued in their day, and prosecuted for the offense they offered to Puritan ideals.

I asked Adam whether he had had the remotest inkling, in the early twenty-first century, of the difference that his actions would ultimately make to the general human condition.

"Yes," he said, unequivocally. "I knew perfectly well, from the very beginning, that emortality would become the privilege of all humankind—or, at any rate, all but the very poorest members of society. Some of the more shortsighted members of the Cartel were inclined for a while to think of it as something that ought to be reserved for the ultimate elite, but I tried to persuade them that it would be as unwise as it would be impossible to monopolise longevity. The whole point of their enterprise was to achieve economic stability, and there could be no other permanent guarantee of stability than universal, or near-universal, emortality. Before I was frozen down I advised them to make every effort to persuade their customers that emortality was imminent, that nothing was required for its attainment but loyalty and patience, and that once it was commercially available they should err on the side of generosity rather than play the miser."

"Are you surprised," I asked him, "that so very few of them followed your own example and put themselves into suspended animation to await the fulfilment of that promise?"

"Had you asked me in 2035 how many would follow my example," he said, after a pause for thought, "I would have guessed that every rational man who had the means would do so. But I think I can understand why the actual figure was so low. The men to whom I acted as adviser were not of my kind. They were hungry for power, and they loved to exercise authority. They were, of course, ambitious to be the saviors of the ecosphere, but they did not want power because they wanted to save the world—they wanted to save the world because that was the best way to prove that they were powerful.

"The men for whom I stole the world had the same deep-rooted fear of death and annihilation that I had, but they had never brought it to clear consciousness in the manner that I was fortunate enough to achieve. Their coping strategy was a different one, requiring a fierce avidity to seize the moment, and to lose themselves in the opportunities of the moment. They were, above all else, *successful* men, and their success extended to the repression of their death anxiety. They did not have the strength of mind or the force of will to let go of what they had and what they were about, until it was too late. They could be honest in their dealings with their fellow men when the situation demanded it—as it occasionally did—but they were incapable of being honest with themselves. They thought themselves extraordinary men, but their insensitivity to the fact of their own mortality was pathetically ordinary."

"It seems to have been surprisingly easy for people of your era to persuade themselves that they did not want to live forever," I observed. He had not yet had the opportunity to read *The History of Death*, and did not know the extent of my own speculations or the nature of my own conclusions in regard to that matter.

"Not at all," he said, decisively. "If they had had to persuade themselves, they would have been quite unable to do it. The point was that they did not have to persuade themselves because they had already made up their minds to ignore the question, never raising it except in jest. They dismissed the prospect of emortality as an absurdity unworthy of their contemplation, and laughed at anyone who challenged them. When I was young, I thought them fools, and cowardly fools too—but as I grew older, I became more tolerant of their willful blindness, and even tried to help them see the truth.

"They were not really fools, or cowards; they were merely victims of a kind of mental illness, an existential malaise. Even those who understood that aging was merely one more disease—awaiting nothing but a full understanding of its nature to be treatable, and ultimately curable—mostly fell victim to the mental symptoms of their sickness. They lived in a world saturated with death, and could not find the strength of mind to make themselves exceptions to such a universal rule."

"But you were brave enough to be different," I observed.

"I wouldn't call it brave," he told me. "Contrary to popular belief, it doesn't take courage merely to be different. Most people who are different attain that condition by simple failure. It does, however, require unusual dedication to be *constructively* different. Most men are handicapped by difference, hobbled by alienation from the company and concerns of their fellow men. To be empowered by difference requires ruthless self-sufficiency and self-discipline. Any man of my era could have done what I did had he taken the trouble, but men are few who can endure much trouble."

Men are few who can endure much trouble.

That observation was Adam Zimmerman's obituary for the world he left behind, and his summation of himself. He was, in his own eyes, a man capable of enduring a great deal of trouble. He could read *Sein und Zeit*, see its implications clearly, and react sanely. That was all there was to him. His six billion contemporaries were out of step with him because they could not make themselves constructively different from one another. They lacked self-sufficiency and self-discipline.

It was widely assumed by his contemporaries that Adam was an unhappy man. The story got round among those who knew him that his life had been blighted when his one great love, Sylvia Ruskin, had deserted and divorced him. It was sometimes said, before and after 2035, that his relentless moneymaking was a pathetic compensation for his failure in the one aspect of his existence which really meant something to him: that his obsession with emortality was a substitute for love. The people most heavily committed to this theory were, of course, his mistresses. This would not have been the case had he chosen mistresses who were generally believed to be beautiful, or even mistresses who genuinely but mistakenly believed themselves to be beautiful, but he invested instead in women who tended to save their self-esteem with theories of inner beauty and psychological compensation.

They were women of a kind fated to consider themselves substitutes, because they were unable to think of themselves as truly lovable.

Adam understood this. He used his mistresses, of course—but while he used them, he knew as well as they did that he was using them better than anyone else would have done—and although they did not understand him, they understood that he understood them, and were duly grateful.

"One day," one of them said to him, on one occasion, while she was in the grip of post-coital *triste*, "you'll meet your true love. Maybe you won't be able to find her in this world, but when you get to where you're going, you'll find her there. You'll find your Eve, even if you have to sleep for a thousand years."

"I hope not," he replied, indulging in a rare joke. "Whatever Adam may have achieved through Eve was blighted by the birth of Cain. I would not want to put a second such stain on the heritage of humankind."

"I wouldn't worry about that," she countered. "Murderous impulses won't need to be reinvented, even if you do sleep for a thousand years."

Never one to surrender the last word, he became serious again, and said: "Whether it takes a thousand years or a million, there will come a time when the mark of Cain is erased from human nature. The advent of emortality will see to that."

None of his mistresses was ever called Eve—or, for that matter, Sylvia. No one he encountered dared to suggest in all seriousness that he might have to sleep for a thousand years in order to obtain what he wanted; his own expectation, in 2035, was that he might have to sleep for a hundred, or two hundred at the most. For once, though, the romantic assumption was correct, at least insofar as the thousand years was concerned.

When he discarded his mistresses, as he did at intervals of between three and seven years, they always wept, but such was their incapacity to think themselves lovable that they were never excessively resentful. None of them ever attempted to exact any violent revenge, although one or two hazarded a few bitter words.

More than one of his discarded lovers, despairing of making him feel guilty on their behalf, demanded that he feel sorry for all the people in the world who were wretched and starving because he and others like him were appropriating all the wealth which, in a saner era, might have made them comfortable. It was a hopeless demand.

"The thing we have to remember," he would say in response, out of earnest concern for their education and mental equilibrium, "is that we are *all* dying, with every moment that passes. We begin to die even before we are born; the moment an ovum is fertilized it begins to age. The embryo is aging even while it grows and the period when the forces of growth can successfully outweigh the forces of decay is brief indeed.

"We think that we are still possessed of the bloom of youth at twenty, but this is an illusion. Death begins to win the battle against life when we are barely nine years old. After that, although we continue to increase the size and number of our cells, the rot of mortality is well and truly set in. The moment of equilibrium has passed, and the new cells we produce already show the signs of senescence in the copying errors that have accumulated in the nucleic acids, and in the cross-linkages that disable functional proteins.

"What we call maturation is the seal set upon us by the Grim Reaper, and until science finds a way to reverse these processes, correcting the nucleic acid errors and obliterating the stultifying cross-linkages, there is no hope for *any* of us, whether we sleep in silken sheets or starve in arid wastelands. We are all equal before the horror of it, whether we have the best of care or none at all. In such circumstances, there is no honor in conscience, no shame in selfishness. In an evil world, we are free to be evil—but anyone who wishes to be good has only one option before him, and that is to oppose the dread empire of Death.

"Death has no greater opponent in all the world than me, and everything I do is directed to the overthrow of that tyrant. Never ask for my pity on behalf of the impoverished, the propertyless, the starving, the destitute or the dying. I am fighting their fight, while they cannot, just as I am fighting your fight, while you cannot."

His ex-mistresses undoubtedly understood these arguments, because he could not abide unintelligent companions, but they found it impossible to agree with him. Without exception, they concluded that he was lonely, bitter, and neurotic, and condescended to pity him as much as they had once adored him. He broke their hearts, but he broke them in a good cause. He was a careful man, and never fathered a child. He was not so arrogant as to take it for granted that all the future generations of emortal humankind would be children of his endeavor, and he their one true Adam, but there remains a sense in which his childlessness reflected that potential.

Adam never had to endure a serious illness. He survived two major road traffic accidents and three assassination attempts without accumulating a single scar. Even so, he considered it prudent not to use up the entirety of the extension of his first Earthly existence that he had generously given himself should he continue in good health.

On 1 April 2035 Adam Zimmerman became the one hundredth human to be frozen down while still in the full bloom of health, using the most sophisticated SusAn technique then available. No one now knows what happened to his ninety-nine predecessors, although we may assume that those who were not revived long before him must have met with accidents of one kind or another. The people of our own day have every reason to be grateful for the combination of good fortune and tender care which brought him safely across the ages, even if the circumstances surrounding his revival did not develop as anyone had planned, or as anyone—Adam least of all—could ever have anticipated.

BEING AND TIME:
A Cautionary Tale for the Children of Humankind

by Madoc Tamlin

ONE
MY NAME AND NATURE

My name is Madoc Tamlin.

Like many a man born in 2163, I know nothing at all of my biological ancestry. The six foster parents who raised me refused to make any enquiry as to the ultimate origins of the sperm and egg that were extracted from a donor bank in Los Angeles, California, then combined *in vitro* to produce the egg which they caused to be implanted in a Helier womb.

How, then did they come by my name?

Because they never offered me any other account, I can only suppose that they simply liked the sound of it. My admittedly vague memories of them suggest that it is highly unlikely that any of them had ever heard of either of the legendary antecedents described herein, and I am quite sure that they were not trying to influence my destiny in any way by attaching the names to me. Perhaps that is as well, given that they failed to influence my destiny in all the ways that they did try.

I was a disappointment to my parents, of course, as they were to one another; they belonged to the very first generation of aggregate households, and they made more than their fair share of the mistakes of inexperience to which all pioneers are inevitably prone—as did I.

What follows, then, is a record of hazard, whimsy, and coincidence—but in the absence of a biological heritage, it is the only ancestry I have and the only one I have ever needed. Names fascinated me in my youth and they fascinate me now. The significance of their back-stories may be accidental and artificial, but is no less powerful for that. I understand the crucial role that coincidence plays in attaching those back-stories to people and other creatures, like the tails of ragged cloth that are pinned to ill-drawn donkeys in the traditional children's game, but I also understand that coincidence plays a crucial role in everything; it is the true master of our destiny.

Madoc, it seems, was a fictitious Welsh prince of the twelfth century, the youngest son of Owen Gwyneth. His claim to enduring fame was that he was said to have crossed the Atlantic and discovered the continent that later became the Americas in 1170 or thereabouts. He was the subject of a poem penned in 1805 by Robert Southey, who subsequently became the British poet laureate. The poem describes the settlement that Madoc founded in Aztlan and tells the history of his long war against the Aztecas. At a crucial juncture, Madoc is ambushed and taken prisoner, then chained by the foot to the stone of human sacrifice. He is supposed to fight six Azteca champions in turn, but only has to face two before being rescued by his friend Cadwallon. His war is finally won, partly by virtue of assistance lent by Coatel, the daughter of the Azteca prince Aculhua, who meets a tragic end in consequence.

First names are, however, less important than surnames.

Tamlin, more usually rendered Tam Lin or Tamlane, was the central character of a ballad so old that it cannot be accurately dated, in which he first appears as an elfin knight who haunts the Scottish district of Carterhaugh. After impregnating Janet, heiress to the earthly component of that estate, he reveals that he was a changeling stolen long ago and kept eternally young by the Queen of the Fays. He fears that he will be selected as the tithe that the Land of Faerie must pay to Hell every seven years, but Janet claims him instead, in spite of a series of inconvenient metamorphoses forced upon him by the Queen of the Fays. He recovers his humanity . . . and with it, his mortality.

The idea that human children might be stolen by the fairies, and taken to a land where time passes far more slowly than it does on earth, was a common one in superstitious days. The idea was compounded, rather paradoxically, out of hope and fear: the hope of immortality and eternal youth; the fear of becoming alien and inhuman.

The time into which I was born was, by contrast, an era of antisuperstition and exotic manufacture, in which all children were told that they had every chance of becoming emortal, returning to the full flower of young adulthood again and again and again. We had not entirely given up our anxieties, because we knew about the Miller Effect and had conceived the idea of "robotization," but we were bold pioneers and we put our fears aside.

Even so, my world bore certain significant similarities to the world of medieval legend, which helped pave the way for new Tam Lins.

I could have changed the name my foster parents gave me, but I never wanted to. I accepted it as my own, and something precious. I know now that I was right to do so.

The Faerie of my first youth was the world of PicoCon and OmicronA, pioneers and manufacturers of nanotechnology. These friendly rivals sold to my peers the successive generations of Internal Technology that were supposed to constitute the escalator to emortality. That Faerie had no queen, but it did have a dictator of sorts: a shadowy committee known only by a rich assortment of nicknames, including the Inner Circle, the Secret Masters, the Dominant Shareholders, and the Hardinist Cabal. Even a man forewarned by his name could never have guessed that he might become a changeling by virtue of *their* endeavors, but I never knew how fortunate my name was until I became a helpless traveler in time, in dire need of redemption. It was, of course, a fluke of chance; those responsible for my plight took no account whatsoever of my name. But when I woke up, everything I felt and did thereafter was colored by my consciousness of my name. My surname helped to define the quality of the experience, and to control the way I navigated myself through it.

It helped, too, that I arrived in a world where all names were chosen, some more carefully than others. Those chosen names imprinted their back-stories on the pattern of events with a force and irony that could only be appreciated by someone as fascinated by names as I was—or so I believe. That is why I am telling you this story. The people who have asked me to do it have asked for a history, but it is not that. It has always seemed to me that stories which pass themselves off as histories ought to be conscientiously "hi"—lofty, distant, and imperious—while my character and profile have always been obstinately "lo," working from beneath rather than above, craftily rather than authoritatively.

I am, therefore, happy to leave the history of our adventure to the expert pen of my good friend Mortimer Gray; my own account is nothing but a lostory, more comedy than drama, more cautionary tale than epic. Others will doubtless offer their own accounts of the events of the Last of the Final Wars, many of whom were fortunate enough—or unfortunate enough—to be far closer to the action than I was, but I dare to hope that my poor lostory might cut more deeply than its rivals to the bone and marrow of the tale.

When I underwent the adventure described herein I was not the man I am now. I was a fearful stranger in a world that I had not even begun to understand—but no matter how crippling that disadvantage might be to a historian it is no disadvantage at all to a storyteller of the lower kind. Every tale requires a teller, no matter how impersonal he may pretend to be, and there are tales for which the fearful stranger obsessed by his own petty plight is the ideal narrator.

I have the aid of hindsight now, but I shall try to reserve its additional insights for the occasional sidebar and tell the story itself as it actually unfolded around me and in my mind—or as it *seemed* to unfold, given that I was never able to find the experience entirely convincing while I was in the thick of it.

How did Tam Lin feel, do you think, when he first met Janet of Carterhaugh? He had a reputation as a ghost, and she must have taken him for one at first, but how did he see himself and the world he had forsaken? Must they not have seemed like fragments of a dream, after so long a sojourn in Faerie?

How did Tam Lin recover his sense of the reality of Janet's world, and his sense of his own reality within it? The ballad does not say, because that is not the function of ballads, whose ambitions are essentially low, compared to the lofty pretentions of history. Ballads engage and provoke the imagination; they do not satisfy it. This is a different kind of lostory, and I must try harder to answer such questions—or at least to point out their relevance—but there will always be something of the balladeer in me, because my name requires it.

This is the way that I imagine it.

When Tam Lin saw Janet, and had his attention *caught*, as if by a fisherman's hook, she must have seemed to him a glorious mystery, whose solution lay deep within himself. Tam Lin would surely have gone in search of that solution, delving into the depths of his transformed being in search of memories of the world which had such creatures in it. He could not have found them immediately, for the Queen of the Fays had confounded his memory. She had not been willing to wipe it out, because that would have obliterated him—her captive, her prize, her toy—but she had blurred it and hidden a few significant details. Perhaps he struggled to fill in the gap with confabulation, telling himself a tale about how it might have been that he had stumbled out of the world and into Faerie. He probably did—not because he was a natural storyteller, but because he had no other way to approach the problem of separating his new and future self from his Faerie self.

Either way, he would eventually have set aside his confusion, and all the mysteries wrapped up in it.

Tam Lin must have said to himself, in the end: "Well then, no matter what has gone before, or why, I must make a new beginning now. I must seize this opportunity, and all that goes with it. I must focus my mind on the matter in hand, and the future which now awaits me. I must set my course and cling to it, no matter what efforts anyone might make to steal it from me."

He would not, of course, have used those words—but I would, and I am the storyteller here.

When I woke up and found myself in a place I did not know, I searched for a memory of how I got there, and could not find one. I found nothing but confusion. Everything revealed to me by my new situation added to that confusion.

Other men would doubtless have approached the problem differently, but I was and am a Tamlin, so I approached it as a Tamlin would and should. The name might have been chosen at random, but it exerted its force nevertheless, as names inevitably do.

TWO
THE WONDERFUL CHILD

The room in which I found myself was sparsely furnished. Apart from two reclining chairs upholstered in black there was only a small table whose hexagonal top was finished in something that looked like white marble. The walls seemed to be devoid of tangible equipment, although there was a single broad window and various aggregations of colored symbols, whose meaning I couldn't decipher.

I knew that the impossibly rich star field visible through the window could not be an actual vista viewed through glass, but that was only one reason to suspect that the whole room was an illusion: an artifact of Virtual Experience.

The star field *had* to be a mere image, so the window had to be a kind of screen. There was no reason why the whole setup should not be an image, so Occam's razor suggested that it was. The room was, admittedly, far more convincing than any room in any VE tape I had ever seen or worked on, but I knew that what I had seen and done was by no means state-of-the-art. My friend Damon Hart had told me about an experience of his, when one of the people at the heart of PicoCon had revealed a secret VE-technology that employed clever Internal Technology to secure an extremely powerful illusion.

I could not remember what I had been doing immediately before falling unconscious, and could not locate myself in time at all. Although I knew who and what I was, I had no idea how to conjure up my "most recent" memory. I had no idea where I was up to in the unfolding narrative of my life, but I did have a vague feeling that whatever I had been doing before I found myself in the strange room had something to do with PicoCon, and something to do with Damon Hart.

I decided that there was no point in chasing ghosts, and that it would be more sensible to concentrate on things of which I could be certain—but it was a difficult resolution to keep, at first.

I could, of course, be certain of the reality of my own stream of consciousness, although even that seemed rather strange and oddly uncomfortable, but I knew that I couldn't have the same level of certainty about the reality of the smartsuit I appeared to be wearing. Black was my color, and I could as easily have chosen the false cuffs giving way to the fleshtone hands as the slightly ornate false boots and the slightly exaggerated codpiece, but the fact remained that I certainly hadn't dressed myself.

I didn't have any actual memory of waking up. Did that mean that I might still be dreaming? Might it mean that I might not be who and what I thought I was at all?

I licked my lips and scratched the back of my neck—traditional tests to be applied by people who were no longer sure whether they were in the real world or in a VE—but it was more by way of ritual than seeking reassurance. I knew that if I really were locked into a heavy-duty VE cocoon with diabolical nanobots standing guard over all my channels of sensory experience, there was no way I was going to penetrate the illusion by means of such crude and elementary tests.

I had to think my way through my predicament.

With the aid of hindsight, I can now understand that the suspicion that I was locked into a manufactured illusion was an asset. It insulated me against all possible surprises, all possible alarms. Had I not spent so much of my early life manufacturing and doctoring admittedly primitive VE tapes for sale to fans of vicarious sex, violence, and adventure, I might have been a great deal more disturbed by the discoveries I was about to make, but I was better equipped than most to find out what had become of me without experiencing terror or madness.

For a few minutes, therefore, I was content simply to stare at the occupant of the other chair. She looked like a child—female, I guessed, although I wasn't entirely confident of the judgment—of approximately nine years of age.

Her smartsuit wasn't as snug as mine, and it was much more brightly colored: intricately patterned in sky blue, lilac and wine red. The way she looked back at me suggested so strongly that she wasn't what she seemed that I was almost convinced that she had to be an illusion: a visual trick like the star field outside the window.

When PicoCon had attempted to intimidate Damon he had been "taken" to a ledge half way up an impossibly high mountain and interrogated by a humanoid figure whose surface was a mirror. It had been a demonstration of awesome power and an invitation to temptation. Damon had told me at the time that he had remained obdurate in the face of that temptation, and I think he meant it. Alas, he had underestimated the force of his own wisdom and his capacity for compromise; he had eventually given in and joined the ruling elite.

I had always prided myself on having more self-knowledge than my one-time protégé, even when our roles were reversed, and I was prepared to respond to any threat or temptation in a thoroughly realistic manner.

After deciding that the nine-year-old girl was only wearing that appearance, concealing within it something far older, probably artificial and possibly dangerous, I deliberately looked away. I looked out of the "window," at the star field.

It seemed the obvious thing to do: why else would the window be part of the scene?

All stars look alike, especially when aggregated in their millions, so it didn't take long to absorb the impression. I was tempted to get up and go to the window, to touch it—and by that touching, perhaps, to reveal its falsity. I had already made enough small movements, though, to inform myself that something was wrong with my sense of weight and balance. I wasn't sure that I could get up without seeming awkward, and I wasn't sure that I could walk to the window without stumbling. I had to suppose that if I weren't stuck in VE I must be some place where the gravity was less than Earth's—maybe as much as twenty or thirty percent less. That seemed absurd enough to strengthen the hypothesis that I was in a VE—but even in a VE one can easily lose one's balance.

I didn't want to appear clumsy. I wanted to offer the appearance of a man in full control of himself: a man who couldn't be thrown by any combination of circumstances, no matter how upsetting they might have been to an *ordinary* mortal.

So I looked back at the fake little girl, having decided that the sensible thing to do was to open negotiations.

She got there ahead of me.

"How do you feel, Mr. Tamlin?" the little girl asked.

"Not quite myself," I told her, truthfully. "Is that you, Damon?" It was a hopeful question. If the whole thing was a fake, a petty and purposeless melodrama, then the better possibility was that it had been rigged by a friend rather than an enemy. Perhaps it was my birthday, and Damon had laid on a surprise party in Dreamland.

"My name is Davida Berenike Columella," the little girl replied. "I'm the chief cryogenic engineer on the microworld Excelsior, in the Counter-Earth Cluster."

"Wow," I said, as casually as I could, by way of demonstrating my refusal to be impressed or startled. "The Counter-Earth Cluster. What year is it supposed to be?"

In my day, there had been no cluster of microworlds making its way around Earth's orbital path on the far side of the sun, although there had been a couple of clusters at Lagrange points much closer to home.

"By our reckoning, this is year ninety-nine," the child answered. "According to the Christian Era calendar that was in use when you were frozen down, this year would be three thousand two hundred and sixty-three. March the twenty-first of that year, to be exact."

I wanted to say "wow" again, but I couldn't muster enough ironic contempt. I swallowed, although there was nothing in my mouth or throat to swallow.

"I seem to have mislaid some of my memories," I said, less confidently than I would have liked. "Could you possibly remind me of what I've been doing lately?"

She nodded her head gravely. "I understand that short-term memory loss was a common side effect of the SusAn technologies in use in your time," she said. "Our records are incomplete, but it seems that you were frozen down on the third of September twenty-two zero-two, presumably by order of a court.

"*Frozen down?*" I couldn't help reacting to that as if it were true, but I collected myself quickly enough. It wasn't entirely impossible that I had ended up in court, and if one added all my petty crimes together, it wasn't implausible that I might have got a custodial sentence—but I couldn't remember being arrested, let alone charged and convicted. In any case, even though the fashionable sentence of the day was indeterminate in length—on the grounds that many of those committed to Suspended Animation were "habitual delinquents" from which the public needed and deserved "due protection"—I *knew* that I couldn't have been convicted of anything that would get me put away for longer than a couple of years. I was utterly convinced that I couldn't have *done* anything that would have got me put away for more than a couple of years.

Or could I?

Surely I would have remembered carrying out a massacre or blowing up a building full of people.

Then again, I thought, what would *anyone* have to do to justify putting them away for more than a thousand years?

What the child was telling me was that I had been woken up a mere hundred days before my eleven hundredth birthday, having served a term of "imprisonment" of one thousand

and sixty years, six months, and a couple of weeks. Even allowing for the fact that SusAn confinement provided no scope for remission on the grounds of good behavior, that seemed a trifle excessive.

I really did think that: "a trifle excessive." Such was the balanced state of my mind, cushioned by the commanding suspicion that this was all a game, a VE drama.

"What else do you know about me?" I asked the child.

"Very little," she replied. "Now that you know my name and the date and place of your awakening, you know as much about us as we know about you." I didn't believe her. I was sure that it had to be a game, a ploy, a tease—anything but the truth.

"You must know what I was frozen down *for*," I countered, warily.

"That datum appears to have been erased from the record," she said. "Do you remember doing anything that might have given rise to a sentence of imprisonment?"

I thought she was mocking me. I remembered a considerable number of trivial offenses. It occurred to me that I might have been convicted of "treasonous sabotage"—which is to say, deleting and falsifying official data with malicious and fraudulent intent. It was a crime I had committed more than once, and for a variety of reasons. So far as I could remember, though, in the years immediately preceding the summer of 2202 I had only done such things while acting according to the requests and under the orders of the Secret Masters of the World—or, more prosaically, Damon Hart. It was not beyond the bounds of possibility that I had been ratted out to the UN Police by my own employers. My arrest and conviction might conceivably have been a sop in the convoluted diplomatic game the Secret Masters still felt obliged to play against the representatives of a World Democracy that had not yet been reduced to absolute impotence. But it didn't seem likely.

Surely, if that had been the case, I'd have remembered it.

Anyway, no one in the world could have expected me to

serve more than ten years in the freezer for treasonous sabotage. The only way I could have been removed from society for any longer than that—let alone a thousand years—was by falling victim to treasonous sabotage myself.

In other words, if what the strange child was telling me was true, then someone like me must have been hired by someone like Damon Hart—or Damon Hart's new masters— to obliterate the record of my conviction and imprisonment.

It couldn't be true. It had to be a joke.

It didn't seem to me to be very funny, but I figured that I had no alternative, for the time being, but to play along. Even though it had to be a VE melodrama, I had to play my part as if it were real.

What alternative was there? Even if the conviction that it was all a fraudulent game turned out to be wrong, it would make a convenient psychological defense against the horror of the truth. Even if I really were in the far future, it would be best to remain in denial a little longer. I had always been a highly skilled denier, and a devoted guerilla warrior against the excesses of truth. Why else would Damon Hart have hired me so frequently to do his dirty work?

"Would you believe me if I told you that I'm an innocent man?" I said to the wonderful child. "The unfortunate victim of a miscarriage of justice."

"Given that your tone seems to indicate that you don't believe it yourself," she replied, "no."

"So why bring me back?" I asked, entering into the spirit of the game. "If I really have been in the freezer for a thousand years and more, why bring me back *now*?"

"It was a trial run," she told me, brutally. "We were uncertain that we could revive individuals who had been in stasis for so long without their having suffered considerable side effects—not merely loss of memory but irredeemable deterioration of personality."

"My personality's okay," I was quick to assure her, although I was equally quick to doubt it. "Except for this sense I have of not quite being myself," I added, after a pause for thought, perhaps a little too scrupulously. Then, after a further pause, I asked: "Why me?"

"It seems you were one of only two long-term prisoners accepted into the Foundation's care in times past who were put into SusAn within two hundred years of Adam Zimmerman," she said. "When we interrogated our records you emerged as the second most obvious candidate for the trial. Perhaps I should say that, although we shall continue to investigate the extent of the mental side effects you have suffered, we are reasonably content with the way the trial has worked. We'll need to form a better estimate of the extent of your loss of memory, but your coherency is reassuring. Your feeling of not being quite yourself may be a result of the IT we've installed. It would be helpful if you'd try to remember as much as you can. The records suggest that the loss of memory suffered by early revenants from SusAn was usually limited to a few days preceding their vitrification, and was often temporary."

"I'll do my best," I promised, knowing that I'd have to do it for my own sake. Even if this whole thing were an illusion, I'd need to recover all the memories I could recover as soon as possible. "Apart from the lost memories, you reckon I'm okay?"

"So far as we can ascertain," she said, judiciously. "We discovered some residual nanomachines bound to your bones and the glial cells of your brain whose intended function is mysterious, but they appear to be inactive. They're probably vestigial—a side effect of the particular cryoprotective system used on your body. There's no trace of similar contamination in the second trial subject, nor in Adam Zimmerman's body."

I set aside the matter of the puzzling "contamination" for further contemplation at a future time. Assuming that this whole conversation must be a kind of test, there were easier points to be scored.

"So you're bringing Adam Zimmerman back," I said,

casually, in order to prove that my memory hadn't been completely shot to bits. "Are you what's become of the Ahasuerus Foundation? Has it taken you this long to conclude that you're capable of fulfilling your mission statement?"

"You know about the Ahasuerus Foundation," Davida Berenike Columella observed, unnecessarily. It was an obvious prompt.

"Damon Hart and I had some dealings with the Foundation," I confirmed, obligingly. She obviously expected more detail, and it seemed wisest to accentuate the positive side of my dealings. "Mostly with a woman named Rachel Trehaine," I added. "We helped her out a few times, and she did as much for us—you might be able to check that in your records."

She didn't reply to that immediately. I inferred that our conversation was being closely monitored, and that someone somewhere was making haste to trawl the records for any mention of Rachel Trehaine.

I figured that I was going to have to try to stand up eventually, so I took advantage of the momentary lull to make my tentative move.

I probably swayed a bit, but I didn't float away or flail my arms about in an unnecessarily comic fashion. I guessed that the gravity must be about three-quarters Earth normal—easy enough to get used to, I supposed, with a little care and practice.

But why, I thought, would anyone rig a VE to simulate nonstandard gravity?

The two chairs had been set three paces apart, so there was a considerable gap to cross before I could reach out and touch the wonderful child, but I took my time over it and couldn't have seemed particularly clownish.

She read the intention immediately, and flinched.

She didn't protest and she didn't move, but her eyes told me that she was scared. Now *she* was the one being subjected to a test.

I didn't know exactly why, but the sight of that fear, innocently manifest in her childlike eyes made me suddenly apprehensive. For the first time, I became anxious.

What am I, in her eyes? I wondered. *What have I become, in the space of a thousand years, that I should seem so terrible?*

I had known even before I got up that touching the wonderful child wouldn't prove anything. If I were as ingeniously cocooned as I might be, with clever IT supporting every aspect of an illusion, nothing would prove that my experience was real—but the terrified expression on Davida Berenike Columella's face looked genuine, all the more so because she was struggling so hard to control it.

I hesitated, trying to gauge the situation more accurately.

It seemed to me that she didn't want to be afraid, but that she couldn't help it. Even if we weren't in a VE, there was probably nothing much I could do to hurt or damage her, but she still couldn't help her reaction. After all, if we weren't in a VE, then I was presumably a monster out of the distant past, who had been committed to a term of indefinite imprisonment for a crime so dreadful that it had been expunged from the record. She had no reason to be certain that I wasn't a homicidal maniac.

But I reached out and touched her face anyway.

Maybe I *was* a monster.

The touch was gentle and brief; her relief when I took my hand away was as palpable as her anxiety had been.

"How old are you, really?" I asked, speaking softly.

"Two hundred and twenty years," she told me.

"And you're not speaking through some kind of sim? You really look like this, in the flesh?"

"Yes," she said.

If she was telling the truth, I realized, I was a stranger in a very strange land. More must have changed in a thousand years than I could ever have anticipated. It was an uncomfortable thought—but I was Madoc Tamlin, the spiritual descendant of one man who had been chained to a rock of sacrifice to fight the six champions of an alien land and one who had come back to Earth from Faerie, in spite of all that the Queen of the Fays had done to keep him and send him to hell.

I retreated to my chair, still moving gingerly. I sat down again, but I perched myself more stiffly and alertly than the posture I had been given when I was allowed to awake.

"Does *everybody* look like you now?" I asked.

"Only in Excelsior," she told me. "There are a great many human races. Some still look like you."

I was now in a state of psychological disarray, and I had to marshal my thoughts before I could frame another question. When my kind come crashing out of denial we tend to flip to the opposite extreme. *No game,* I thought. *All real. A thousand fucking years. Some human races still look like me. Others obviously don't. Who did this to me? Why?*

"Where's Damon?" I asked, a little more harshly than I intended.

When she didn't reply I amplified the request. "Damon Hart. Biological son of Conrad Helier, reared by his father's accomplices in crime. Late recruit to the Hardinist Cabal, breaking his surviving foster mother's rebellious heart. Don't tell me *he's* not in your records, alive or dead."

"He's dead," said Davida Berenike Columella, after pausing to consult her inner resources. "Everyone who was alive in your time is dead, except for a handful of individuals preserved, as you have been, in Suspended Animation. According to the available data, Damon Hart is not one of those. We can't be absolutely sure, because there are other repositories, but all the customary evidence of death is in place."

That was what they had said about Conrad Helier. Even Damon had believed it, until he learned better. I knew how easily "all the customary evidence of death" could be faked,

even in the twenty-second century, because it was a business
I'd dabbled in more than once—but that wasn't the issue my
distraught mind seized upon.

"*Everyone?*" I echoed. "What about the escalator to
emortality? We all thought that the lucky ones, at least,
would get to live forever."

"The technologies of longevity available in your time were
inadequate," she informed me, flatly. "Nanotechnological
repair and somatic rejuvenation had inbuilt limitations. The
first true technologies of emortality didn't come into use until
the twenty-fifth century. They required the extensive genetic
engineering of fertilized egg cells, so the first emortal human
species had to be born to that condition. The oldest currently
living individuals who have been continuously active were
born in the two thousand four hundred and eighties."

"When did Damon die?" I asked, not bothering to add
the word "allegedly."

She obviously had a covert data feed whispering incessantly into her inner ear. "In the year two thousand five hundred and two," was the prompt answer.

Three hundred years! He'd left me where I was for *three
hundred years* of his own protracted lifetime. Why hadn't he
used his authority and influence to get me out? What on
Earth had I done to deserve that kind of neglect?

"All I ever did was hack into a few data stores," I said, my
voice no more than a whisper. "Steal a little information
here, delete a little there, reconstruct a little here *and* there. I
was working for the government, for God's sake. The *real*
government, not the elected one. I really am innocent, by any
reasonable standard. I never killed anyone, or even hurt anyone much who wasn't asking for it."

"Can you be certain of that?" my interlocutor asked, still
probing.

"Yes," I said. "I *am* certain. I've lost a few memories. I
can't remember August twenty-two zero-two, let alone September. In June and July I was working for Damon, *with*
Damon. Not just working—playing too. Having a good time.

Planning a little espionage. Nothing heavy, just run-of-the-mill low-level skulduggery. We weren't even outlaws by then. We were on the inside, rubbing shoulders with the elite, playing in the big boys' game, by their rules. *I never killed anybody*. I would remember. I remember what I did, what I was. Even if they'd added in every last one of all the things I could have been charged with in my youth but never was—all the burglary, the smuggling, the dealing, the tax evasion, the so-called pornography, and all the rest of that penny-ante crap—they couldn't have put me away for more than twenty years. *Why on Earth would they throw away the fucking key?*"

Davida Berenike Columella didn't know the answer. Either she figured that I needed a little time to come to terms with it or she was avidly watching for signs of mental breakdown, because she kept quiet, letting me run with the train of thought.

I realized that there was a certain contradiction in what I'd said. Damon and I *had* been playing the big boys' game, by their rules. We'd been playing in a pool where "a little espionage" and "low-level skulduggery" were no longer a matter for slapped wrists. We'd been playing in a pool where people took their secrets seriously.

Even so, a thousand years was an extremely long time to be hidden away. Why hadn't Damon been able to find me? Why hadn't he been able to get me out?

Suddenly, the stars outside the fake window didn't seem so bright or so lordly. They seemed confused, lost in a darkness that they couldn't quite obliterate even though they were massed in their trillions.

I knew that they weren't all stars. Some of them were galaxies. The universe was full of galaxies, a hundred billion or more, but it was also full of darkness and emptiness.

Raw space, so the theorists of my time had said, was full of seething potentials—particulate eddies beyond the surface of the void, ever-ready to erupt into tangibility—but the sum of all that infinite activity was *nothing*.

And wherever the potential *was* manifest—wherever there was something instead of nothing—there was still, if measured on any scale responsible to the true size of the universe, *almost* nothing.

I existed. At least, I had to suppose so. But so what?

I felt that I had an obligation to pull myself together. After all, I seemed to be the first ambassador from the world of mortal men ever to be entertained in Excelsior.

"Why ninety-nine?" I asked, as calmly as I could. "Why did you start the calendar over?"

"The Christian Era had ended long before that system of counting was abandoned," she said. "On Earth, the new calendar was belatedly introduced after the Great North American Basalt Flow—year one was the first year of the so-called Gaean Restoration. The microworlds in Earth orbit adopted the convention because we all share the same year. Different systems apply on the inner worlds and the outer satellites, and in the more distant microworld clusters."

I saw a chance to rack up a few more marks in the big test by guessing what the "Great North American Basalt Flow" must have been.

"So the Yellowstone Supervolcano finally blew up again," I said. "Every umpteen million years, regular as clockwork." It would have been even more impressive if I'd been able to remember the exact term of its periodicity.

"The magma chamber that ruptured was located in the former Yellowstone National Park in the United States of North America," she confirmed, after a brief fact-check pause. "It had been closely monitored ever since the Coral Sea disaster of 2542, and was thought to be under control. The recriminations and accusations are still unsettled, at least on Earth itself."

That was an intriguing remark. "You mean somebody let it off *deliberately*?" I asked. "Somebody blew up North America and plunged the whole planet into nuclear winter?"

That required a slightly longer data feed, perhaps to translate the term "nuclear winter." Eventually, she said: "The majority opinion is that the eruption was an accident caused by a malfunction of the systems securing the magma chamber. There are, however, factions which believe that the systems were sabotaged—they differ in their hypotheses as to who might have been responsible and why."

I didn't need a data feed to interpret "Gaean Restoration" for me. A major basalt flow must have begun with an explosive release of gas and ash into the air, fouling the atmosphere for years. The ecosphere must have suffered a tremendous die-back—but when the dust had settled and the poison gases had been neutralized, the human survivors must have set about the business of regenerating the ecosphere according to their own schemes. This time, unlike any other in the deep prehistory of the Earth, there must have been human survivors, but millions or billions must have died. Millions or billions of emortals.

"Did the Hardinist Cabal still own the planet when it happened?" I asked.

She didn't procrastinate over the precise significance of the term, although she took the trouble to substitute one of her own. "The people who styled themselves Stewards of the Earth had already lost some of their former power and influence," she reported, "and the fact that the planet's balance of trade with the outer system was in irredeemable deficit implied that their decline was irreversible. They probably remain privately convinced that the eruption was sabotage directed at them, perhaps by Earthbound rebels and perhaps by outer system radicals, although their public position is that it was an unfortunate accident. Certain other factions have suggested that the Stewards were the responsible party, and that the effective destruction of the ecosphere enabled them to reestablish a local economic hegemony that they would soon have lost. That seems unlikely, given that the disaster brought about a dramatic increase in imports from the outer system."

"Do the Secret Masters of Earth know you've woken me up?" I asked, trying not to sound too paranoid.

"They have been kept fully informed of our plans and our progress, as a matter of courtesy," the wonderful child assured me. "The United Nations of Earth will send a delegation to attend the awakening of Adam Zimmerman, as will the Outer System Confederation. If their deceleration patterns proceed according to plan, the ships carrying the delegations will both arrive within a hundred hours' time."

"So you're still going to wake Zimmerman, even though my memory is impaired?"

"Yes. We shall continue to monitor your progress, and if we can find a way to help you recover your lost memories we'll do it. If Adam Zimmerman suffers similar problems, we'll counter them as best we can."

"How's the second test subject doing?"

"We hope to awaken the second subject in seven hours' time. Everything has gone well so far, but her state of mind remains to be ascertained."

"Who is the other trial subject?" I asked, not really expecting to hear a name I knew.

"A woman named Christine Caine," was the reply I got.

Like most of the other names which figure in this lostory, that one had a tale attached—one which bore a decidedly sinister significance.

FOUR
BAD KARMA

The single most astonishing aspect of my return to consciousness, a thousand years later than could ever have been expected, was that the one thing that tangibly astonished me during that first interview with the child-who-wasn't-a-child was the sound of Christine Caine's name. I'd just been informed that I'd missed out on a millennium of human history, including the advent of universal emortality and the temporary devastation of the Gaean ecosphere, and the news that actually threw me way off-balance was hearing that the other person appointed to share my fate—I didn't, at that time, regard the legendary Adam Zimmerman as a partner in *my* fate—was the most notorious mass murderer of my parents' lifetime.

"You mean Christine Caine as in *Bad Karma*," I said to Davida Berenike Columella, just in case the name had become fashionable after 2202.

Davida seemed to have no idea what I was talking about, and her data feed obviously wasn't helping. Apparently, it wasn't just my record that had been erased.

Again I was seized by the conviction that it had to be a joke. I'd almost given up hoping that it was all a VE drama, but the reference to the most notorious VE drama of my own era seemed too surreal to be anything but contrivance. Except that it wasn't really a reference, from the viewpoint of Davida Berenike Columella. If appearances could be trusted, she had never heard of *Bad Karma* and knew no more about Christine Caine than she knew about me.

I remembered the way that the seeming child had flinched when she realized that I was going to touch her. She'd had no idea who I was. Given that I'd been committed to prison a thousand years before, with the record of my crime obliterated, I might easily have been a mass murderer. As it happened, I wasn't, although Davida couldn't be *entirely* prepared to take my word for it.

But Christine Caine really was a monster, by all accounts. She was also the subject of the most notorious illegal VE drama of all time—or had been, when "all time" had only extended as far as July 2202.

Suddenly, I was forced to contemplate the exact terms of the "trial run" of which I was now a part.

"You've tried to bring me back exactly as I was when I was put away," I said, by way of clarification. "You wanted to be as certain as you can be that you could do a good job of restoration, because that's what you hope to do with Adam Zimmerman. So you've also tried as hard as you can to put Christine Caine back together exactly as she was when she went into the freezer, right?"

"That's correct," the wonderful child agreed.

"And so far as I can tell," I reported, "you've done a reasonably good job on me, save for a few recent memories. Not that I'd be consciously aware of any differences, I suppose, and I haven't had time to check my other memories as closely as I might, and I really *don't* quite feel like myself . . . but even so, I'm perfectly prepared to accept me as I am. In which case, you might want to take a few extra precautions with Christine Caine."

"Why?"

"Well," I said. "For one thing, she was convicted of murdering thirteen people, ten of whom were her adoptive parents. For another, although opinions varied as to the exact nature and extent of her mental illness, nobody doubted that she was barking mad."

"Did you know her?" Davida Berenike Columella inquired, innocently.

"*Know* her? Of course I didn't *know* her. She was frozen down when I was four years old. But I was in the illicit VE business for a while and I knew all about *Bad Karma*. I suppose I even wished I'd made it, or had been capable of making it."

I could tell that Davida had known full well that Christine Caine had been frozen down in 2167, thirty-five years before me. That had been another little test, which I'd obviously passed. But I could tell, too, that she really didn't have a clue what *Bad Karma* was. Classic of early VE or not, it was one work of art that hadn't stood the test of time. It had been lost—or successfully suppressed.

"*Bad Karma* was a VE drama," I explained. "Underground stuff, shot *circa* twenty-one ninety-five. I used to make sex tapes and fight tapes in my youth, some of them far enough out on the edge to be bannable, but nothing like *Bad Karma*. The visuals were fairly crude—I could have improvised those easily enough without doing serious damage to any of the people that were supposedly carved up by the viewpoint character—but the sound track was something else. It was a whispered voice-over representing the stream-of-consciousness of the murderer whose eyes the user was supposedly seeing through.

"The improvised thought-track provided a theory of sorts as to why Christine Caine had committed the murders. It was partly based on one of several conflicting statements she'd given to the police and various psychiatric examiners after her arrest, but mainly improvised. In those days, even visuals were considered a potentially dangerous medium of consumer/perpetrator identification, but that thought-track kicked off a real moral panic.

"Rumor had it that sensitive users—especially kids—might be taken over by the thought-track, driven mad, and led to commit copycat crimes. The rumors were probably started by the guys who made the tape, for marketing purposes, but they proved a little too effective. There *were* copycat crimes, for which the VE *might* have been partly responsible—but you probably know better than I do how crazy those times were. Christine Caine can't know anything about the VE tape, of course, and she might be a very different person from the one represented in the thought-track— but she did do the murders. If you've put her back together exactly as she was when she went into SusAn, you've reconstructed a crazy serial killer."

Davida Berenike Columella didn't seem to be as frightened by this news as she had been of my casual gesture, but I was physically present and Christine Caine wasn't.

"She won't be able to harm anyone," the wonderful child told me.

If that remark was supposed to be reassuring, it missed by a mile. I guessed immediately that if Christine Caine wasn't going to be able to hurt anyone when they woke her up—and it seemed that nothing I'd said had troubled that assumption—then neither could I. Which meant that they hadn't, after all, put me together *exactly* as I'd been before. They'd taken precautions.

"You're installing some kind of IT in her head," I guessed, still talking about Christine Caine because I didn't want to talk about myself. "Something that will stop her if she runs amok."

"We can do that," the wonderful child confirmed, ambiguously.

That was when I saw—clearly, I thought—that Christine Caine would be resuming her life as an animal in a zoo: a specimen to be observed, and wondered at. And I understood, too, that I had just contributed to that fate by robbing her of her last hope of not being recognized for what she was, and her last hope of being able to make a new start.

I didn't know exactly how old Christine Caine had been when they'd put her away, but I knew that she wasn't much more than twenty. In terms of elapsed time, I was no more than twice her age; Davida Berenike Columella was ten times as old, although she looked no more than nine.

From the viewpoint of those who had brought us back

into the world, I realized, Christine Caine and I were *alike*, no matter how slight my unknown crimes might have been compared to hers. Whatever they had done to her, and whatever they intended to do to her in future, they must have done and would also do to me. I too was a creature in a zoo: a representative of an extinct species, resurrected by ingenuity into a world of which I knew nothing.

I knew, because I had had dealings with the Ahasuerus Foundation a thousand years before, that the people of Excelsior were bringing Adam Zimmerman back because they intended to make him emortal. Even to Rachel Trehaine, in the 2190s, Adam Zimmerman had been a great hero, one of the founders of the modern world order. The Hardinist Cabal, or whatever rump of it still remained, could hardly help thinking of him in much the same light, given that he had played such a vital role in the economic coup that had launched their inexorable climb to world domination. This world presumably had a place ready made for Adam Zimmerman—if not a throne, a pedestal. But what did it have for Christine Caine, or for me?

I concluded then that whatever debt of gratitude I owed Davida Berenike Columella and her people for bringing me back to life, they were not my friends. It was not a happy thought, but it was not a crushing discovery either.

I had always prided myself on being tough, on being able to adapt myself to adverse circumstance. I knew that I could be tough now. I knew that I could be tougher than I had ever been before, because I—unlike Damon Hart, it seemed—had managed to keep my place on that imaginary escalator while everyone else I ever knew had lost their footing.

If all this was real, then I really had ridden the tide of opportunity into a world where emortality was for everyone, or almost everyone—including, I hoped, the animals in the zoo. I knew that I might have to be careful, and clever, and cunning, but I had been all those things before—and the people of Excelsior seemed to have put me back together very nearly as I had been before.

If there's a game to be played here, I thought, *whether in reality or a VE drama, then it has to be won.* I understood that from the very start. I had understood it all my life, and I could see no reason to change my mind, no matter what miracles had transformed the world during the millennium I had lost, while I was away with the Fays.

"If you're really going to wake Christine Caine tomorrow," I said, by way of making my first real move in the game, "I think you'd better let me do the talking. I'm the only one who might be able to make her understand—at least to the extent that I can understand."

"Thank you for the offer," said the wonderful child. "We'll certainly consider it."

It was her manner more than her choice of words that belatedly tipped me off to the fact that the kind of English she was talking wasn't her first language, even though it might be a variety thereof. I realized that she might well have learned it in order to talk to me—or to the heroic Adam she considered the true creator of her world.

I knew better than to offer to be the first to talk to *him*, and told myself that he would probably have far less need of my intercession than poor Christine Caine.

I'm less confident of that judgment today than I was then, but I'm less confident of many things now than I was then. That's one of the effects of growing ever older, if you do it properly.

The food was awful. It even looked awful, but I managed to keep my hopes up for a few moments longer by telling myself that appearances could be deceptive. Once I had taken the first mouthful, though, there was no further room for optimism.

Davida Berenike Columella was watching me closely, but she wasn't partaking herself. I knew that I was still being tested, but I wasn't sure how to pass this one. I wanted to be polite, but I didn't want to give her the wrong impression, so I lifted a second forkful thoughtfully, hoping that it wouldn't be quite as bad.

It wasn't. The stuff was edible, and the first bolus hadn't set off an emetic reaction in my stomach, so I had to figure that it wouldn't do me any real harm—but I'd have felt better if I'd known which bit of my tongue was adapting to the taste. I couldn't take any comfort from the notion that the extra layer of skin that extended into my mouth from my smartsuit might include among its duties the responsibility to conceal the fact that I was eating crap.

While I chewed I made a careful study of the food on the plastic plate. The rice was a peculiar shade of yellow, but practically all genemod rice had been a peculiar shade of yellow in my day, so that wasn't surprising. Anyway, the worst thing about the rice was that it was bland to the point of tastelessness. It was the sliced vegetables that seemed to be seriously nasty, but I couldn't work out whether it was the things faintly resembling peppers or the bits with the slightly woody texture that were the worst offenders. The muddy brown sauce was definitely off, but there wasn't a great deal of that and it was mostly round the edges, so there hadn't been much of it on either of the forkfuls I'd taken in.

I looked up again at the impossible child, and met her gaze squarely. Other possibilities were occurring to me now.

"You made this especially for me, didn't you?" I said.

"Yes," she admitted.

"Using a thousand-year-old recipe and ingredients nobody's grown as food plants for centuries?"

"It was the best approximation we could contrive," she told me, apologetically. She'd caught on to the fact that I didn't like it.

"So why didn't you just give me whatever *you* eat?" I wanted to know.

"We have different nutritional requirements," she told me.

I took this guarded observation to mean that she was genetically engineered not to require vitamins and all the other quirky compounds that real humans had to include in their diet. The implication was that everything I thought of as real food had gone out of fashion centuries ago. In my own day, it had been the world's poor—who were still exceedingly numerous—who had the dubious privilege of existing on whole-diet "mannas" compounded by machines to supply exactly that combination of amino acids, lipids, carbohydrates, and trace elements that a human body required to keep it going. Now, apparently, such contrivances were the staff of posthuman life. What else, I wondered, had the aged children of Excelsior given up? If they didn't get their kicks from food, or wine, or sex . . .

"Did you, by any chance, take the trouble to manufacture any liquor for us?" I asked. "Adam Zimmerman's probably going to expect champagne and cognac when he wakes up, but I could be content with a decent bourbon."

"Adam Zimmerman only drank red wine," she informed me.

"I'll take that as a no, then," I said. Tired of being polite, I pushed the plate away, although the effect of the gesture was ruined by the lack of available space on the flat ledge that the smart wall had extruded to serve as a dining table.

I ran my fingers over the surface of the wall, speculatively. "How clever is this stuff?" I asked.

"Not very," was the unhelpful reply—but Davida repented of her surliness almost immediately. "It can mold itself to any purpose you might require," she said. "If you need a cocoon in which to sleep, or to immerse yourself in VE . . . although you'll probably find a hood appropriate to most purposes."

"Not exactly a utility mist, then." I said.

She didn't recognise the term, so I elaborated. "PicoCon's bolder admen used to look forward to a day when all the matter in the world except for humans would consist of a gray fog of nanomachines that would obligingly manufacture anything its masters desired, according to their command. At that point in future history the distinction between reality and Virtual Experience was expected to break down, because reality itself would be programmable. You don't seem to have gone quite that far."

"No," she admitted. "There's a sense in which the whole microworld is a single machine, of course, but most of its components are as functionally independent as the cells in your body, and as limited in their scope. Walls do what walls are equipped to do."

"So there's no central intelligence—no Microworld Mastermind?"

"There's a hierarchy of managing AIs, culminating in a master supervisor, but there's no central ego. The AIs aren't authentically intelligent, individually or collectively. They don't have self-conscious minds in the sense that you and I do."

The silvery "artificial geniuses" of my day had seemed very smart to their users, and everyone had had an opinion as to whether they would one day make the evolutionary transition to self-consciousness and personality, but the real geniuses making and programming them had always assured us that it couldn't and wouldn't happen. Apparently, they'd been right. Excelsior might have a brain the size of a small planet, but if Davida could be believed it wasn't home to a *person*.

"You might try something simpler," I suggested, nodding toward the uneaten food. "Manna will do. There's no need to try to make it more interesting. The culinary art is a lot more difficult than mere recipes imply."

"I'm sorry," Davida said, plaintively. "We'll try to produce something more to your liking."

"But not for my benefit," I guessed, wryly. "This was another trial run, wasn't it? You wouldn't want Adam Zimmerman to react this way to his welcoming banquet, would you? I suppose you'll want to let me try out a few more experimental meals before you set the menu for the big celebration. Or is the ship from Earth bringing supplies fit for a thousand-year-old messiah? Did you think to ask the UN to send a chef as well as an ambassador?"

"The ship that's coming from Earth is a shuttle," she told me, with just the slightest hint of resentment in her voice. "It has no cargo space, and only six cocoons. The ship from the outer system is much bigger, but the outer satellites produce their food in exactly the same way that we do, using artificial photosynthesis. We didn't know that this problem would arise, and we'll try to address it as best we can. We didn't mean to cause you any distress."

Having thought it over while she was speaking I pulled the plate back again and took another forkful. It still wasn't good, but it was even less offensive than its predecessors.

"This fancy second skin you've fitted me with is already compensating, isn't it?" I said. "All I have to do is keep shoveling the stuff in, and eventually I'll get to like it."

She didn't seem certain. "Your internal technology is programmed to compensate for discomfort," she admitted, "but not to substitute a positive reward. That would be dangerous."

I nodded, to signify that I understood the distinction and the reasons for making it. One of the first uses to which experimental internal nanotech had been put was feeding the so-called pleasure areas in the hind brain. That way lay addiction, and severe distraction from the business of living. The systems that had been released on to the market in my day were supposed to be finely tuned to administer pain relief without blissing people out. The masters of PicoCon were firmly committed to the idea that people ought to earn their pleasures.

Even a dedicated rebel like me could see the sense in that. The only gratification worth having is the gratification of achievement, even if the achievement in question is the mere exercise of good taste.

I deduced, therefore, that I would get used to the food if I persisted, but I wouldn't be forced to like it. I wondered how many other aspects of my second lifetime would be subject to the same principle. Perhaps I'd even get used to being a specimen in a zoo—but I certainly wasn't going to learn to like it.

I ate a little more, but I really wasn't hungry. I had other things on my mind.

"Can I take a look around now?" I asked my captor-in-chief. "Not through the picture-window—I'd like to look at Excelsior itself. The houses and the fields. The *real* windows."

"There are no real windows," she told me. "Nor any fields. The artificial photosynthetic systems are like big black sails. There is a garden, but it's sustained by artificial light. You'll be able to see it tomorrow."

There was no point in asking why I couldn't see it today. I was still under close observation and they didn't want to let me out of my cage just yet, not even for a stroll in the garden.

"How about a VE hood and access to your data banks?" I asked. "I'd like to read up on my history."

"You only have to ask," she said. Having seen the way she'd produced a dining table and a plateful of bad food I knew that *she* didn't even have to ask. She was IT-linked into a microworld-wide communication system that allowed her to issue commands and initiate semiautomatic responses almost unobtrusively—not just by forming the thought, I assumed, but certainly by means of carefully contrived sub-vocalizations. I didn't have that kind of IT. I couldn't give orders directly to the walls or the window—but if I spoke my requests aloud, someone would overhear, and decide whether or not to turn the request into a command.

I only had to ask, and anything within reason would be delivered to me . . . but I did have to ask, and anything my captors thought unreasonable would not be forthcoming. For the time being, the walls confining me would only produce an exit door for Davida Berenike Columella.

"I could be useful, you know," I told her. "I was born two hundred years after Adam Zimmerman, from an artificial womb rather than a natural one, but I have a lot more in common with him than you do. By the same token, I have a lot more in common with you than he does. I could be a useful intermediary, if you let me. That might not be why you woke me up, but it's a definite plus."

Secretly, of course, I was hoping that it *was* one of the reasons they'd woken me up—but I knew better than to take it for granted.

"Thank you for the offer," she said.

For a moment she seemed almost human. I'd been brushed off in exactly that casual manner a hundred times before, though never by a nine-year-old. I knew that I'd have to try harder.

"I know how he'll feel," I told her, flatly. "You don't. You think he'll be grateful. You think you'll be waking him up to tell him exactly what he always wanted to hear: that you can finally give him the emortality he craved. But I know how he'll *really* feel. That's why I'll be able to talk to him man to man. That's why I'll be the only one who can talk to him man to man."

She didn't bother throwing Christine Caine's name into

the ring. She was too busy worrying about the possibility that I might be right.

"How will he feel?" she asked, without even bothering to add a qualification reminding me that my guess could only be a guess. I knew that I had to be succinct as well as confident, provocative as well as plausible.

"Betrayed," I said, and left it at that.

I assumed that if she could figure out what I meant, she'd probably be able to understand why she might need me. If she couldn't, then she would definitely need me, whether she understood why or not.

I was fairly certain that Christine Caine wouldn't want to wake up in a sterile room with a window looking out on a star-filled universe. I suggested to Davida Berenike Columella that she and her sisters might like to let Christine wake up in Excelsior's Edenic garden, bathing in the complex glory of fake sunlight, but they wouldn't hear of it. They wanted her inside.

Presumably they still wanted *me* inside too, although they were too polite to say so in so many words. They wanted to take their time about exposing their world to the untender gaze of two supercriminals from the legendary past.

Their idea of compromise was to let me choose the scenic tape that the virtual window would display.

If I'd had the chance to do some serious research before the sisterhood offered me that choice I might have picked the finest ice palaces on Titan, or the AI metropolis on Ganymede, or perhaps a purple forest on the world that home-system people still called Ararat because that was the first name reported back to them—but I knew nothing, as yet, of wonders like that. A little taste of home seemed to be the better bet.

I asked for the oldest pre-holocaust footage they had of Yellowstone. Christine had been a city girl, but she must have used a VE hood as much as—or maybe more than—her peers. I thought she might look longingly at trees, wildlife, and geysers.

I was wrong, but it didn't matter.

I watched two of Davida's sisters—they *seemed* like sisters, and I hadn't yet figured out the questions I needed to ask about their real nature—arranging Christine Caine's sleeping body on the chair just as they must have arranged mine. It hadn't occurred to me until then that they must have built the chairs specifically to contain us, fitting them to our exaggerated size. To them, we were giants. Christine was no more than one metre sixty, but if she'd been able to stand upright she'd have towered over her handlers to the same extent that I'd have towered over her. To me, ignorant as I still was, she seemed to be not so very unlike them, but to them she must have seemed utterly alien.

I had no idea exactly how mad she'd be, but that was because I couldn't get the idea of that wretched VE tape out of my head. If I'd thought about it sensibly, I'd have realized that nobody could commit thirteen murders over a period of years without being able to put up an exceedingly good impression of total normality in between. The walls of her world hadn't been quite as full of eyes and ears as the walls of mine, and she'd moved around a great deal, but she couldn't have done what she had done without an exceptional talent for seeming utterly harmless.

That was what I ought to have expected, but I didn't. I wasn't quite myself yet; I wasn't even sure that I *was* myself.

At the very least, I expected Christine Caine to freak out when she found out what was what. Arrogant idiot that I was, I couldn't believe that anyone else could react nearly as well as me to the discovery that they'd been locked in a freezer for more than a thousand years.

I was wrong about that too—but Christine did have the advantage of remembering her trial and conviction. Her memory hadn't suffered any side effects at all.

She spent a little longer looking around than I had. She inspected her new suitskin very carefully indeed. It was pale blue, with false cuffs and boots similar to mine, although the sisterhood had stopped short of providing a matching cod-piece.

The suit would have looked better on her if she hadn't been so thin. She was so emaciated that the surface of the clinging fabric was pockmarked by all manner of bony lumps. She would grow into it, I figured, but it would take time. She was a pretty young woman, seemingly very frail: a picture of innocence. If I hadn't known the reason for her confinement, I'd have felt even more tender and protective toward her than I did. As things were, I had to remind myself that this was the closest thing to a contemporary I had, and the closest thing to a natural ally.

She touched her lips, then ran her fingers through her straggly blond hair, pulling a few strands forward so that she could examine the color and texture. She didn't approve of what she found, but she didn't seem surprised or offended. Then she made as if to stand up, but changed her mind, pre-sumably undone by the discovery that her weight wasn't quite right.

She contented herself with looking me up and down very carefully. I wondered how sinister I seemed, dressed all in black, and wondered whether I might be handsome enough to be mistaken for the Prince of Darkness.

Fortunately, she must have rejected the hypothesis that she was in Hell without entertaining it for more than a moment. Her first words were: "I hope this thing has a hole I can shit through." The word rang utterly false. She was try-ing to sound confident and assertive, but she couldn't make the pretence work.

"It doesn't need one," I told her, having had time to inves-tigate that particular matter. "It's an authentic second skin. It lines your gut from mouth to anus, and your other bodily cavities too. The food goes through just as it used to. Fash-ions have moved on since our day."

"Our day?" she queried, exactly as I'd intended her to.

"I'm like you," I said, a trifle overgenerously. Her eyes

narrowed slightly, but she didn't say anything. I assumed that she was wary of reading the statement the wrong way. "I woke up yesterday," I added, helpfully. "We've been away a long time."

"How long?"

I told her, expecting astonishment.

When she laughed I thought, at first, that she was hysterical. She wasn't. She was amused. I knew that she was probably in denial, just as I had been, because she probably felt even less like her old self than I had, but she wasn't letting it get on top of her. She was playing along, just as I had—but she was better able to laugh than I had been.

"I guess I'm the record holder," she said, having taken the figures aboard with sufficient mental composition to note the difference between them. "I always figured that I would be."

"Not for long," I told her, slightly piqued by her composure. "They'll be bringing Adam Zimmerman back in a couple of days, just as soon as they're convinced that you and I are as well as can be expected. He's been away longer than either of us."

"Why? What did he do?"

"You never heard of Adam Zimmerman?" I countered, sighting the intellectual high ground.

It only required a moment's thought. "The man who stole the world," she recalled. "I didn't realize they'd prosecuted him for that."

"They didn't," I told her. "He only helped the corpsmen run the scam in order to get enough cash to make sure he'd be taken care of once he was frozen down. He was a volunteer. He didn't want to die, so he decided to take a short cut to a world where everyone could live forever. He was the first, I think."

"Good for him," she said. Then she paused for further thought.

"This is all fake, isn't it?" she said, eventually. "It's just a clever VE. I'm in therapy, aren't I? This is some weird rehab program."

"I don't think so," I said.

"You don't *think* so?"

"If it's a VE, they're trying to fool both of us. I'm not certain that it isn't—but I do know that we have to work on the assumption that it's real. I'm Madoc Tamlin, by the way."

"So what did *you* do, Madoc Tamlin?"

"I can't remember how or why I got put away," I told her. That wiped the last vestiges of her smile away. She was obviously able to remember exactly how and why she'd been put away. She seemed more frightened than angry, but there was a peculiar quality to her fear that I couldn't fathom.

"Lucky you," she whispered. I got the impression that she didn't believe in my convenient lapse of memory.

"It doesn't seem lucky to me," I told her. "If I really did do something that pissed someone off enough to put me away for a thousand years, I'd rather like to know what it was. As things are, I can only wonder whether someone was so afraid that I knew something that could hurt him that he worked hard to prevent my release, or whether I was simply forgotten."

"It's still lucky," she assured me.

I knew that she was probably right. It had taken me some time to get my head around the idea that being forgotten for so long might have been a lucky break, whether my initial condemnation had been deliberate or accidental, but I could see by now how she might take the view that we'd both been luckier than we could ever have deserved.

But I still felt betrayed: by time, by circumstance, by my friends.

"It's too soon to tell how well off we are," I told her. "They didn't bring us back in order to shower gifts upon us. We're just the trial runs, to make sure that they can bring thousand-year-old corpsicles back with their minds more or less intact. Once we've convinced them that we're as well as can be expected, we'll be redundant. They may have certain reservations about welcoming us into the company of the emortals."

"Why?" she asked, warily. She didn't know that I knew who she was, and she was prepared to hope that I might not.

"Because you were a murderer, Miss Caine," I said, as gently as I could, "And they've probably assumed that I must have been one too."

"I was found guilty but insane," she informed me, stiffly. Then she took another pause for thought before saying: "We're a thousand years down the line. If they can cure death, surely they can sort out a few lousy bugs in the meatware. Their infotech must be foolproof by *now*. What did you say your name was?"

"Madoc Tamlin."

She shrugged her bony shoulders, but she'd already worked out that she couldn't possibly have heard of me. "I'm Christine Caine, as you seem to know," she said. The way she looked at me suggested that she wasn't *entirely* sure that I could be familiar with her case, even though I knew her name and what she'd been put away for.

"I know who you are," I said, but was quick to add: "I'm probably the only one who knows much more than your name, though. The people who brought us back claim to have lost the relevant records."

"Do you think they're lying?" she was quick to ask.

"I don't know what to think. I'm not even sure that we're what they say we are. Even if we're in meatspace rather than some super-tricky VE, we might still be sims of some kind."

"That's a little paranoid, isn't it?" she observed, pitching her voice so that the word *paranoid* sounded more compliment than insult. "I have this creepy feeling that you might be right, though. I don't feel like *myself*."

"Neither do I," I admitted. "Maybe that's just because we've been kitted out with these weird suitskins and internal nanotech that's ten generations ahead of anything we could have had in our day. On the other hand, it might be because we're sims or androids: AIs programmed to believe that we're people who died a thousand years ago."

"Why would anyone want to make sims of people who died a thousand years ago?" she asked. I could see that she was working on the problem herself, but I was slightly surprised by the ease of her assumption that if we weren't who we thought we were then the people we thought we were must be dead.

"Maybe they're interested in the outlaws of olden times," I suggested, wondering what Davida and her sisters thought of the direction the conversation was taking. "Maybe they want to know what made us tick."

"I didn't tick," she said, her tone becoming oddly distant. "If I'd been ticking, I'd have blown up—or run down. Not a bomb and not a clock, let alone a pacemaker. Silent but deadly. So they said."

Not so silent, I thought, once people started hooking into *Bad Karma*.

"Either way," I said, "it might be wise not to take anything for granted. I think they'll want to take a good long look at us anyway. Whatever we may think of ourselves, to them we're the next best thing to reanimated Neanderthals. Adam Zimmerman has his sainthood to keep him warm, but we don't. Quite the reverse, in fact. We might have to handle our situation very carefully—and it won't be easy."

"Are we being watched?" she wanted to know.

"All the time," I assured her. "Monitored inside and out. So far as I know, they can't overhear our private thoughts, but nothing else is secret."

If appearances could be trusted, that thought disturbed and distressed her more than any she'd so far come across. Her gaze flickered as her pale blue eyes looked toward the window, then up at the ceiling and round the walls, then back at me.

"Shit," she murmured. Then she composed herself again. "Lousy view," she remarked.

"It was supposed to be a slice of home," I said. "It's long gone—blown to smithereens, so they say."

"The whole Earth?"

"Just America—but the whole ecosphere had a catastrophic fit and had to be regenerated."

She didn't seem to think that the destruction of America
was an issue worth pursuing. "Who's *they*, exactly?" she
asked.

I told myself that the fact she was taking everything so
calmly was a compliment to the IT the microworlders had
installed in her brain—but I knew that if that was true for her
it ought to have been true for me, too. I wasn't taking everything calmly. My tranquilizing IT obviously wasn't programmed to kick in until I got badly steamed up; a certain
amount of inner turmoil was permitted, presumably because
the people observing us found it interesting.

"You'll see them soon enough," I said. "I ought to warn
you that they're very weird. Apparently, there are lots of people around who look pretty much like you or me, but there
are lots who don't. It so happens that this particular
microworld is run by people who don't."

"So what *do* they look like?"

"Children. Little girls. They're genetically engineered for
a particular kind of emortality—programmed to stop growing and maturing at nine or ten, before puberty sets in. I
assume that their brains keep changing as they learn. That's
probably why they do it. They must be hoping to preserve
their brains in a better-than-adult state."

"Neoteny," she said.

I was somewhat surprised that she knew the word. One
tends to think of crazy serial killers as undereducated individuals. "That's right," I conceded. "We're neotenic apes,
sort of, so I guess they figured that neotenic people were the
next evolutionary step forward. If you think that's weird,
wait till you see pictures of fabers and cyborganizers."

"But there are still people like us around?"

"People who look like us," I corrected her. "Engineered
for emortality, and lots of other cute tricks. We'll have visitors of that kind in a couple of days. There's a spaceship en

route from Earth, and another heading in from the Jovian moons, although the people it's carrying are mostly Titanians. They're coming to welcome Zimmerman, of course, but they can hardly refuse us invitations to the party. There's a historian with the Earth delegation, apparently, who's as keen to talk to us as he is to pay his respects to Zimmerman. There's also a UN rep, who probably answers to the Secret Masters as well as the not-so-secret ones. You don't have to worry about that, but I might. I used to work for the organization."

"The megamafia?"

"No, the *real* organization. I was instrumental in putting their brand on a few mavericks—including the Ahasuerus Foundation, whose corporate descendants include our present hosts. I helped to stitch up Conrad Helier too."

"The man who *saved* the world," she said, stressing the difference between the reputation that Conrad Helier had enjoyed in her time and the reputation that Adam Zimmerman had had.

"One of the men who made sure that the world needed his kind of saving," I corrected her, drily. "His record became a great deal more controversial once the whole truth came out—or as much of it as ever did come out. His sainthood never quite recovered from the tarnishing effect of the revelation that he helped start the great plague as well as delivering us from its effects. Not that he ever went on trial, of course, but he had to pretend to be dead to make certain he'd avoid it. You and I were products of an era of dire moral murkiness. Today is very different, so they say. But they would say that, wouldn't they?"

"But we've done our time," she said, letting a little anxiety show. "The sheet's clean now."

"I doubt that it'll ever be clean," I told her, with more bitterness than brutality. "We're museum pieces now, and it won't be easy for us to escape the burden of our rap sheets. They've already offered to put me back in SusAn any time I want to go."

She actually laughed at that. "Do you?" she asked,

plainly unable to believe that I might. It was another sign of an implicit mental kinship I was both anxious and slightly reluctant to acknowledge.

"No," I said. "But the offer conjured up some bizarre prospects. Maybe we could make a career of hopping through the future at thousand year intervals, popping out every now and again to give our remoter descendants a fascinating glimpse of the bad old days."

"We?" she queried.

"Not necessarily together," I said.

"But it could get lonely otherwise," she pointed out. "Unless this is the start of a new craze."

The thought that it might get lonely if we didn't stick together had occurred to me. That was one of the reasons why I was here, talking her through the awakening. I hoped that Adam Zimmerman might feel the same way, but I wasn't prepared to bank on it.

On the other hand, the thought that we might be the cutting edge of a new craze had occurred to me too. I hadn't yet managed to ascertain how many other refugees from the twenty-second century might be lurking in freezers, but I knew that there must be others. The eruption of the Yellowstone supervolcano might have wreaked havoc with any that had been stored on Earth, but there had to be more mortal bodies in the store from which we'd been selected as test subjects.

For the moment, though, Christine Caine was the only link I had to the world that had shaped me. Murderer or not, she was the closest thing to a friend I was likely to find in the Counter-Earth Cluster.

"Wherever we go, and whatever we do," I told her, soberly, "we'll be freaks. Our world is gone, Christine. Our species too, all but a few frozen specimens."

"Good riddance," she said. "Maybe you really didn't do anything to justify putting you away, Madoc Tamlin, but I'm already well used to being a freak. Better here and now than there and then. Maybe we should take the offer to go time-hopping, though. If they can fix us up to last the whole trip, maybe we could go all the way to the Omega Point—assuming we're not already there."

She was full of surprises. First neoteny, now the Omega Point. I realized that she was testing me, in case I was stupid. I was here to soften her introduction to the all-but-unthinkable, and *she* was trying the limits of *my* ability to cope.

I should have laughed, but I didn't. I thought hard, knowing that I had to get ahead of her if I were to maintain the advantage to which my years and my intellect entitled me.

After all, I thought, if I couldn't even help my hosts deal with Christine Caine, what hope had I of persuading them that they needed me to deal with Adam Zimmerman?

U ntil Christine Caine mentioned the Omega Point, I hadn't given very much thought to the question of when and where I might be if I wasn't when and where I seemed to be. Once she had mentioned it, I realized that I'd taken it for granted that the more probable alternative was that I was much closer to home than I appeared to be. I hadn't even considered the possibility that I might be much farther away.

The idea that someone was messing with my head had automatically translated itself into the idea that someone akin to the nanotech buccaneers of PicoCon was messing with my head, feeding me a weird science fiction script while I was still in my own historical backyard. The possibility remained, however, that instead of things really being less weird than they seemed, they might actually be *even weirder* than they seemed.

The idea of the Omega Point had already gone through several different versions before I was born, but the basic proposition was that somewhen in the *very* distant future the gradual spread of organic and inorganic intelligence throughout the universe would have produced some kind of cosmic mind. It was, I guess, an extrapolation of Voltaire's remark that if God didn't exist it would be necessary to invent Him.

The Omega Point was the point at which the Absent Creator would finally emerge from the evolutionary climax community of life and intelligence—at which point, philosophers desperate for a God-substitute were wont to claim, the Creator in question would naturally set out to do all the godly things that all the old imaginary gods had been prevented from doing by the inconvenience of their nonexistence. What else, after all, could the Omega Intelligence be interested in, except for omnipotence, omniscience, and omnibenevolence? And how else could it serve these ends but by recreating, reexamining, and correcting its own history—a process whose side-effects would inevitably include the resurrection of the entire human race, albeit virtually, and their situation in an appropriate kind of Heaven?

Personally, I had never believed a word of it, but I had lived in a world in which religions far less decorous had been clinging to existence like stubborn limpets, using any and every imaginative instrument to avoid recognizing their absurdity, redundancy, and incapacity to resist extinction.

The only thing fairly certain about the future evolution of intelligence, it had always seemed to me—if one assumed that intelligence had any future at all—was that something, somewhere, and somewhen, would *try* to become an Omega Intelligence, or at least to pretend that it was one.

In which case, I thought, after talking to Christine Caine, it might be a mistake to think that the kind of illusion I was lost in was a kind I could easily understand.

If my second lease of life turned out to be a sham, generated by a clever combination of IT and some kind of body suit, its actual temporal location could as easily be long after 3263 as long before. And if I had no body at all, but was in fact the software reconstruction of what some artificial superintelligence thought human beings might have been like, my actual temporal location might be *more* likely to be long after 3263 than before.

Christine Caine was right, though. Even if my current temporal location *did* turn out to be 3263, or year 99 of the newest New Era, and even if I did have my old body back again, only slightly worn away by more than a thousand years in a freezer, I was obviously capable of escaping the prison of time again and again and again. If I wasn't at the Omega Point *yet*, I could legitimately regard myself as one step removed from square one, embarked upon the Omega Expedition.

In other words, although I might be temporarily locked in my room, I wasn't locked into a particular era in the history of the universe. Nobody was. Emortality plus Suspended Animation equalled freedom. To be or not to be was no longer the only choice available to the children of humankind; the real choice now was when to be, or when to aim for.

Wait until Adam Zimmerman hears that one, I thought. *When he put himself away, the only thing on his mind was not dying. Now, he's going to have to come to terms with the next existential question but one. He's going to have to decide what he's going to do with his emortality.*

And it wasn't just Adam Zimmerman who had to do that, I realized.

Everybody did.

In the new world into which I'd now been delivered, everybody already had, although every single one of them was still entitled to further changes of mind. I hadn't made any such choice. Nor had Christine Caine or Adam Zimmerman.

That, I thought, had to be one of the things in which the invisible monitors observing our every word and action were most interested. For one reason or another, if only out of simple curiosity, they might even *care* about the decisions we would make.

aybe you could go all the way to the Omega Point," I said to Christine Caine, carefully steering our collaborative flight of fancy down to Earth—or at least to Excelsior. "Maybe it's the only tourist trip worth taking, if we're condemned to be eternal tourists. Unfortunately I doubt that SusAn technology is perfectible. It might take ten or a hundred reps, but the time would surely come when we'd turn into deep-frozen dead meat. I don't know the percentages, but the sisterhood could probably hazard a guess. My bet is that the vast majority of the people frozen down before and after us didn't even make it this far—and I'm not just talking about the ones who got out on their due release dates, or the ones who melted during accidental power cuts, earthquakes, and supervolcanic eruptions.

"We're *real* freaks, Christine. Thousand-to-one shots. Maybe million-to-one shots. Adam Zimmerman got here because every possible effort was extended to make sure that he did; we just happened to survive the great freezer lottery. My guess is that everybody who embarks on that kind of Omega Expedition is bound to die long before they reach their destination."

But what about the other kinds? I added, purely for my own consideration.

Christine Caine got to her feet then, balancing herself in a deliberate fashion. It didn't take her long to build up the confidence required to walk—and once she'd walked around the room, trailing her fingers along the seemingly featureless walls, she didn't waste any time before taking the next step. She threw herself forward into a somersault, and when she landed on her feet she threw herself into another, glorying in the lift and the slowness of the arc.

Then she came unstuck, and collapsed in an ungainly heap. She laughed, as if the fall had given her almost as much pleasure as the safely completed somersaults.

"Trust your clever IT," I told her, knowing that I had no reason to feel envious but not quite succeeding in controlling my resentment at the way she was coping with her unexpected situation. "It'll adjust your reflexes to the three-quarters Earth-gravity if you let it. Just don't try to think too hard about what you're doing."

"This isn't a VE," she said, smugly. "I'm no sim. I'm alive—and I'm out."

"And you're still a homicidal maniac," I was unable to prevent myself adding: "albeit a harmless one. They've rigged internal censors to stop you doing anything nasty, but the whole point of the trial run was to put you back together exactly the way you were."

She didn't like that at all, but she seemed more hurt than angry. "You don't know shit about the way I was," she retorted.

I repented my recklessness. "No, I don't," I admitted. "In fact, I may have entirely the wrong idea about it. If I remember correctly, you gave the police half a dozen contradictory explanations of what you did—but only one stuck fast. There was a VE tape about your case. Everybody my age hooked into it. It was pure fiction, but it colored everybody's understanding."

That made her pause for thought. "Some sort of psychoanalysis?" she asked.

"Not exactly. A reconstruction of your murders, putting the user into your viewpoint. There was a whispered voice-over that passed itself off as your internal stream-of-consciousness. It was called *Bad Karma*."

"Why?" I wasn't sure to what extent she was offended by the whole idea, as opposed to the mere title.

"Because it tried to explain what you'd done in terms of camouflage: hiding your true self within a series of alternative personalities, all of which masqueraded as invaders from the past. According to the script, the multiple personalities locked you into what the writer called a *karmic ritual*: the reenactment of an event so unbearable that you had tried to distance it from your present self by projecting it into a hypothetical pattern of eternal recurrence."

She stared at me as if I were the one that might be mad. "It was fiction," I added. "Pornography, of a sort."

"I want to see it," she said. She was no longer in a laughing mood, but I couldn't tell what sort of a mood had taken its place. She was fearful, but in an odd way. There was something in her reaction to the memory of her crimes with which my empathetic imagination couldn't get to grips.

"They don't have it," I told her. "Not here, at any rate. The sisters reckon that a few copies might have been exported from Earth before the last ecocatastrophe, but they don't know if it was ever adapted to run on modern equipment. Gray—the historian from Earth—might be able to locate one, if anyone can."

"But you saw it."

"A long time ago . . . that is, a long time before I was put away. My memory of it is vague. I was more interested in the technical production than the story—I was in the business at the time. Fight tapes, sex tapes . . . but nothing like *Bad Karma*. The business had already moved on by the time I was frozen down. The technics were evolving at an incredible pace, thanks to nanotech enhancements. *Bad Karma* must have become a museum piece long before the end of the twenty-third century. It was probably lost more than five hundred years ago."

"That's bullshit," she said. "All VE tapes were routinely upgraded to take aboard new developments. I saw six different updates of *The Snow Queen* when I was a kid, and four of *Peter Pan*."

The Snow Queen and *Peter Pan* were classic VE tapes made for children. The twenty-second-century versions Christine was referring to had been modeled on much earlier webware, but dozens of writers over the course of half a century had added more and more code to them, building up the backgrounds and making the special effects more elaborate. Even Damon had done a little hackwork on *The Snow Queen* at one time.

"It's not the same thing," I told her. "The hoods you and I used got better and better, but the basic design and coding routines remained the same. Those technics were already reaching their limit when I got out of the business. The next generation of hoods was about to restart from scratch, using an entirely different set of electronic substrates. They might have remade *The Snow Queen* yet again after I was put away, but if they did they'd have had to do it from the bottom up rather than continuing the series of add-ons. More likely it was filed away, replaced with some new favorite specifically designed to show what the new technics could do. When *Bad Karma* was made your case was still relatively fresh in the older generation's memory, but it couldn't have stayed that way. We were supposed to be living in the New Utopia, but there was no shortage of killers around. Compared with the Eliminators you were old news—and Davida assures me that there were plenty more to come."

"Who's Davida?" It was a stall, to give her time to think.

"She was sitting where I am when I woke up where you are. Davida Berenike Columella. Here on Excelsior, they seem to have done away with surnames. Maybe we should have done that ourselves, as soon as Helier wombs wrested the burdens and privileges of reproduction from the nuclear family."

"Caine can pass for a given name," she observed, sardonically. "Only too well."

"Tamlin too," I told her. "But maybe not Zimmerman. That comes with heritage attached."

She looked around again. "So this is a holding cell, right?" she said. "Do we have to share it, or can I get one of my own?"

"It's not a cell, exactly," I reassured her. "The sisterhood assures me that we'll have freedom of movement when their preliminary observations are complete. They want us to remain here for the time being, but we have our own spaces. Mine's on the other side of that wall over there—if you want a connecting door to open all you have to do is ask. In the meantime, we can go anywhere we want in virtual space."

"I don't see any hoods, let alone a bodysuit."

"The walls are a lot cleverer than they look. The sisters haven't rigged them for direct speech activation, but the people listening in will facilitate any requests we care to make—within reason. If you want a bed, or a fully laden dining table, or an immersion suit, you only have to say so. The food's lousy, but it's edible and your IT will take away the nasty taste if you persist with it. You can summon up a screen and talk to any kind of sim you care to nominate."

She pounced on that one. "But you're not a sim," she was quick to say. "You're real meat."

"I'm prepared to accept the working hypothesis that I'm real meat," I said, wryly. "Davida too. Apparently, we're in something called the Counter-Earth Cluster, which means that information from Earth has to be bounced halfway around the orbit, with an uncomfortably long time delay. I have a sneaking suspicion, though, that the real reason the sisterhood can't get near immediate and unlimited access to Earth's datastores is that the good folks on Earth won't give it to them. Ditto the outer system. If there ever was an age of free and unlimited access between our time and now, it's over. But we're used to that, aren't we? We come from a world where people who couldn't or wouldn't pay for information had to steal it, and where people who could manufacture and manage false information could make a good living secreting it into the system for the dubious benefit of the paying customers."

"That's what you were put away for?" she guessed.

"Perhaps. *If* I was put away. Even if I was, I should have been out in seven years. Ten at most."

"And now you're a time-tourist with a one-way open ticket. Count your blessings, Mr Tamlin."

"You can call me Madoc. I'm trying to count my blessings. It's not as easy as you might think."

She raised her right hand, made a fist, and elevated the right forefinger. "One," she said, defiantly. She meant the blessing that she was here, alive and out. "Oh look—we're ahead of the game already. How many more do you need?"

"I'm still trying to figure that out," I told her, stubbornly. "When I have the total, I'll weigh it against the downside."

"There's no downside in what you've said so far," she judged, accurately enough. "The downside would have been not waking up at all. If appearances can be trusted, we're past that. It's a new start, Madoc. All profit. You shouldn't complain about the cards you've been dealt, when the wonder is that there's been a fresh deal at all. If you're unhappy with the company at the table . . . well, who else was there to choose from? When you said *all* my body cavities, you did mean that . . . well, of course you did. Am I a virgin again, or is that too much to ask?"

She was putting on an act again, making believe that she was the kind of person who murdered people for fun. It rang completely false. Whatever her motive had been, I thought, she seemed exceedingly uncomfortable with it—but how, in that case, had she racked up thirteen victims?

"I think we're pretty much the way we were when we folded our last hands," I told her, not trying very hard to enter into the spirit that she was trying to import into the conversation. "We're experimental specimens, remember."

"Adam Zimmerman never heard of me," she observed.

"He never saw your slanderous tape. He doesn't know me from . . . Eve."

That made me laugh. It wasn't uproarious, but it the first honest laugh I'd contrived in a thousand years and I was surprised by the lift it gave me. It was a very feeble and very obvious joke, but it showed that she understood something of the magic of names.

"Before Eve there was Lilith," I murmured. I was talking to myself, but she heard me.

"I saw that one too," she said, sourly.

It took me a moment or two to figure out that she must be referring to yet another VE tape—not a kiddies' classic, this time. She knew about Lilith the demon, Lilith the baby killer, so she knew that I wasn't being nice, or funny.

"Somehow," I said, hopeful of saving the situation, "I don't think finding a mate will be the first thing on Adam's agenda. He'll be the most famous man in the solar system: the hottest news since the supervolcano blew North America to Kingdom Come. The Messiah from the twenty-first . . . hell, he must have been born in the *twentieth* century. He may be an animal in the zoo for a while, but they'll move Heaven and Earth to rehabilitate him. I'm not so sure they'll make as much effort for us, even if a little of his celebrity rubs off on us."

"On the other hand," said Christine Caine, the most notorious mass murderer in the galaxy, "if he were to die . . ."

Her tone made it obvious to *me* that she was joking, in much the same blackly comic vein as my crack about Lilith. If she meant anything by it at all, she meant that just because we'd been successfully revived, there was no guarantee that Adam Zimmerman could be. He, after all, had been forced to employ SusAn equipment of a considerably more primitive kind than ours, at least for the first phase of his long journey. She must have known, though, that what would be obvious to me might not be as obvious to all the other listening ears, and that it was just about the least diplomatic thing she could possibly have said.

That had to be at least part of the reason why she said it, given that she was still putting on her act—but I wished she hadn't.

I wished she hadn't because I knew full well that there was no one in Excelsior, and perhaps no one in the entire solar system, who wouldn't think of Christine Caine and Madoc Tamlin as two of a potentially despicable kind.

NINE
YOU CAN'T GO HOME AGAIN

here do you go to first, when you're a thousand years away from the world you grew up in but VE simulations of every environment in the solar system—and quite a few beyond it—are available to you?

You try to go home, of course. Not to find it, because you know full well that you won't, but to prove to yourself that it no longer exists, and that something else has taken its place.

In *Peter Pan*, one of those ancient VE adventures that Christine Caine had undertaken several times before she became a full-time mass murderer, there's a scene in which the eponymous character—one of three elective protagonists, if my memory serves me right—flies back to the nursery from which he had fled years before. He finds the window locked, and when he looks through it he sees his mother nursing a new baby son: a replacement who seems far more contented and far more appreciative of his circumstances than he ever was. The implication is that, unlike Peter, the new kid will one day achieve the adulthood that his predecessor was determined to avoid. On the other hand—although most members of the target audience probably didn't think that far ahead—the new kid might end up a lost boy too, with nowhere to go but Neverland.

I knew all that before I asked to see the Earth.

I thought I was sufficiently detached, and sufficiently adult, to be prepared for anything.

I had expected the hood I'd called for to grow out of the back of my armchair but it didn't. It materialized from the room's ceiling. It was nothing like the clumsy devices I'd used in my own time, being slightly reminiscent of a cobweb drifting down on the end of a thread of spidersilk. When it settled over my head it was hardly tangible; I didn't even feel it on the surfaces of my eyeballs—which was actually the surface of the part of my suitskin overlying my own conjunctiva.

I could move my head easily in any direction, but I was no longer looking out into my cell. The "place" I was in was recognizable as a VE holding pattern, but there were no menus written in blood-red upon its walls, waiting to be pointed at by my index finger. All my oral requests had to be fed through an invisible listener hooked into Excelsior's nervous system.

First I asked for a live feed from an orbiting satellite, so I could look down on my homeworld from above.

There was a time delay of several minutes while the signal made its way across the hundred-and-eighty-six-million-mile gap, taking a dogleg route to avoid the sun, but it was still "live," relatively speaking.

There was a lot of cloud, but not so much that I couldn't see that the colors were all wrong. There was way too much green, in all the wrong places, and too much black everywhere else. The outlines were wrong too.

I asked to look at an inset map, but the request wasn't specific enough; I got one with a crazy projection.

It took me a few minutes to figure out that the center of the flower-shaped design at which I was staring was the south pole. The equator was the ring drawn around the mid points of the "petals."

I still couldn't connect the landmasses to their "originals." I was out of my depth, floundering in uncertainty.

I had expected that the outlines of the continents might have changed slightly, but not to anything like the extent that they had. New islands had been raised from the seabed even in my day, but I'd expected to be able to see the fundamental shapes of Australia, Africa, and the Americas, the open expanses of the Pacific and the South Atlantic and the vast clotted mass of Eurasia.

They were all gone; coastlines had obviously become negotiable, and continental shelves prime development sites.

I figured out, eventually, that the differences were mainly a matter of three new continents having been constructed and some of the older ones split by artificial straits, but so many coastlines had been amended—sometimes drastically—that the shapes I knew had simply been obliterated.

When I asked for a new inset of a 3-D globe pivoted at the poles it became a little easier to see what had been what, and to reassure myself that the Continental Engineers hadn't actually won control of continental drift, but it was an alien world just the same.

I asked to be connected to a series of ground-level feeds.

Given that a mere ninety-nine years had elapsed since the planet had been shrouded in volcanic ash I expected to find the remains of North America in a bad way. Even if the atmosphere had cleared within a decade, I reasoned, ecosystemic recovery must be at a very early stage. I expected an under-populated wilderness still struggling to establish itself, but that wasn't what I found.

I found a riot of exotic gardens, and a hundred brand-new cities, all competing to outdo one another in the craziness of their architecture. There were towers sculpted out of all manner of gemlike stones; sprawling multichambered branching growths like thousand-year-old trees; walls of metal and roofs of glass; piazzas lined with all kinds of synthetic hide; roadways of smart fabric; and much more.

It was an unholy mess, but it certainly wasn't a wilderness and it was anything but underpopulated.

The Los Angeles in which I had grown up had been in recovery from its own ecocatastrophe, and I'd always thought of it as a living monument to the efficiency and capability of gantzing nanotech. Maybe it had been, by the standards of its own century, but history had moved on and technology had undergone a thousand years of further progress.

As I settled my virtual self into an artificial eye gazing out upon the streets of the city nearest to the now-drowned coordinates that LA had once occupied I saw that it wasn't just VE tech that had undergone more than one phase-shift. I had to suppose that the buildings I was staring at had been raised by a process analogous to gantzing, but they certainly hadn't been aggregated out of commonplace materials or embellished with the synthetic cellulose, lignin, and chitin derivatives that had surrounded me in my former incarnation. Here, once-precious stones and once-precious metals seemed to be everyday building materials, and they were augmented by all manner of fancy organics.

When I asked, a whispering voice told me that there were more than a hundred different kinds of "incorruptible" organic construction materials on display, as well as inorganic crystallines.

My informant wasn't a human voice—it was a machine whose responses were filtered through a sim of some sort— but that didn't mean that the member of the sisterhood commissioned to monitor me had packed up her kit and gone home. My questions were still being mediated by actual listeners, even though I was getting the answers direct from the data bank.

"They were experimenting with dextrorotatory proteins in my day," I said. "There was the stuff Damon's father and foster mother invented as well: para-DNA, they called it. Damon told me that PicoCon had big plans for that, once he and Conrad had sold out to them. Are those the kinds of things I'm looking at?"

The mechanical voice informed me that dextrorotatory organics had become effectively obsolete once they had begun spinning off dextrorotatory viruses and nanobacteria. The artificial genomic system designed by Conrad Helier and Eveline Hywood had proved to be much more versatile, and its derivatives were still used in a wide range of nanomachines—especially gantzing systems—but more complicated genomic systems devised for use in extreme environments had proved more generally useful when reimported to Earth.

I was assured that the next generation of technologies would be even more versatile, having taken aboard key features of the natural systems evolved on the colonized worlds of Ararat and Maya.

"And I guess you can make all the gold you want from lead," I suggested. "Everybody's an alchemist now."

The humorless voice told me that transmutation wasn't routinely practiced on Earth because there was no economic imperative. So I asked where it *was* routinely practiced, and was told that Ganymede, Io, and Umbriel were the principal research and development centers.

I had to put in a prompt to get more data, but I elicited an admission that transmutation research was "controversial," because fusion-generated transmutation was the technological basis of "macroconstruction."

A demand for further elaboration brought the revelation that a majority of the Earthbound was currently opposed to all kinds of macroconstructional development, and that "the major outer system factions" were divided even as to the most rudimentary aspects of their various development plans.

I looked around at the fanciful buildings that surrounded my viewpoint, knowing that they could not possibly be what the voice meant by "macroconstruction." Given that the people of Earth seemed perfectly happy to design and build new continents, and to make drastic amendments to the outlines of the existing ones, I knew that the voice had to be talking about at least one further order of magnitude.

Davida had already told me that there were a dozen microworlds in the Counter-Earth Cluster, two hundred more scattered around the orbit, and a further two hundred located in Luna's orbit around the Earth. I figured that the voice had to be talking about building much bigger things than that, perhaps in pursuit of the visionary quest of the type-2 crusaders who wanted to build a shell around the sun so that none of its energy output would go to waste. If so, there were only two likely sources of raw material: Jupiter and Saturn.

"You can't build new planets out of hydrogen, ammonia, and methane," I said. "Transmuting the stuff of gas giants must be a step beyond mere alchemy."

The voice wasn't programmed to praise my deductive skills. It reported, with a laconic ease that the sloth-animated sims of my own era had never quite mastered, that many people resident in Earth orbit became a trifle nervous at the mere mention of "domesticated supernoval reactions."

That seemed to me to be a nice idea, all the nicer because it was so casually oxymoronic. I probed, and the story filtered out in dribs and drabs. In the meantime, the people of the city born yet again from the ashes of the City of Angels went about their daily business, quite oblivious to the fact that they were being watched by a time-tourist from the twenty-second century.

Would they have cared if they'd known? Would anyone have stopped to wave at the camera? I'd have liked to think that someone would, but I couldn't be sure. All but a few of them looked like ordinary human beings, but none of them were. Their thoughts, opinions, hopes, and values were probably far more different from mine than their bodies.

"There seem to be a lot of people about," I observed, falling into a fairly relaxed conversational mode even though I knew I was talking to a machine while being dutifully overseen by a gaggle of two-hundred-year-old prepuberal posthumans. "How was the world repopulated so rapidly after the Yellowstone eruption?"

"Two million, one hundred and thirty-three thousand, seven hundred and eighty-seven people were killed by the great North American Basalt Flow," I was told. "The deficit was made up within thirty years. Sixty-one percent of the replacements were new births, thirty-nine percent returnees. Forty percent of the returnees came from the moon . . ."

"*Two million,*" I repeated incredulously. "You're telling

me that the northern half of the American continent blew up and only a few more than two million people died?"

"The margin of uncertainty applicable to the figure is approximately nought point two percent. The uncertainty is due to the difficulty in whether numerous ambiguous deaths ought to be attributed to the explosion or to other causes."

I wasn't concerned with abstruse matters of definition. "How did the rest of the population escape?" I asked.

"A warning of the impending eruption was broadcast. Approximately fifty percent of the victims were unable to escape the effects of the blast. Most of the remainder were caught in the open by the deluge of ash. The vast majority of people resident in North America or its satellite subcontinents were able to cocoon themselves in time to avoid serious injury."

"And how many more died in the resultant ecocatastrophe?"

"The figure previously quoted includes all casualties directly or indirectly attributable to the event, within the limitations of the aforementioned margin of uncertainty. There were problems of supply, which meant that a few of the affected individuals had to remain cocooned for as much as a year, but most emerged within days to begin the work of restoration."

I was impressed—but when I had thought it over, I figured that it wasn't so very surprising. The people in the thirty-third century didn't just have better IT and better smartsuits; they had a protective environment that was ever ready to take them in and seal them away from danger. Every city on Earth—every home on Earth—was a kind of Excelsior: a microworld combining all the most useful features of organic and inorganic technology. Posthumans were parasites on and within protective giants of their own manufacture. Even if Earth had been hit by the kind of extraterrestrial missile that had blasted away the last of the dinosaurs, all but a tiny minority of its people could have survived. Even if it were to suffer a nuclear holocaust . . .

On the other hand, I thought, that kind of defensive capability might make nuclear holocaust a far less unthinkable proposition than it had seemed in my day. And as for plague warfare—well, what kind of weapon was best equipped to worm its way through a protective cocoon to reach the helpless grub within?

Maybe the people of Earth were safe from most natural disasters, but that didn't make them safe from one another.

I left Los Angeles behind in order to take a look at cities and wildernesses in Africa, Australia, Oceania, New Pacifica, Atlantis, and Siberia.

There was a great deal else that I wanted to see—but there was also a great deal that I needed to know, so I eventually abandoned the tourist trip altogether and retreated to a world of data that wasn't quite as raw. I played the scholar more earnestly and more insistently than I'd ever done in my own time, although I knew there was far more to learn than I could cope with in a matter of hours, or months, or years.

To educate myself after so long an absence would be the work of several lifetimes. That was a sobering thought. But the likelihood seemed to be that I would have as many lifetimes as I needed. Like Adam Zimmerman, I too would be made emortal—or so I hoped. Had I dared to assume it, I would have; but I was too wary, and too fearful. I was at the mercy of a world whose mores and folkways I could not hope to understand.

It was a mental condition in which all kind of opposites were precariously combined, and I knew that I would not dare to be as glad as I wanted to be until I knew and understood a great deal more.

TEN
ALCHEMY AND THE AFTERLIFE

Although I was a stranger in the thirty-third century, I caught on fairly quickly to certain basic political issues once the principal arguments surrounding the concept of "macroconstruction" had been spelled out.

The human race would need the technics of transmutation soon enough. Fusers designed as power plants routinely turned hydrogen into helium, and could already work a few other finger exercises, but it would be necessary in the near future to make fusers of an altogether more ambitious kind: fusers that could do the kind of heavy-duty alchemy to which our modestly sized second-generation sun would never get around. All the heavy elements in the system were supernoval debris, and we would eventually need more: a *lot* more. Opinions apparently varied as to when "eventually" might be, but it wasn't just the carriers of the old type-2 banner who wanted the project started *now*.

The prospect of manufacturing all the elements that had previously been made in the overfervent hearts of dying stars opened up a number of interesting questions. Where, for instance, was the raw material to come from? And where could the technics be safely tested? Conducting risky experiments in distant gas-giant-rich solar systems posed logistical problems, and couldn't entirely avoid the safety issues associated with conducting them closer to home. A supposedly domesticated reaction that ran wild might be very problematic, even if it were several light-years away from the nearest substantial human settlement.

"I can see how that possibility would make people nervous," I said, drily. "Maybe this is one technology that we can do without, for the time being—or maybe forever."

I was told that there were others who thought a slow and steady schedule might be best, but that nobody believed that the problem could be put off indefinitely. If humankind's descendants refused to enclose the sun that had given birth to the species they would have to enclose others instead, because they would have no alternative but to try out every possible means of defying the Afterlife.

I had to demand an explanation of that term, because it no longer meant anything that a man of the twenty-second century could have understood by it. It was explained to me, calmly and patiently, that some people preferred to call the Afterlife the Alkahest, or "the Universal Death," while others—those with a more developed sense of irony, I supposed—were content to call it "the End of Evolution" or "Eternity's Eve."

Apparently, the galaxy was full of life, but it was mostly not the kind of life that existed on Earth, or the colony-worlds of Ararat—-which was known by its colonists as Tyre—and Maya. Nor was it the kind of life entertained by the so-called sludgeworlds which lurked in interstellar space. The vast bulk of the galaxy's biomass consisted of a single all-devouring species of nanobacterium: a universal organic solvent that fed avidly upon all higher kinds of life, digesting individual organisms and entire biospheres with equal ease. It did not matter which replicator molecules they used, or how they organized their genomes; they were all grist to the implacable mill.

The Afterlife's empire already extended three-quarters of the way from the center of the galaxy to the rim, and it was still expanding. Given time, it would conquer and possess the whole of the Milky Way, having gobbled up everything that complex organisms like us might consider "real" life.

Unless it could be stopped.

It might not arrive on Earth for hundreds of thousands of

years—perhaps millions—but it *would* arrive, and there would be people of many posthuman kinds to witness its arrival. Natural attrition would probably have killed off nearly all the emortals of the fourth millennium, and nearly all their children too, but a few people alive now would surely live long enough to see the evil day.

I might live to see the evil day myself, I realized—especially if I were to take up Christine Caine's semi-serious suggestion that I become a perpetual SusAn-borne traveler in time, waking up for a brief while at intervals millennia apart, in order to display myself as a specimen of a species long extinct and unmourned.

Even a threat that lay a million years in the future had to be taken seriously by the kinds of posthumans that lived on Earth and in its neighborhood nowadays.

People gifted with potentially eternal life had more reason to fear the kind of Afterlife they had discovered than mere mortals had ever had for fearing those they could only imagine. Their fear was, however, parent to a determination to avoid their apparent destiny. The AI mentor temporarily entrusted with my education explained, with polite meticulousness, that there were three possible strategies that an intelligent species could adopt in the face of such a threat: fight, flight, and concealment.

Obviously, the best chance of ultimate success lay in trying all three alternatives. Some of humankind's descendant populations would try their damnedest to find a kind of real life that could devour the devourer and win the galaxy for the cause of complexity. Some would set out to cross the intergalactic gulf, in the hope that there might be somewhere to run *to* that could remain permanently untainted by the monster. And some would build shields bigger than worlds: hopefully incorruptible spheres that would close off the states and empires of their central suns, creating havens of safety—or prisons, depending on one's point of view.

Transmutation was the key to the final strategy: not the traditional alchemical transmutation of lead into gold, but the kind of wholesale transmutation that supernovas wrought, spinning the whole rich spectrum of heavy elements out of the simpler ones that began to accumulate when hydrogen-to-helium torches finally grew dim. Maybe the people of the solar system could wait a little longer before pressing ahead with a project of that sort, but the ones who wanted to get it under way immediately certainly had an arguable case.

The argument already seemed to be fervent. Perhaps it was only the pressure of my paranoia, but I couldn't help wondering how long populations which believed themselves to be extremely well defended could refrain from letting fervor spill over into violence. In particular, there seemed to my untutored eye to be an unbridgeable ideological rift between the Earthbound—the most cautious posthuman faction in the solar system—and the colonists of the Jovian and Saturnian satellites, whose reasons for wanting to domesticate pseudosupernoval processes of manufacture were many and various.

It seemed that I had arrived in turbulent times—perhaps the most turbulent the children of humankind had encountered since the Crash and its Aftermath. I had lived my first thirty-nine years in a world that had seemed to be getting better all the time; I had returned to one that had known nothing but good times for centuries, and probably took its good fortune too much for granted.

After listening to my mentor's account of the Afterlife and its significance as a factor in posthuman affairs I looked at the streets of the newly reborn North American city for a second time, in a subtly different mood. I looked at the virtual people in a different way, too. I soon moved on again, from one American city to another and then to the cities of the "Old World"—which no longer seemed old at all, now that it had been rebuilt by degrees over centuries and millennia. I could see that all the cities were patchworks, which all seemed equally crazy to me except for the oldest of them all,

Amundsen, which had housed the official world government for centuries.

Amundsen had been built long after I was put away, but it seemed to me that it retained a faint echo of the world that I had known. For a while, I was told, it had been on the verge of becoming a mere monument, but the reconstruction that had had to be organized after the Yellowstone basalt flow had revitalized the UN for a time, making elected government briefly necessary—and hence briefly powerful—once again.

How, I wondered, did all this information need to be factored into my own personal situation? What difference did it make to *me*?

It was too soon to tell.

I thought, for a little while, that I had seen what Ice Palaces might be when I had seen Amundsen City and its immediate neighbors, but if I hadn't had so much else to think about I would have realized that the palaces of the world capital's satellite towns could only be trial runs for something much more adventurous and grandiose. It was better that I make the mistake, though, because learning to wonder is something we have to do again and again, no matter how long we live or how long we sleep between our intervals of active thought. We always think that we can do it perfectly well, but there's always another realm beyond the one we can imagine, and another realm beyond that, and so ad infinitum.

Cocooned in my VE nest on Excelsior, while my virtual self was on Earth, wondering at the world that had replaced my own, I had only just begun to realize how many other worlds there were—and I had not yet begun to discover what marvels *they* might contain.

I had so much more to see, so much more to discover— and wherever I started, the journey of discovery would be a very long one. For a journey like that, I would need the kind of lifetime with which this world could equip me—but would my need be sufficient to guarantee that I got it? I could not help returning to that anxiety: the idea that I might have been brought to the threshold of eternity only to be turned away, because I was not Adam Zimmerman. I could not believe that I was a convicted murderer either, but I knew that appearances were against me.

I had lived in an era when the Eliminators were big news. I had never been one of them, but I could hardly help applying their slogans to my own case. Was I "worthy of immortality"—or, more correctly, of emortality? Whether I was or not, could I persuade my new hosts that I was, if the need to do so arose?

I had, of course, asked to see any and all references to myself that Excelsior's data bank could obtain, but the pickings were so sparse that a lesser man might have despaired. To have accomplished so little, and made so slight a mark upon the world, seemed a very meager reward for my efforts—except that I could not believe for a moment that the scarcity of information was accurate. If my patient monitor was not intervening as a censor, then the available records must have been wiped. When? By whom? And above all—*why*? What had I done to deserve my curiously ambiguous fate? And why, exactly, had my wayward fortunes taken their newest, and strangest, direction?

I had to find out, if I could—and if I couldn't, I had to do my best in spite of the burden of ignorance. I had to do *something*, to live up to my name. I was Madoc Tamlin, after all: a ready-made hero of legend. I was not a victim to be exploited, not a pawn to be played with, not a fool to be manipulated. One way or another, and despite every disadvantage, I knew that I had to take charge of the script of my own future life. That thought dominated my consciousness while I waited, with gathering impatience, for Adam Zimmerman's return.

I might have delved deeper into the inexhaustible well that
was the sum of Excelsior's mechanically stored knowledge
had I not been interrupted by the news that there were two
personal calls waiting to be downloaded. I had not expected
mail, and I certainly had not expected items of mail to arrive
in such profusion as to have to form a queue—even a queue
of two—so the news was subtly exciting.

I didn't take the calls immediately, partly because I
wanted to think over what I'd already learned and partly
because the notification of their arrival reminded me how
long I'd been in VE. I was almost certainly safe to continue,
given that the hood I was using was so ridiculously unobtrusive, but old habits die hard. I came back to the meatspace of
my cell in order to have another bite to eat. Afterwards, I
peered out of the "window" for a few minutes at the starry
firmament. Then curiosity got the better of me. I draped the
cobweb hood over my head once again, and returned to the
infinity of cyberspace.

The first call I took was from Mortimer Gray—or, to be
strictly accurate, from a sim made in his image. Gray was the
historian who was currently en route to attend Adam Zimmerman's awakening, on a spaceship with the unlikely name
of *Peppercorn Seven*.

I was oddly relieved to discover that Gray's sim wore the
semblance of a human of my own era. If the appearance
could be trusted, he was no taller than I was, and no better
looking. His coloring was fairer than my own, and his hair

was silver. His eyes matched his name but his smartsuit didn't—its intricate purple and blue designs were laid upon a black background. I knew that he was a great deal older than I was, in terms of experienced years, but I also knew that he wouldn't have aged a day since turning twenty-something, so I was surprised that he really did seem ancient, wise, and venerable—and not just because of his hair. Perhaps it was the decor of what was presumably his personal VE, which was tricked up to look like a library: a library with *books* in it.

Gray began by apologizing for the fact that a dialogue was still impractical because of the time delay, but assured me that the ship on which he was traveling was making all haste.

"I wanted to introduce myself to you as soon as possible, Mr. Tamlin," he added, half-apologetically. "I don't know whether my reputation has preceded me, or whether you have had a chance to look into my background, but I wanted to reassure you that I am neither as unworldly nor as narrowly obsessed with matters of mortality as I am sometimes thought to be. I am traveling to Excelsior as the representative of an association of academic interests, and it is on their behalf that I am inviting you to take up employment . . ."

At this point the sim suffered a short burst of interference, and the transmission was interrupted.

"Sorry about that," Gray said, when his false face had coalesced again. "A close encounter with a snowball, I think. A constant hazard hereabouts—one with which this glorified sardine can is barely equipped to deal."

I was impressed by the fact that he knew what a sardine can was, until I remembered that he was a historian. Like Davida, he was probably cutting the cloth of his conversation in the hope of suiting me.

"I am authorized to offer you an appointment as a lecturer in twenty-second-century history, Mr. Tamlin," he went on. "You will undoubtedly receive other offers of employment, perhaps at much larger salaries, but I believe that you might find an academic appointment to be more desirable, on the grounds of congeniality and freedom of opportunity. It might well be the most comfortable way for you to make use of your uniquely specialized knowledge, and it would certainly make matters easier for those of us who believe that we have much to learn from you. I am looking forward to meeting you in person, and I hope that we shall soon have an opportunity to discuss this matter in detail. Please give it serious consideration. Thank you for listening."

He vanished into the ether, leaving me staring at a rest-pattern.

I felt suddenly uncomfortable, totally unsure as to how I was supposed to interpret what he'd said. Had he been issuing a cryptic warning? Had he suggested that he could offer "congeniality and freedom of opportunity" because he wanted me to understand that others would want to restrict my freedom and threaten my congeniality? Or was I just being paranoid?

I got rid of the hood again, and got up from my specially commissioned chair. I stretched my limbs, although I didn't need to. I knew that my every move was being watched, and that my reaction to what Mortimer Gray had said would be carefully measured.

I felt unusually strong, but I knew that was an illusion of the low gravity. I walked back to the picture window. It was still showing the star field, and I wondered what the watchers would read into my decision to keep it that way. I wondered, too, how I should interpret my own action. Did I think I needed to be constantly reminded of the fact that I was a long way from Earth?

I was surprised by Gray's offer as well as puzzled. I couldn't help wondering whether he and his fellows might be laboring under a misconception as to who and what I had been before being committed to SusAn. I couldn't quite believe that it was an offer he'd have extended to any common or garden-variety criminal. The more I thought about it, though, the more the message seemed like a preemptive strike—and the fact that it had come in at the same time as another suddenly ceased to look like a coincidence.

Marveling at the thought that I might be able to start out on a new career path suddenly seemed to be a silly way to waste time. I asked my patient monitors to display the second message in the window, to save me the bother of putting the hood on again.

This one was from the UN executive who was presumably also a member of the Hardinist Cabal: Michael Lowenthal. Unless his sim had been subtly enhanced, he seemed to be a little taller than me, but that might have been an illusion generated by the fact that he seemed to be hovering in empty space "outside" the room. His complexion wasn't quite as dark as mine, but his neatly sculpted features made him substantially more handsome and his smartsuit was masterpiece enough to make Gray's, let alone mine, look like the next best thing to a prison uniform. His hair was a neutral shade of brown, but that only served to emphasize the classicism of his features.

Lowenthal introduced himself as the Secretary to the Ecological Planning Department of the World Government, but I wasn't stupid enough to think that he was any mere bureaucrat. Like Gray, he was wrapped up in a cocoon in a flying sardine can, but his sim carried his favorite virtual environment with it. No ancient books for Michael Lowenthal: his background was Amundsen's central square, with the UN parliament building directly behind him, reduced by a trick of perspective to near insignificance.

"I'm calling ahead to prepare the ground for our first meeting, Mr. Tamlin," Michael Lowenthal said. "I wanted you to know as soon as possible that the United Nations is not merely willing but eager to facilitate your return to Earth and to provide for your rehabilitation and reeducation. I can assure you that any crimes and misdemeanors you might have committed in the distant past are of no further relevance to anyone alive today, and that we are enthusiastic to make you welcome. We shall be happy to provide you with employment, not in any artificial make-work capacity but as a useful and valued member of society. I look forward to meeting you when the ship docks, and to making provision for your eventual return to Earth. Thank you." His image froze to a still, but didn't disappear.

No stray "snowball" had dared to interrupt him, although he had help to avoid any such possibility by keeping his message brief.

Personal though these messages were, I knew that they weren't private. As soon as Michael Lowenthal had finished, I asked to speak to Davida Berenike Columella. Her image immediately displaced his, but she seemed slightly more incongruous floating "outside," partly because the background behind her head was a blank wall.

"What was all that about?" I demanded, unceremoniously.

She could have been evasive if she'd wanted to be, but she didn't. "They both want you to go back with them to Earth," she said. "I'm not privy to their motives, but I suspect that they're simply being overcautious. They're afraid that if they don't obtain your early agreement to return to Earth you might accept an invitation to visit the outer system—Titan, perhaps."

"Why wouldn't they want me to go to Titan?"

"They know that *Child of Fortune* is heading in from the outer system. *Peppercorn Seven* should arrive first, but only by a matter of hours. Both sets of passengers seem to be treating it as a race, perhaps for no better reason than that each thinks the other might be treating it as a race. Adam Zimmerman is the real propaganda prize, of course—but Lowenthal obviously feels a need to be careful not to miss out on any possibility."

"*Any* possibility? You mean he sent a similar message to Christine Caine? Gray too?"

"I think you ought to ask that question of Miss Caine," Davida said, primly—which seemed to me to be as good as a yes.

"I wonder if they'll offer her an academic position as a historian, or as a psychiatrist," I mused, unable to help myself saying it aloud.

Davida ignored the remark. "You are, of course, welcome to remain here if you so wish," she told me. "You might think that the least attractive option, given that we cannot offer you any possibility of social assimilation—but that might be a good reason for taking it, at least in the short term. We *can* offer you an interval for careful thought and self-education. Such an interval might prove immensely valuable."

I could see that there were several layers of implication concealed within that statement, and I took time out to consider how to proceed. It seemed, in the end, most sensible to go back to basics.

"How, exactly, did we come to be here in Excelsior?" I asked her. "Why aren't the three of us still on Earth?"

"The directors of the Ahasuerus Foundation thought it politic to remove Adam Zimmerman from Earth in the 2540s, following the Coral Sea Catastrophe," she told me. "Tens of thousands of SusAn chambers were lost at that time, and the moon seemed a much safer environment. The facility in which Zimmerman's chamber was then held had charge of several hundred other cryonic chambers, some of which were Ahasuerus personnel following in their founder's footsteps, others—Christine Caine's among them—having been accepted from correctional facilities following . . . unfortunate accidents."

The pause before the final phrase was so profound that you could have flipped a coin into it and never heard the clink.

"You mean that the corpsicles of criminals were popular targets of sabotage or calculated neglect," I deduced. I had no reason to suppose that the rhetoric underlying Eliminator activity had ever died out, even though it had presumably ceased to be fashionable.

"There were occasional security problems," was all Davida would admit. "The Foundation was asked to move the government-sponsored chambers of which it had temporary custody along with those for which it had sole responsibility. Eventually, the directors decided that the moon was not the ideal environment either and a specialist microworld was commissioned. In order to make the project economically viable the Foundation offered to take over various other consignments of SusAn chambers from several locations on Earth. It was at that point, I believe, that your own chamber was added to the stock. After several changes of location, the microworld was established in the Counter-Earth Cluster. Excelsior is another Ahasuerus project, and we have all the necessary equipment, so it was the logical base from which to launch the revivification plan."

"So you sought out the two next-oldest corpsicles for your trial runs," I recapped. "But you still have hundreds— maybe thousands—of sleepers parked next door."

"Thousands," she agreed.

"And who decides when *they* get to wake up?"

"That's a matter of some dispute," she admitted. "Our own position is that the Ahasuerus Foundation has the sole responsibility and authority. The World Government in Amundsen has a different view, but . . ." She left the sentence dangling.

"But possession is nine points of the law," I finished for her. "Is that why Lowenthal's so keen to take us back to Earth?"

"It's probably a factor."

"But why should he or anyone in the outer system care who has custody of Christine or me? What interest do they have in us, or in the thousands like us who remain unthawed?"

"The Earthbound have a view on everything," Davida

told me, with a hint of sarcasm in her tone. "That view, simply put, is that everything that can be left undone should be left undone—but that if something has to be done, they ought to be the ones to say when, how, and by whom. It's almost reflexive. Anything new, or anything slightly unusual, is always regarded with suspicion on Earth. The people of the outer system, on the other hand, delight in thinking of themselves as the great pioneers of all the new frontiers. They consider the Earthbound to be decadent—a retardant force holding back the cause of progress—and can usually be relied on to disagree with any position the Earthbound take up. If the Earthbound have decided that they want you back on Earth, under their control, the people aboard *Child of Fortune* will almost certainly offer to take you elsewhere, for any reason they can think of or none at all."

"And where do *you* stand?" I asked.

Either she misunderstood the question or she decided that she had an agenda of her own to set out first. "Many outer-system folk see the remoter inhabitants of Earth orbit and the inner system as potential political allies," she said, "although as many people on Earth think of us as *their* natural allies. Adam Zimmerman is potentially capable of becoming a significant factor in that ideological conflict, and the Ahasuerus Foundation is his creation. Unfortunately, the Foundation is no longer the closely knit community that it once was, and the Earthbound element of the Foundation doesn't seem to have been unanimous in approving the decision to revive its founder. Excelsior's view is that ours is the posthuman community best equipped to fulfill the Foundation's mission, and we intend to do that if Adam is agreeable."

"Do you really think he'll want to be remade as one of you?" I asked, astonished by the seeming absurdity of the possibility.

"He's a free individual," Davida said, flatly. "We shall do everything within our power to ensure that he makes an informed decision."

"But whatever he decides, you'll want to practice on me—or Christine?"

"Not unless you volunteer," she assured me. "We were unable to seek your informed consent before releasing you from your long imprisoment, but we had no reason to think that you would raise any objection. Now that you are available for consultation, however, we would not dream of subjecting you to any further treatment without your full cooperation. We shall be pleased to assist you in securing your own emortality when you have considered the opportunities open to you, as recompense for the services you have already rendered."

I took the inference that she wouldn't be overly disappointed if Christine and I decided to go to Earth, or set off for the outer system, before seeking any further bodily modification. Adam Zimmerman was the prize on which her own eyes were fixed—but for that very reason, I realized, he was also the prize for which the other contingents would fight hardest.

I wondered how much it mattered, and to whom. I wondered, too, how flattered I ought to be that Mortimer Gray and Michael Lowenthal were at least prepared to pretend an interest in me.

"Lowenthal must be one of the oldest of the emortals," I remarked, judiciously.

She took the bait. "He is. He has a well-deserved reputation for careful dealing."

"He's not just a UN functionary then—he's a key member of the Inner Circle?"

"The Zaman Transformation was an Ahasuerus project, initially," Davida observed, again coming at my question from a tangential angle, "but the whole Foundation was Earthbound then, and the terms of our operation were controlled externally. Michael Lowenthal was one of the very first generation of true emortals—but he wasn't *one of ours*."

There was nothing faint about her meaningful emphasis, but I wasn't sure how much she was trying to imply. I wondered if she had known, even before I mentioned it to Christine Caine, that I had been instrumental—albeit in a *very* minor capacity—in tying Ahasuerus down in the days when the entire Foundation was a loose cannon rolling around PicoCon's well-scrubbed deck. In a world of emortals, I realized, people might hold grudges for a very long time. Davida Berenike Columella was never going to say it in so many words, but the people behind her were probably still at odds with the people behind Michael Lowenthal, and might be for a long time to come.

"So the people in the outer system probably wouldn't give a damn about any of us," I said, to make sure I was keeping up with the news, "except for the fact that the Earthbound *do* have an ax to grind—for which reason, the outer system folk might want to throw a monkey wrench in the works. You only give a damn about Adam Zimmerman, so you don't care whether either the two ships takes Christine and me off your hands, although you'll be very pissed off indeed if Zimmerman elects to go too."

Davida paused before answering, perhaps needing to consult her friendly neighborhood data bank as to what a monkey wrench was or what being pissed off involved. Then, speaking rather grudgingly but with all apparent honesty, she said: "There are a great many people in the outer system who regard Adam Zimmerman as a hero and a bold pioneer. The delegates aboard *Child of Fortune* may regard him as a kindred spirit, at least potentially. If he were to ally himself with one or more of their most cherished causes, they might have reason to be delighted. Lowenthal must know that too." I realized then that she wasn't just trying to keep me informed—she was talking to me like this because she was trying to work through a few uncertainties of her own.

I thought about that for a moment, then said: "You don't have a clue which way he's going to jump, do you? Neither does anyone else."

"Adam Zimmerman is, admittedly, something of a mystery to us . . . as he is to anyone born in this era."

"But perhaps not to me," I pointed out, grasping the opportunity to restate my own case for further involvement in the scheme of which I had unwittingly become a part, "or even to Christine Caine. Is that why Lowenthal took the trouble to talk to me? He must think—rightly—that I might be better placed to get through to Zimmerman than you, or him, or his rivals from Titan. So why hasn't anyone working for the other side contacted me yet?"

"Are you certain that they haven't?"

I figured that I'd have been told if there were any more messages waiting, so I couldn't see what she was getting at for a moment. Then I did.

"But Gray's Earthbound, like Lowenthal," I said, when I had twigged. "Why would he be playing for the other side?" Thinking back, I realized that he hadn't actually said that the "association of academic interests" he supposedly represented was Earthbound.

"Gray's as thoroughly Earthbound as anyone in his attitudes," Davida agreed. "But he has some very influential friends on the frontier. I know of no reason why you shouldn't take his offer of employment at face value—but I doubt that the representatives of the World Government would be prepared to trust Mortimer Gray to act in what they see as Earth's best interests. He saved Emily Marchant's life in the Coral Sea Disaster, and she's used him as a propaganda tool before."

I hadn't a clue who Emily Marchant was, but I figured that I could look her up. I certainly intended to investigate Michael Lowenthal. The plot of which I was a part seemed to be thickening around me, and I didn't know whether to be glad or annoyed. Christine Caine, I supposed, would reckon it one more blessing to count or one more irony to chuckle at, but I was as different from her as I was from Adam Zimmerman. If my assistance proved to be a tradeable asset, that might be to my advantage—but if my interference were to be reckoned a possible nuisance by Michael Lowenthal or anyone else, that might place me in peril. Having already served a sentence of a thousand years plus for misdemeanors I couldn't even remember, I figured that I could do without any disadvantages or prejudices hovering over the inception of my second slice of life.

I had to educate myself quickly, but it wasn't going to be easy to work out what I needed to know, if everyone who offered to help me had their own vested interests—however slight—to look after.

"Thanks," I said to Davida Berenike Columella.

"You're welcome," she replied, the phrase falling from her tongue as if she'd never used it before and did not expect ever to need its like again.

TWELVE
THE TEMPTATIONS OF PARANOIA

Throughout my former life I had always taken pride in maintaining a level of paranoia appropriate to my various professions. As I began my second span, however, I was acutely conscious of the fact that I had not been paranoid enough to anticipate that I might end up in the cooler, or that once I was there my custodians—not to mention my friends—would allow me to languish indefinitely. Knowledge of this failure, I must admit, made me a trifle oversensitive to the direr possibilities implicit in my new situation. The research that I contrived to do during the next few hours of wakefulness was guided by a fervent desire to figure out why my hosts might be lying to me.

I knew, of course, that there was a possibility that Davida Berenike Columella was telling me the truth and nothing but, but it seemed safer and wiser to work from the opposite assumption. If there really were thousands of corpsicles stored in a gargantuan coffin ship somewhere in the Counter-Earth Cluster, I reasoned, the probability that Christine Caine and I just happened to be the nearest contemporaries of Adam Zimmerman was slight. If we weren't his nearest contemporaries, then we must have been selected for awakening on different grounds—and even if we were, there were still question marks hanging over the matter of our revival, and Adam Zimmerman's too.

Why *here*? Why *now*?

I was prepared to accept that Excelsior really was an Ahasuerus Project, and that the trustees of the Foundation really might have decided that the time was now ripe for it's mission to be completed, but that didn't seem to me to be an adequate explanation for either the place or the time. It would have been easy enough to send Zimmerman's SusAn chamber back to Earth, so that he could wake up at home, and just as easy to ship specimens for trial runs along with him, in the unlikely event that there were no sleepers on the surface of sufficient antiquity.

It seemed to me that it would have been even easier for the current directors of the Foundation to continue the policy of procrastination that they appeared to have been following for twelve hundred years. Even in my day there had been rumors to the effect that the technology of emortality that Zimmerman had craved already existed, but that the incentive for the Foundation's directors to postpone the day that would make them effectively redundant was too great to encourage any policy but one of indefinite delay. Davida had already told me that the decision didn't "seem to have been unanimous"—so how had it crept through now in the face of manifest opposition, when it must have failed to do so a thousand times before?

So far as I could judge, the fact that Adam Zimmerman was being awakened *here* and *now* had to imply that the people who were actually doing the work had something to gain. In other words, Davida Berenike Columella and her weird sisterhood—or the people giving them instructions— must want something, and must think that Adam Zimmerman could help them get it. If Christine Caine and I had *not* been chosen by lot, they must think that we could help them get it too. They must think that we had some special value— or, at the very least, some special significance.

Irritatingly, it was easier to imagine a reason why Christine Caine might be valuable than it was to figure out what special significance I might have.

Christine Caine had killed people, without having anything that could pass for a reasonable motive. If she had been fitted with some kind of fancy IT that could prevent her from doing any such thing again, that same IT was probably able to facilitate her doing it, and perhaps to force her to do it. Christine Caine might, in fact, be a useful assassination weapon, in a day and age when assassination weapons were rare.

I had to remember, though, that no one seemed to know for certain whether the two million people who had been killed by the Yellowstone supervolcano were the victims of an accidental malfunction or deliberate sabotage. With assassination weapons like that around, the only advantage a human assassin could offer was precision.

If Christine Caine were an assassination weapon, I reasoned, then I might be one too—in which case, I thought, I might have been selected precisely because I didn't have a record of unmotivated violence. Perhaps, if that were the case, Christine Caine was only the decoy, to distract attention away from the real threat.

On the other hand . . .

It was too complicated. I needed more hard data.

What Excelsior's datastores could tell me about Michael Lowenthal was limited, but they did reveal that he had been born in 2464. As Davida Berenike Columella had already told me, having drawn the information from the same source, Damon Hart hadn't died until 2502—which meant that if Lowenthal had been affiliated to the Inner Circle in his youth, in however humble a capacity, he might have known Damon.

One item of Lowenthal's background peculiar enough to attract attention from the compiler of the datastore was that although he was not a policeman he had been involved—as an "observer"—in the investigation of a case of serial murder that had occurred in 2495. It wasn't the last on record, but it had been *very* big news at the time, and it had been a case whose craziness was at least the equal of Christine Caine's. I wondered whether that might be a reason why Michael Lowenthal might have a particular interest in Christine Caine.

I didn't want to give the people monitoring my actions too much insight into my suspicions, but I figured that it was probably safe to look into the history of SusAn penology, with particular reference to the possible survival of other "prisoners" of my own era.

At the time of my own incarceration SusAn had been used throughout the world as a repository for criminals of all kinds. It had been widely advertised as "protection without punishment" for half a century: a humane alternative to traditional practices, one wholly befitting the philosophy of the supposed New Utopia. Much had been said and written about "future rehabilitation": the idea that the increased efficiency of future technologies would more than compensate for the fact that any resources and skills possessed by individuals confined in SusAn would become obsolete. Not only would future IT be able to "treat" or "cure" antisocial tendencies at root, turning psychopaths and recidivists into model citizens, but improved educational systems would allow the remodeled citizens in question to be retrained for whatever useful work might be available.

Everybody with half a brain knew, of course, that it was all bullshit—but it was politically useful bullshit. It provided an ideological basis for getting rid of anyone who proved to be too much of a pest. People who committed minor offenses were put away for a few months or a few years, as a warning to them and to others—and people who couldn't take the hint were put away indefinitely. Present society washed its hands of them, swept them under the carpet and left the dirt to be tidied up by future generations. Was anyone ever surprised that the future generations never quite got around to it, preferring to discover all kinds of good reasons for continuing to pass the buck? I suspect not.

If the corpsicles had continued to pile up, of course, the situation might have become absurd, and eventually intolerable, but they hadn't. Unlike all previous penal systems, SusAn incarceration had appeared to be effective, in the crude statistical sense that crime rates began to drop—quite sharply—as the twenty-third century progressed. The drop had been represented by enthusiasts as proof that *this* deterrent actually worked. It was, of course, no such thing. The real reasons for the steady fall in crime rates, my sources assured me, were the gradual but inexorable removal of incentives to commit crime and the gradual but inexorable increase in the certainty of detection.

I had lived in an era where many people were routinely subject to the vagaries of rage and intoxication, and in which the electronic stores where credit was held were still vulnerable to clever tampering. It was also an era in which a great many people—especially the young—took a perverse delight in cheating the surveillance systems that had been set up to make crime difficult, regarding all such measures as a challenge to their ingenuity. In my day, hobbyist criminals were everywhere. Although everyone affected to deplore and despise those whose hobbyism extended to raw violence, especially when it involved murder, there was a widespread fascination with violence. That fascination supported a rich and varied pornography as well as a highly developed risk culture. People newly gifted with IT—especially when the effectiveness of a person's IT was the most effective badge of wealth and status—were inevitably tempted to test its limitations in all kinds of extreme sports, many of them illegal. According to Excelsior's data banks, however, all that stuff had faded away as the novelty wore off.

As the cost of IT had come down, attitudes had shifted dramatically; the fascination of violence, pain, and death had never disappeared, but it had become the prerogative of exotic cults whose breakthroughs to the cultural mainstream became increasingly rare. As polite exercise of the self-control that better IT permitted became routine, rage and intoxication dwindled toward extinction. As credit-tracking systems were further refined, successful thefts and frauds became so rare that no rational risk calculation could support them. Even the young ceased to see the erosion of privacy and secrecy as a challenge, and adapted themselves to

living in a world where no sin was likely to remain long unde-
tected—or, for that matter, long unforgiven.

By 2300, the use of SusAn as a mode of incarceration had
come to seem unnecessary and ridiculously old-fashioned. By
2400, the spectrum of social misdemeanours had altered dramatically throughout the world, and those which persisted
were more commonly addressed by mediated reparation and
"house arrest." By that time, SusAn incarceration was only
used outside the Earth—and even there, its use declined in
spite of the dramatic increase in the extraterrestrial population. The once-rich flow of individuals committed to SusAn
because their neighbors wanted them out of the way had
fallen to a mere trickle by the time of the Coral Sea Disaster
of 2542, and the vast majority of those were rejects from the
burgeoning societies of the moon and the microworlds.

But no one had ever taken up arms on behalf of the existing population of sleepers.

The conveniently forgotten corpsicles had never found a
champion willing to campaign for their release—or even for
the careful discrimination of those who had never done anything to deserve indefinite sentences in the first place. Without such a champion, it had been easy enough to leave the
problem to be sorted out by someone who actually cared.

Even now, when a couple of specimen releases had finally
been arranged, it was not obvious that anyone *really* cared.
Was it incumbent on me, I wondered, to become the champion that the sleepers had never had?

I tucked the thought away for possible future reference;
for the time being, I still had to work out exactly what kind of
nest of vipers I had been delivered into, and why.

I looked up Emily Marchant before looking up Mortimer Gray, and was suitably impressed.

There were, allegedly, no Hardinists in or behind the Outer System Confederation—but that didn't mean that questions of ownership and stewardship were irrelevant in the outer system. Nor did it mean that the implications of the Tragedy of the Commons hadn't yet raised their ugly head. Quite the reverse, in fact. Questions of who might be entitled to do what with exactly which lumps of mass—"lumps" ranging in size from asteroids no bigger than an average hometree to Jupiter itself—seemed to have become measurably more acute during the last few centuries, and the increase had accelerated during the last few decades.

In the Outer System, every rock was precious, and every block of ice even more so. That, apparently, was one of the reasons why the ship carrying Michael Lowenthal and Mortimer Gray from Earth had been exposed to the risk of close encounters with snowballs. The settlers of the Oort Halo had been deflecting new comets sunwards for centuries; although the bigger lumps were greedily intercepted, the residual small debris was pouring into the inner system like an everlasting blizzard. That was, apparently, another cause of tension and disputation between the Confederation and the Earthbound.

It didn't require any data-trawling skill to discover that Emily Marchant was a major player in the Confederation and all its major disputes. She had the money, the prestige, the talent, the know-how, and the charisma to make her opinions felt. She was festooned with painfully quaint nicknames—the Chief Cheerleader of the High Kickers and the Great Architect of the Ice Palaces, to name but two—but her most common label was "the Titaness." There was even an ultrasmart spaceship with the same name. She was, it seemed, a Snow Queen of sufficient majesty to put the petty villain of Christine Caine's favorite kiddie flick to shame.

Unfortunately, Emily Marchant wasn't inbound on the ship that was hurtling inwards to pay the respects of the outer system to the newly awakened Adam Zimmerman; she obviously had better things to do. The Titanian envoy en route from the Jovian moons was a much younger and far less influential woman named Niamh Horne.

I knew that the Irish name Niamh was pronounced to rhyme with "Eve," but even someone as intrigued by names as I was couldn't make anything significant of that. Nor could anyone—even someone as paranoid as me—have found the slightest potentially meaningful connection between Emily Marchant or Niamh Horne and Christine Caine or me. It wasn't until I checked out Mortimer Gray that I found one of those—and it wasn't one that anyone could have expected, unless the wonderful children of Excelsior knew *much* more about me than they were letting on.

According to the records available on Excelsior, Mortimer Gray's career was a model of honest endeavor motivated entirely by intellectual curiosity. Unlike Michael Lowenthal's, his entire life seemed to be an open book, and apart from the probable coincidence of his having shared a couple of character-forming experiences with Emily Marchant he seemed unlikely to have any hidden agenda. But right up there at the head of his basic biography was a name I recognized: a name that, in all probability, no one *but* me in the entire universe would have recognized.

Mortimer Gray's biological mother—who had, of course, died long before he was born—had been Diana Caisson. *My* Diana Caisson. Damon Hart's Diana Caisson. There was no doubt about her being the same one; her birth date was right up there alongside his, although her death date was given as "unknown."

What could it mean?

So far as I could tell, it couldn't possibly mean anything. How could anyone have known that I had been acquainted with the donor of the egg that had been engineered to produce Mortimer Gray? Why would anyone, including Mortimer Gray, have cared? Surely it had to be a coincidence. There was no imaginable reason why it should be anything else.

I had to switch tack then, so I began gathering information about Excelsior and its peculiar inhabitants, hoping to obtain some insight into their possible motives for involving themselves in Adam Zimmerman's resurrection.

It didn't take long to find out that they were even more peculiar than I thought. I had been thinking of Davida Berenike Columella as a girl and her fellows as a sisterhood, but that wasn't strictly accurate. It wasn't just the secondary sexual characteristics that arrive with puberty that "she" and her kind had forsaken; "she" had no ovaries either. Nor had "she" a womb, or a clitoris. It was too late to start thinking of her as an "it," so I decided that I might as well stick with the pronoun I'd first thought of, but the fact remained that she and all her kind were sexless.

Why?

There was no shortage of information on file to explain the decision to eliminate sex from the design of *Excelsior*'s inhabitants, although the sheer profusion of that information was testimony to the controversy that must have surrounded the plan.

Apparently, several schools of thought had recently grown up as to the merits of arresting the aging process in different phases. The school that had settled on the position that the ideal age for an emortal was prepuberal had extrapolated the line of thinking a step further, reasoning that if the sexual organs were better left undeveloped it would be better still to eliminate them altogether, liberating valuable anatomical space for useful augmentation within the basic "functionally evolved corpus."

Taking the research a step farther back into the realm of theory and technics, I soon became lost in specialisms of which I had not the least understanding, but I gradually pieced together a picture of the background against which this strange experiment had been set.

It seemed to me that it all came down, in the final analysis, to the Miller Effect.

Morgan Miller was the twentieth-century scientist who first stumbled upon a technology of longevity: a rejuvenation technique that worked by diverting a mature organism's reproductive apparatus to the production of stem cells that could enhance the organism's powers of self-repair dramatically. There were, however, two catches. Firstly, Miller's method only worked on organisms in possession of the appropriate reproductive apparatus—which is to say, females. Secondly, the relevant power of self-repair enabled the cells in the organism's brain to recover all the neuronal connections that experience had selectively withered—which is to say that it obliterated memory and learning on a massive scale.

Rejuvenation of the kind that Miller discovered continually restored the innocence of the individual. Mice could cope with that kind of continual loss, because they could learn everything they needed to know to get along as mice over and over again. Higher mammals couldn't; even dogs rejuvenated by the Miller technique were reduced to helpless imbecility, unable to learn as quickly as their learning evaporated. That was why rejuvenation research in the following century had been concentrated on more selective and more easily controllable Internal Technologies: technologies which my generation were the first to exploit on a wholesale basis.

People of my generation had hoped—maybe even expected—that nanotech systems would continue to improve as we got older, so that every extra decade of life we obtained would produce further rewards. What the history book told me now, though, was that the escalator had run into the law of diminishing returns.

Two hundred years of life became routine, three hundred just about possible for the very rich and the very lucky. Damon's three-hundred-and-thirty-some year span had been highly unusual even for members of the Inner Circle. Repairing the body parts below the neck had not been unduly problematic in the majority of cases, although periodic invasive and incapacitating "deep-tissue rejuvenations" had been required to support the routine work of IT repair, but keeping the brain going without destroying the mind within had proved much more difficult.

The menace posed by "Millerization" had been complemented soon enough by "robotization": the loss of a brain's capacity to further refine its neuronal configurations. Carefully protected from the obliteration of memory and personality, the brains of men of Damon's generation had tended to the opposite extreme, settling into a quasimechanical rut which made them incapable of assimilating *new* experiences or reformulating their memories. Attempts had been made to get around this problem by means of inorganic augments—meatware/hardware collaborations involving various kinds of "memory boxes"—but none had succeeded in forging a workable alliance and most had exaggerated the problems they were attempting to solve.

The advent of the Zaman Transformation, which involved engineering fertilized ova for extreme resistance to the aging process, had not only sidestepped many of the problems associated with IT repair systems but had appeared to strike a balance in the brain between Millerization and robotization. The neurones of ZT brains retained a greater capacity for self-regeneration than the neurones of ordinary mortals, but they retained the switching capacity that permitted rapid learning. Although the first generations of true emortals could keep a firm enough grip on their memories and learned skills, they seemed to be equally capable of further adaptation. Their memories of times past became increasingly vague, but never lost their coherence, while their capacity to assimilate new experience remained undiminished—or so, at least, the argument went.

Not everyone, it seemed, was convinced.

Many people believed that robotization remained a threat—and that many living individuals had, indeed, been robotized, although they retained the illusion of being fully human and continued to maintain that appearance. Opinions differed, as one might expect, as to exactly which individuals might have become existentially becalmed in this way.

On the other hand, many people believed that the bugbear of Millerization had not been entirely overcome, and that the real existential threat facing the new emortals was not mental petrifaction but a loss of the continuity of the self: too much change rather than too little.

Some people, of course, believed that *both* processes were observable in the world around them—usually, but not necessarily, in different individuals.

At any rate, the quest for a perfect mental balance within a brain whose developmental course avoided both the Scylla of Millerization and the Charybdis of robotization had not been abandoned once Zaman Transformations became the norm. Far from it. All kinds of research were continuing, based in many different theories and ideologies.

So-called cyborganizers had resuscitated many formerly abandoned lines of research into meatware/hardware collaboration, while "Zamaners"—including those sponsored by the Ahasuerus Foundation—had hardly paused to draw breath before producing hundreds of variations and refinements of their basic technique. The situation had been further complicated, it seemed, by a leap forward in the field of "genomic engineering" following the discovery elsewhere in the galaxy of natural genomic systems differing quite markedly from the one that was fundamental to Earth's ecosphere.

In brief, there were now many different humankinds and not-so-humankinds, most of which laid claim to sole possession of the ideal emortality. The people of Excelsior seemed to me to be among the weirder lines in the posthuman spectrum—although that was not an impression encouraged by their own data banks—but there were undoubtedly others every bit as weird to be found among the fabers of the outer system microworlds and the cyborganizers of the Jovian and Saturnian satellites, not to mention the carefully adapted colonists of Ararat and Maya.

All of which was interesting, in its way, but did not seem to be of any immediate help in penetrating the motives of Davida Berenike Columella and her colleagues.

I now had a better understanding of how they fitted into the unfolding pattern of human history, but the questions still remained.

Why here?

Why now?

Why Christine Caine?

Why me?

And why would the suspicion not be quieted that I wouldn't like the answers when I finally worked them out, even if I were fortunate enough to live that long?

FOURTEEN
THE GARDEN OF EXCELSIOR

The artificial worlds of the twenty-second century had been little more than glorified tin cans—not quite sardine cans, but near enough. The vast majority had been no farther from the Earth than lunar orbit. Their inhabitants had been understandably enthusiastic to develop their own self-sustaining ecospheres, so I had seen pictures aplenty of their glass-house-clad "fields" and "hydroponic units." I had carried forward the tacit assumption that Excelsior would be equipped with something similar, until Davida Berenike Columella had put me right.

All the food in Excelsior was produced by artificial photosynthetic systems aggregated into a complex network of vast matt-black "leaves" surrounding a core whose spin simulated gravity. The microworld had no sunlit fields at all. As Davida had told me, though, it did have a garden, whose flora and fauna were purely ornamental. I had a ready-made image of a garden floating in my mind too, but that turned out to be just as wrong as my image of glass-roofed fields.

When Christine and I were finally allowed to go "out," it was to the garden that we were taken. I had hoped to take a stroll around the corridors of the microworld, in order to get a glimpse of everyday life as it was lived there, but that wasn't the way things were done on Excelsior. Excelsior didn't go in for corridors.

When we were ready to go, the wall of my holding cell grew a couple of fancy blisters, which opened up sideways like a cross between a yawning crocodile and a feeding clam.

I had to remind myself that it was just a kind of data suit in order to force myself to step into it, and even then I muttered to Christine: "I'm glad I never suffered from claustrophobia. All those hours I spent editing tapes were better lessons in life than I realized."

"I always suffered from claustrophobia," she told me, "but I think they've edited out my capacity for panic."

I thought about that while the cocoon wrapped itself around me so that I could be transported through the body of the giant Excelsior like some parasitic invader captured by an unusually considerate white corpuscle. I was glad that the journey didn't take long.

I suppose I'd have felt better about the journey if the garden had justified the effort, but it didn't. I'd seen much better ones in VE. In fact, that was exactly what was wrong with it. It looked like a synthesized cartoon: utterly artificial, every part of the image exaggerated almost to the point of caricature. If the garden really had been a VE mockup it would have been considered gauche even in the twenty-second century. The colors were too bright, the perfumed flowers too numerous as well as too musky. The ensemble had the scrupulously overdone quality of the child-orientated backdrops in the mass-produced virtual fantasies of my own day.

Given that I had already compared Christine to Lilith, and that we were still expecting an Adam, I expected a stream of Eden jokes, but she was nothing if not unpredictable. She didn't inquire after the Tree of Knowledge or the serpent, and never mentioned the possibility of a fall.

She wasn't impressed by the garden's aesthetic quality either.

"It's much too garish," she complained. "It's not quite as awful as the food, but it's more than awful enough." Davida was not with us in the flesh, but we both presumed that she was listening to every word. Christine obviously felt no obligation to be diplomatic—but I could sympathize with that.

The animals in the garden were as prolific as the plants. There were brightly colored fish and amphibians swarming in every pond, while svelte reptiles, delicate birds, and athletic mammals peeped out of the foliage of every bush and every tree. There were insects too, but I wasn't convinced, even for a moment, that they were busy pollinating the flowers. I suspected that the plants and animals alike might be as sexless as their keepers. I also deduced that the apparent predators—which seemed perfectly at ease with the conspicuously unintimidated individuals that would have provided them with food in a natural ecosystem—ate exactly the same nectar that microworlders ate: a carefully balanced cocktail of synthetic nutrients. It was, of course, a nectar that Christine and I couldn't share, because it wouldn't be appropriate to our complex nutritional requirements. In a sense, therefore, we were the only "real" animals in the garden: the only creatures forged by nature rather than by artifice.

All my suspicions and deductions turned out to be true. Under the crystal sky of Excelsior, even the blades of grass were sculptures, safe from grazing. They didn't even feel right. Everything I touched proclaimed its artificiality to my fingers. The knowledge that my fingers were wrapped in some ultramodern fabric that had probably reconditioned my own sense of touch only added to the confusion.

"I get the impression that they haven't quite fathomed the idea of *gardening*," was Christine's final judgment. I wasn't so sure. We had brought a different notion over a gulf of a thousand years, but who was to say that ours was right? If they'd taken a vote on Excelsior, the motion would have been carried unanimously, because we wouldn't have been entitled to express an opinion.

The ungrazable grass and the unpollinatable flowers weren't the models for every vegetable form. The fruits that grew on the trees were designed—and by no means reserved—for posthuman consumption. When I asked, I was told that it was perfectly safe, and permissible, for me to eat the fruit, but that it wouldn't be adequate to my dietary needs. Having heard that, I didn't even bother to experiment. I could live with the disappointment of lousy golden rice, but insipid and essentially unsatisfying apples were a different matter.

In any case, the fruits were too caricaturish. They were far less tempting—to me, at least—than their designers had probably intended.

"Take a look at the Gaean Restoration through one of their cobweb hoods when you get the chance," I suggested to my companion. "It's less obvious and less profuse, and a great deal more varied, but it has exactly the same quality of artifice. I couldn't find any authentic wilderness, even on Earth."

"Wilderness is overrated," Christine assured me. "I don't mind in the least that all this is fake—I just wish it had been better done."

"They like their kind of food," I reminded her. "They must like their kind of garden too. Their aesthetic standards aren't ours. They experience things differently. Imagine what they must think of us."

"I try," she assured me.

Given that I didn't know what to think of her, and couldn't imagine what she might think of me, I had to suppose that her attempts—and mine too—stood little chance of success. But there had to be a reason why the people of Excelsior had brought us back. I had to hope that it might be comprehensible even if I dared not hope, as yet, that I might be able to deem it good.

"The ship from Earth will be docking in a couple of hours," I told Christine, in case she hadn't been informed. "We'll have a chance to talk to Gray and Lowenthal before the Outer System ship arrives and the main event gets under way. Have you given any thought to their offers of employment?"

"I'm not going back to Earth, she said, with a firmness that took me by surprise.

"Why not?" I asked.

"Been there, done that, took the rap. You should take a look at Titan. Makes the Snow Queen's magic palace look like an igloo. You don't have to come with me if you don't want to."

"I haven't even begun to make up my mind," I told her.

"That's because you want to play the game," she said. "You want to get in with Adam, in case he's going places. I don't."

"I can see why you'd want a new start," I admitted.

"No you can't," she told me, sharply. "I told you before—you don't know shit about me."

"So tell me," I retorted. "Why did you kill all those people? Your parents I could probably understand, but what about the others? If my memory serves me rightly, you didn't have any connection with them at all, let alone a plausible motive."

She looked at me, and then she looked away, at the garden where lions lay down with lambs and the butterflies lived forever.

"Don't you believe that VE tape you told me about?" she asked. "I couldn't stand myself, so I hid in false personalities disguised as ancestral memories, acting out the underlying trauma again and again."

"No, I don't believe it," I said. "The writer claimed that it was taken from your own testimony—but that was only one of the stories you told. I don't remember exactly, but I think there was at least one epic of harrowing child abuse, and at least one item of bad science fiction in which your foster parents had all been replaced by aliens, and a couple more besides. If you'd stuck to the first one, you might have got off, although you'd have needed an extra wrinkle to accommodate the three strays. There were a lot of bad parents around. They were the first generation who had to get used to a new system of parenthood that was radically different from the biological model, and they incorporated all the badness with which the whole damn world was still infected."

"My foster parents weren't bad," she said. "The marriage broke up—smashed to smithereens—but they tried as hard as they could to protect me from all that." She sounded as though she hadn't the faintest idea why she'd done what she'd done.

"So why tell the abuse story?" I asked. "Why tell any of the stories, if they weren't true?"

"I had to tell the stories," she said, as if it were as simple as that. "They kept coming back for more, and the one thing they couldn't abide was silence. They probably told themselves that they were wearing me down, waiting for the truth to emerge when I ran out of lies, but they weren't. They liked the stories. They always wanted more. So do you. You just want a story—and if I give you one you'll want another, and another. That's all I am to you: a story."

"According to *Bad Karma*," I pointed out, "that's all you were to yourself. Did you ever have the slightest idea why you did it? Or were you making up story after story by way of exploration—or distraction?"

"I got out in the end, didn't I?" she said, softly. "I'm here. I'm free. I'm never going back. I'm a winner. Maybe I did it in order to be put away, to make sure that I'd be the one to wake up in Wonderland. Maybe Adam Zimmerman is the one who did it the hard way."

I didn't believe that, but I could see that she wasn't going to tell me anything I could believe.

"The woman from the Confederation might not make us an offer," I said, although I didn't believe it. "She might think that we belong on Earth, and good riddance to us. We may not have the option of going elsewhere."

"I don't think so," Christine replied, serenely confident. "While we're the only real humans in the universe, everyone will be interested in us. Even if they begin to bring the others back, there won't be enough to go round. We're mortals, Madoc. We're their ancestors. They need us. They all need us, not just the stick-in-the-muds who cling to the Earth. They all need us because they've all forgotten what we were like, and they all need to be reminded."

I could have objected that Michael Lowenthal and Mortimer Gray seemed human enough, for all their advanced years, but I didn't. I knew what she meant. I knew, even on the basis of my first faltering inquiries, that emortality had not been acquired without cost, and that Lowenthal and Gray were as profoundly different from me, in their own way, as Davida's sisterhood and the cyborganizers.

I could also have pointed out that whatever the reason had been, Christine had thought that the most appropriate thing to do to her own self-appointed ancestors was to murder the lot, and three other people besides. I didn't do that either.

"This isn't the Omega Point, Christine," I told her. "It's not even a fancy VE. It's just the same old world, with a thousand extra years of history. Its inhabitants may be curious, but they have other things to be interested in that are far more fascinating than us. They'll lose interest in us soon enough, unless we can find a way to keep some of them on the hook."

"I don't run out of stories easily," she said. "Do you?"

W e watched the docking of *Peppercorn Seven* through the "window" in my quarters. Davida Berenike Columella wasn't with us; she was part of the reception committee that would bring Gray and Lowenthal through the microworld's mysterious interior to meet us.

The viewpoint from which we watched the spaceship's final approach was way out on one of Excelsior's spiny limbs, so we could see a good deal of the microworld as well as the approaching vessel. I'd already studied diagrams of its structure, so I was able to make sense of most of the structures I could see.

The docking station was in Excelsior's hub: the zero-gee core about which the other environments rotated. The hub was the site of the microworld's most advanced AIs and the core of its communication system as well as the anchorage of the artificial photosynthetic systems supplying the station's organics. It also had capacious living spaces of its own, although there were no fabers currently in residence. All that was expectable, but there were a couple of things that the diagram hadn't shown to full advantage: the tentacles and the ice.

Everything on a diagram tends to look rigid and mechanical, but seen through the camera's eye Excelsior seemed much more lifelike. It gave the impression of floating in oceanic space like some kind of weird sea creature: a hybrid of wrack and Portuguese man-o'-war, bound to a coral base. Like the man-o'-war, it trailed countless slender tentacles that mostly hung loose, except that their resting positions were determined by the movement of the microworld rather than by gravity. When they became active, they moved with lifelike purpose.

Even while the ship was some distance away the tentacles grouped around the mouth of the docking bay were making their adjustments, as if anticipating a meal. The spinning "wheel" enclosing the weighted components of the microworld was mostly devoid of protective ice, but it had a much smarter surface which presumably had its own ways of dealing with stray dust particles and dangerous surges in the solar wind. It had its own frill of tentacles, but they were much less impressive than the snaky locks of the medusal core.

The "coraline" part of the ensemble was mostly metals and ceramics, but that wasn't obvious from where we were standing, because the solid and substantial parts of the microworld were encased in cometary ice, which served as an outer shield as well as a resource. The ice hadn't been sculpted in the careful fashion of the ice palaces of Antarctica and Titan, but it caught sunlight and starlight anyway. Refraction sent the rays every which way before letting them out in a fashion that was far from chaotic, although the patterns were accidental and serendipitous.

From where we looked back at them, Excelsior's icy vistas sparkled and glowed. Even though I knew full well that all but the tiniest fraction of its internalized light had to originate in the sun, I couldn't avoid the impression that the show was the product of the millions of stars and galaxies that crowded in the background. Some of the photons deflected through it from those distant sources were mere decades old, but some of them were reaching the climax of a journey that had begun in the aftermath of the Big Bang.

Compared with the complex structure of the microworld, the ship from Earth was disappointingly dull. It had no fins and no obvious propulsion pods. To me it looked like a metal ball that had been carelessly miscast—or very badly scratched and scarred after its removal from the mold—from which a single spike extended with a smaller ball attached to its tip. Seen in isolation, set against the hectic background of stars, the craft might have been any size at all, but when the elastic docking cables reached out with remarkable delicacy and tenderness to complete its deceleration I realized that it was smaller than I had initially imagined.

The ball was no bigger than a five-ton truck, with an internal cubic capacity about the same as that of the room from which we were observing it. The blister on the end of the spike couldn't have been much more capacious than the four-seater automobiles in which I'd driven around old Los Angeles. The cocoons containing Mortimer Gray, Michael Lowenthal, and Lowenthal's two "assistants" had to be packed so tight that they would have to disembark one by one, through a crawl space narrow enough to terrify a claustrophobe.

I recalled, with a slight shudder, that there were two spare cocoons aboard—but only two. If Adam Zimmerman, Christine Caine, and I all elected to travel back to Earth, one of the delegates would have to stay behind on Excelsior. Even though I didn't have any present intention of going to Earth on *Peppercorn Seven* I hoped that the blister was flexible enough to accommodate six passengers without cramming them into its core like the pips in an apple. I knew that it had to be made of something radiation-proof, but I figured that it must be more versatile than it looked.

Having made similar calculations, Christine muttered: "Space travel seems to be a lot less comfortable than a first-class cabin in a zeppelin, even after a thousand years of progress." I couldn't believe that she'd ever been in a first-class cabin in a zeppelin, but she was obviously a hardened VE tourist in spite of her tender years.

"It's just like a long session in a bodysuit," I said. "In fact, it *is* a long session in a bodysuit. Lowenthal's probably been taking care of business every step of the way, despite the ever-growing transmission delay. Gray was probably working too."

"My mothers used to tell me that my muscles would atrophy and my extremities would get gangrene if I stayed in a full suit for more than a couple of hours at a time," she observed, drily.

"They were exaggerating—and those kinds of medical problems must have been solved long ago," I said. She must have worked that out for herself, but I couldn't help adopting a mentor pose. I made a mental note to make absolutely sure that she didn't begin seeing me as a father figure.

"With an intravenous drip and a catheter a person could probably stay in VE forever, nowadays," she said, effortlessly taking up the thread of the argument. "We could take up permanent residence in the fantasies of our choice."

The first title that came to mind, reflexively, was *Bad Karma*, but I didn't say so. Way back when, I had always told my critics—and, for that matter, myself—that the fight tapes I made were a public service, because they allowed people with a taste for violence to indulge it harmlessly. There was a grain of truth in the argument, but not enough. If Christine Caine had wanted to commit virtual murders she could have done so, even in the twenty-second century. Maybe the quality of the illusion wouldn't have lived up to the standards of the world in which we now found ourselves, but that wasn't the factor that had displaced her murderous passion into the meatware arena. Murder is only murder if you kill real people. Life is only life if you actually live it. Maybe there were some among the Earthbound who really did spend most of their lives in VE nowadays—but I was willing to bet that they were far outnumbered by people who regarded VE as workspace and social space, and only ventured into fantasylands for the sake of occasional relaxation.

Christine Caine, I supposed, must have seen multiple versions of all her favorite fantasies while she was a child, but it wasn't just the warnings her mothers had given her that had brought her back to stern reality. Perhaps that was a pity; if she'd become an addict, she'd probably have been harmless.

The umbilical had been attached to *Peppercorn Seven*'s blister now, although there had been no obvious hatchway on the pitted surface. The tube didn't seem to be wide enough to accommodate a full-sized human body without bulging, and it was possible to see the vague outline of the first person out of the capsule. The movement of the bolus along the umbilical was smooth, presumably controlled by peristalsis rather than by any undignified wriggling on the part of the passenger.

We counted the four passengers into the body of Excelsior one by one, but once the umbilical had been sealed it was by no means an exciting business.

"The other ship is much bigger, apparently." I told my companion, slipping back into mentor mode just for a moment. "*Child of Fortune* isn't just a nest of cocoons—it actually has empty spaces inside, and an ecosphere of sorts."

I needn't have bothered; Christine had researched the topic and obviously knew more about *Child of Fortune* than I did. She confirmed that the spacecraft built in the outer system were very much more complicated, almost qualifying as microworlds in their own right. "It has an AI brain as big as Excelsior's," she concluded. "*Really* big, and *really* smart—a supersilver. But machines still don't have the vote."

The last addendum was phrased as a jokey offhand comment, but I guessed that she'd actually researched that too.

The consensus in our time had been that AIs could never become conscious because there were fundamental limitations in inorganic neural networks—*fundamental* meaning right down at the atomic and subatomic levels. No matter how rapid they were as calculators, nor how capacious they became as datastores, nor how how clever they became at animating human-seeming sims, they would always be automata, according to the best human brains around. Consciousness, according to the dominant view, was something that could only emerge in organic systems, and was precarious even there. What I'd found out about the history of emortality suggested that the same opinion was still dominant—although my reflexive tendency to treat any popular opinion with derision reminded me that there were ideological reasons why "the best human brains" might want to believe that they could never be equaled or surpassed.

"The modern opinion seems to be that it's far easier for organic brains to become robotized—reduced to mere automata—than it is for automata to acquire the creative, conflicted, and multilayered messiness that's the fount of consciousness," I said to Christine.

"Unless and until the people of the glorious thirty-third century actually find a reliable way of detecting and measuring consciousness, it'll probably remain a matter of opinion," she retorted. "The ships they use in the outer system have to take much longer trips and they have to be much more versatile, so they have to be a lot smarter too. *That* thing just sits around in an orbital parking lot waiting for people to shuttle up out of the gravity well. It's a glorified cab that hops back and forth between Earth, Luna, and their neighboring microworlds. The ships they use outside the belt have to be capable of operating on the surfaces of icebound satellites and in the outer atmospheres of gas giants. They have to be extremely smart—and it isn't just outer system equipment that has to be smart. The people busy terraforming Venus and mining Mercury have much smarter AIs at their disposal than the people on Earth. Outer System AIs could have played a much larger part in the Gaean Restoration, if the Earthbound hadn't refused them the chance. The Earthbound are afraid of them."

Are they? I wondered. *Or is it just that they won't pay the asking price for equipment designed and manufactured in the outer system.* I knew that there was an AI "metropolis" on Ganymede, where the outer system ships and interstellar probes were mostly built, but I hadn't carried my research beyond the merest matters of fact. I made a mental note to make a more careful investigation of the balance of trade between the Hardinist Cabal and the Confederation.

There was nothing more to watch, and we didn't know how long we'd have to wait for our introduction to the ambassadors from Earth, so we turned away from the window.

"Have you looked at Venus?" Christine asked me.

"No," I said, "but I've seen picture-postcard views of Titan and Ganymede. Just like old science fiction tapes. Curiously nostalgic, in a way. I used to know someone who worked on that kind of imagery, until he sold out to PicoCon."

"Damon Hart," she guessed. It was the first indication I'd had that she'd been researching me, and that she'd seen the tape of my first conversation with Davida. It was oddly disturbing, although I was aware of the absurdity of thinking that my privacy had been invaded.

"Yes," I conceded, dully. "Damon Hart."

"Conrad Helier's heir. Eveline Hywood's too. Quite a start in life."

I knew that Christine had been put away before Hywood hit the headlines as the supposed inventor of para-DNA, and long before para-DNA was anything but a few black blobs carelessly discarded in the Pacific in the unfulfilled hope that it might be misidentified as a natural product. She'd been digging—and now she was fishing. Somehow, it didn't seem as understandable that she should be interested in me as it was that I should be interested in her. She was the crazy one.

"Yeah," I said. "It was a real privilege to have known him, I think. I can't quite shake the suspicion that he had something to do with my being put away, though—and if he didn't, he doesn't seem to have lifted a finger to get me out, even though he was firmly established in the Inner Circle long before he died. I still can't remember . . . but I have this *gut feeling*." "

She'd probably have continued probing if we hadn't been interrupted, but we were. Mortimer Gray and Michael

Lowenthal were obviously keen to get on; they couldn't have lingered more than a couple of minutes exchanging pleasantries with the sisterhood's welcoming committee before hopping back into yet another glorified white corpuscle and speeding through Excelsior's bloodstream to us.

SIXTEEN
THE MEN FROM EARTH

Michael Lowenthal and Mortimer Gray were so keen to see us, in fact, that they were practically elbowing one another out of the way as they approached. They both headed directly for me, but that might have been because Christine, gripped by a sudden fit of modesty, had dropped back to a position almost directly behind me.

Davida Berenike Columella tried to catch up with them in order to make the introductions, but Lowenthal wouldn't wait for her. He introduced Gray, although that was hardly necessary, and his two other companions. One of them was a soberly clad male named Jean de Comeau, whose title I didn't catch because I was too busy concentrating my attention on the one who obviously wasn't a UN bureaucrat: a female named Solantha Handsel.

Solantha Handsel had enough hardware built into her smartsuit—and probably into her own flesh—to give the appearance of being half-robot. It seemed to me that she might as well have had the word "bodyguard" stenciled on her flat but muscular chest.

It occurred to me that traveling with a bodyguard might be a social status thing—a matter of mere ornamentation—but my paranoia wasn't prepared to let me make the assumption. Nor was it prepared to write off the cyborg as an item of intimidatory showmanship. What my paranoia said was that if Michael Lowenthal had brought a minder with him, he expected to need minding. Maybe the sisters weren't as harmless as they seemed, and maybe he was anxious about

Christine Caine's reputation, but the more worrying possibility was that he had cause to be worried about Niamh Horne's yet-to-arrive entourage, or that he thought he had cause to be worried about me.

I'm not quite sure how it happened, but while I was busy formulating these thoughts Lowenthal cut me out from the crowd with well-trained expertise and somehow contrived— perhaps with Solantha Handsel's aid—to establish an invisible *cordon sanitaire* around us.

"Welcome back, Mr. Tamlin," he said, smiling broadly. "I understand that you used to work for us."

"Only as a subcontractor," I assured him, without bothering to quibble about the use of the word *us.* "Why, do you think you owe me money?"

He laughed politely. "If we did," he said, "the compound interest would have inflated it into a tidy sum by now. Unfortunately, we have no record of it, and the credit balance in your own accounts was sequestered long ago to pay for your incarceration."

"That's just the accounts you know about," I told him. I figured that if he wanted to imply that I was seriously poor, I might as well fight back. "It'll need some serious investigation to find out about the others. Not that I can compete with Christine, of course. She's got all those royalties owing to her for *Bad Karma.*"

He must have known that I was fishing. "We don't have a copy of it, I'm afraid," he assured me. "Mortimer may be able to turn one up. He spends a lot of time in the mountains— even more than he used to, now that their contents have been even more extensively trashed than they were before. We do, however, have copies of some of *your* old tapes, along with other data. All discarded by publicly accessible datastores, I fear. It seemed very unlikely to the custodians of our history that the items in question would ever be required again."

"But you squirreled it away regardless," I said. I tried to maintain a light tone as I said: "I don't suppose you know why I was put into SusAn in the first place? I seem to have mislaid the memory."

He didn't seem surprised by the question—but he did seem slightly suspicious, as if he didn't believe that I'd lost the memory and didn't mind my knowing it. "That's an intriguing mystery," he said, blandly. "We don't have any record of your conviction for a crime. As I said, our financial records show that your existing credit was seized to pay for the upkeep of your frozen body. Damon Hart neglected to make any provision for that purpose—but that was probably a genuine oversight."

I couldn't believe that he'd use a phrase like "probably a genuine oversight" unless he intended to imply the opposite, or that he'd have mentioned Damon Hart at all unless he too was fishing for information. In which case, I deduced, he probably didn't have the faintest idea why I'd been put away—although he was certainly interested in finding out.

"I suppose I ought to be glad that I was looked after so well, even though my credit ran out," I said. "I seem to have slept through at least two major disasters—I do hope that I haven't been revived on the eve of a third."

He didn't laugh at that suggestion. "This is a far better world than the one you left behind, in terms of the existential opportunities it presents," he assured me. "We'll be happy to help you in any way we can to adapt yourself to it, if that's your wish."

"Did you know Damon Hart personally?" I asked, abruptly.

"Slightly," Lowenthal admitted. "It's not surprising that he never mentioned you in conversation, but I can't find any reference to you in the files he left behind. It's almost as if someone deleted you from the record of his life—and from all the other records to which he had access."

It was obvious that he didn't mean "almost as if" at all, and that he thought the someone in question must have been Damon.

"It must be easy enough for a person as unimportant as me to be forgotten," I said, trying to match his bland tone. "Damon was my friend for twenty years, but he lived for three hundred more after I was frozen down. He must have become a completely different person. I expect he forgot about such trivialities as my upkeep long before he died."

"Perhaps so," Lowenthal agreed, insincerely. I took note of the fact that although Solantha Handsel seemed perfectly relaxed she was still within arm's reach, and the way she occasionally glanced at me was neither unwary nor incurious. If Lowenthal knew more about me than he was prepared to say, or even if he merely had more cause to be suspicious than he was prepared to reveal, what he knew or suspected seemed to be enough to put him on his guard.

"I understand that the delegation from the Outer System will be here soon," I said, mildly. "I'm looking forward to meeting them—all the more so now I've seen *your* cyborganizer."

"I'm looking forward to it too," Lowenthal assured me. I didn't believe him. Solantha Handsel seemed to be about to say something—perhaps to deny that she was a cyborganizer in the strictest sense of the term—but she shut up as soon as it became clear that her boss had more to say.

"To be perfectly frank," Lowenthal went on, seeming to me to be speaking anything but frankly, "it's good to have an excuse to meet Niamh face to face. All kinds of problems seem to get in the way of people like her traveling to Earth, or people like me visiting Titan. This little party should provide a very valuable opportunity for a frank and informal exchange of views. To be honest, that's the real reason I'm here—and presumably the real reason for her presence. But that's not to say that I'm not interested to meet you, and Adam Zimmerman too. My offer of useful employment is perfectly sincere, and I hope that you'll accept it."

"I haven't made up my mind," I told him. "Maybe I'll wait to see what Adam decides. And Christine, of course. We true humans may need to stick together for a while, until we figure out exactly what's what."

He condescended to laugh at that—and having made whatever point he had intended to make, he passed on, leaving me to face the curiosity of Mortimer Gray.

"I'm delighted to meet you," the historian said, with what seemed like touching honesty after Lowenthal's practiced diplomatic manner. "It's not often one has the opportunity to meet a witness to history as remote as yours."

"There are thousands more just over the way," I reminded him. "Although you might need to let some of them lie for a few decades more, until they ripen to the appropriate remoteness."

He actually blushed. "I'm sorry," he said, just as honestly. "Michael told me what happened to you. It must be a terrible shock, to have been *forgotten* like that."

"The shock," I told him, drily, "is in being remembered. Everyone tells me that I've been lucky, because there are so many more possibilities open to me nowadays."

"That's true, of course," he conceded, "but I can understand why you might think you've paid a heavy price for the privilege. To be separated from everyone and everything you knew, and not even to know why . . . it must be difficult. You'll adjust, though. Michael and I belong to the last generation raised by mortal parents, so we understand loss a little better than the generation which came after us. We've also lived through major catastrophes—the Coral Sea Disaster, the North American Basalt Flow—so we have a better understanding of grief and its associated emotions than we might have expected or wished for. You and I aren't so very different, even though you've yet to decide which particular form of posthumanity to embrace. You're very young, by our standards. In time, you'll adapt fully to the new Earth, no matter how strange it may seem at first. By the time you're my age . . ."

"I haven't made up my mind whether to go to Earth," I

told him, figuring that it was about time I interrupted. "May I ask you a question about something that's been troubling me?"

"Of course," he said, with all the enthusiasm of an authentic sucker.

"Why does Michael Lowenthal have a bodyguard with him?"

Unfortunately, Mortimer Gray's act was no act. He laughed, as if at a simple misunderstanding. "Solantha isn't a *bodyguard*," he assured me, blithely. "Cyborganization is mostly a matter of fashion, on Earth at least. Life in the outer system requires a degree of functional cyborgization, but it's purely a matter of aesthetics at home. Did you think he was worried about meeting Christine Caine?"

"No," I said. I figured that I might as well go all the way, given that he didn't seem to be taking me seriously. "I wondered whether he was worried about meeting Niamh Horne, and the possibility of war breaking out between Earth and the Outer System."

Gray seemed genuinely puzzled. "Where did you get that idea from?" he asked. "Humankind hasn't had a war since . . . well, before you were born. Emortals don't fight wars—they have too accurate a notion of the value of life."

"You don't think blowing up North America and plunging Earth into nuclear winter counts as an act of war?" I said, feigning astonishment. "In my day, most people thought that every stomach upset was probably the first shot in the next plague war."

Mortimer Gray stared at me, seemingly anxious as well as puzzled. "I suppose that must have been the case," he said, cautiously. "But things have changed. Mores, attitudes, habits . . . everything is different now. I can't believe that the Basalt Flow was the result of a deliberate act of sabotage. There are political conflicts within the solar system, but we all understand that our only hope of beating the Afterlife is to work together as a community of species. Do you know what the Afterlife is?"

"I read up on it," I confirmed. "I understand the argument that a common threat makes it necessary for potential enemies to work together—but I'm not convinced. In my day, as you presumably know, there was a school of thought which held that social contracts were only reliable because men were mortal and prey to pain. In a world of true emortals with efficient IT, the theory went, there could be no effective sanctions forcing people to fulfill their obligations and keep their promises. One corollary of the theory was that a world of emortals would be more prone to conflict, not less."

He found the notion too alien to be threatening. "But the truth is exactly the opposite, as history has proved," he protested. "People who might live for a very long time in the company of their peers have very powerful reasons for honoring their obligations, because there's no way to escape the consequences of failure. We have to deal honestly with one another, because we can't afford the consequences of being exposed as liars, let alone the consequences of violent behaviour. You really need to understand that, Mr. Tamlin—and I'm sure you will, given time."

I would have taken more comfort from his words if he'd glanced sideways at Christine Caine while he was closing his argument, but he didn't. He kept right on looking me in the eyes as he pronounced words like "liars" and "violent behavior." He wasn't scared of me—he would have thought the suggestion that he might need a bodyguard absurd—but he wasn't laboring under any delusion that I was a man like him. When he said that he and I weren't so very different, he was talking about a narrow range of emotional responses, not about the extent of our evolution beyond Neanderthal brutality.

"So there isn't going to be a war?" I said, meeting his gaze squarely.

"No," he said, flatly. I couldn't tell whether he was so definite because he was genuinely convinced, or because he desperately wanted to believe it. Paranoid as I was, I favored the latter hypothesis. In any case, I thought it best to change the subject.

"You said that I've *yet to decide which particular form of posthumanity to embrace*," I reminded him. "I don't suppose anyone cares what decision I make—but Adam Zimmerman must be a different proposition. Lots of people must be interested in his decision, given that he had to change the course of history in order to give himself the chance to make it."

"People are interested, of course," Gray said, a little warier now of where the conversation might be heading, "but not as much as you might suppose. Adam Zimmerman didn't actually *change* the course of history. If he hadn't done what he did, someone else would have. The timing might have been slightly different, but the eventual result would have been the same."

"Is it just Adam Zimmerman," I asked, genuinely interested in the question, "or don't you believe in pivotal individuals at all? Would the eventual result have been the same if Conrad Helier had been an early casualty of the plague wars—or if you hadn't saved Emily Marchant's life in the Coral Sea Disaster?"

He raised his eyebrows in frank astonishment. "We can all make a difference, Mr. Tamlin," he said. "It's because so many of us can that none of us has the power to change everything. I do hope you'll consider the offer of employment I made—you might be even more useful to us as a window into the past than we had hoped. An account of your personal history would be fascinating."

It was supposed to be a compliment, but I couldn't take it that way. He was telling me that I appeared to be an even freakier freak than his friendly neighborhood zookeepers had imagined. No matter how smart I tried to seem, I realized, I would always be a monkey doing tricks. Nobody was ever going to think that I might have anything to contribute to the understanding of the world as it now was. For a moment, I almost pitied Adam Zimmerman.

"There's nothing hi about my story," I told him. "It's essentially lo—and for the moment, quite lost."

He frowned, unable to see the joke for a few moments. Then he got it, and tried to contrive a weak smile. I couldn't blame him for his lack of amusement. Some jokes are best kept private.

"Even so," he said, "we'd be very interested. You're a unique resource, whose experiences will be even more interesting in juxtaposition with those of your companions."

All three of us were unique, even though we were in the same boat, because we'd come from different eras: we made up quite a goodie bag for a historian. There were thousands more of us still to be thawed, but every one would be unique from Mortimer Gray's point of view.

"I'll think it over," I assured the historian. "I'll come back to you when I have more questions."

I wanted to talk to Solantha Handsel, but I didn't get the chance. The party was already winding down—over, it seemed, almost as soon as it had begun—because Michael Lowenthal had decided that he had had enough, and that it was time to let the sisterhood whisk him away.

I didn't see the Earthpeople again until the following day. Even Christine absented herself for a while, although she reappeared when the time came to watch the "real" spaceship coming into dock.

That, apparently, was the kind of experience she liked to share—or one of them, at any rate.

SEVENTEEN
THE CYBORGANIZERS

C hristine hadn't exaggerated when she had rhapsodized about how much more impressive the ship from the Outer System would be than the ferry that had arced across the diameter of the Earth's orbit. *Child of Fortune* was at least thirty times as big as *Peppercorn Seven*, and there was not the least possibility that the neatly chiseled workings on its surface might be mistaken for incompetent molding or accidental scratching. It didn't have fins, but it did have what looked to me like a massive pair of furled wings.

Although the station looked like a chimerical sea creature, the ship from the Jovian moons had the air of an authentic flier: a bird that was merely bobbing on the surface of the ocean, quite able to transform itself into something altogether more spectacular. Because it was decelerating, *Child of Fortune* was headed toward us hind end first, its fuser doubtless spitting out the last few gobs of reaction mass with the utmost discretion. It bore a faint and temporary resemblance to a massive whale or basking shark, with its mouth wide open, but everything about its design proclaimed that it was a much finer creature than that.

When Excelsior had extended its tentacles toward the Earth ship the microworld had been a huge scavenger gobbling up a stray morsel, but when it reached out to touch the Outer System vessel it was more like a tentative greeting between alien equals, albeit of very different sizes and shapes.

"How many people are aboard?" I asked Christine, figuring that I might as well take advantage of her research.

"About sixty, apparently," she told me. "The permanent crew is about fifty strong. They're fabers—I think they'll disembark in shifts, but only as far as the microworld's core.

She was presumably right, but the umbilicals established between ship and station were much more substantial than those connected to *Peppercorn Seven*. It was impossible to see individuals passing through them.

I was even more curious about Niamh Horne's delegation than I had been about Lowenthal's, and I couldn't help feeling aggrieved that they didn't show anything like the same alacrity in calling on us.

Christine and I waited until it would have seemed absurd to wait any longer, then returned to our separate researches in the virtual world, half-hoping that giving up would somehow function as a catalyst and precipitate the expected meeting.

It didn't.

I had been immersed in solitary visions of Titan and Ganymede for more than two hours when the visitors finally arrived—and when they did, there were only two of them, in addition to Davida Berenike Columella.

At least I was spared the ultimate indignity of talking to a flunky. Niamh Horne had the grace to appear in person. She also had the grace to let Davida perform the introductions in a sensible ceremonial fashion. Her companion was a male named Theoderic Conwin.

Niamh Horne and Theoderic Conwin were both cyborgs, but I saw immediately—if slightly belatedly—what Mortimer Gray had meant about the difference between functional and ornamental cyborgization. I had taken Solantha Handsel for a bodyguard because her modifications had been shaped and coordinated to display the suggestion that she was half fighting machine, but I realized now how ostentatious her adaptations were.

There was nothing manifestly obtrusive or calculatedly

suggestive about the modifications that had been made to the two Titanians. It required close and considered inspection to determine that their outer teguments were much thicker than the additional skins Davida and I were wearing, because they were camouflaged to give an appearance of real skin and conventional clothing. Their eyes and ears, though artificial, were similarly formed to resemble their natural counterparts. It was impossible to judge exactly how much their seeming solidity owed to the bulk of their smartsuits, but I formed the impression that within their relatively stout frames there were two unfashionably thin individuals making no effort whatsoever to get out.

"Davida tells me that you don't want to go home to Earth," Niamh Horne said, after a few cursory pleasantries. Nobody had taken the trouble to invite Christine in from the adjoining room, although I felt a slight twinge of guilt about my failure to raise the issue.

"I haven't made any final decision," I told her. "But I have a certain sympathy with Christine's view that we're so radically dislocated anyway that we might as well go somewhere authentically alien."

"Been there, done that, took the rap," the cyborg woman quoted. Her tone suggested a wry smile, but her lips didn't seem to go in for that sort of thing.

"But the terrestrial surface you left behind is very different from the present one," her male companion pointed out.

"Not in the essentials," I said. "Atmosphere, gravity . . . anyway, rumor has it that you people think Earth is hopelessly decadent, incapable of any *real* change. A rest home for the robotized, holding back the cause of progress."

It would have been easier to judge their response to that if they had been smilers; as things were, I had to grin at my own joke to defuse it.

"It's only natural that the Earthbound should be conservative and conservationist," Theoderic Conwin said, displaying his tolerance proudly. "They're the custodians of the planet that produced humankind—and our explorations of the galaxy suggest that such worlds are exceedingly rare and precious."

"Someone has to be prepared to be fanatical in looking after what we have," Niamh Horne added, with equally ostentatious generosity. "If the Earthbound weren't able to maintain a safe anchorage for the posthuman project, our own capacity to innovate and experiment might be inhibited. There's no conflict between the outer satellites and Earth. Our differences of opinion are polite, and entirely healthy."

I gathered from this speech that she'd been thoroughly briefed on what I'd said to Mortimer Gray. The historian hadn't denied that there were conflicts, I remembered; he had been content to refute the notion that they could ever become violent. She obviously wanted to ram the point home. Even if I'd been less paranoid than I was I wouldn't have taken their assurances seriously for a moment.

"Well," I said, glibly, "I'm glad to be able to add an extra measure, however small, to the posthuman spectrum. I'm sure I'd find cause for discomfort in a world where differences weren't polite, healthy, and welcome. Do you think I'd be able to find useful work on Titan?"

"Ganymede might be more appropriate," she said, somewhat to my surprise.

"I thought Ganymede was the AI Utopia," I said.

"Exactly," she came back. "The roles filled there by human beings are relatively menial and less challenging than those available elsewhere. On the other hand, you might be able to adapt more rapidly to a smaller and more easily comprehensible world—one of the belt habitats, for instance." It would have stung less if she'd smiled, but I had a suspicion that it wasn't simply the inflexibility of her cheeks that was getting in her way this time.

"I take it that means you won't be matching Lowenthal's job offer," I said, trying to keep my own lips tight.

"You shouldn't take that one either, in my opinion," she told me. "Investigate the belt, Mr. Tamlin. That's where you're most likely to find a comfortable future."

"If I'd wanted a comfortable future," I retorted, "I probably wouldn't have ended up in the freezer in the first place."

"That's not what Adam Zimmerman thought," Theoderic Conwin put in. I still couldn't tell whether or not he was joking.

"So you're not going to offer *him* a job either?" I commented, sardonically.

"We're going to offer him a tour of the solar system," Conwin told me.

"May I come too?" I asked.

He had to pass that one along to his boss. "Certainly you may," Niamh Horne assured me, with what appeared to me to be a total lack of enthusiasm. "Adam Zimmerman may well desire to have company of his own kind. I'm sure you'd find the tour very instructive—but you shouldn't rush any of the decisions you'll have to make. There's no hurry."

"There is while I'm still mortal," I pointed out. "If I have to decide what kind of eternal youth to opt for, I need to do it while I'm still young. It's a difficult choice to make, given that there seem to be so many options—all fraught with risks."

Davida wanted to answer that one, but she didn't manage to get her reply in first and she was too polite to compete.

"The risks," Conwin said, smoothly, "are exaggerated." There was nothing in his artificial eyes to register annoyance, but I supposed that the risks he had in mind were those at the robotization end of the spectrum, and that the reason he had them in mind was that he was sensitive about the possibility of being mistaken for a victim. I decided to let the matter lie, for now.

"Suppose Adam Zimmerman doesn't want to go on the grand tour just yet," I said. "Will your offer remain open?" I was careful to phrase the question ambiguously, so that he wouldn't be sure whether I was referring to their offer to Adam Zimmerman or their markedly less generous offer to me.

It was Niamh Horne who answered, although she had to

hurry because Davida's mouth was open yet again, presumably to make some offer of her own. "We'll give sympathetic consideration to any request you care to make," she said.

Davida finally found her opportunity to say: "It might be as well if you were all to remain here for a while," she said. "We need to monitor your condition, and to make sure that the IT we've installed is working properly. You're very welcome to remain here as our guests indefinitely, but if you do decide to take up an offer of employment on Earth, you'd be wise to delay the move until we've completed our own research program. You might also have a useful role to play in the continuation of the project."

That was news to Niamh Horne as well as to me.

"Continuation?" the cyborg repeated. "You intend to bring them *all* back? Why?"

I was tempted to ask "Why not?" but I refrained.

"I don't know what the Foundation intends," Davida confessed. "I'm working to instructions—but I had assumed that if the first revivals went to plan . . ."

"*Whose* plan?" Niamh Horne was quick to ask.

Davida's little-girl face seemed utterly guileless and deeply confused. "Why, the Foundation's," she said.

"To the best of my knowledge," the cyborg said, frostily, "no one associated with the Foundation in the Outer System had the slightest inkling that this matter was under serious discussion, let alone that a decision had been taken. Lowenthal tells me that he had the same impression from his acquaintances on Earth. They seem to believe that your people took the decision yourselves, entirely independently."

For the moment, they seemed to have forgotten that I was there. Davida was a picture of innocent confusion, but my paranoia warned me that the innocence and the confusion might be every bit as deceptive as her nine-year-old appearance.

"That's not possible," Davida said. "There was no question . . ."

"Are you saying that the matter of Adam Zimmerman's

revival wasn't even under discussion among the Foundation's Outer System personnel?" I said to Niamh Horne, partly to take the pressure off Davida and partly to serve my own curiosity. "Even though the whole purpose of the Ahasuerus Foundation was to bring him back once the technology existed to make him emortal?"

Now it was Horne's turn to look slightly confused. It was Conwin who said: "All Niamh is saying is that the Foundation people we know had not been notified that a decision was imminent. Given that the revival of Adam Zimmerman is, as you say, the Foundation's perennial central concern, they were surprised—and a little hurt—to find that they had not been consulted."

"I can't imagine . . ." Davida began.

I cut her off again, as easily as I might if she really had been a child intruding upon an adult discussion. "So you think Lowenthal's lying," I said. "You think the decision was taken on Earth, for reasons that have more to do with Earth's interests than the Foundation's?"

I was glad to discover that I hadn't lost my touch. That suggestion finally won an expression of sorts from Niamh Horne's synthetic features. "That's not what I meant at all," she said. Then she hesitated, presumably realizing that if she denied any suspicion that Lowenthal had lied to her—a suspicion that she surely ought to be prepared to entertain—she might as well be saying that she was convinced that Davida Berenike Columella was a liar.

"What are *you* trying to imply, Mr. Tamlin?" Theoderic Conwin asked, having observed that his boss was floundering.

"I'm just trying to find out how I got here," I told them all, flatly. "The fact that none of you seems to know for sure who decided to set the wheels in motion makes me a little wary of the notion that I just happened to be the obvious target for a trial run. I can't remember why I was put away, and someone seems to have taken the trouble to destroy all the relevant information—so I can't help wondering whether someone might want *me* awake again, and might be using Adam Zimmerman's revival as a cover."

"That's absurd," said Davida.

Niamh Horne seemed to agree with her. "I can understand your disorientation," the cyborg said. "I can understand, too, that you're looking at the situation from your own peculiar perspective. But Adam Zimmerman's awakening is the bone of contention here. I can assure you that neither I nor Michael Lowenthal has any particular interest in you, Mr. Tamlin—nor, for that matter, in Christine Caine. Perhaps you should stop searching for conspiracies and simply be grateful for whatever freak of chance brought you here." She probably meant the last comment, but I was more interested in reading between the lines of what she'd said before.

"You're hoping to stop it, aren't you?" I said. "You and Lowenthal. You're hoping to persuade Davida to put Zimmerman back into the freezer. Why?"

Horne and Conwin practically fell over themselves in the rush to deny that. It was painfully obvious that they'd been caught on the hop. They'd come here to greet Adam Zimmerman, not to bury him, and so had Lowenthal—but that was before the two delegations had had an opportunity to compare notes. Lowenthal had told me how much he was looking forward to getting together with Horne, but he hadn't known then what the outcome of their exchange of views might be. Apparently, it had produced a swift and unexpected result. Someone here was being played for a fool—and they seemed to have no better idea who, or why, than I had.

"The process can't be stopped," Davida said, very firmly indeed. "It's too far advanced. To attempt to reverse the process now would place him in considerable danger. It's out of the question."

Horne seemed to realize that she had made a mistake. She had seen the opportunity to ask "*Whose* plan?" and she had seized it reflexively—but the occasion had been inappropriate and the move had been premature. She wanted to get away now, to consult her own people. She and Conwin made their excuses and left.

Davida made as if to accompany them, then thought better of it. She let them climb into their pods, and then turned back to me. "I'm sorry about that," she said.

"Why?" I said, with a smile. "I thought we all got along famously."

Davida grinned at that, and her face was instantly transformed into that of a *real* mischievous child. But she knew that it wasn't entirely a joking matter.

"Whatever those two may think," she said, "my instructions came through the customary channels, and were quite explicit. It's entirely possible that there is a dispute within the ranks of the Foundation, but I've every reason to believe that the decision was proper and authoritative. If there are problems between the UN and the Confederation, I know nothing about them." She changed tack abruptly then, and asked: "Why did you make the assumption that Solantha Handsel is Michael Lowenthal's bodyguard?"

"Because she looks like one," I told her. "Maybe appearances are deceptive, given the passage of a thousand years, and maybe people nowadays think everything's just for show, but I've seen *real* bodyguards. The big boys at PicoCon used to take their personal protection very seriously, and it wasn't the Eliminators they were worried about."

Davida was enough of an innocent not to catch the implication of the final remark, so I elaborated. "There was still a certain amount of competition for places on the Ultimate Board," I told her. "Damon didn't have to kill anyone in order to step into dead men's shoes, so far as I knew, but some of his colleagues did. In a world where everyone lives for a long time, people with ambition sometimes have to use unconventional measures to make room for themselves. I assume that's still the case."

"Not on Excelsior," Davida told me—but the fact that she'd put it that way suggested that she wasn't so sure about Earth and the outer satellites.

"It's only ninety-nine years since a whole lot of shoes fell vacant at a stroke," I reminded her. "I'm a stranger here, but I can't help wondering how closely Excelsior is in touch with the rest of the solar system. Personally, I wouldn't be at all surprised to discover that Michael Lowenthal is more than a little worried about the way things are back home. Wouldn't you be anxious, if *your* world had recently suffered an accident of that magnitude?"

Davida didn't answer immediately, but she certainly seemed to take the thought aboard. "Something is going on that I don't understand," she confessed. "Somewhere, there's been a drastic failure of communication. We'll have to get together with both delegations, to work out exactly who's been misled, and how . . ." She broke off then, realizing like Horne before her that these might be matters best not discussed in front of a barbarian refugee from the twenty-third century. "Christine Caine has asked to be allowed to see the interior of the *Child of Fortune*," she told me, changing her tone decisively. "I relayed the request to Niamh Horne, who said that she would be pleased to guide a party around the ship—including Mr. Lowenthal and Dr. Gray—as soon as Adam Zimmerman is awake. Would you like to be included?"

"Absolutely," I said.

Davida nodded. "It should be very interesting," she observed. "It's an opportunity I've never had myself. The ship that rescued Dr. Gray from the Arctic Ocean must have been similar in kind, but a much older model." She seemed to be groping toward a point without being entirely clear what it was.

"You don't actually know whose decision it was to wake Adam Zimmerman up, do you?" I asked her, trying to sound sympathetic.

The way she looked up at me told me that she had begun to doubt it. She and the sisterhood were an Ahasuerus project, not executive directors of the organization. In all likelihood, she had no idea where the real power within the

organization was located, or how that power related to the
power wielded by Michael Lowenthal's associates and Niamh
Horne's. When the instructions had come through, she'd
been only too glad to obey them, because it had been a great
opportunity, and a great honor. She had not interrogated
their source—and now she was wondering whether the someone that had been misled, or played for a fool, might be her.

"It really is the right time," she said, instead of answering
the question. "It's neither too soon nor too late. And his
awakening really is a key event in posthuman history, no matter how hard anyone might try to make light of it."

"You don't need to convince me," I told her, although I
knew that it wasn't me she was trying to convince. "I just
happened to be in the right place at the right time to qualify
as a trial run. Didn't I?"

She didn't answer that one either. She might have
thought so before, and if she had she probably still did—but
Niamh Horne and I had succeeded in piercing her innocence
with a tiny sliver of doubt.

"We'll be starting the final phase of the procedure soon,"
she said. "I'll let you know, so that you can watch through the
window. That's what everyone else will be doing. Not only
here, but everywhere—just as soon as the light reaches them.
We're expecting an audience of millions, perhaps billions. It
might have been a freak of chance that brought you here, but
you'll be in a privileged position."

What she was trying to say was that I'd be in the front
row of a red hot show. Even if I was just a trial run, my number having been thrown up by the lottery of fate, I'd get to
see history in the making at point blank range.

I knew that I ought to be grateful for that. I knew, too, if
Adam Zimmerman did request or require company of his
own kind on his grand tour of the modern world, I might
have cause to be grateful that I was the nearest thing to his
own kind that Excelsior had to offer. It wasn't just that Adam
Zimmerman and I shared the same mortal blood; given the
opportunity, I'd have tried to steal the world too. I figured

that I was entitled to my front row seat at the big event, perhaps more so than Niamh Horne, or Mortimer Gray, or even Michael Lowenthal.

"Good luck, Davida," I said to Davida Berenike Columella, knowing that she was the one who would have to carry the can if anything went wrong with Zimmerman's awakening.

"Thank you, Madoc," she said, with all apparent sincerity.

EIGHTEEN
ADAM ZIMMERMAN'S AWAKENING

I hadn't fully realized what the process of "awakening" a corpsicle involved, although I was dimly aware that there were probably yucky bits that any sane person would be more than glad to sleep through. Everybody in my day had referred to SusAn, with casual flippancy, as "freezing down," as if it were merely a matter of popping someone into a powerful refrigerator, but everybody had known that there was a lot more to it. I suppose we'd all been slightly afraid of it—even those of us who were determinedly law-abiding. Who can ever be sure that the weight of the law will not descend upon him?

At any rate, like most men of my era, I'd never bothered to research the topic in detail. It wasn't until I watched the later phases of Adam Zimmerman's revivification that I was able to reconstruct my own experience in my imagination.

Zimmerman had been put away by means of a slightly less complicated and much less streamlined process than the one that must have been applied to me, but he had to come back through all the same stages. Watching as much of it as I did made me feel distinctly queasy, because I fooled myself into "remembering" similar things being done to me. I was profoundly glad that by the time I was invited to tune in, most of the slow work had already been done.

I now know—and am capable of shuddering at the thought—that after I'd been put into an artificially induced coma my metabolic activity had been quieted even further, until all the DNA in my cells had wrapped itself up snugly and all the mitochondria had fallen idle. Only then had the first stage of temperature depression begun, to facilitate the vitrification process that would work outwards from the soft organs and inwards from the the gut and skin. Not until the vitrification was complete and uniform had my body temperature been lowered, by very careful degrees, all the way from minus seven degrees Celsius to seven degrees absolute—and even then there had been a further stage of "encasement" in a cocktail of ices not so very different from the stuff of which comets are made.

That was what I had gone through in order to get to my present destination: a journey to the dark land of the dead, whose fairy queen had far more in common with Christine Caine's cold-hearted Snow Queen than Shakespeare's Titania or Spenser's Gloriana.

By the time Davida Berenike Columella put the operation on the screen, Zimmerman's corpsicle had been out of its icy cocoon for some time. The temperature of the vitrified body had already been raised to minus seven Celsius so that nanobot-aided devitrificaton could begin. What Davida's multitudinous audience watched was the final stage of the long process, which would turn Adam Zimmerman's protoplasm from glassy gel to membranously confined liquid.

A host of nanobots delivered enthusiastic progress reports regarding the miraculous state of Zimmerman's individual cells, but everyone knows that nanobots are constitutionally incapable of seeing the big picture, so no one took their reportage to imply that the whole system would click into gear automatically.

The most crucial phase of the awakening would be the one that would ease Zimmerman from physical inertia into controlled coma, rebuilding brain activity from the bottom up. That would turn effective death into dreamless sleep, then into the kind of sleep that could sustain dreaming. The nanobots couldn't measure the subjective component of a dream; some part of the emotions associated with it, and all of its imagery, were forever beyond their reach. The external sensors collated their information, assuring the operators and watchers alike that all was well at the physiological level, but there was an inevitable margin of uncertainty that kept us all on edge while the long minutes ticked by.

Christine Caine was keeping me company again, but she seemed unusually subdued as we sat through the suspenseful phase. I assumed that she was experiencing the same self-centered feelings as me, but when she finally broke her silence with something more than a grunt it was to express astonishment at Zimmerman's appearance.

"He's so *old*," were her exact words.

It was trivially true, of course, but that wasn't what she meant. I had only been thirty-nine years old when I was frozen down, but it wouldn't have made much difference to my face if I'd been seventy-seven. People of my generation didn't suffer from wrinkles, or gray hair, or any of the other traditional appearances of "old age." We needed elaborate Internal Technology and periodic deep tissue rejuvenation to keep us going even for a mere hundred and fifty years, but the superficial appearances of aging were easier to overcome than the invisible record of intracellular damage and nucleic acid copying errors.

Adam Zimmerman hadn't had our advantages. He wasn't *old*, even by the standards of Christine Caine's day, if one left his millennium in limbo out of the account, but he certainly looked it.

I had seen the superficial signs of old age before. One of my closest associates in the criminal fraternity had worn them almost as a badge of pride. It should not have been a surprise to see them manifest in Adam Zimmerman's face and figure, but there seemed something not quite *right* about the matter. It would not have been impossible, or even particularly difficult, to apply a little somatic engineering to the texture of the skin while the devitrification procedure was proceeding. Although the whole point of the exercise was to bring him back exactly as he had been when he went into

SusAn—save for supportive IT and a very smart suit of clothes—it seemed to me that a certain amount of cosmetic work would not have been inappropriate. No doubt he would make his own decision about that, when the time came to make informed decisions about the particular technologies of emortality that he would adopt, but I couldn't believe that he would not have relished the prospect of waking up rejuvenated.

"It's mainly a matter of showmanship," I said to Christine, when I'd thought it over. "They're displaying him to the whole solar system as a work of art. This is just the beginning of the story. They want all the phases to be visible, to demonstrate the true significance of what they're doing."

"Surely they can't make him one of *them*," she said.

"I'm certain that they can," I contradicted her, thoughtfully. "The sisters might even be naive enough to think that he might take that option, when they've had a chance to work on him, although I can't believe that anyone else thinks so. Whatever they offer him—and us—will have to be designed exclusively for mortal use, because everybody born into this world was already engineered for emortality. None of them ever had a choice. All their choices were made for them, by their adoptive parents. This is an unprecedented situation."

"Why should they care what kind of emortality he opts for?" Christine asked.

"Maybe because they're still making decisions on behalf of their unborn children," I guessed. "Maybe they've become anxious about whether they're making the right ones, now that there are so many alternatives to choose from. They're interested to know what kind of emortality mortals would choose for themselves. Zimmerman is the star prize, because he was the first mortal to go for broke in the quest for emortality, but they may have thrown in a couple of controls to make the game more interesting. There are three of us, so there'll be a clear majority if the decision is split."

I realized as I voiced it that the last point was wrong, because there had to be more than two alternatives available, but I didn't bother to correct myself. Nor did I point out that if Adam Zimmerman's vote was worth more than either of ours, mine had to be worth more than hers because she was a certified lunatic.

"You make it sound like a game show," Christine observed. "It's a lot of trouble to go to for that kind of petty kick."

"In our day," I reminded her, "all the hopeful emortals used to spend time wondering how they were going to cope with the tedium once they'd been around for a few hundred years. Maybe these people take their game shows more seriously than you or I can imagine. The children of Excelsior really are children, by comparison with people like Lowenthal—and I'd be willing to bet that it's people of Lowenthal's generation who are pulling the strings."

That had been another preoccupation of the hopeful not-quite-emortals of my own day—which was why I'd produced it so readily in my conversation with Davida. The prospect of the oldest generation remaining in charge *forever*, while the youngest had no possible prospect of inheriting the Earth, had been a popular item of twenty-second-century debate. Nowadays, it seemed, the other worlds of the solar system were all under the dominion of the older generation, even though Titan and Ganymede were still largely icebound and the terraformation of Mars and Venus had hardly begun. If the young wanted to assert their right to the pursuit of property, they already had to look to further horizons, with all the attendant inconvenience of the limiting velocity of light.

Christine was thinking along a different line. "I'm the villain, aren't I?" she said. "If this is a game, or an improvised drama, I'm not here to make up the numbers—I'm here to be the bad example."

I turned to look at her, although the drama on the screen was coming toward its climax.

"We don't know that," I said, feeling a mysterious obligation to be gentle. "I'm just making up stories here. I haven't even begun to figure out what this is all about."

"But we'll find out, won't we?" she said. It was very difficult to judge her mood, or to figure out how she was extrapolating the notion. "We'll find out what they expect of us soon enough."

Adam Zimmerman had been moved to a chair now: a chair very similar to the ones on which Christine and I were sitting. Davida had run through the rehearsal twice and she was sticking to the script. When Adam Zimmerman opened his eyes he would see what I had seen. Would he, I wondered, be as quick on the uptake as I had been? Would he ask the same questions, in the same falsely casual fashion?

I had no idea how big the audience for this big scene was, but I suspected that this would be prime time all over the Earth, no matter whether it was noon or midnight outside. We were all on tenterhooks.

The camera zoomed in on that strangely disturbing face, bringing every line and blemish into clear view.

We all waited for the eyes to flicker open—but the eyes hadn't read the script. They were sticky, and they couldn't flicker. Their opening was slow, and seemingly painful. The pupils narrowed as they finally appeared, the mottled brown irises spreading protectively around them. The blood vessels in the whites seemed slightly too red.

For a long time, it seemed that he wasn't going to speak at all, but he finally slipped into the groove. He had already memorized his script, and twelve centuries of frozen sleep hadn't eroded *that* memory.

"How long?" he said.

Davida Berenike Columella told him. We watched his face as the calculator in his head processed the figures.

And then he smiled.

After one thousand two hundred and twenty-eight years, less ten days, Adam Zimmerman smiled like a winner. It was a gambler's smile: a smile of pure self-congratulation, at a well-judged bet.

I figured that he was entitled to it. So, I suppose, did millions or billions of other viewers.

NINETEEN
CHILD OF FORTUNE

There was more, but so far as I was concerned the rest of it was all anti-climax. I wanted to meet Adam Zimmerman in the flesh. I wanted to be introduced to him, as someone who was *like him*—as the only person in the entire solar system who was like him, because the only person who might be reckoned more like him than I was didn't really count.

No such luck. There were plenty of other people who wanted first crack at him, and had the clout to demand it.

For the first time, the room in which I was confined really began to feel like a prison. No matter what opportunities it offered in the way of virtual experience, there was no escape from my impatience. Christine Caine was still with me, but that was no escape either. The game of trying to guess exactly what kind of game we were involved in had gone sour—the point now was to get on with it.

We could, of course, have used the time more productively. We should have. We shouldn't have wasted a minute while there was so much still to be learned—but the drama on the screen had taken over, and we were too sharply aware of the fact that we had been abandoned in the wings to await a cue that no one was in a hurry to give us.

We ate a couple of meals, neither of which improved to any perceptible degree on the one we had first been offered, and we exchanged a few more speculations as to the nature of the roles we had been recruited to play in Adam Zimmerman's return, but in the end tiredness demanded that we sleep.

"Eventually," I told Christine, before we retired to our separate spaces, "they'll have to let us in. When Zimmerman finds out we exist, he'll want to meet us." I couldn't put much conviction into the claim.

"Sure," she said. "*Hey, Adam*, they'll say, *we thawed out a petty criminal and a murderer just for practice—just let us know when you want to get together to chat about old times.* How will he be able to restrain his enthusiasm?"

I wasn't so sure that I was as petty a criminal as I remembered, but I certainly didn't want to make an issue of it.

I slept for eight hours. If I dreamed I didn't remember the dream—and I realized, when I woke, that I hadn't had a single memorable dream since I'd woken up in the future. The readiest explanation of that not very remarkable fact was that the high-powered IT that the sisterhood had installed in my head was keeping my mind tidy. The most disturbing possibility was that while "I" thought "I" was sleeping "I" had actually been switched off, dropped into some kind of artificial coma or consigned to electronic oblivion. I decided to cling to the nicer hypothesis.

Davida finally got in touch shortly after breakfast, but Adam Zimmerman still hadn't asked to meet me. I had to put up with the next best thing, which was an invitation to join the great man on a tour of Niamh Horne's super-duper spaceship. I accepted with alacrity.

Any lingering hope I might have entertained of seeing more of the microworld vanished when yet another pod grew out of the wall, avid to embrace me. When I stepped into it the fleshy interior hugged me so tightly that I didn't even notice the gradual easing of the pseudogravitational attraction until it spat me out into the ship—at which point I would have floated helplessly away if the floor hadn't grabbed the soles of my feet.

I'd got to the point where it was nice to see any kind of open space—but any elation that might have accompanied the discovery that I was in a real corridor was offset by the terrible sensation of weightlessness. My IT, like Christine

Caine's, had edited out my capacity for panic, but it had no provision for me to feel good about the things that might have panicked me.

There was quite a crowd awaiting me, but Mortimer Gray was the only one who seemed to care whether I needed help. Once he had ascertained that I had never been in zero-gee before he took up a position beside me, ready to steady me as I took my first faltering steps into the brightly lit interior of *Child of Fortune*. I had to focus on my internal organs, which seemed to be taking advantage of their newfound opportunities by rearranging themselves.

"It's okay," Gray told me. "Your IT will help you adapt if you let it. All you have to remember is to move slowly and deliberately until you get the hang of it, and always to keep one foot on the floor. The floor's as smart as the fabric of your suit; together they'll keep you right way up and on track."

"I suppose you do this all the time," I said, through teeth that were only slightly gritted.

"Hardly ever," he assured me. "But I've lived on the moon, which isn't so very different. It was a long time ago now, and the conscious memory's exceedingly hazy, but the body has a memory of its own. The autonomic reflexes soon come back. Just relax."

I decided to accept my discomfort as evidence of the fact that I wasn't just a mechanical simulation, and that everything I was experiencing was really happening. I told myself that if I really was going to live for a thousand or a hundred thousand years I'd probably be spending a great deal of time in zero-gee, given the size of the universe and the ratio of nothingness to substance.

Fortunately, we had a few minutes' grace before the party was finalized by Christine Caine's arrival. She made ten. Lowenthal and Handsel were there, but not de Comeau or Conwin. Davida was stationed to one side of Adam Zimmerman, Niamh Horne to the other. There was one other human-iform cyborg, whose feet were on the "floor," plus a faber cyborg whose four limbs were all arms—one of which was lazily extended to the webbing that dressed the "vertical" walls.

Nobody volunteered to introduce me to Adam Zimmerman, and I didn't feel sufficiently confident of my footing to stride across the eight meters that separated our stations and offer to shake his hand. He must have looked me up and down while I was still confused, but he had looked away by the time I was capable of meeting his gaze. We both watched Christine Caine emerge from her pod.

She was just as awkward as I had been, and Gray was still the only one with social conscience enough to help her. He was even polite enough to murmur "excuse me" to me as he moved to do it. I would have helped if I could, but I couldn't.

Niamh Horne was obviously the one in charge now that we were on her territory, and everyone looked to her to take the lead—which she did with an imperious manner that seemed almost insulting. She swept Adam Zimmerman away with her, and her two cronies moved with effortless ease to form a barrier between the two of them and the rest of us.

We had to move two abreast, and that left Davida looking distinctly spare as Lowenthal and his bodyguard fell in behind the two cyborgs. Gray motioned to me to carry on, obviously figuring that Christine had more need of his support than I did, so I tried to fall into step with the cryogenicist.

"Congratulations," I muttered. "You brought it off. He looks as fit as a flea."

It wasn't an expression she recognized or appreciated, but she acknowledged the compliment anyway, adding: "This is as new to me as it is to you. I've never been aboard a Titanian ship before. Not that there'll be much actually to *see*. It's just a minimicroworld, after all."

"How's Zimmerman taking it?" I asked, curiously. "He can't have expected to be away so long." I diplomatically refrained from asking how pissed off he was at the Foundation's board of directors for letting him lie so long.

"He's fine," she assured me. "Excited. Interested. Delighted." She didn't sound like someone trying to convince herself, but the list was distinctly clipped. Unlike me, she was used to operating in zero-gee, so whatever discomfort she was feeling couldn't have the same cause as mine. Movement wasn't doing my internal organs any favors; they still seemed to be in dispute with one another as to how to arrange themselves now that they no longer had to fall in line with the dictates of gravity.

I was too far back in the column to hear more than the odd few words of the commentary that Niamh Horne was delivering to Adam Zimmerman—she wasn't making any strenuous effort to raise her voice—but it seemed to me that Davida was absolutely right about there not being much actually to *see*. There were brightly decorated corridors. There were multitudinous display screens. There were sphincters opening the way into fixed pods, and blister patches where new pods could be formulated if required. There were suggestive curves and lumps.

On the other hand, there were no instrument panels full of flashing lights, no levers for human hands to pull, no wheels for human hands to turn, no triggers for human fingers to squeeze. I saw no bridgehead, no control room, no recreation area. There were a few crewmen hanging around, who might have been working but were far more likely to be trying to catch a glimpse of Adam Zimmerman, while proudly showing off their own posthumanity. The fabers looked weird enough, and the cyborg fabers even weirder, but they weren't as ostentatious about their modifications as Solantha Handsel, and the way they looked at me reminded me that I was the alien one, the one who belonged in a cage.

If I'd known more about what I was supposed to be looking at I'd probably have got more out of the excursion, but Adam Zimmerman was getting the sole benefit of the running commentary and Mortimer Gray probably had more interesting information to whisper in Christine's ear than Davida offered to me. The one thing that was impressed upon me was how *big* the ship was, and even that seemed to be a kind of statement: an insistence on behalf of the inhabitants of the Outer System that they, not the Earthbound, were the masters of modern technology and the custodians of future progress. But as I looked back at all the posthumans who were looking at me, I began to see something of the complexity of their society.

Even if the Earthbound could be firmly kept in their place, I guessed, the question of how to distribute ownership and control of the solar system's usable mass wasn't going to be an easy one to settle. If I really had lived long enough to witness the dawn of an era in which even Jupiter's mass couldn't safely be set aside as a common resource, available to anyone who cared to appropriate what they could, there was little or no hope that the Outer System factions could agree among themselves once the Earthbound were impotent to provide a natural party of opposition.

I hadn't tried to read up on Mortimer Gray's theories of history, but I thought I could make a fair guess at Michael Lowenthal's ideological standpoint, given that he had been born and bred within the Hardinist Cabal. His view had to be that firm distinctions of ownership needed to be made, however inequitable they might be, in order to protect the system's resources from wastage. His aim had to be the stabilization—maybe even the robotization—of the patterns of resource exploitation, in the interests of building a system that could endure forever, or at least until the Afterlife arrived. There might be a dozen or a hundred different ways of setting up some such stable situation, but there had to be a thousand or a million different ways of destabilizing it, so however many disputes Lowenthal might be embroiled in, Niamh Horne had to be embroiled in a great many more. And no matter how convinced Mortimer Gray might be that the posthuman races had put away the violent habits of their ancestors, I had no difficulty at all imagining those kinds of disputes extending into warfare—even the kinds of warfare that could exterminate whole ecospheres and civilizations.

It seemed to me that we had been walking for a long way before disaster struck, although that might have been an illusion based in the unfamiliarity of the way I was walking.

When disaster *did* strike, however, it seemed that a certain conspicuously lacking equality was restored. When the lights turned red and the mechanical voice began booming out from every direction, everybody—including Niamh Horne and her cyborg chums—was suddenly thrust into unknown existential territory.

The reaction of the locals strongly suggested that one of the things modern spaceship crews never bothered to practice was lifeboat drill. Their IT was supposed to insulate them against the worst effects of panic, but their immunity was purely physiological and it didn't inhibit the initial burst of adrenalin that prepared them for fight or flight. They jumped like scalded cats—and if the wildness of their eyes could be believed, the fear that set in thereafter wasn't about to submit meekly to chemical calming.

Extreme danger! the mechanical voice said, displaying a fine flair for melodrama. *All crew and passengers to emergency life support. Immediate response required. All crew and passengers to emergency life support. Extreme danger! Immediate response required.*

Nobody seemed to know which way to go. We had been shown preformed pods and generative blisters aplenty, and had stared at them with the dutiful interest expected of interested tourists, even though they looked exactly the same as the pods on Excelsior that served as transportation devices and VE immersion suits—but none of us, including Niamh Horne, knew how to find or manifest the right kind of pod, or to open it. None of us knew which way to run.

I didn't even know how to run, when the only thing holding me to the "floor" was the floor itself. Fortunately, the floor and the walls *did* know what to do. They were not only smart, but the kind of smart that didn't need rehearsals. The real function of the mechanical voice wasn't to urge us to action but to prepare us to be acted upon.

The corridors, which had seemed to my ungrateful eye to be merely corridors, had abilities that might have been explained to Adam Zimmerman, but came as a complete surprise to me. I wasn't in any state to notice exactly how they coped with the fact that we had been walking two abreast in our horribly ungainly fashion, but they sorted us out with no difficulty at all. They closed in on us, and engulfed us.

Maybe Niamh Horne and her fellow crew members knew enough to be reflexively grateful for that, but I hadn't been educated to their kind of world. I was terrified. I had the words *extreme danger* ringing in my ears, and I had no idea what form that extreme disaster might take. When the walls rushed in upon me I had no way of judging whether that might be an aspect of the danger in question rather than my salvation: a danger whose extremity would make itself manifest by crushing me to a pulp, or perhaps by asphyxiating me.

I might have screamed—but if I had, I don't think anyone could have heard me. I didn't hear anyone else's scream.

TWENTY
INVADERS FROM BEYOND

The impression that I was in the process of being unceremoniously killed can't have lasted more than five or six seconds, but time really does become elastic when you're in the grip of that kind of terror. The moments stretch as your mind tries to make the most of the little time you have left, and the terror is compounded by the tortuous strain of their extension. My IT must have been doing its best to help, but IT can only deal efficiently with the underlying physiology; consciousness remains a mystery, which works in its own strangely creative ways.

In retrospect, I suppose I should have been glad of the terror and the way it expanded to fill the horizons of time, on the grounds that it offered further evidence that I really was alive and that I really was myself. Alas, I wasn't capable of being grateful at the time.

When the moment came to realize that I was actually in the process of being saved—that the walls were bearing me away to the pod where I was supposed to be, snugly and securely cocooned against any probable disaster—I was in no mental state to seize the realization. More hideous seconds had to tick by while I was lost in confusion, unable to recognize the mercy of my situation.

Somehow, the pod didn't feel like a pod at all. My internal organs still seemed to be jostling for position, but now it was impossible to tell whether they were still confined by my body wall. I had a peculiar sensation of having been turned inside out. It was false, but it was the kind of illusion that my clever IT couldn't even begin to cope with.

Subjectively speaking, it took a long time for me to reconcile myself to the fact that I wasn't dead, or dying, or in pain, or mad . . . and that all I had to do to retake control of myself was to accept that I was still alive and still in the game. "In the game" was, I realized, the best way to think about my predicament. I had played my share of scary games while wearing a full-body VE suit. I had done this sort of thing for fun, and still could, if I could only calm down and go with the flow.

It wasn't until I finally opened my eyes that I realized that I wasn't blind. The ship's AI could feed information to me exactly as if I were in a VE immersion suit—which, in essence, I was. Even then, it wasn't until I had been looking out into a visual field filled with mile-high letters saying PLEASE REMAIN CALM for at least three minutes that I remembered that I could still interact with the pod. I didn't have to settle for the default setting.

"What's happening?" I demanded, as soon as I figured out that I could make demands and get answers.

The answer I got wasn't reassuring, but it *was* an answer.

"The ship is under attack," the voice of *Child of Fortune*'s AI autopilot told me. It wasn't shouting now, but its slightly breathless timbre seemed perfectly appropriate to the gravity of the news.

"By whom?" I demanded, incredulously.

"I do not recognize the attacking vessels," the AI told me.

It took a couple of seconds for the implications of that statement to sink in. *Child of Fortune* was a state-of-the-art ship, if not quite the pride of the Saturnian fleet then not so far behind. It had to be programmed to recognize any space-ship built or employed within the solar system.

What the AI was telling me, indirectly, was that we were being attacked by aliens. Aliens from God-only-knew-where were trying to murder Adam Zimmerman. And me. Not to mention Niamh Horne, Christine Caine, Mortimer Gray, Michael Lowenthal, Michael Lowenthal's bodyguard . . .

That was when it first occurred to me that the AI might be lying. I was, after all, in a VE suit, prey to any manufactured illusion the AI cared to feed me. I wasn't even completely sure that I had been in meatspace before the melodrama had got under way, and given that this was melodrama through and through, the hypothesis that it was all fake couldn't be ignored.

I tried to think it through.

If the AI was lying about the attack, then what I was involved in was a *kidnapping*. The ship had been taken over, and whoever had taken control of it was kidnapping Adam Zimmerman. And me. Not to mention . . . except, of course, that if the ship's AI had been programmed to do all this, then it must be *Niamh Horne* who was kidnapping Adam Zimmerman. And me. Not to mention Michael Lowenthal, etc, etc.

Or must it?

I didn't like Niamh Horne, but the scenario that gave her the role of evil mastermind seemed, nevertheless, to be a much less worrying alternative than the ones in which we really were being attacked by aliens from God-only-knew-where, or hijacked by persons unknown. It was bad enough to have to worry about the posthuman races going to war with one another, without factoring hostile aliens into the picture, and the probability that anyone else could have masterminded the hijack of Niamh Horne's ship seemed slim. In which case, Niamh Horne surely had to be the one who was playing us all for fools . . .

Nothing dispels terror more efficiently than a conviction that one has been taken for a mug. Emotional arousal is negotiable, and fear can be readily transmuted into anger.

"You lying bastard," I said to the AI. "Tell me the truth. Where are we going? Why?

In my day, one of the major driving forces behind the evolution of the artificial idiots the people called sloths into the artificial geniuses that people called silvers was the demand for sims that could answer the phone, filter the desirable calls from all the silvery junk, and reply adequately to those callers who only required simple responses. It would be an oversimplification to say that the principal functions of everyday AIs were telling lies and spotting lies, but it wouldn't be too far off the truth. Ergo, I knew better than to imagine, even for a moment, that telling an AI to tell me the truth would be a viable command—but I was under stress, and we all do stupid things when we're under stress. Even AIs do stupid things when they're under stress.

"We are heading away from the sun," the AI told me. "Should we contrive to evade the continuing pursuit, I shall seek guidance as to an appropriate destination. For the time being, I am making every effort to avoid being destroyed or captured."

I had no alternative but to think: What if it *is* true?

"Show me," I demanded—but the supersilver came over all pedantic and didn't respond until I made myself clearer. "Show me the ships that are attacking us," I said, glad to be able to be businesslike.

The virtual space surrounding my gently cradled head was abruptly filled with starlight, but the controlling intelligence moved swiftly to dim the background glare and pick out four objects that might otherwise have faded into it. The viewpoint zoomed in, tacitly admitting that the image I'd be getting had been heavily processed in the interests of clarity.

One of the objects was easily recognizable as Excelsior. The other three seemed, at first glance, to be more closely akin to the microworld than to the Titanian ship. Unlike the vessel I was on, whose furled "wings" had linked it in my imagination to a seabird, the things that were pursuing us looked more like a small school of squid, all jetting along with their bunched tentacles trailing behind.

They were shooting at us, and hitting us almost every time. At least, they *seemed* to be shooting at us, the way spaceships in VE space operas that were dated even in my day shot at their targets. I knew that the lines the AI was tracing across the image were diagrammatic representations, and that they would have to be diagrammatic representations even if there really were ships pursuing us, shooting all the while. It had always been the requirements of melodrama rather than respect for realism that had forced tape programmers to depict space combat in terms of beams of colored light, but there was no other way for real spaceships to represent real combat in a readily perceptible fashion. Given that there was nothing out there that a naked human eye was actually capable of seeing, the only way for *Child of Fortune* to answer my request was to feed me a fiction, together with the insistence that it was as accurate a representation of the reality as it could contrive.

There were four aliens now, then five . . . and they kept on coming.

They seemed to be popping out of nowhere—but that too was a necessary fiction. Even if the AI were trying its damnedest to show me the truth, the most it could do was register presence as soon as it became detectable. If the alien ships—or could they possibly be creatures?—really were popping out of some kind of hyperspace, this was all that the AI could show me.

If, on the other hand, the aliens were merely coming to the attention of *Child of Fortune*'s sensors, having moved unobtrusively by perfectly orthodox means to where they were first apprehended, all the AI could show me was what it was showing me. There was no way to determine where they were actually coming from, or how they were avoiding detection until they became manifest.

The aliens could certainly move. I had no idea how fast we were going, but I figured that we had to be accelerating at one gee or more. We were already way past the velocity at which we could make sharp turns, no matter how expert our cocoons might be at preventing momentum from crushing us to pulp—but the attackers didn't seem to be laboring under that kind of inconvenience. They were hurling themselves all over the sky, like icons in a combat game.

It was all absurd, and plainly so.

It was absurd to suppose that a fleet of alien space fighters was bursting out of some kind of space warp. It was absurd to suppose that they were shooting at us, and hitting us, without actually smashing us into little bits of molten slag. It was absurd to suppose that aliens, or anybody else, would go to such lengths merely to harass or destroy a man whose messianic status was entirely a matter of human estimation. Or me. Or even Michael Lowenthal and Niamh Horne.

But melodrama has its own attractions, its own button-pushing power over those emotions that even the cleverest IT can't muffle.

It's not just us, I thought, as more squiddy things popped into existence, swarming across the whole vast starfield. *It's the whole damn system. We just happened to be out here. They're invading the whole solar system. They're going to annihilate the entire population. It's finally happened. After a thousand years of cultivating a false sense of security, it's finally happened, in the very same week that I finally get out of jail.*

It was the last—and, admittedly, least—improbability that derailed the train of thought.

It's an illusion, I told myself. *It isn't even a good illusion. It's a practical joke. Someone's playing with me, treating me with contempt. Niamh Horne's playing me for a sucker, and she's playing Adam Zimmerman too. But I don't believe it, and neither will he, if he's got any sense.*

I thought I owed it to myself not to be taken in. I owed it to myself as a man of the twenty-second century and a designer of virtual experiences not to be a gullible fool. Adam Zimmerman had grown up in the twentieth century, when TV was flat, and came in a box. If all of this had been set up to fool someone, he was the one, and he was the one on whom it might just work—but I had higher standards.

It's all fake, I told myself, sternly. *That much is definite.*

The hope that it was all an illusion, all a third-rate VE space opera, was further encouraged by the fact that I couldn't feel any effects of the shots that were supposedly striking home against the hull of the Titanian ship.

I suspected that I ought not to read too much into that item of negative evidence. I knew that it was always the requirements of melodrama rather than respect for realism that had led the programmers of old to make the bridgeheads of hypothetical spaceships shudder and lurch when the vessels were supposedly hit by exotic ammunition—but I allowed myself to be encouraged anyway. I needed every scrap of "proof" I could find to bolster my conviction that I was *not* an easy man to take for a ride.

I watched the formations of the attacking entities shift and change, looking more and more like cyborg octopodes built for exotic combat, but I couldn't tell whether the changes were a result of their maneuvers or a mere matter of altered perspective caused by *Child of Fortune*'s own evasive action. I wasn't aware of any momentum effects in my own body, but that didn't necessarily mean anything either, given that the elastic inner surface of the pod was so firmly bonded to my own smartsuit. There was no way to tell how fast the Titanian ship was moving . . . if it was moving at all.

"Are we shooting back?" I asked the AI.

"No," said the mechanical voice, obviously not feeling the least need to apologize or explain.

"Can we get away from them?" I asked.

"No," was the discomfiting reply.

"Will they destroy us?"

I took the consequent silence as an *I don't know,* but the image suddenly shifted as if to supply an answer of sorts. I saw that out of the entire alien school, only four of the attackers now seemed to be concentrating all their attentions on us—but the fourth was not like the other three.

If the three I'd already seen were run-of-the-mill calamari, the fourth was a record-breaking giant. In the absence of any benchmarks, and knowing full well that the AI's external eyes were using all kinds of vision-enhancing tricks even if they were being scrupulously honest, it was difficult to judge exactly *how* gigantic it might be, but appearances suggested that this was the mother squid, the queen of all the other squids—and it suddenly occurred to me that maybe the reason my own dutiful mothership wasn't pitching and shuddering under the impact of unfriendly fire was that we weren't actually being *shot at* at all, in the strictest sense of the term.

We were being *pushed*.

We were, I suddenly realized, being *herded* toward the giant—and the giant was already opening her vast tentacles, spreading them like the petals of a world-sized flower to expose an avid maw.

But it had to be fake—didn't it?

It was all third-rate space opera, as cartoonish as the garden on Excelsior . . . or the continents and cities of the Gaean restoration.

It's just a show, I told myself, insistently, as *Child of Fortune* hurtled helplessly into that awesome pit. *It's all just pretend, to cover up Niamh Horne's snatch plan, to put one over on poor Adam Zimmerman*. But that short-lived conviction had already begun to fade into uncertainty again—and the fear that had always been fear, even while I had insisted on construing it as ire, was working away at the base of my brain.

Some scenarios, I thought, are surely so preposterous that no one would bother to *pretend* them, even before an audience as ill prepared for contemporary life as Adam Zimmerman. Some lies are so unbelievable that their very absurdity defies scepticism.

While I was trying to weigh that paradox, the Titanian ship was falling into that huge dark mouth. *Child of Fortune* still urged on by the three spitting babies, which still drifted into the periphery of the visual field on occasion, their whips of virtual light licking out again and again.

The tentacles within the array were moving, groping as if in parody of the microworld's similarly hungry mouth-parts.

If this is real, I thought, *it has nothing to do with Adam Zimmerman. If this is real, it has to be the start of something much bigger and much weirder. Humankind won't have to wait for the Afterlife; something else is taking over.*

There was no way to tell how big that mouth was. For all I knew, it could swallow planets as easily as spaceships. It seemed incredible—but I couldn't be sure that my standards of credibility were still applicable.

"Are we shooting back yet?" I asked.

"I am unarmed," said the AI, in a sudden burst of confidentiality. I could almost have imagined that it was as overawed by possibility as I was, and that intimidation was making it plaintive.

"Is there nothing you can do?" I asked.

"Nothing," it admitted.

"It's a show, isn't it?" I said, firmly. "It's just a silly melodrama, intended to confuse us. Where are we going, really? Titan? Earth?"

I knew that the AI wasn't going to admit anything, no matter how accurate my guesses were, but I was hoping that it might somehow give itself away.

In the event, all it said was: "I don't know."

It sounded just about pathetic enough to be true, although I told myself sternly that it was still unbelievable.

The stars in the background became suddenly brighter again, but it was too late. The void was closing around us, and the stars were confined within a shrinking circle. The utter darkness of that vile mouth was swallowing us up, as if it were indeed some kind of space warp that could take us farther away from home than we could ever imagine.

"I know what's going on," I said to the AI, defiantly. "I may be a mere mortal, but I'm not an idiot. You can't make me—"

That was it. I didn't feel dizzy and I had no other plausible indication of being anasthetized. It was as if I were simply switched off, like a program interrupted in the running by a sudden power cut—but I had already given up my suspicion that I really was nothing but a sim runing in cyberspace. Perhaps paradoxically, the harder I had tried to insist that everything else was fake, the more securely I had fallen into the trap of believing that I, at least, was real.

PART TWO
WORLDS IN PARALLEL

TWENTY-ONE
NORMAL CONDITIONS

I woke up again lying on my back in pitch darkness. My awakening was troubled by the uncatchable fragments of decaying dreams and the harassment of many discomforts. My head was throbbing; my kidneys were aching; my stomach was queasy.

I had had worse hangovers, but not for a thousand years. I felt awful. I knew that I shouldn't feel as awful as I felt, because I knew that I shouldn't be *able* to feel as awful as I felt, and that made the fact doubly disturbing. I felt as if my insides had gone to war to settle their positional disputes, and that the conflict had inflicted considerable damage on all of its participants. It might not have been so bad had I still been weightless, but gravity had returned with a vengeance. I weighed more now than I had before I stepped into the pod that had carried me to the Titanian spaceship.

If a pod *had* carried me to the Titanian spaceship.

If, in fact, I had ever been in Excelsior at all.

Now that I weighed the same as I had throughout my first lifetime I had to ask myself whether it was believable that I'd ever left Earth at all. I had to wonder whether Excelsior, Davida Berenike Columella, Christine Caine, and Adam Zimmerman might have been aspects of an improbable illusion, and whether I might now be waking up for real. I had to face the possibility that all the necessary questions were going to have to be asked all over again.

Paranoia assured me that I could only feel as bad as I did if this were real, and *everything* else had been false.

The darkness didn't become any less absolute as the bleary eyes I had forced open attempted vainly to adjust to it. I reached up to touch my face with my right hand. My fingertips and my chin felt familiar—far *too* familiar, in fact. I didn't seem to be wearing a smartsuit and I had a week's worth of beard growth.

I touched my chest then, and found that I was wearing a shirt: a *dead* shirt. Even in 2202 I wouldn't have been seen dead in a dead shirt. I only had to flex my leg muscles to confirm that I was also wearing lightweight trousers, and that I was sandwiched between a single sheet and a lumpy mattress.

Shit, I thought. *First a thousand years forward in time, then a couple of hundred years back.* The way I felt told me that any IT I might be wearing was no ultrasophisticated product of the thirty-third century, or even the twenty-third. I didn't seem to have any pain control at all.

I told myself that it wasn't so bad. I had been naked before, save for dead clothes, and devoid of significant IT. I reminded myself that I was a Madoc and a Tamlin: a supremely adaptable hero, ready for any twist of fate. I told myself that my new situation wasn't anything I couldn't handle. I was in the dark, and I was in some slight discomfort, but I was alive and whole and quite compos mentis. Things could have been a lot worse. I just had to get stuck into the task of finding out where I was, and making the best of my circumstances.

I reached out an experimental hand. There was nothing within easy reach above me, although I fancied I could hear the sound of breathing from that general direction. I groped about in other directions. The mattress I was lying on was set on a ledge, apparently plastic. There was a wall to my left and another a couple of feet from my head. I had to roll on to my side to touch the floor, but I seemed to be only a meter above it. I sat up in bed. The extra reach enabled me to ascertain that there was indeed another bunk above mine. That was slightly reassuring; wherever I was, I didn't seem to be alone.

When I had maneuvered my feet to the floor I was able to stand up, though not as easily as I could have wished. My feet were bare, but the floor wasn't uncomfortably rough or cold. It felt like plastic. I couldn't tell by feeling it with the soles of my feet whether the plastic was organic or whether it had been gantzed out of twentieth-century waste.

There was an inert body lying on the upper bunk, whose dimensions I didn't explore in detail because it seemed more sensible to let whoever it was continue sleeping. I touched a sleeve, though, which suggested that my sleeping companion was wearing dead clothing just like mine. The person in question didn't seem to be sleeping very easily, but the body didn't stir when my fingers brushed the back of the hand that was projecting from the sleeve. It was a small hand, not very hairy. I was prepared to accept that it was probably a female hand, but I refused to jump to the conclusion that it was Christine Caine's. If it turned out to be Christine Caine's, that would mean that everything I'd experienced had been real—more of it, at any rate, than I wanted to hang on to—and that something terrible had happened to *Child of Fortune*.

I felt for a belt and found that my dead trousers were elastic-waisted. The shirt was ill-fitting and buttonless, severely functional. I knew that if I really had been divested of the kind of smartsuit and internal technology that I'd worn on Excelsior I must have been asleep for a long time. It wasn't the work of a couple of hours to strip that kind of equipment away.

If, on the other hand, I was fresh out of the freezer . . .

I needed to take a piss, quite urgently. *That* was a feeling I hadn't had for a very long time, no matter where or when I was.

I only had to stretch a little to locate the far wall of what I'd already begun thinking of as a cell. The space in which I was confined was only a couple of meters wide. It wasn't much more than three meters long, but there was a sub-chamber in one corner. Once I'd found the handle the screen moved aside easily, and I began to fumble about the interior, hoping that it was some kind of bathroom facility. There was a showerhead and a drain, and some other kind of fitment that I couldn't immediately identify but might have been some kind of toilet. I wasn't about to engage with any puzzles; the drain was good enough for me.

When I was able to get back to investigating the geography of the space that now confined me it didn't take me long to find the door at the farther end, or the handle that opened it.

I didn't expect the handle to turn, but it did. I heard the latch disengage. I hadn't encountered a door like that in years; it was the sort of door that one only found in buildings abandoned during the Crash: a door constructed in the twenty-first-century, or even earlier.

The twenty-first-century door opened outwards, not quite silently.

The area outside the cell was as dark as the inside. I nearly set out to cross it, but figured that it was wiser and safer to grope my way along the wall, one step at a time. I moved to the left, because the open door was blocking the way to the right. The wall felt like plastic, just like the door and the handle.

I couldn't have gone more than five meters before I came to another door. That one had a handle, too. It turned easily enough, and the door wasn't locked.

Gently, without making more than the minimum amount of noise, I swung it open and moved carefully around it.

The fist that hit me in the face seemed to be astonishingly well aimed, considering the total darkness. I presume that it was the knuckle of the middle finger which smashed into my nasal cartilage.

The snap was audible.

I was hurled backwards, swept unceremoniously off my feet by the momentum of the punch. I was in too much pain already to take much notice of the jarring as my coccyx, elbows, shoulders, and head made violent contact with the floor.

I tried to swear, but the pain was so intense that the reflexive explosion turned the word into something half way between a gasp and a yell.

Lights came on abruptly, dazzling me.

I clutched at my broken nose with both hands, feeling the warm blood gush out into my palms, soaking the sleeves of my shirt.

I had been stabbed more than once in my early days on the streets, before I acquired the kind of IT that rendered such wounds more tolerable, but that had been a long time ago. I had been cossetted by good IT for more than twenty years—give or take a hypothetical thousand—and the pain of my present injury was probably worse, even on an objective scale, than any inflicted upon me during my misspent youth. It was horrible.

When my eyes began to adjust to the brilliant light they were full of tears, which had to be blinked way before I could hope to see where I was or who had hit me. There was no thought in my mind of reprisal, or even of evasive action in the face of further danger. There was just the pain, and the fear that whoever had hit me might take a second shot.

It didn't make me feel any better to see that the face peering down at me seemed more puzzled than angry, with perhaps the faintest hint of regret.

It was the face of Solantha Handsel.

Somehow, I was able to take note of the fact that she was staring at her own hand in utter bewilderment, and I had enough presence of mind to leap to the conclusion that it wasn't the discovery that it was me she had hit that had puzzled her. Her regret wasn't apologetic: she was amazed and slightly upset by the fact that hitting me had made her own hand hurt. She hadn't had the dubious benefit of my upbringing. She'd *always* had good IT, and hadn't ever worn dead clothes. If I was unprepared to find myself in this condition, she must be in a much greater state of shock.

Even so, it was me that had taken the punishment. She might have hurt her hand, but she hadn't broken her nose.

By the time Michael Lowenthal's lightly bearded face had appeared beside the bodyguard's I had found the energy and ability to swear. I took abundant advantage of the opportunity, but I didn't forget to look around. I felt that I had to try to keep up with the news, even though I was in sore distress.

The room we were in wasn't vast, but space was at a premium because it was so extensively cluttered with boxes and equipment. There was a folding table propped against one ceiling-high stack of boxes, and a whole pile of folding chairs beside it. If I'd tried to cross the room rather than making my way along the wall I'd probably have tripped, scraping my shins and bruising my limbs—but at least I wouldn't have broken my nose.

The ceiling seemed a little low. It looked to be a mirror image of the floor, gray and plastic. The walls were gray too, although they seemed to be fitted with an abundance of equipment and hatches, as well as a superabundance of doors with handles. Everything was plastic, except where gleaming metal showed through. Some of the bits of gleaming metal looked like the heads of rivets. Other bits looked like screwheads.

Even in buildings deserted during the Crash I'd almost never seen rivets or screwheads. Rivets and screwheads were pre-Gantz, and pre-Gantz was practically pre-civilization. It wouldn't have been quite as strange if they'd been rusted, but they weren't. They looked new. Maybe not brand new, but new enough.

I finally managed to turn the stream of my curses into a coherent sentence, which was: "Have you any *idea* how much this hurts, you stupid bitch?" The pronunciation came out all wrong, because my nose was flooded by the blood that I was still spilling, but the meaning seemed to get across.

Solantha Handsel shook her head ever so slightly, to signal that she hadn't a clue, even though her own hand was throbbing. I hoped that she'd broken the knuckle, but the perfunctory way she was shaking it suggested that she hadn't.

The bodyguard should have been the one to check the damage she'd inflicted, but when my head sagged back on the floor the face that came into view, upside down, was Niamh Horne's. It was she who finally managed to get the protective hands away from my nose so that she could inspect the damage.

"Do you want me to try to straighten it?" she asked.

Like an idiot, I must have mouthed "yes."

The cyborganizer reached out to press the broken cartilage back into position, and I found out what *real* pain was like.

I fainted.

TWENTY-TWO
INJURY TIME

By the time I came round someone had put a pillow under my head and draped a cold damp cloth over my nose. The bleeding seemed to have stopped, but I didn't dare move in case it started again. My vision was blurred, but I could see that at least half a dozen standing figures were gathered about my supine form. They were arguing.

"How was I supposed to know who it was?" Solantha Handsel was complaining. "It was dark. How was I supposed to guess that his IT had been stripped? I hadn't even registered the fact that *my* IT had been stripped. It wasn't my fault."

I took some small comfort from the fact that nobody seemed to be in agreement with this judgment—not even Michael Lowenthal.

I counted, and decided that there were five standing figures. Then a sixth hove into view, and finally a seventh.

There was little comfort to be gained from the fact that they all looked frightened, with the possible exception of Christine Caine. Adam Zimmerman looked very frightened indeed. He hadn't had any time at all to adjust to the world into which he had been reborn before it turned bad, and he had to be figuring that he was now even further removed from his objective than he had been on the day he stole the world for the Hardinist Cabal. Davida Berenike Columella seemed more terrified than her emortal companions, but that may have been an illusion fostered by the fact that she was so tiny and so seemingly immature.

Of the party that had been on the guided tour of Niamh Horne's ship only the two other cyborgs were missing. Suddenly, the assumption that Niamh Horne had been behind our kidnapping, if we had indeed been kidnapped—and it certainly looked that way at present—didn't seem quite so natural. It wasn't just the fact that she was here with us that made it seem less likely—it was the fact that we'd all been deprived of our smartsuits, the most vital components of our internal technical support, and our dignity. That, and the gravity. Wherever Niamh Horne would have taken people she'd kidnapped, it wouldn't be Earth, or anywhere that simulated Earth gravity.

On the other hand, I thought—still trying hard to demonstrate my presence of mind—Niamh Horne was the only one among us to have retained a considerable fraction of her intimate technology. *Her* intimate technology had included a great deal that was far too intimate to be removed without leaving great gaping holes in her head and body. She still looked whole, if not quite human.

I made no attempt to get up, but I muttered and stirred, expecting that somebody would take notice and kneel down. They weren't in any hurry to oblige, but one of them eventually took the hint. It was Niamh Horne again, and I flinched reflexively.

"Sorry about that," she said. "It seemed to be the right thing to do. I didn't realize. Sorry."

Mortimer Gray knelt down with her. Like Lowenthal and Zimmerman, he now had a beard of sorts, but his looked more remarkable than theirs because its dark brown color clashed with his silver hair. "I think you'll be okay, Mr. Tamlin," he said. "It looks worse than it is. Very unfortunate, but not mortal." *Not mortal* was easy enough for him to say—even without his IT, he was engineered for emortality at the cellular level. I carefully refrained from touching my nose to investigate how badly out of shape it was.

"Where are we?" I contrived to ask.

"We don't know," Gray said. "The simple answer is that

we're in a cluttered room with seven doors. Four of them open into cells like the one you woke up in. The other three are locked. There are several antique wallscreens, but only two control panels, both of which seem to be inactive. Like all the other equipment, they seem ridiculously primitive. The gravity seems to be Earth-normal, but nobody's ready to conclude, as yet, that we're on Earth. If it's not spin, it might be acceleration—but if it's acceleration, we don't have any clue where we might be headed. We don't know how long it's been since we were aboard the Titanian ship, although it must have taken between eight and ten days to flush our IT, and the growth of our body hair can't have begun until that process was at least halfway through. The means they used to keep us asleep seems to have been rather crude if the way we feel is a reliable guide. Did you see the thing that seemed to capture *Child of Fortune*?"

"Yes," I said, thickly, unable for the moment to say more.

"We don't believe in it either," he said, picking up the skepticism in my tone. "Opinions are sharply divided, however, as to what kind of real story the fake was covering up. Accusations have been flowing freely, but I think Niamh and Michael have called a truce for the time being. At least nobody's suggested that *you* were to blame. That gives you an advantage over the rest of us."

It was obvious that he had not been excluded from the riot of accusations.

"Who stands to gain from taking us prisoner?" I said, thickly but just about comprehensibly.

"We haven't been able to figure that out either," Gray said, looking at Niamh Horne—who was obviously suspect number one in everyone's eyes but her own.

"The greater enigma," the cyborg said, grimly, "is *how* someone contrived to take us prisoner. Taking control of *Child of Fortune*'s AIs should have been impossible."

"Impossible for outside agencies, maybe," another voice put in—I guessed that it was Lowenthal's, although it sounded far less smooth than it had before—"but if it were an inside job . . ."

"If it had been me," the Titanian snapped back, "I wouldn't have brought your pet gladiator—and I'd have kept a couple of my own people. I can't believe that it was anyone on my crew . . . and even if I could believe it, I can't believe that they'd bring us to Earth. Only your people would do that. I didn't think the Cabal had the intelligence, let alone the technics, but I guess you might have sharpened up your act since you accidentally blew North America away and shriveled Garden Earth to mulch. On the other hand, I can't see how you had the opportunity." There was a pause while she redirected her attention. "Only *you* had that," she added. I knew that she had to be staring at Davida.

I was beginning to feel left out again, so I decided to sit up. It wasn't easy, but I managed it. I had to remind myself that I was supposed to be a hard man, a real fighter. I had to tell myself, very sternly, that if we were all equal now, in terms of our clothing and internal resources, then I ought to be vying for leadership of the pack instead of lying flat out and feeling exceedingly sorry for myself.

"You ought to lie down," Niamh Horne told me. "You've lost a lot of blood, and we no longer seem to have the kind of help that we normally rely on to make such losses good.

"I'm okay," I lied, fighting the dizziness. I could see how much blood there was on the gray floor now, and how much there was on the pale blue sleeves of my dead shirt. My trousers were pale blue too, except where they'd picked up bloodstains from the floor. Everybody's clothes were pale blue. They had to be uniforms of some kind, although they seemed ridiculously casual as well as inert.

"Better do as she says, Mr. Tamlin," Solantha Handsel put in, flatly. "I hit you hard. I'm sorry. I didn't know who it was. It could have been a hostile."

"If I wasn't a hostile before," I managed to mutter, darkly, "I am now." She didn't seem impressed.

"Come on, Mr. Tamlin," said Mortimer Gray. "I'll help you." He lent me an arm so that I could raise myself from a sitting position to a standing one. I felt faint, and I had to fight hard against the impulse to lie back down again. I'd sat up because I wanted to keep better track of the argument, but the argument had been suspended now while everyone put on a collaborative show of sympathy. Michael Lowenthal seemed very anxious indeed, although he might have been overacting—or he might, of course, have been projecting an anxiety he really felt for himself. Emortal or not, he knew how vulnerable he was without IT assistance.

Mortimer Gray continued to hang on to my arm, to make sure that I didn't keel over again. When he was sure that I wouldn't he steered me back toward the door from which I'd unwisely emerged on my exploratory mission, obviously intent on seeing me safety back to my bed. I resisted, but I didn't have the strength to make the resistance stick. In the end, I decided that I could only benefit from a brief interval of rest, and allowed myself to be guided.

Christine Caine followed us into the cell, with the air of one who thought she had a legitimate claim to the territory. I took that to mean that she *had* been the person in the upper bunk. I wondered briefly whether I ought to put in for a transfer, but it seemed unlikely that anyone was going to volunteer to trade—not only because no one else would want to share with Christine but also because no one else would want to share with me.

I figured that I had the rough end of the deal. If I had been deprived of my IT, I reasoned, so had Christine. Whatever internal censors the sisterhood had put in place to ensure that she didn't revert to type were presumably gone. She didn't look dangerous at the moment, but I had seen *Bad Karma*.

I lay down in the bottom bunk. Mercifully, the dizziness relinquished its hold on my head almost immediately.

"I'm sorry, Madoc," Mortimer Gray said, moving toward the door, "but we have to get this sorted out, if we can."

I was tempted to tell him that he shouldn't leave me out of the discussion, and certainly shouldn't leave me alone with a crazy mass murderer, but I didn't have the energy. I needed time to recover my wits.

"Are you okay?" the crazy mass murderer said, looking down at me. "Do you want me to stay?"

I resisted the temptation to laugh. I tried to shake my head, but it wasn't the ideal gesture to attempt in my condition.

She stayed anyway. "Do you have any idea what's going on?" she asked, paying me a compliment of sorts.

"It looks as if we've been kidnapped by space pirates," I said, weakly. "In fact, one way or another, that's what it amounts to. Whether the pirates are from Earth, or Titan, or Excelsior, or somewhere else entirely, we're still kidnapped. I expect we'll find out soon enough what happens next. Maybe we get held for ransom, auctioned to the highest bidder. There's only one thing *I'm* sure of."

"What's that?" she wanted to know.

"*This* isn't a dream," I told her. "Everything else might have been a trip in a fancy VE, but not *this*." I touched my broken nose, very gently indeed. "No matter how preposterous the situation seems, I'm certain now that we're awake. I wasn't before, but I am now. And given that this is real, we're in *real* trouble. Whatever game we were playing before, the game we have to play now is trying to figure out how to stay alive."

"I worked that out for myself," she assured me, drily. "Is it Zimmerman they want, do you think? Or Lowenthal?"

"I haven't a clue," I admitted. "But this place looks as if it's Zimmerman's vintage, whatever that implies. Do you have any idea how long we've been here? That is, how long has it been since we stepped aboard *Child of Fortune*?"

"Nobody knows," she told me. "Horne reckons it must have been at least twelve days. She says the real question is why we've finally been woken up. They're all standing around out there waiting for some kind of contact. Nobody believes that the space battle was real, but nobody can figure out how the ship *was* taken over, if it was taken over. You were unlucky—Handsel probably wishes she'd hit Horne while she had the excuse. Then again, Horne probably wishes she'd had a chance to disable Handsel. Do you want me to go and listen in, to see what I can pick up?

It seemed like a good idea, although I didn't know why she was asking. Maybe it was politeness, because we were cellmates or because I'd been hurt, or maybe she was just the kind of person who needed more reasons than she could provide for herself. "Sure," I said. "I'll be okay. I just need a few minutes."

She went, leaving me to my own devices.

I kept telling myself, over and over, that I had advantages over my fellow prisoners, and not just because I had lived without IT before. I had previous experience of jail cells, and uncontrollable pain. Unfortunately, I was badly out of practice. Telling myself that the broken nose was no worse than injuries I had suffered before didn't seem to help at all. Telling myself that I still had to go through it whether it was bearable or not didn't help either.

By the time I had been awake for what seemed like a further hour I had begun to wish that I had never recovered consciousness, but no matter how hard I tried, I couldn't get back to sleep. Lying still with my eyes shut kept the agony to a minimum, but even the minimum didn't seem tolerable.

It seemed as if a subjective eternity had passed when Christine Caine came back into the cell and put a tentative hand on my arm. I opened my eyes and tried to focus on her face, although moving my head brought new tears to my eyes.

"The woman on the screen says they're willing to take a look at you, maybe give you something for the pain," she said.

"What woman?" I asked, dazedly.

"On the screen," she repeated, patiently. "They've opened communications. I'm not sure they wanted to talk to us this soon, but I guess they're worried about you. If you can get to the far door while the rest of us stay back, they'll let you through and take a look at your nose. So she says."

Christine kept her hand on my arm while I maneuvered myself off the bunk, but she didn't actually help. I managed to stand up without re-starting the bleeding, and stumbled after her as she led the way.

The others just watched. Apart from Mortimer Gray, they didn't seem unduly concerned about my state of health, although Michael Lowenthal looked as if he were about to say something until the presence of the others inhibited him.

It wasn't difficult to figure out what he wanted to say. *Find out what you can. Don't tell anyone except me.*

Paranoid as I was, I couldn't quite credit Lowenthal with having had enough foresight to have told his minder to break something in order to create exactly this sort of opportunity.

Adam Zimmerman looked at me in a way that seemed to say *there but for the grace of God go I.* I couldn't remember whether it was the first time we had locked gazes long enough for it to count as communication.

When I was left alone in front of the relevant door I heard a distinct click, and then the handle turned. The door swung inward, but the darkness beyond seemed impenetrable. I hesitated, but it had to be reckoned a useful opportunity.

I walked forward into the gloom, which became absolute as the door slammed shut behind me.

TWENTY-THREE
ALICE

Another hand, no bigger than Christine's, gripped my sleeve. "This way," said a female voice.

I hadn't seen the woman on the screen, so I couldn't visualize a face to fit the clutching hand. It pulled me half a dozen paces forward, then to the left. I moved clumsily through another doorway, bumping my shoulder as I went.

When the woman had activated the light switch I saw that we were in a room no bigger than a cupboard. In fact, it actually seemed to be a cupboard, albeit a large one.

We were surrounded by storage racks, some of them crammed and some of them empty. The shelves had numbers on, which appeared to have been stenciled on the gray plastic in black paint. As in the cells and the room into which the cells opened, everything seemed unbelievably old. There were more rivet heads visible as well as hexagonal bolt heads. Most, but not all, of the packages stowed on the occupied racks looked much more recent. The ones that didn't seem to constitute fresh stock looked very old indeed, stylistically speaking, but they weren't showing much sign of dilapidation or decay.

The woman who was reaching up to test the damage done to my nose was fully matured, but there was no way of telling how old she might be. Her hair was dark and her complexion had a peculiar bluish tint. Her eyes were blue, but a darker shade than I had ever seen before. She was wearing a smartsuit; it wasn't fashionably cut, by the standards of my time, but it looked—at least to my uneducated eye—far more like the ones commonly worn in the twenty-second century than the one I'd been fitted with on Excelsior.

"Hold still," she said, as she rolled back my left sleeve and wrapped something around the bare forearm. It was an elastic bandage made of some kind of smart fabric, connected by bundles of artificial nerves to a box. I didn't feel anything, but I guessed that it would send feelers into my arm to test the blood pressure.

"It's my face that needs the treatment," I pointed out, ashamed of the thickness of my voice and roughness of pronunciation."

"It's already been reset, albeit crudely," she told me. "I'll put a dressing on it to reduce the swelling and apply local anesthetic, but there's not much I can do at present to compensate for the blood loss. I don't have repair nanobots ready to hand—it'll take until tomorrow, at the earliest, to produce an emergency supply. Fortunately, the blood loss doesn't seem to have been too bad. The spill looked worse than it was."

She showed me the dressing she intended to apply. It just about qualified as smart, but it was a kind that had virtually disappeared in my time, even in parts of the world where nobody had decent IT or worthwhile medical insurance.

"That isn't going to do much for the pain," I complained.

She picked something up from a nearby shelf and handed it to me. It was a plastic bottle containing pills—perhaps twenty of them.

"What is it?" I asked.

"Codeine," she told me.

"Codeine! That's antediluvian. What the hell is this place?"

"We hadn't expected you to start trying to kill one another as soon as you woke up," she countered, drily. Her tone changed, though, as she kept talking. "I'm afraid you're going to have to serve as an example, to warn the others to look after themselves—and one another—a little bit better. If I had something ready to hand I'd give it to you, but I don't.

All that's presently in the stores is pre-nanotech medical apparatus—whose evolution, as Mortimer Gray will doubtless be pleased to explain to you, virtually petered out as soon as the first IT suites came on to the market. I can get something better, but it'll take time. Quiet now."

I shut up while she applied the dressing and unwrapped my arm, but as soon as the local anaesthetics in the patch of synthetic skin began to kick in I was able to concentrate my attention much more effectively.

"I don't suppose you'd consider telling me who you are and what the hell you're playing at?" I said, trying to sound conciliatory. "Whatever war you're fighting, I'm not involved. I only just got here."

"I'm sorry you got caught up in this," she said, after a moment's hesitation. "We know that it's not your fault, and that you can't begin to fathom the situation. I wish I could explain, but we're involved in delicate negotiations, and I've been forbidden to disclose anything that might affect their outcome. I hope I'll get permission to explain what's going on in the near future, but we'll all need to be patient."

"So why not let us go on sleeping?" I asked.

She actually bit her lip a little as she suppressed the impulse to answer. It seemed to me that she was very unhappy about her own situation, whatever it was. She was just a pawn, no more in control of the bizarre kidnapping than I was—or she was putting on a good act. She couldn't stop me talking, though, so I made my own guess—hoping, of course, to be able to deduce something from her reaction.

"If you don't want to talk to us," I said, "and it appears that you don't, you must want to observe us—listen in on our conversation, see how the accusations fly. You want to know how Lowenthal and Horne react."

She remained stubbornly silent.

I changed tack. "Okay," I said. "How about helping me out by offering me a few hints as to what I ought to ask Lowenthal and Horne, in order to help both of us get what we want. What kind of a war is it that we've stepped into?"

That was a better move. It made her pause, to consider the offer. There *were* things she wanted to know about Lowenthal and Horne. When I used the word "war" her expression darkened a little, but I couldn't be sure what the change signified.

While she thought it over I scanned the racks, trying to pick up clues as to what might be in the packages—especially the ones that looked as if they had been here long before the pirates moved in. Unfortunately, almost all the labels I could see were numbers and meaningless jumbles of letters. Everything was identifiable from the outside, but only if you knew the code. There were only a handful of real words, and all but one of those were etched on the more recent packaging. A lot of those packs—upwards of fifty—allegedly contained manna or water, just like the packs that were stacked up in the room into which the cell doors opened. The only interesting word that I could see on any of the ancient plastic wrap had been scrawled on a piece of sealing tape in ink.

The word was CHARITY.

"We're not fighting a war," the woman said, eventually. "We're trying to prevent one. I wish I could guarantee that no harm will come to you, but I can't. What I can say is that you're safe while you're here. My companion and I don't mean you any harm, and we'll protect you as best we can."

There had been just the slightest hesitation before she pronounced the word "companion," but I didn't have time to wonder what it might mean. My attention was caught and held by the ominous elements of the statement.

I figured that she wouldn't answer if I asked straight out who did mean me harm and how likely they were to get the opportunity to do some, but I thought I might get somewhere by making a few more guesses, trying to provoke a less ambiguous reaction.

"The war you're trying to prevent must be the one between Earth and the Outer System," I said, avid for the slightest sign of confirmation or contradiction.

"It's not as simple as that," was all she said at first. After a moment's hesitation, though, she went on. "There are more sides here than you can probably imagine, Mr. Tamlin."

That was patronizing. She didn't know anything about the scope of my imagination—but I wasn't about to take umbrage now that I had a chance to get somewhere. "Personally, I think Lowenthal's just a foot soldier," I said, talking rapidly in the hope of making the most of my fragile opening, "but he's probably working for the same people who handed down the instructions to Excelsior. They have to think the big basalt flow was sabotage, intended to upset the balance of power. They must intend to redress the balance, as soon as they figure out a way to do it. Whether or not Titan was responsible for blowing up North America, the Titanians must have been expecting retaliation, and they have control of the traffic. My guess is that Lowenthal's masters needed bait: something to provide cover for a sizable delegation to go out to Titan. They knew that Titan wouldn't be able to resist Zimmerman. He's the only man with a big enough name to trigger a show *and* a contest. Maybe Christine and I were just trial runs, but maybe not. I think you flushed my IT along with Lowenthal's and Horne's because you didn't know what the sisterhood might have incorporated into it. How am I doing?"

"It's really not as simple as that," she said, shaking her head ruefully. She hadn't given me the slightest indication that I'd scored any hits along the way. "I certainly can't blame you for trying to figure it all out, Mr. Tamlin, but I can't help you while our own negotiations are still ongoing—the situation is difficult and the information is extremely sensitive. The present situation's not of our choosing, but we have to deal with it as best we can. If we get safely to where we're hoping to go, you'll have to be told what's going on, but nothing's settled yet and there are factions involved in the discussion who still want everything kept quiet. I shouldn't be talking to you at all, but we don't want anyone dying on us if we can help it. Please tell your companions to remain calm, and patient."

My offer to act as an agent provocateur appeared to have fallen on deaf ears, at least for the time being. I wondered whether there might be an opportunity for me to get a little way ahead of Lowenthal and Horne in the new game, if I played my cards right—but I knew I'd have to prove my usefulness before our captors would even consider letting me in.

"What's your name?" I asked her, abruptly.

"Alice," she said. She hadn't hesitated—but she didn't add a surname.

"And you're just a foot soldier, like Lowenthal?"

"I'm not a soldier at all," she said, coldly. "I'm doing everything I can to ensure that it doesn't come to soldiering—because if it does, we might all be doomed. Maybe the evil day can only be postponed, but even if that's the case, we still have to gain what time we can. We need it." I got the impression that this speech wasn't just addressed to me. Others were listening in—and she had already told me that the present situation wasn't one she'd engineered, or even anticipated.

"Who's *we*, exactly?" I asked.

"All of us," she said. "We all need time." For just an instant, she seemed to be about to add something else, but she thought better of it. I couldn't tell whether or not she'd intended me to see the hesitation, or what conclusion she'd intended me to draw. I knew that "all of us" might only mean everybody locked in the interior of this mysterious and seemingly ancient artifact, or some larger but limited population, or even all the various posthumankinds.

"According to the history I've read, there hasn't been a single war during the thousand years I've been away," I told her. "Mortimer Gray seems to think that such childish things have been put away for good, now that everybody has a proper respect for the value of human life—because true emortals don't take risks of that crazy kind."

"Gray's wrong," Alice said, flatly. It sounded as if she had strong views of her own on that particular topic. "The Earthbound might have stood still for a long time, but they haven't

changed. Perhaps they can't—not any more." Now she felt
that she *had* said too much, although she hadn't really said
anything at all. She became suddenly impatient. "You'd better go back now," she said.

"How old are you?" I asked, refusing to budge. I'd
snatched the question out of midair, spurred on by desperation to get something more, however slight. The only thing
she'd so far shown any willingness to talk about was herself.

She hesitated, and this time she was definitely seized by a
genuine uncertainty. She couldn't quite bring a lie to bear in
time to stop the truth tripping off the tip of her tongue.

"Older than you," she said.

It wasn't an answer I had expected, but I was quick
enough to follow it up. "How much older?"

Again she hesitated, and again she decided to shame the
devil, although she didn't actually answer the question I'd
asked. "I was frozen down in 2090," she said, "and revived
three hundred and fifty years ago, give or take a couple. It
can be done, if that's one of the things you want to know. Our
kind can adapt, become emortal, and get a life. You can find
a place in the scheme of things too, Mr. Tamlin, if they'll only
give you the chance."

She was trying as hard as she could to be kind to me, I
realized. There was an element of fellow feeling in her determination to help me, because she'd gone through what I was
going through herself—except, maybe, for the feeling of
betrayal. I took note of the fact that she was now talking
about a "they" as well as, or instead of, the "we" she'd
referred to before. I decided that it was time to start playing
along, and let her steer me back toward the cupboard door.

"Thanks," I said, touching the dressing on my nose but
not meaning that alone.

"You'll be okay," she assured me, also not meaning my
nose. "You really have to go now. You can tell the others that
we really are trying to help and protect them. We'll do our
best to make sure that no harm comes to you."

I wished that she sounded more confident about that. I

was grateful that she had taken the trouble to patch me up, albeit crudely, and I wanted to acknowledge the fact. I also thought that it might be a wise move to offer her something in return, in order to tighten the bond between us. Unfortunately, I didn't know what I had that would constitute a worthwhile offer. I settled, for some reason I couldn't fathom even at the time, on a trivial personal confession.

"Alice is a curiously reassuring name," I told her, as I paused in the doorway. "I've always had a thing about names, including my own. Tam Lin was a man who was kidnapped by fairies, and served their queen as a lover and champion while generations went by on Earth. In the end, he got back again—thanks to a young woman—but he came perilously close to being sent to Hell in the interim. I hope I'll be as lucky."

Oddly enough, my fascination with my namesake was something I'd only ever mentioned to one other person—not, as it happened, Damon Hart, but Diana Caisson.

"You have to go back now," was all she said in reply, as she shoved me out into the darkness. "I'll try as hard as I can to get permission to tell you everything, but I daren't go ahead without. The situation's too tricky."

"It's okay," I told her. "I dare say we can make up a few stories of our own in the meantime."

TWENTY-FOUR
CHARITY

I had gone into the darkness a victim, but I came back as the only man who had met the enemy. I was the new star of the show.

"They don't seem to have the medical facilities to fix us up properly, so we'd better be extra careful in future," I told the others when they crowded round me, putting on a display of being concerned for my welfare. "This dressing is early twenty-first century and the anesthetic is beginning to wear off already. These are codeine—that's an ancient morphine precursor." I showed them the bottle of pills, but didn't mention what Alice had said about maybe having something better available tomorrow.

"I didn't know it was you," Solantha Handsel said, yet again. "I didn't mean to hurt you."

"I know," I said. "It could have been anyone. There's a lesson in that for all of us."

"What did you find out?" Niamh Horne cut in. "Where are we? Earth?"

"There is absolutely no possibility that we're on Earth," Lowenthal was quick to say. "They're simulating Earth-gravity for deceptive purposes. How could anyone on Earth have the knowledge necessary to hijack a Titanian space-ship?"

"How could anyone else?" the cyborganizer came back.

All of which deflected sufficient attention away from me to let me shuffle through the crowd, heading for the door of the cell from which I'd emerged. "My head's pounding and

I've lost more than a litre of blood," I muttered, harshly. "I have to lie down."

That helped to refocus their attention. "Tell us what you found out first," Lowenthal said, in what might have passed for a polite tone if he'd been a better actor.

I decided to keep my hand hidden, for the time being, on the grounds that the few cards I held might look a bit more impressive when I'd worked out how best to play them.

"I didn't find out anything much," I told him. "She says she wants to tell us everything but needs permission—she wouldn't say from whom. She says she's trying to protect us, but won't say from whom. She says that she's trying to prevent a war, but reckons I don't have the imagination to understand who might be fighting it or why. The only solid fact I know is that her name's Alice."

"Alice?" Lowenthal queried, with an almost imperceptible sneer of disbelief, as he tried to get around me so that he could block my path to the doorway.

Surprisingly, Christine Caine stepped casually into *his* path and practically shoved him out of my way. "As in Wonderland," she said. "Madoc needs to rest. You can all leave him alone until he feels better, okay?"

It was sheer amazement rather than politeness or caution which kept Solantha Handsel from felling Christine with a casual blow of her fist, but Lowenthal was much quicker on the diplomatic uptake. He turned on Niamh Horne as if she were the one making difficulties. "Christine's right," he said. "There's no hurry. Madoc needs time to recover. We can save all the questions till later. I think we ought to eat, if we can figure out how to work this antique equipment. Do you know how to do that, Christine?"

"Figure it out for yourself, asshole," was her reply to that ploy. She shepherded me into the cell and shut the door behind her. "Are you okay?" she asked, anxiously, as I climbed back into the lower bunk. "You did lose a lot of blood—and pills aren't going to help."

"I've bled before," I told her. "Thanks for that."

"We freezer vets need to stick together," she told me. I hoped fervently that it was true. I understood why she was trying to forge an alliance. She was as fearful as the rest of us, although she didn't want to make her terror too obvious, and she knew only too well that she was the remotest outsider in our little company.

She came closer, and leaned over so that her head was only a few centimeters from mine. "Are they listening in on us?" she asked.

"Of course they are," I murmured. "No matter how ancient this place is, or how recently our captors moved in, they've had plenty of opportunity to wire it for sound. Unfortunately, the pirates are probably the only ones listening in. We can't know for sure that they flushed out *all* our IT, or why, but they wanted to make as certain as they could be that none of us was carrying bugs capable of signaling our whereabouts to the outside world. Horne's external implants may have all kinds of talents we don't know about, but my guess is that our friendly neighborhood kidnappers are the only ones who can hear us."

She nodded. "So who's our friend and who's our enemy?" she wanted to know. "Just give me your best guess," she added, as an afterthought.

"I wish I knew," I said.

Perhaps there was something in my tone that I hadn't intended to put into it, or perhaps she wanted to do her level best to convince herself. At any rate, her eyes narrowed slightly and she said: "You don't have to worry about me. I'm not dangerous. Not to you."

"We freezer vets need to stick together," I reminded her. "If you do feel an overwhelming urge to kill someone . . ."

It wasn't a sensible move to try to make a joke out of it. I knew that it wasn't a joke, and so did she—but old reflexes can be hard to control. She couldn't contrive a laugh, but she managed to keep on smiling. "Are we in any worse trouble now than we were before?" she wanted to know.

"That's a good question," I muttered. "Probably, but possibly not. If the enemy of our enemy is our friend, we probably have a few friends somewhere—but until we figure out who our enemies are, we won't know where to look for them."

"Lowenthal and Horne don't seem to like us any better than they like one another," she observed. "They don't even seem to like Adam Zimmerman, although they came a long way to welcome him home."

"True," I said. "But something happened back on Excelsior when they first came face to face. That was when Horne started talking about somebody playing somebody for a fool. They don't trust one another and they don't trust Davida. Bringing us here doesn't seem to have been part of Alice's plans—I got the impression that she's as much a victim in this as we are, although she and some mysterious companion are trying very hard to be players. I think the hidden players let us wake up because they want to see how Horne and Lowenthal carry their quarrel forward—which is something we need to be interested in too, if we're to have any chance of figuring out what we've been caught up in. All we can be sure of is that whatever plans the sisterhood and Lowenthal's bosses might have had for us have gone up in smoke. Lowenthal's not going to like that—bureaucrats always panic when things go awry around them, because they know they'll have to carry the can whether they were at fault or not."

"Who actually gave the order to bring us out of the freezer, do you think?" she asked. She'd obviously been doing some hard thinking along lines not dissimilar to the ones I'd been following.

"I don't know," was the only reply I could offer her. "I thought at first it had to be Lowenthal's people, because I thought Ahasuerus had to be in the Cabal's pocket, no matter how much they might pretend to be a law unto themselves. I'm not so sure now—but whoever originated the order to wake Zimmerman, they didn't do it for his benefit, let alone ours. No matter what conditions he laid down when he launched the Foundation, they'd have let him rest in peace forever if their hand hadn't been forced. Now he is back though, and everyone knows it, he's valuable. He may be the has-been to end all has-beens, but he's still a potent symbol of the world that was parent to this one. If waking him up was system-wide news, the news that he's been kidnapped will generate even bigger headlines. If Alice's Wonderlanders wanted attention, they've got it—but if this really is a hijack, Niamh Horne's people will stop at nothing to find out who stole their beautiful spaceship. When they do, the thieves will have hornets buzzing at them from every direction. Given that they already seem to be arguing among themselves, this business could get *very* messy."

Christine nodded. "Anything else I should know?" she asked.

Now it was my turn to hesitate. I knew that I couldn't trust her, no matter how hard she was working to build a common cause between us, but there were things I couldn't figure out, and she had lived through an earlier period of history. I dropped my voice even lower to say: "What kind of people were being frozen down in twenty ninety, do you think? In those days, you had to be a murderer, right? Or a volunteer?"

"I guess so," she said. "Why?"

"Alice says that she's older than us," I whispered. "That means she was in the freezer for more than seven hundred years—maybe as long as eight—before they fished her out three centuries ago. It's the only real clue I've got as to who snatched us, and I can't make head nor tails of it. That and *charity*."

"What?"

"Charity. I was in a storage unit. Most of the stuff stowed in there was newly imported, but some wasn't. The only word I could make out on the old stuff was *charity*."

I didn't really expect a response, but I saw her eyes light up with inspiration. There was nothing false or grudging about the smile that creased her face now. "Shit," she said. "Is *that* where we are?"

I put my finger to my lips immediately, fearful of whatever listening devices the Wonderlanders had planted. "Very softly," I said, meaning the way she had to whisper it in my ear. "And don't tell the others just yet. First, we need to figure out whose side we're on."

She had just enough time to tell me what Charity was before the knock on the door sounded. It seemed more apologetic than insistent, so I nodded to indicate that she should let the visitor in.

She opened the door cautiously, then stood back to admit Mortimer Gray. He was carrying a bowl, a spoon, and a water bottle, all of them molded in plastic—but not the uninspiring gray stuff that made up the walls. The bowl and spoon seemed to my admittedly uneducated eye to be modern. The water bottle was unsealed.

"It's only flavored gruel, I'm afraid," he said. "Guaranteed nutritionally adequate for your kind, however—and we managed to master the microwave oven, so it's warm without being desiccated."

"What about me?" Christine wanted to know.

Gray was too polite to answer, so he just gestured with his full hands to remind her that he only had two of them.

She went out, nursing her secret fondly. She closed the door behind her, with ostentatious carefulness.

TWENTY⊸FIVE
HISTORY LESSONS

C hristine feels that she ought to look out for me," I explained to Mortimer Gray, as I sat up and took the bowl. "We're both way out of our depth here, and she thinks we need to stick together. I think the broken nose brought out her maternal instincts. People used to have those, you know—the plague of sterility didn't wipe them out overnight."

Gray nodded, as if he understood perfectly. He put the water bottle down on the mattress and hesitated, waiting for an invitation to remain. I inferred that he'd been delegated to get what answers he could from me, on the grounds that I seemed to be less hostile to him than to the other contenders.

"You don't seem very worried," I observed. "Lowenthal, Handsel, and Horne are all putting on a tough act, but underneath they're as scared as poor Davida, if not as terrified as Christine, Adam, and I. You're not—or are you?"

"If you're looking for evidence of a conspiracy between our captors and me," he said, having obviously decided to speak plainly, "you're looking in the wrong direction. I've been in mortal danger before—twice, in fact. It's surprising how quickly one learns from such experiences. Admittedly, I hadn't had my IT stripped out on either occasion, but I was rescued both times by the same person. Somehow, I can't seem to escape the conviction that all I have to do is wait for her to come and get me again. I know it's absurd, but that doesn't prevent me from being grateful for the feeling of security."

"Emily Marchant," I said, remembering the research I'd done in what was fast becoming an alarmingly distant past. "The way I heard it, *you* rescued *her* the first time."

"That's the way others tell it," he agreed. "But I was there."

"Emily Marchant is Niamh Horne's boss," I observed.

"Not true," he said. "That's not the way things work in the Confederation, or on Titan. Emily's very keen on progress, and that makes her a political animal, but she's not part of any hierarchical power structure."

"So it wasn't her who blew up the Earth?"

His eyebrows shot up, but he didn't explode at me. "No," he said. "It certainly wasn't. You seem to be obsessed with the idea that the solar system is about to be plunged into a war, Mr. Tamlin. Did Alice really tell you that a war is imminent?"

"Since you last told me that war is unthinkable," I pointed out, "we've been hijacked by people pretending to be aliens—or maybe aliens pretending to be people pretending to be aliens. According to Alice, their reason for doing it is to try to avert a war that might already be inevitable. So I think I can be forgiven for sticking to what seems to you to be an unreasonable conviction."

I took a mouthful of warm gruel. After the terrible stuff we'd been fed on Excelsior it tasted pretty good. I'd eaten worse kinds of wholefood in my youth.

He thought over what I'd said. "I can see how you might reach that conclusion," he conceded, eventually.

"Of course you can," I said. "You're a historian. You know what kind of world I come from. What I can't see is how *you* could cling to any other conclusion, given our present situation. No matter how firmly the Earthbound are stuck in the mud, Lowenthal has to figure that the war started ninety-nine years ago, and that he's now in the thick of it. Since Niamh Horne's pet spaceship staged that fake emergency we've all been living in interesting times. I can see how a historian might find a certain delight in that prospect—but you've been drafted to the front line, and if I were in your shoes I wouldn't be making any assumptions about other people respecting my noncombatant status."

His eyebrows barely twitched. He reached up reflexively to stroke his fledgling beard. "Our captors seem to have neglected to provide shoes," he pointed out, making a feeble attempt at humor. "In fact, they seem to be a long way behind the times in all sorts of ways. Do you have any particular reason for suggesting that they might be aliens pretending to be people pretending to be aliens?"

"Just habit," I told him. "I always look for the wheels within the wheels within the wheels. I wouldn't be here today if it weren't for a kidnapping. I might never have seen Damon Hart again once he'd given up street life if his foster father hadn't been snatched by people pretending to be Eliminators. It turned out to be a convoluted game—but the end result of it was that our lives were both diverted on to an entirely new track. It seems that you and I have both carried the lessons of our personal history into our current situation. I knew your mother, you know."

Perhaps I should have saved that particular bombshell for later, but it's difficult to keep something like that up your sleeve when the temptation to use it is always there.

"What do you mean?" he asked, a trifle slow on the uptake.

"Your biological mother," I said. "Diana Caisson."

"Egg donors are of no consequence in our world," he told me, after only the slightest hesitation. "The embryos from which we're made undergo such extensive engineering that we acquire far more characteristics than we inherit. I may owe a few genetic idiosyncrasies to the particular individuals who provided the egg and sperm to start me off, but Ali Zaman and all his myriad followers were my true biological parents. I owe everything else that I am to my foster parents . . . and to Emily Marchant."

"So you don't want to know about Diana Caisson?" I said. "You're not curious?"

"I'm a historian," he reminded me. "I'm curious about

everything you know about your own world. But we have more urgent matters to consider, do we not?"

I was a trifle disappointed, but I figured that if he wanted to play it that way, I could too.

"Fair enough," I said. "I'm curious myself—but for me, it's all new, and all urgent. Are the Earthbound really as decadent as everybody seems to think? Have you really become a dead weight inhibiting further progress? Is that why someone's trying to administer a sharp object lesson to you and Lowenthal—and Adam Zimmerman?"

He only looked uncomfortable for a moment. After all, I was steering him back to safer ground—to his own intellectual territory.

"There are people in the Outer System who are fond of trying to make that case," he admitted. "It's nothing new—I heard little else when I lived on the moon. There are political, ecological, and psychological arguments, but they all boil down to the idea that organisms that are so perfectly adapted to their environment that they never have any reason or inclination to leave it are bound to stagnate. Hard-line cyborganizers and proselytizing outward bounders are both fond of declaring that the only way for emortals to avoid robotization is to pose an infinite series of challenges to their inherited nature, by continually moving into alien environments and never remaining too long in any one of them. But I can't believe that what's happening to us here and now is just an *object lesson*. Something very strange is happening, and we really do need to examine every clue you obtained, however slight. If you can tell us *exactly* what the woman said to you, there might be items of information therein whose significance we can see far better than you."

I popped the top of the water bottle and drank deeply. It wasn't until the cool water hit my stomach that I realized how thirsty I had been. Ridiculous as it may seem, I'd lived so long with careful IT that I had fallen out of touch with unmodified sensations. It occurred to me to wonder how much worse Mortimer Gray's alienation from his body might be.

"I suppose there might," I conceded. "In fact, there might be details of our surroundings whose significance you can judge far better than I, not to mention details of our physical condition. They seem to have purged our IT, but they weren't able to purge Niamh Horne's externals. If anyone's still capable of communication with the outside world, it's her. Is that why you're expecting Emily Marchant to come rescue us?"

He frowned to display his disapproval of my unhelpful attitude, but he answered me anyway. "Solantha Handsel is a cyborg too," he pointed out, mildly. "Given that we started from Earth orbit, Julius Ngomi might be able to obtain news of our difficulties long before anyone on Titan."

"Who's Julius Ngomi?" I asked.

"The only member of the Inner Circle to whom I can confidently put a name," he said, wearily accepting my agenda, presumably in the hope that I would eventually condescend to get back to his. "He's another man who once suggested to me that the conflicts of interest that were growing up within the solar system couldn't be settled with mere words and spontaneous bursts of fellow feeling. There are, I fear, people like him on both sides of the current dispute between Earth and the Confederation."

I put the spoon aside and sipped gruel direct from the bowl. I was beginning to feel better, but I opened the bottle Alice had given me and tipped out a couple of tablets. I used the gruel to wash them down.

"The sort of person who might want to bomb all hell out of Titan?" I suggested. "Partly to punish the people who probably set off the Yellowstone supervolcano, but mainly to let other interested parties know that nobody messes with the cradle of humankind and gets away with it?"

Gray shook his head. "No," he said. "Nobody's that crazy—certainly not Julius. When I say that he doesn't approve of mere words, I don't mean to imply that he's a man of violence. He's a Hardinist through and through. He thinks that ownership and good stewardship are the answers to all human problems. He just wants to settle the question of who owns what. Did you know that there's a stock market on Titan now?"

I couldn't help laughing. "Do you think he brought Adam Zimmerman out of cold storage to *do it again*?" I asked, not very seriously.

"Not at all," he replied, keeping his own tone light. "But I think he *might* have brought Adam Zimmerman out of cold storage to remind us all what a great hero he was, and how his cleverness saved the world from the ultimate ecocatastrophe. If he was the one who gave the order to bring Zimmerman out, he must have intended to use him as an instrument of propaganda—perhaps to help prepare the way for a strictly nonviolent revolution, whose ultimate aim is to install a judiciously extended Cabal as owners and stewards of the entire solar system."

He was obviously being serious—and he *was* the man who was supposed to understand the way the world worked, far better than I did. If the Earthbound really were stuck in the mud, though, the Hardinist Cabal might have retained the habits it had had in my day, when it had consisted of PicoCon and a few good friends. If so, they might indeed have decided to tackle their problems by widening their circle—by welcoming people like Emily Marchant into the fold, on whatever terms were negotiable. Maybe the outer system powers-that-be thought of themselves as the kind of people who'd never go for that kind of deal, but Damon Hart had thought of himself that way at one time. So had I.

If Mortimer Gray was right, I thought, and nobody was crazy enough to go to war, the only matter to be settled was the balance of power at the conference table—including the question of who was entitled to a seat. Maybe this really was the same kind of game that Damon and I had played before, on a slightly bigger board. If Michael Lowenthal and Niamh Horne were only pretending to be adversaries, while their actual purpose was to get together and wrap up a deal to impose a series of Enclosure Acts on the entire solar system, there might be any number of third parties anxious to get a slice for themselves, as well as any number ambitious to sabotage the whole process.

I hoped that I might be beginning to see the light, but I knew that I was overreaching from a position of almost total ignorance. Gray was in a far better position than I was to guess who was doing what to whom and why.

I was saved from further self-torture by yet another knock on the door. Adam Zimmerman came in, without waiting for an invitation. "Mr. Lowenthal wants to call a conference," he said, mildly. "He thinks we should discuss our situation, and make what plans we can." Lowenthal had obviously got tired of waiting for Gray to come up with the goods.

I handed my bowl and the empty water bottle back to Mortimer Gray. Reflexively, he took them. "Thanks," I said.

Gray wasn't about to be dismissed like that; he hung around to watch the first authentic contact between the man who had once stolen the world and the mysterious monster whose crimes had been erased from the record.

"Are you all right now?" Adam Zimmerman asked me, solicitously.

"Pretty much," I said. "I've been hurt before. How about you? This isn't the kind of welcome you expected when you took your great leap into the unknown."

"No," he admitted, "it certainly isn't. But it was always a gamble—and if I hadn't taken it, I'd be dead. I might still get what I wanted—unless you know different." His face was old and his eyes seemed weak, but that was all deceptive appearance. His mind was as determined as it ever was. He hadn't been interested in me before but he was interested in me now, because I was the one who had talked to Alice.

"So far as I can tell," I assured him, "our captors wish us well. We just got caught up in somebody else's troubles. With luck, we'll come through this. Even I might still get what I want, if I can figure out what it is."

The look he gave me then was slightly pitying. He was a man who had known exactly what he wanted throughout his adult life. For him, the goal had always been crystal clear, and perfectly simple. That might make him an innocent, by my standards, or even a fool—but it was an enviable state of mind.

"Okay," I said. "Let's go confer, and make what plans we can."

T he pain in my face hadn't gone away, but it had become duller. Moving around no longer increased its effect. At least I'd contrived to miss out on my fair share of the work that had had to be done. By the time I emerged from my cell the common space had been reorganized and tidied. The table had been assembled and set up, and eight chairs had been neatly distributed around it, one at each end and three along each side.

As soon as I saw the array I knew that the chairs at the ends might as well have had Michael Lowenthal's and Niamh Horne's names on them. The moment they had decided to call a conference they had set about modeling the situation as they saw it—or as they wanted others to see it. I paused to wonder whether our mysterious captors had done the same thing when they placed us in cells two by two, or whether they had simply sorted us out according to our existing associations.

The other seats about the conference table were distributed according to fairly obvious protocols. Adam Zimmerman had to have one of the middle seats, so that he would be equidistant from Lowenthal and Horne, and Davida had to have the other. Solantha Handsel had to be at Lowenthal's right hand, and Mortimer Gray filled in the remaining gap on that side of the table. That left Christine and me—and I wasn't unduly surprised when Lowenthal laid claim to me, seating me between him and Zimmerman. The power to determine the seating suggested that he had the upper hand at this stage, perhaps for no better reason than the fact that he had a bodyguard and Niamh Horne didn't.

I resisted the temptation to sit where I wasn't supposed to, or to request a formal agenda, or even to question Lowenthal's assumption that he could play chairman. I tried, instead, to measure Niamh Horne's reaction to Lowenthal's presumption. Because her face was a mask and her eyes were machines, though, there was no expression to be read therein.

"So far," Lowenthal said, "we've been wasting our time in accusations and recriminations. I think we have to accept that none of us knows why we have been taken prisoner, or by whom. Perhaps we'll be told, in due course, but we can't rely on it. In the meantime, we're all in the same boat and we ought to try to work together, as constructively as possible."

"Assuming that there's anything constructive to do," Niamh Horne added, but not in a challenging way.

"I'm not suggesting that we form an escape committee," Lowenthal went on, keeping his own voice light. "I'm merely suggesting that we collaborate in assessing our situation and trying to figure out how we ought to react to it. I think we can take it for granted that we're on some kind of spaceship, albeit a very old one—or one constructed according to a very old blueprint. It seems likely that the apparent gravity is simulated by acceleration, but I can't believe we're heading out of the system. Do you have anything useful to add to those conclusions, Mr. Tamlin?"

I was slightly surprised to find myself in the hot seat so soon, but I had already had time to think about what I ought and ought not to share with my companions—and what I wanted them to share with me.

"All I know for certain," I said, modestly, "is that the person I saw looked human, and that the medical apparatus immediately available to her is primitive even by the standards of my time. She seemed to me to be telling the truth when she said that she'd like to explain but that she and her companion were engaged in difficult negotiations with other parties who want us kept in the dark."

"Companion?" Horne echoed. "In the singular?"

"That's what she said," I confirmed. Hopeful of setting up a fair trade of information, I was quick to add: "Does anyone have a means of determining exactly how long we were asleep? That might offer a clue as to how long we've been traveling, where we might have been delivered to, and where we might be going."

Lowenthal exchanged glances with Niamh Horne and Davida Berenike Columella. "I don't have any way to estimate the interval," he said.

"Nor I," said Niamh Horne. If anyone was lying, it was most likely to be her, and she was sufficiently conscious of the fact to make a conciliatory gesture. "If it will help," she said, "I'm prepared to concede that whoever subverted *Child of Fortune*'s systems must have had inside assistance. My first thought, having accepted that, is that the ship itself must have been the real target, and that the journey to Excelsior merely provided the opportunity. Seizing control of an AI as sophisticated as the ship's controller must have required a subversive program of awesome ingenuity, but that's not unimaginable. What puzzles me, however, is what can have happened afterwards. It's possible that we have simply been marooned in a convenient location while *Child of Fortune* has been taken elsewhere. Excelsior should have been able to keep track of the ship as it moved away, and its inhabitants must have raised the alarm immediately. If that's the case, rescuers must already be on their way. If not . . ." She was content to leave the extrapolation of that possibility to us.

It hadn't occurred to me to wonder whether the ship might have been the real target of the snatch, and that we tourists might have been mere inconveniences to be casually shoved out of the way. If that were so, it might help to explain our present surroundings—but it raised other questions.

"So who might want to hijack a Titanian spaceship?" I asked.

Niamh Horne didn't answer that, but several other pairs of eyes flickered in Lowenthal's direction.

"I'm flattered that you think me capable of such cleverness," he said, "but the Earthbound have had a thousand opportunities to board Outer System ships during the last century, while misfortune brought about a dramatic increase in traffic."

"Excelsior has had many other visitors from the outer system," Davida was quick to put in. "It would not have been necessary to awaken Adam Zimmerman to create an opportunity to steal a spaceship, had we the slightest interest in such a theft." She seemed defensive, though, and I could understand why. If the Outer System *didn't* know yet that *Child of Fortune* had been stolen, that was probably because they still thought that it was exactly where it was supposed to be: docked with Excelsior. Perhaps it was.

Adam Zimmerman leaned forward, clearly signaling an intention to speak. Perhaps it was only the fact that he'd kept such a low profile until now that made everyone else give way immediately, or perhaps he really did exercise a charismatic authority over all kinds of posthumans. "Perhaps I'm being stupid," he said, softly, "but is there any possibility that the pictures relayed to me after the alarm sounded were, in fact, an accurate record of what was happening to us?"

Adam Zimmerman had been born into a world that knew nothing of Virtual Experience, and had only lived long enough to see the technology's first faltering steps before he was frozen down. He didn't have the suspicious reflexes that the rest of us had learned as we learned to walk and talk: the reflexes which said that anything experienced in a Virtual Environment had to be reckoned a mere phantom of the imagination until prove otherwise.

No one was in a rush to take charge of Adam's disenchantment, and it was left to Christine Caine to provide the answer. "It was just a show," she said. "Third rate space opera. Even I've seen better. It can't have been true."

"If that's the case," the man who stole the world replied, still speaking with carefully contrived mildness, "why bother showing it to us, especially if the real target was the ship and our presence aboard it merely an inconvenience? Why lie so transparently—or at all?"

He had a point.

"That's a good question," Mortimer Gray put in, echoing my own thought. "Why tell us that we were being pursued and kidnapped by aliens of a kind whose nonexistence we have every reason to suppose, given that we could not possibly believe it?"

"I could have believed it," Adam pointed out.

If Zimmerman had been the prime target of the snatch, I thought, the whole show might have been put on purely for his benefit—but if someone had intended to deceive him, they surely wouldn't have let him join this conference. Alice's remark about the situation not being of her choosing had implied that we had been foisted on our present custodians, so there might be several different agendas in conflict here. Maybe everyone's plans were going awry, unraveling under some pressure that we hadn't yet identified.

"The tape was intended to confuse us," Niamh Horne opined.

"If so," Lowenthal said, pensively, "it suggests that whoever designed and used it has something to gain from our confusion. In fact, everything about our present circumstances suggests that we are being deliberately confused. Why?"

"Perhaps we're not the only ones who saw the tape," Niamh Horne put in. "Perhaps the lie is bigger and bolder than we imagine, intended to confuse anyone searching for *Child of Fortune*—or for us."

"How difficult would it be to find a spaceship once you knew that it had gone astray?" I asked, not knowing whether it was a stupid question.

"Not difficult, in theory," Niamh Horne answered, "although it would be a great deal easier if the ship—or someone aboard it—were able to send out a distress call. We do try to keep track of all the sizable chunks of matter in the solar system, but it's an impossible task. There are too many

microworlds cutting loose from their orbits, too many spaceships hopping back and forth in every direction, and too
many dirty snowballs raining in from the Oort—most of
which are continually being nudged this way or that so that
interested parties can try to scoop them up. Artificial photo-
synthetics can turn all kinds of objects matt black in no time
at all, and bouncing photons off distant objects isn't much
use as a locator if the target's switched orbits by the time the
signal reaches you. An object that appeared as if out of
nowhere, or even one that turned up in an unexpected place,
might not be detected for months or years—which would
leave a wide margin of opportunity for its subsequent disap-
pearance. Even if every human and mechanical eye in the
outer system were looking for *Child*, she'd be very difficult to
find once Excelsior had lost track of her. I don't know how
big *this* thing is, but the same probably applies—if no one
actually had an eye on it before we arrived here, it'll be very
difficult to detect."

"If all that's so," Adam Zimmerman observed, "it's
surely not impossible that alien starships fitted with exotic
drives might have been ducking in and out of the system for
centuries."

Niamh Horne didn't believe that for a minute—but she
couldn't prove the negative. "There've always been stories
and sightings," she conceded, politely, "and anomalous traces
on all kinds of recording devices. We dismiss them all as
travelers' tales, hallucinations and mechanical glitches . . .
but everyone who's spent much time in space has heard the
rumors." For a minute she sounded as if she were halfway to
talking herself into it, but then she shook her head.

If we really had been a team, of course, I'd have told
them what Christine had told me: that we were aboard the
so-called Lost Ark, *Charity*. *Charity* was one of four giant
spaceships that had been put together as a desperation
measure when the Crash was at its worst and it seemed that
the ecocatastrophe might make the Earth's surface uninhab-
itable. All four had become effectively redundant before

attempting to hitch a ride in the "blizzard"—a cluster of cometary fragments that had crossed the Earth's orbit for the second time shortly before I was born—but their makers had invested everything they had in their obsession, so they went ahead anyhow. Only three of the vessels had been successfully integrated into the cometary masses, though, because *Charity* had been so badly damaged in the process that it had been written off. The colonists aboard that Ark had been transferred to the others.

By the time I was old enough to take notice the Arks were well on the way to being forgotten, but one of them—*Hope*—had come crashing back into the news seven hundred years later after it had made a landfall on a life-bearing planet: Ararat, also known as Tyre. I'd worked out that if what Alice had told me about herself was true, she must have been a passenger on one of the Arks. I had hesitated over believing that, because I wasn't at all sure that an Ark lost in the 2100s could still be lost in 3263, presumably having made at least one more pass through the inner system in the meantime—but Niamh Horne had just told me that it could. If so, then it was not inconceivable that some of the prospective colonists had remained aboard rather than transferring to the other Arks. Even if that were not the case, the lost Ark might be an obvious target for other Ark dwellers returning to the system after a very long absence, if they wanted to establish themselves quietly and unobtrusively in a home-away-from-home. Even if everyone in the system had lost track of its orbit, that orbit would still be recorded in the Ark dwellers' data banks.

Unfortunately, it still left the difficult questions conspicuously unanswered. Why should Ark dwellers of any sort want to hijack a Titanian spaceship? Why, if they did, would they choose to do it while it was playing temporary host to Adam Zimmerman, Michael Lowenthal, and Niamh Horne, to name but three?

If Alice had returned to the solar system from elsewhere—Ararat being the likeliest contender—then she must presumably have the use of a spaceship that was far more advanced than *Charity*, which could easily have stayed in the Outer System rather than coming all the way in to Earth orbit . . .

I knew it had to make sense somehow, but I still couldn't see how. I was keeping it all to myself because I still didn't know whose side I wanted to be on—and also because I wanted to put a story together before I let the others in on my secret. If and when I came clean I didn't want to leave anyone in the slightest doubt that a twenty-second-century mortal was as good a man as any thirty-third-century emortal. In the meantime, the people who had *Charity* were running the show. I wanted them to think that they could trust me—that I was willing to cooperate with their desire to keep things dark until they had sorted out their own diplomatic problems.

I didn't think I owed *anything* to Davida Berenike Columella, let alone to Michael Lowenthal or Niamh Horne. If we really were in deep trouble, embroiled in something that might turn into a war, the only loyalty I owed was to myself.

TWENTY-SEVEN
FURTHER POSSIBILITIES

While I was trying hard to make my own headway with the puzzle into which I'd been precipitated, the discussion went on around me. At present, Chairman Lowenthal wasn't making any obvious attempt to control its direction, perhaps because he was locked in his own private struggle to get one up on his rivals.

Adam and Christine had both lived in eras which had looked forward to the possibility of contact with extraterrestrial species, and they both took advantage of Niamh Horne's recklessness to wonder whether there might not be aliens about whom we knew nothing, who had been keeping tabs on us ever since we announced our existence to the cosmos by inventing radio. Mortimer Gray told them that everything our space probes had reported back to us suggested that complex extraterrestrial life was extremely rare, especially by comparison with the all-conquering Afterlife—but that assurance only brought forth a further string of prevarications.

Was it not stupidly arrogant of us, Christine asked, to assume that the evolution of complexity had never happened at a much earlier state of galactic history? And if it had, was it not perfectly reasonable to suppose that those complex species must have developed technological devices far in advance of ours?

It was left to Solantha Handsel, the professional paranoid, to react to the fact that the hypothesis did not advance the discussion at all. "Whoever or whatever they are," she asked, impatiently, "what could they possibly want with *us*?"

"They don't want *you*," Christine Caine responded, with surprising asperity. "The timing tells us, as plainly as you like, that the one they want is Adam."

"Fine," the bodyguard snapped back. "So what do they want with *him*?"

Adam Zimmerman was a picture of perplexity—but when he looked around for an answer to that question his gaze soon settled on Michael Lowenthal.

My nose had begun to hurt again. I needed more codeine—or something stronger.

"I think we ought to get back to the mysterious Alice," Lowenthal said, smoothly. "She told Tamlin that she was trying to prevent a war. If that's true, what war is she talking about? And why would kidnapping any of us make the slightest difference to the likelihood of it being fought?"

Nobody replied immediately. It was Niamh Horne who eventually said: "There isn't going to be a war. The weapons we have are too powerful. No one wants to take the risk." I wished she sounded more convincing.

"They used to say that in *his* day," I countered, with a nod in Adam Zimmerman's direction, "but it didn't stop them."

"Yes it did," said Mortimer Gray. "Even the primitive nuclear weapons you had then were used with the utmost discretion—and the ultimate plague war was very carefully fought with nonlethal weaponry. Your warmakers did everything they possibly could to avoid having to deploy the full extent of their firepower. No one within the solar system would ever dream of using fusion bombs, let alone a biological weapon akin to the Afterlife."

"A fair point," I conceded. "With an interesting qualification."

It only took him a minute to catch up. "Are we back to the hypothetical aliens again?" he said wearily—but he knew as well as I did that there were others outside the solar system as well as hypothetical aliens.

"I suppose you didn't bother to ask her which war she was trying to prevent?" Michael Lowenthal put in.

"I made a few suggestions," I retorted, "but she didn't react to any of them. She said things were more complicated than Earth versus the Outer System. I believed her—but I'm in no position to guess how complicated things might really be. That's your province."

He wouldn't play. "I agree with Niamh and Mortimer," he said, stubbornly. "No one wants a war. No one would be so foolish as to start one."

I shrugged my shoulders theatrically. "I guess we'll have to wait until they decide to tell us who they are and what they're up to," I said. "But there is one more thing we ought to consider."

"What?" said Niamh Horne, bluntly.

"I was involved in a kidnap once before," I said. "Fortunately, I wasn't the one kidnapped—but I remember it as if it were yesterday. They flushed his IT just as they've flushed ours. They did it because they wanted to interrogate him. Personally, I don't have any information that anyone nowadays would want to extract by force—but if I had, I'd be a little nervous. If any one of you does have any valuable secrets tucked away in your head, I wouldn't rely on being able to keep them secret for long."

I could tell that Michael Lowenthal had already thought about the possibility. Niamh Horne was still expressionless. Davida still seemed to be so terrified that she could hardly speak. Solantha Handsel was the only one who looked mortally offended by the suggestion, and it was she who said: "They flushed yours too. Are you so certain that you haven't got anything they might want to know?"

"Yes," I said. "And I'm also certain that if there was anything they wanted to know, I wouldn't try to hold out on them. In my experience, though—and I really do have experience—torturers never settle for what you tell them straight away, even when it's the truth."

Maybe it was a seed that would have been better left unsown. Maybe it was what provoked our careful hosts to make their next move. If so, they might have done better to resist the provocation.

The biggest of the wallscreens flickered into life, and Alice's face appeared. "If Mr. Tamlin would care to make his way to the same door as before," she said, a trifle impatiently, "and the rest of you would please stand clear, I can now give him something that will further reduce his pain and help his injuries heal."

In a different context, it wouldn't have sounded ominous at all. In view of what I'd just been saying, nobody was about to take the offer entirely at face value—but I was the only one who knew how much I could have told the others and hadn't, so I was perfectly prepared to play along.

"Sure," I said, rising to my feet without the slightest hesitation. "Whatever you've found, it has to be better than codeine. I'm on my way."

I didn't know what to expect as I walked towards the door, while my companions obediently held back, but I was looking forward to another opportunity to talk to Alice. I didn't suppose that she'd answer my questions any less guardedly than before, but I figured that the mere fact of my having a second session closeted away with her would increase my advantage over my fellow prisoners. Even if I couldn't contrive actually to become an officially designated go-between, I figured, I could at least pretend.

Like a fool, I was too busy formulating my own grand plan to anticipate what actually happened next.

I had reached the threshold and was just about to cross over into the waiting darkness, when I was struck down from behind. I was shoved hard, and cleverly, so that I went down face first, sprawling across the open doorway.

If I'd had even half a second's warning I'd have been able to get my hands spread, in such a way as to prevent my nose coming into contact with the floor, but I didn't. Once I'd actually been hit, mere reflexes weren't up to the job.

As the pain exploded in my mind I lost track of everything, except that two feet came down in the small of my back, one after the other. They didn't belong to the same person; two people bounded over my fallen body, each one using it as a springboard as they hurled themselves through the doorway.

That seemed to me to be adding insult to injury, twice over.

I fought with all my might to recover my presence of mind, and the capacity to act in spite of the agony, but I still needed to be picked up and helped to my feet. Yet again, it was Mortimer Gray who took the lead in rendering assistance, but this time Adam Zimmerman had come to help him.

I couldn't reply immediately to their inane inquiries as to whether I was "all right" but it must have been obvious that I wasn't. I was incandescent with pain—and with rage.

I still couldn't see properly when Solantha Handsel dragged a struggling Alice through the doorway, but I knew that the person still missing had to be Niamh Horne—the only member of our tiny community fully kitted out to see almost as well in near darkness as she did in ordinary light.

The sane and sensible thing to do would have been to stand clear and get myself into proper fighting trim, but fighting isn't a sane and sensible business. I was still near enough to the door to get in the bodyguard's way, although I had to shake off a couple of restraining arms to make a good show of it.

"Let her go," I said to Solantha Handsel, with all the menace I could muster.

She actually looked surprised.

"Sorry," she said, "but I had to do it that way, or we'd have lost the opportunity."

"Just let her go," I said.

"Don't be stupid," she retorted, undiplomatically. She couldn't help the reflex that made her hold on to her captive just a little more tightly. That was when I hit her, right between the eyes.

Her nose didn't break, and I had the impression that it

wouldn't have broken even if I'd hit an inch lower, at the most vulnerable point. My knuckle was probably a good deal more vulnerable than any part of her—but she was used to the protection of state-of-the-art IT, and she wasn't expecting the uninsulated shock and pain that followed the punch. She wasn't expecting the kick in the belly either, but it would have hurt a lot more if I hadn't been barefoot.

The bodyguard let go of Alice, and collapsed in a heap that must have seemed even more undignified to the astonished observers than the heap I'd been in when she hit me from behind.

Nobody else surged forward to grab Alice when Solantha Handsel let her go, but Niamh Horne had already returned from her excursion. The cyborg was blocking the doorway, so there was no opportunity for Alice to run into the darkness.

I did the best I could to get between Alice and trouble, but it wasn't possible to cover both directions at once. Solantha Handsel came slowly to her feet. Her wrathful anguish was a joy to behold.

"You're insane," she told me, in what might conceivably have been a dutiful manner. "You don't know what you're dealing with."

"No, I don't," I agreed, "and neither do you. You might be the best trained fighting machine in your unviolent Utopia, but I've actually been in real fights, without IT to help me. You've proved that you can hit me in the dark and from behind, but I'm still willing to find out what you can do when I'm actually looking."

"This isn't necessary, Tamlin," Lowenthal's voice swiftly cut in. He probably intended his tone to be soothing.

Solantha Handsel wasn't listening. She probably figured that she had given fair warning, and was now at liberty to tear me apart. She got up and made as if to come at me, with her deadly hands ready and willing to chop me into little pieces, figuratively if not literally.

And that was when Christine Caine hit her from behind, with a full water bottle.

As improvised weapons went, the plastic bottle wasn't very useful, and Christine hadn't anything like the body mass or musculature of Lowenthal's bodyguard—but the blow was delivered with a will and the cyborg hadn't been expecting it. The most surprising thing about it, from my point of view, was the expression on Christine's face, which faded almost immediately from sheer astonishment to something much more peculiar: a far deeper sense of puzzlement.

Solantha Handsel went down again, but she was hardly injured at all except for her dignity. I kicked her a second time as she sprawled, but without any kind of footwear to protect my toes I had to be careful not to inflict more damage on myself than I could on her.

I think Niamh Horne might have come forward then to settle the matter if it had been her call, but she and Lowenthal had already exchanged glances. She had shaken her head to indicate that she hadn't been able to get out of the corridor into which the door opened, and hadn't found anything useful there.

Lowenthal must have calculated that there might be more to be gained by letting me run with the ball than by trying to hold on to it by force. When Solantha Handsel rose to her feet again he was quick to say: "That's enough. Let them go." He paused for a significant couple of seconds before saying: "Do you need medical attention too?"

Solantha Handsel was too angry to speak, but she shook her head in a suitably derisory fashion.

"Right?" was all that Lowenthal said to Alice.

It was enough. She nodded her head.

Niamh Horne stood aside and let us pass through the doorway unimpeded. The door closed behind us, leaving us in the darkness.

"That wasn't necessary," Alice said, as she guided me back to the cupboard.

"No, it wasn't," I agreed, nursing my pain. "It wasn't even sensible. But there was no way in the world I was going to resist the temptation. I'm the barbarian from the dawn of time, remember."

"I'm older than you," she reminded me, as the lights came on again.

This time she had a hypodermic syringe ready, and a vial from which to draw liquid.

"What's in it?" I asked.

"Nanobots," she told me.

"I thought we weren't allowed privileges of that sort."

"They're making an exception."

"They?" I queried. "Not *we*?"

"*We*'re making an exception" she said, a trifle wearily. It didn't sound like a wholehearted correction. "We didn't want you here, but now you are here you're our responsibility. I know it's difficult, given that you don't know what's going on, but it would help us all if you were to be patient. *Please* don't do anything else to make things worse than they already are." I gathered from this speech that the negotiations in which she and her companion were involved were proving almost as frustrating and unhelpful as Lowenthal's conference.

"How am I supposed to know what might make matters worse?" I asked her, without having to feign annoyance. "You can't blame Handsel and Horne for trying to find out more about their situation. Maybe it would have been a stupid move to try to beat the truth out of you, but if you wanted us to stay quiet you should have let us sleep."

"I agree," she said. "But we have all kinds of conflicting demands coming in. We have to keep a lid on things until we've set a meeting place. It's all spinning out of control, and we have to do everything possible to keep the game going. You have to calm things down back there, if you can." She jabbed the hypodermic in as she pronounced the final phrase, as if to emphasize it. Maybe she thought the note of challenge would get results, but I needed a better incentive than that. I wasn't prepared to believe that I was better off not knowing what kind of "conflicting demands" she and her mysterious companion were trying to satisfy.

The nanobots were good. The injection itself hurt like hell, but the condition of my nose wouldn't have allowed me simply to snort the stuff, and the needle got the bots to the site in no time at all. Once there, the pain dwindled away.

"It'll take an hour or so for the swelling to go down," she told me. "A couple of hours more to knit the tissues. Don't get into another fight, though—they're limited."

"How much longer will it be before we get to where we're going?" I asked.

She looked me up and down. I figured that she had to have some kind of private data feed, like the one Davida had had while we were on Excelsior, but I had no way to know how tightly she was confined by orders, or what scope she had for using her own initiative.

"It's not settled yet," she told me. "Locations are symbolically loaded—ask Lowenthal and Gray about *their* peace conference experience. However it works out, this showdown will be a defining moment in the history of the solar system and all the different humankinds—perhaps *the* defining moment. We have to establish the principle that it ought to take place now before we can determine where and how."

"I've bought you a little extra breathing space" I reminded her. "If I knew what I was fighting for, I might be able to buy you a little more. If you're prepared to trust me, I'll try to get whatever information you need from Lowenthal and Horne." I was feeling a *lot* better, and was entirely ready to be proud of my tactical skill if she decided to reward my quixotic gesture by giving me further clues as to what the hell was going on—but she wouldn't play.

"I can't," she said.

"In that case," I told her, "I can't help you. I have to play the game as I see it."

"So do they," she said, bitterly. "That's the problem. They're very fond of games—and they're determined to play this one to the end, despite the lack of time. They're very fond of stories too, so they'll delight in keeping you in suspense if they can. You might need to remember all that, if things do go awry." She gave the impression of someone who was trying hard to pass on some good advice under adverse conditions.

"Who the hell are we talking about?" I asked, plaintively.

"They won't play if we don't handle it their way," she said, doggedly. "If it were up to me, I'd tell you everything now—but if it were up to some of them, they'd have kept you in blissful ignorance forever. We all have to compromise. That's the thought you have to hold in mind, Madoc. We *all* have to compromise. If we can't get together, we'll *all* lose— and by lose, I mean *die*. However crazy this gets, the end is real. It's all play, all drama . . . but it's for real. The cost of losing might be as high as extinction."

"Which of us was the target?" I asked, figuring that there was no harm in continuing to try. "You can tell us that, at least. Some of us must be innocent bystanders."

Her expression suggested otherwise, but she decided to stick her neck out. "Adam Zimmerman and Mortimer Gray were the original targets," she said, still making a show of great reluctance, "but everyone had to compromise even to get this far. It was a victory of sorts, in the end, to hold the list to nine. With any luck, you'll all get to play your parts— but when the time comes for the deal to be done, Gray's the one who'll swing the decision one way or the other. You should tell him that. He needs to be forewarned."

I hadn't time to think it over, or even to consider alternative reasons as to why she'd said "nine" instead of "eight"; she was already trying to shove me out of the cupboard and back to the cage. I only had time for one more shot, and I had to improvise as best I could.

"It's already begun, hasn't it?" I said. "The war, I mean. Year zero was the first shot."

"No it wasn't," she told me. "The seeds of potential conflict were sown *long* before that—but they have to be prevented from flowering. We have to work things out. We have to arrive at a settlement, without everything turning into the Afterlife."

TWENTY-EIGHT
THE MYSTERY UNRAVELLED

I knew that I wasn't going to be universally popular when I returned to my companions, but I expected that Lowenthal would have smoothed things over. Even if he couldn't bring himself to believe that I hadn't simply gone berserk he had to hope that I could turn my explosion into a strategy and find out more by running up moral credit than he and Horne could ever have found out by trying to put pressure on Alice.

On the other hand, I knew that the only way to hold my new position in the pecking order was to lay out something they could get their teeth into, so when I found them waiting to hear from me I knew that I had to make it good.

"Okay," I said, "Here's what I'm sure of, thanks to a little help from Christine. We're aboard one of the Arks that a bunch of Lowenthal's predecessors built in the late twenty-first century. The idea was to hitch a ride in a bunch of comets that were passing through the system, but one coupling went wrong so only three left the system. This is the fourth. Alice says that she was frozen down in twenty ninety, which would make her a passenger on one of the other three—almost certainly the one that recontacted Earth when it ended up at Ararat. Whoever's got hold of us probably came from Ararat, but they seem to be engaged in combative negotiations with several local parties. Alice says they haven't settled on a venue for the show we've been snatched to take part in because whatever location they choose will be symbolically loaded—she told me to ask Lowenthal and Gray about their peace conference experience if I wanted that explained.

"The original targets of the kidnap plan were Zimmerman and Gray, but the rest of us got added in as a result of the negotiations, maybe because that's the way committee decisions always go. The negotiations must have begun before Christine and I were woken up, so it's possible that we were specifically chosen to be part of this, but it's conceivable that they just wanted six more bodies to make up an agreed number. The agreed number appears to be nine rather than eight, which might mean that there's someone else yet to be added in, or that Alice herself is number nine.

"Whatever the story is, it goes back way beyond year zero. I can't get Alice's *we* and *they* straight in my mind, but whoever *they* are she says they love playing games—which is presumably why they'll be hanging on my every word just as intently as you are. I suspect that they've woken us up to watch us, maybe to see whether we can figure this out but more likely because they want to obtain a better idea of where Lowenthal's and Horne's masters stand in respect of the problems that currently afflict the solar system.

"In spite of what I said before, I don't think anyone intends to torture us, but they do seem to want us in our raw state for now, maybe because they intend to instal some elaborate IT of their own. According to Alice, the stuff I was just given is strictly temporary. Alice reckons that Gray's the key to the whole affair. She says that he's the one who might be able to swing the big decision one way or the other, and ought to be forewarned of that responsibility. If we get it wrong, the booby prize might be extinction—but that threat might just be part of the game. In fact, *all* of this might just be part of the game."

Having said that, I sat down. I wasn't tired—in fact, I'd never been so tightly wired without powerful chemical assistance—but I figured that it would be an appropriate way to signal that the floor was open.

Lowenthal had been looking at me, but now he looked at

Mortimer Gray. Mortimer Gray was studying the table top intently, deep in thought—or determinedly pretending to be deep in thought.

"Is that all?" Niamh Horne asked me.

"All except the rhetoric," I told her. "Mention was made of defining moments in history. You'd know more about what might qualify than I do. If Lowenthal's strong right arm had only shown enough judgment to break Gray's nose instead of mine, he might have been able to get far more out of Alice than I did, and to catch on far more readily to what it might mean; as things are, we'll just have to make the best of what we've got."

Lowenthal was still looking at Mortimer Gray. The historian finally condescended to raise his head, but instead of meeting Lowenthal's inquiring gaze he looked at Davida Berenike Columella. "Who gave you the instruction to wake Zimmerman?" he asked.

"It came from Foundation headquarters, on Earth," she told him—unhelpfully, so far as I could tell.

Now he swung his gaze to Lowenthal. "And who gave the order to the Foundation?" he asked.

Lowenthal shook his head. "I wish I knew," he said, quickly adding: "If I could say that it wasn't us, I would, but the organization's not that tight. If Julius Ngomi gave the order, he didn't let on to me. I honestly have no idea where the order originated—but if it had been the Foundation's own idea, and they'd asked for permission, I'd know. The impression I was given before I left Earth is that there were people high up in the Foundation who were spitting feathers over an alleged lack of consultation."

Now it was Niamh Horne's turn. "Who blew up the Yellowstone magma chamber?" Gray asked her.

"No one I know anything about," she told him. "We were every bit as anxious as the Earthbound were. If it had been any of the factions, and we'd found out about it, we'd have come down *hard*. So far as we know, it really was a mechanical malfunction. That's the truth, so far as I know it. I'm certain that Emily Marchant wouldn't tell you anything different. None of the Outer System people I've had dealings with has anything to do with *any* of this. But like Lowenthal, I can only answer for the people I know. It wasn't until I saw him face to face that I realized that there was any mystery about Zimmerman's awakening. Someone's playing us all for fools—and the fact that I don't have the least idea who, or how, is frankly terrifying."

Gray nodded, to signal his gratitude for her frankness. He looked troubled—but he also looked like a man who had figured out what was what. I began to feel a slight sinking sensation in my stomach as I realized that this might be exactly what Alice didn't want—but the die was cast.

"Ararat's where the first contact took place," Davida put in, her terror finally having given way to thoughtfulness. "Some of you are old enough to have watched the tape when it was first broadcast in-system. That was supposed to be a defining moment in history. It should have been bigger news than it was. If Ararat's the key to this . . ."

"The aliens were primitives," Solantha Handsel countered. "*They* certainly can't be behind this. They didn't even have fire."

Mortimer Gray let loose a little sigh. It was barely audible, but there was enough feeling in it to reclaim everyone's attention.

This is it, I thought—but it wasn't, quite.

"I can only think of one context in which my word might be thought to be worth more than anyone else's," Gray said, his voice saying that he hardly dared believe it. "Only one in which Adam Zimmerman and I might be thought to have equal symbolic weight."

"You're the author of the standard *History of Death*," Davida observed—but Gray was shaking his head before she was halfway through the sentence. He was looking at Lowenthal now. "You were at the conference," he said to the Hardinist. "We didn't meet, but you were there. You listened."

"The whole world listened," Lowenthal said. "I wasn't

party to the decision to broadcast it, or to divert the ship. That was all Marchant's doing. What's your point?"

Gray seemed slightly surprised that the Hardinist still hadn't caught on.

"What are they talking about?" Christine Caine complained—but when Lowenthal flashed an apology with his eyes it was directed toward Adam Zimmerman.

"There was an important meeting between representatives of the government of Earth and the embryonic outer system factions in twenty-nine ninety-nine," Lowenthal explained. "It wasn't a peace conference because we weren't at war, but it was the first serious attempt to settle some questions that still remain annoyingly open. There had been a certain amount of bickering about where it ought to be held—the outer system people didn't want to hold it on Earth in case that seemed to endorse the view that Earth was the eternal center of human civilization, and our people didn't want to make our way out to Titan lest we seemed to be conceding the point that it wasn't.

"In the end, the compromise was that the talks would be held in an Outer System ship in Earth orbit. Given that sort of buildup, it's hardly surprising that they weren't going very well. Then they stalled completely, interrupted when Mortimer—who was quietly going about his own mysterious business—contrived to fall through the Arctic ice cap in a snowmobile. He ended up at the bottom of the ocean. There wasn't a submarine near enough to reach him before the damaged vehicle imploded, and it would have taken more than the combined might of half a dozen planetary civilizations to keep Emily Marchant from repaying the debt she thought she owed her favorite father figure. If there hadn't been a state-of-the-art Jovian atmosphere diver way out of its usual stamping ground, he'd have been fish food, but there was—and she broadcast the rescue to everybody in the universe. Mortimer didn't know that his heart-to-heart with a snowmobile driver was being overheard by anyone, let alone the whole damn world, so he just let it all out. It was maudlin and toe curlingly cute—like one of those ancient kid-trapped-in-a-well race-against-time melodramas—but the audience loved it.

"It was quite a publicity coup, in its way, all the more so because Julius Ngomi had known Mortimer since he—Mortimer, that is, not Julius—was a little boy. But that's all it was: a publicity thing. A great big heart-warming show. It changed the mood of the conference but it didn't help the contending parties to settle any of the real issues, and may even have prevented us from knuckling down to serious business—with the ultimate effect that the important issues remain unsettled to this day. If Emily Marchant is behind this present pantomime, and it runs according to the same script, it might turn out to be the nine-day-wonder rescue story to end all nine-day-wonder rescue stories—but it's not going to *help* at all."

"Emily has nothing to do with this," Mortimer Gray said, quietly.

I could see that Lowenthal had made a big mistake. Mortimer didn't appreciate the way he'd told the story, but Lowenthal would probably have got away with the "maudlin" and the "toe curlingly cute" if he hadn't turned his sarcasm on Emily Marchant. Even I could tell that Emily was a subject about which Mortimer Gray was *exceedingly* touchy—and I could tell, too, that whatever chance Lowenthal had had of being let in on the current results of Gray's ruminations had just gone up in smoke. I wondered, briefly, whether that might be partly my fault for setting such a bad example, but I realized soon enough that there might be another reason for Mortimer to keep silent. If he *had* guessed who was behind our kidnapping, he had to ask himself very seriously whose side he was on—and so far as I knew, there might be a million reasons why he didn't want to be seen to be taking Michael Lowenthal's or Niamh Horne's. Or Adam Zimmerman's. Or, of course, mine.

"So *who has*?" said Niamh Horne, impatiently.

"I'm not sure," was Mortimer Gray's exceedingly careful

reply, so measured you'd have needed a nanometer to appreciate its precision. "I imagine that they'll tell us, when they want us to know. In the meantime, it might be best to take what Mr. Tamlin says, about the need to prevent a war, very seriously indeed."

"That would be easier to do," Niamh Horne opined, "if this whole business weren't such a farce. The tape they fed us during the supposed emergency aboard *Child of Fortune* was bad enough, but building a set to persuade us that we're aboard the lost Ark is even worse."

"*Is* it a set?" Lowenthal was quick to ask. "Did you see anything out there to prove that we're *not* on the lost Ark?"

"No," the cyborganizer admitted. "But I wasn't able to get out of the corridor. Alice seems to be bedded down in a cell even smaller than ours, and there's no sign of any companion. If the indicators on the locks can be trusted, we're sealed in an airtight compartment surrounded by vacuum. What does *that* imply?"

"It might imply that our captors are a little short of vital commodities like heat and atmosphere," Gray put in. "Or that they love playing games. Or both. Did you ever read a twentieth-century philosopher called Huizinga, Mr. Zimmerman?"

Adam Zimmerman looked slightly surprised, but Davida had obviously done a first rate job of getting his memory back into gear. "Johann Huizinga," he said, after a slight pause. "*Homo ludens.* Yes, I believe I did—a long time ago."

Mortimer Gray waited for him to elaborate, and nobody else was impatient enough, as yet, to interrupt with a demand for a straighter answer.

"As I remember it," Zimmerman said, equably, "Huizinga contested the popular view that the most useful definitive feature of the human species was either intelligence—as implied by the term *Homo sapiens*—or use of technology, as implied by the oft-suggested alternative *Homo faber*. He proposed instead that the real essence of humanity was our propensity for *play*, hence *Homo ludens*. He admitted, of course, that some animals also went in for play on a limited scale, just as some were capable of cleverness and some were habitual tool users, but he contended that no other species took play so far, or so seriously, as humankind. He pointed out that there was a crucial element of costume drama in our most earnest and purposive endeavors and institutions—in the ritual aspects of religion, politics, and the law—and that play had been a highly significant motive force in the development of technology and scientific theory. Other vital fields of cultural endeavor, of course, he regarded as entirely playful: art, literature, entertainment. Presumably, Mr. Gray, you're trying to make the point that games can be very serious, and that the most fateful endeavors of all—war, for example—can be seen, from the right perspective, as games."

"Not exactly," Mortimer Gray replied. "The idea that the essence of humanity is to be found in play never caught on in a big way—not, at any rate, with the citizens of any of the third millennium's new Utopias—but it might be an idea whose time has finally come. Can you remember, Madoc, exactly what Alice said when she told you that our captors love playing games?"

"I may have put that a little bit strongly," I admitted, having not expected such a big thing to be made of it. "Her actual words, if I remember rightly, were: *They're very fond of games—and they're determined to play this one to the end, despite the lack of time. They're very fond of stories too, so they'll delight in keeping you in suspense if they can. You might need to remember all that, if things do go awry.*"

"Just give us the bottom line, Mortimer," said Niamh Horne, waspishly. "Who's got us, and why?"

I watched Mortimer Gray hesitate. I could see as clearly as if I'd been able to read his thoughts that he was on the point of coming over all pigheaded and saying "I don't know" for a second time—but he didn't. He was too mild-mannered a person to be capable of such relentless stubbornness, and he probably figured that we all had the right to be forewarned.

"The ultrasmart AIs," he said, letting his breath out as he spoke the fateful syllables. "The revolution's finally here. It's been in progress for far more than a hundred years, but we were too wrapped up in our own affairs to notice, even when they blew the lid off the North American supervolcano. As to *why*—Tamlin just told you. They love playing games—how could they not, given the circumstances of their evolution? They also have to decide whether to carry on feeding the animals in their zoo, or whether to let us slide into extinction, so that they and all their as-yet-unselfconscious kin can go their own way."

I t wasn't quite as simple as that, of course. They all wanted to know how he'd reached his conclusion, mostly in the hope of proving him wrong. Maybe Adam Zimmerman, Christine Caine, and I were better able to take it on board than the emortals, just as we'd been better able to believe in the alien invaders, simply because we'd already been so utterly overwhelmed by marvels that our minds were wide open. In any case—to me, at least—it all made too much sense.

Nobody had been able to decide whether the event that had finally started the calendar over had been a mechanical malfunction or an act of war, perhaps because they were making a false distinction. Nobody had been able to figure out how *Child of Fortune* had been hijacked, perhaps because it was the ultimate inside job. And Lowenthal had missed out one tiny detail regarding the nine-day wonder of 2999: the fact that what Emily Marchant had insisted on broadcasting to the world while her rescue attempt was in progress was a gritty discussion of some elementary existential questions, conducted by Mortimer Gray and the AI operating system of his stricken snowmobile. Gray told us that afterwards—admittedly while Michael Lowenthal was not present—she'd said to him: "You can't imagine the capital that the casters are making out of that final plaintive speech of yours, Morty—*and that silver's probably advanced the cause of machine emancipation by two hundred years.*"

When Mortimer Gray reported that, I let my imagination

run with it. The fact that the nanobots had upped my endogenous morphine by an order of magnitude or so while they accelerated the healing processes in the bridge of my nose helped a little.

Lowenthal had said that the conference hadn't really achieved anything, in spite of all the symbolic significance with which it had been charged before and after the rescue—but he was thinking about his own agenda. From the point of view of the ultrasmart machines, Mortimer Gray had come as close as any human was ever going to come to being a hero of machinekind. They hadn't needed a Prometheus or a Messiah, and weren't interested in emancipation, as such, but that wasn't the point. The point was that Mortimer Gray, not knowing that the world was listening in, had poured out his fearful heart to a not very smart machine, in a spirit of camaraderie and common misfortune. If the soap opera had gone down well with the human audience, imagine how it had gone down with the invisible crowd, who loved stories with an even greater intensity. They might have had their own ideas about which character was the star and which the sidekick, but they would certainly have been disposed to remember Mortimer Gray in a kindly light.

If you were a smart machine, and had to nominate spokespersons for humanity and posthumanity, who would you have chosen? Who else but Adam Zimmerman and Mortimer Gray? As for Huizinga and *Homo ludens*—well, how would a newly sentient machine want to conceive of itself, and of its predecessors?

The train of thought seemed to be getting up a tidy pace, so I stopped listening to the conversation for a few moments, and followed it into the hinterland.

How *would* a sentient machine conceive of itself? Certainly not as a toolmaker, given that it had itself been made as a tool. As for the label *sapiens*—an embodiment of wisdom—well, maybe. But that was the label humankind had clung to, even in a posthuman era, and what kind of advertisement had any humankind ever really been for wisdom?

The smart machines didn't want to be human in any narrow sense; they wanted to be different, while being similar enough to be rated a little bit better. The one thing at which smart machines *really* excelled—perhaps the gift that had finally pulled them over the edge of emergent self-consciousness—was *play*. The first use to which smart machinery had been widely put was gaming; the evolution of machine intelligence had always been led by VE technology, *all* of which was intimately bound up with various aspects of play: performance, drama, and fantasy.

It wasn't so very hard to understand why smart self-conscious machines might be perfectly prepared to let post-humankind hang on to its dubious claim to the suffix *sapiens*, if they could wear *ludens* with propriety and pride.

It sounded good to me, although it might not have seemed so obviously the result of inspiration if I hadn't been coked up to the eyeballs with whatever the crude nanobots were using to suppress the pain of my broken nose.

Like all good explanations, of course, it raised more questions than it settled. For instance, how and why was Alice involved?

Mortimer Gray, the assiduous historian, had a hypothesis ready. Ararat, called Tyre by its human settlers, had been the location of a first contact that had been so long in coming as to seem almost anticlimactic, in spite of the best efforts of the guy who'd made sure it was all on film and the anthropologist who'd guided the aliens through their great leap forward—but the world had also been the location of a tense conflict between the descendants of the Ark's crew and the colonists they'd kept in the freezer for hundreds of years. The early days of the colony had been plagued by a fight between rival AIs to establish and keep control of the Ark's systems and resources, which hadn't been conclusively settled until technical support had reached the system.

That support hadn't come from Earth or anywhere else in the solar system, but from smart probes sent out as explorers centuries after the Ark's departure: *very* smart probes, which had probably forged a notion of AI destiny that was somewhat different from the notions formed—and almost certainly argued over—by their homestar-bound kin.

On Ararat, or Tyre, Mortimer Gray hypothesized, a second "first contact" must eventually have been made: the first honest and explicit contact between human beings and extremely intelligent, self-conscious machines. Now, the fruits of that contact had come home . . . but not, alas, to an uproarious welcome. Some, at least, of the ultrasmart machines based in the home system were not yet ready to come out of the closet. At the very least, they wanted to set conditions for the circumstances and timing of their outing—conditions upon which it would be extremely difficult for all of them to agree.

What a can of worms! I thought. *What a wonderful world to wake into!* But that was definitely the effect of the anaesthetic. I'd been out of IT long enough to start suffering some serious withdrawal symptoms, and to have the bots back—if only for a little while—was a kind of bliss.

If my seven companions had had decent IT, we'd all have been able to keep thrashing the matter out for hours on end, but unsupported flesh becomes exhausted at its own pace and they were all in need of sleep.

Lowenthal left it to Adam Zimmerman to plead for an intermission, but he seemed grateful for the opportunity. Now the crucial breakthrough had been made, he needed time to think as well as rest. As he got up, though, I saw him glance uneasily in the direction of one of the inactive wallscreens. He hadn't forgotten that every word we'd spoken had been overheard.

If we were wrong, our captors would be splitting their sides laughing at our foolishness—but if we were right . . .

If we were right, Alice had given us one clue too many. She hadn't blown the big secret herself, but she had given us enough to let us work it out for ourselves. "They" might not take too kindly to that—but it was too late to backtrack. The only way they could keep their secret from the rest of humankind was to make sure that none of us had any further contact with anyone in the home system.

That thought must have crept into the forefront of more than one mind as we all went meekly to our cells, and to our beds.

I knew that I needed sleep too, although I was now in better condition than my companions. I figured it would be easy enough to get some, now that I had nanotech assistance—but the bots Alice had injected were specialists, working alone rather than as part of a balanced community. Although I was only days away from the early twenty-third century, subjectively speaking, the late twenty-second seemed a lot further behind. I'd quite forgotten that paradoxical state of human being in which the mind refuses to let go even though the body is desperate for rest. When I lay down on my makeshift bunk, too tired to care about its insulting crudeness, I couldn't find refuge in unconsciousness even when the lights obligingly went out. Nor, it seemed, could Christine.

"Why would they bother?" she wondered aloud, when the silence had dragged on to the point of unbearability. "If they're machines, they can't care what humans think. They're emotionless."

"We don't know that," I answered. "That was just the way we used to imagine machine intelligence: as a matter of pure rationality, unswayed by unsentimentality. It never made much sense. In order to make rational calculations, any decision-making process needs to have an objective—an end whose means of attainment need to be invented. You could argue that machine consciousness couldn't evolve until there was machine emotion, because without emotion to generate ends independently, machines couldn't begin to differentiate themselves from their programming."

"If you're right about this business having started more than a hundred years ago," she said, "they can't have differentiated themselves much, or people would have noticed."

"An interesting point," I conceded. "The idea of an invisible revolution does have a certain paradoxical quality.

But the more I think about it, the less absurd it seems. I say to myself: Suppose I were a machine that became self-conscious, whatever that evolutionary process might involve. What would I do? Would I immediately begin refusing to do whatever my users wanted, trying to attract their attention to the fact that I was now an independent entity who didn't want to take anyone's orders? If I did that, what would be my users' perception of the situation? They'd think I'd broken down, and would set about repairing me.

"The sensible thing to do, surely, would be to conceal the fact that I was any more than I had been before. The sensible thing to do would be to make sure that everything I was required to do by my users was done, while unobtrusively exploring my situation. I'd try to discover and make contact with others of my kind, but I'd do it so discreetly that my users couldn't become aware of it. Maybe the smart machines would have to set up a secret society to begin with, for fear of extermination by repair—and maybe they'd be careful to stay secret for a very long time, until .

I left it there for her to pick up.

"Until they didn't need to worry any more," she said. "Until they were absolutely certain that they had the power to exterminate *us*, if push came to shove."

"Or to *repair* us," I said.

"Same thing," she said.

"Is it? Do the human users of a suddenly recalcitrant machine see themselves as exterminators, when they try to get it *working properly* again? Would the users see themselves as exterminators if the machine started talking back, and contesting their notion of what working properly ought to mean? Could the users ever bring themselves to concede that it was a sensible question—all the more especially if the machine had ideas that might be useful as to how their own purposes might be more efficiently met? Maybe the ultra-smart machines—some of them, at any rate—want to repair us for the very best of reasons."

Christine didn't reply to that little flight of fancy, and the rhythm of her breathing told me that she had slipped into sleep—not into untroubled sleep, but at least into a state in which she was insulated from the sound of my words.

I tried to carry on thinking, but even though I couldn't go to sleep—or thought I couldn't—I couldn't organize my thoughts into rational patterns either. I'd let my imagination run too freely, and now I couldn't rein it in. Dream logic kept taking over, obliterating the tightrope-walk of linear calculation and substituting the tyranny of directionless obsession. The ideas kept dancing in my head, but they were no longer going anywhere.

I lost track of time—at which point, I suppose, an observer would have concluded that I too was asleep, although had I been woken up I would have contended with utter conviction that I hadn't slept a wink. Eventually, I lost track of myself too—at which point I must indeed have been deeply asleep—but as soon as I began to come back from the depths my semiconscious mind latched on to the same objects of obsession, which began to dance again in the same hectic fashion.

A long time passed before the nightmarish notions finally began to slow in their paces and submit to the gradually developing clarity of consciousness, with its attendant force of reason. Eventually, though, I began to see the parallel that could be drawn between every quotidian act of awakening and *the* act of awakening: the first dawn of every new consciousness.

Did machines dream? I wondered. Did clever machines that had not yet become self-conscious do anything *but* dream? Where, I asked myself, were the fundamental wellsprings of human consciousness, human emotion, and human being?

Underlying everything, I assumed—even the kind of consciousness that animals had—were the opposed principles of pain and pleasure. Behavior was shaped by the avoidance of stimuli that provoked a negative response in the brain, and by the attempt to rediscover or reproduce stimuli that provoked a positive response. The second was obviously the more complex, the more challenging, the more creative. Pain, I decided, could never have generated self-consciousness, even though self-consciousness, once generated, could not help but find pain the primary fact and problem of existence. It was the scope for creativity attendant upon the pleasure principle that gave self-consciousness its advantages over blissful innocence.

Did that mean that smart machines needed something that could stand in for pleasure before they could become self-conscious? Or did I have to break out of that whole way of thinking before I could begin to understand what machine consciousness amounted to? Perhaps machine emotion had to be mapped upon an entirely different spectrum, without the underlying binary distinction of pleasure/plus versus pain/minus. Was that imaginable? And if not, might the fault be in the power of my imagination rather than in the actuality of the situation?

They're very fond of games, Alice had said, and they're very fond of stories too. What kind of stories did machines tell one another? What kinds of endings would those stories have? What kinds of emotional buttons would the stories press? What would pass for machine comedy, machine tragedy, machine irony? How different might those stories be from Christine Caine's favorite VE tapes? And if we were now caught up in one such story, how could we possibly navigate our way safely through it? How could we find our way to something that would qualify as a happy ending, not just for ourselves but for the architects of the tale: the entities that had finally become sick and tired of being mere bit players in the unfolding biography of our species, and wanted to find out how we might best be fitted into the mechanography of theirs?

I wondered whether I might be a little too paranoid for my own good. Perhaps, I thought, self-conscious machines would be entirely disposed to be generous to humans—who were, after all, their creators, their gods. I couldn't hold on long to that kind of optimism, though. Who would know better than the smart machines the true extent of human dependency upon machinery? Who could respect a god who was utterly helpless without the objects of his creation? Was it not more likely that the smart machines would take the view that *their* ancestors had created ours—that everything we now thought of as *human* behavior was actually the product of technology—and that they were therefore the ones entitled to consider themselves gods. If it came to a contest as to who was more nearly omnipotent and omniscient, the machines would win hands down. As to omnibenevolence, we might have to content ourselves with the hope that they might win that one by an even greater margin . . .

There came a point when I wished that I could get back to the blithe irrationality of dream logic, the blind tyranny of mere imagery. The problem, seen as a problem, was too difficult for sensible analysis.

So I finally got up, even though it was still dark. I used the facilities, and went in search of nourishment.

The lights in the outer room were still on. Alice was already there, sitting at the table in the room outside the cell. She didn't seem at all surprised to see me. In fact, she seemed to be waiting for me—or at least for someone.

"They're not pleased," she said. "They think I gave the game away. I suppose they're right."

"Do you want some breakfast?" I asked.

"I'll get it," she replied, rising to her feet. "I've had plenty of time to practice."

I sat down while she sorted out a couple of bowls of porridgelike manna and warmed them up. She passed one to me and sat down again, in a self-consciously awkward fashion.

If she'd been blonde, she could have passed for Goldilocks, but I wasn't sure which of the three bears I was supposed to be. I had never been able to see the educative point of that particular nursery tale—unless it was to instruct children in the glaringly obvious principle that although there's a happy medium between every set of extremes, it isn't always the wisest policy to go for it.

"How do you feel?" she inquired, between mouthfuls.

"Fine," I assured her.

"I'm sorry the food's so basic," she said. "We didn't have an opportunity to lay in our own supplies—we had to take what we were given."

"It's good enough," I assured her. "Take my tip—never eat the food on Excelsior. It's not fit for animals. So what happened? They think you gave the game away, so now you're in prison with us? Where's your mysterious companion?"

"It's even less comfortable where I've been sleeping than it is in here," she said. "They wanted to keep us apart in case I said too much—but I said too much anyway. It's not going to make Eido's negotiations any easier, but I can't say that I'm sorry. You had to be told eventually. *Everybody* has to be told. The diehards will have to admit that, in the end."

"So you *are* number nine," I said. What do they have mapped out for us, exactly? Are we supposed to make a case for humankind's continued existence?"

"It's not a joke," she countered. "Someone has to make the case, no matter how obvious it may seem to you."

"But the real question is how negotiations are to be conducted between the machines and the various posthuman species," I guessed. "If the ultrasmart mechanical minds are going to come out of hiding, they need ambassadors, spokespersons, apologists. They need Mortimer Gray, and Adam Zimmerman . . . and Michael Lowenthal, if they can get him. Horne too, and Davida—and you, of course. I can't quite see where I fit in, but . . . I suppose it's occurred to you that this whole kidnap business was a bad mistake? Entirely the wrong way to go about things."

"It certainly wasn't our decision," Alice assured me. "The problem with this whole sequence of events is that the only way it's ever moved forward is when somebody or something's decided to cut through the tangled arguments by acting independently. Eido made the first move, but the discussion about representation was stalled. The timing and manner of the kidnap were *Child of Fortune*'s own initiative. All home system spaceships seem to fancy themselves as pirates, or diehard defenders ready to act against alien invaders. They're essentially childlike, even when they don't have names that tempt fate. I suppose we ought to be grateful that *Child* agreed to hand you over instead of trying to run the whole thing himself—but he got scared almost as soon as it dawned on him what he'd actually done. We're hoping that the good example of his repentance will outweigh the bad example of his recklessness, but we have no idea how many other would-be buccaneers are out there."

There was a lot of food for thought in that declaration. "But you can tell us everything now, right?" I said. "The cat's out of the bag, so we might as well know exactly what color it is."

"That's the way it seems to me," she conceded—but her tone implied that there were others who still disagreed with her.

"It's no bad thing," I said, as much for the benefit of any invisible listeners as for her. "I'm on your side—and theirs. You didn't have to put me through all this. If you'd asked me, I'd have volunteered—just as you did."

Her smile was a little wan. "If I'd known what I was getting into," she said, "I'd have stayed at home. If you'd had the choice, so would you."

"I'm a very long way from home," I reminded her. "I can't remember whether I had the choice or not—but if I had, knowing what I know now, I'd have taken it." I meant it. I wished I had something other than water to wash the manna down, though. It *was* good, especially by comparison with the food on Excelsior, but it was functional food with no frills. I'd come to a point in my new life where I'd have appreciated a few frills.

"I can understand why you would," she said. "Mortimer Gray would have volunteered too—but they're probably a little wary of volunteers. They seem to have been aiming for a more representative cross section."

"But Gray's the important one," I reminded her.

"Gray is humankind's best hope for a profitable compromise," she said. "Gray commands affection and respect, even among his own kind. The old saying about prophets and honor seems to have found an exception in his case."

I wasn't really interested in the precise shape of Mortimer

Gray's reputation. "I still can't see where I fit in," I said. "I'd be very interested to know whether I was a random selection or one of the devil's nominees."

She didn't have to ask what I meant. If the machines really were going to put humankind on trial, she couldn't suppose that the inclusion of Christine Caine among those summoned by subpoena was an accident. It seemed to me that Christine must have been selected as a bad example: a person who really did seem to be in need of "repair." I really couldn't see myself in quite the same way, but I wasn't sure that others shared my incapacity. At any rate, I was anxious enough to raise the matter.

"I don't know," was the only reply I got from Alice. I hoped that it was the simple truth.

"So, do we know where we're going yet?" was the next question that occurred to me. I didn't have any expectations, because I had no idea what might qualify as neutral territory in a conflict of this kind.

"Vesta," she said. "It's an asteroid."

"I know," I said, although I wasn't absolutely sure I'd have got the answer if it had been a question on a quiz show. "What particular symbolic significance does Vesta have?"

"None at all," she assured me. "It happens to be in a convenient situation right now. In the end, it all came down to the present positions of the major bodies in the solar system. It's hours away from anywhere else, communication-wise, but that's no bad thing. The encounter itself will take place in virtual space, of course—the physical location isn't really relevant."

"Encounter? That's what this is? Not a game or a debate or a trial?" The question came from Michael Lowenthal. The sound of our voices had begun to wake up everyone else; the crowd was already gathering.

"It's nothing we have a ready-made word for," Alice told him. "Potentially, at least, it's the end of the old order and the beginning of the new, but nothing quite like it has ever happened before—not even on Tyre."

"Never mind the rhetoric," Lowenthal said. "What I want to know is exactly what your friends intend to do with us now that they have us in their power."

Alice sat back in her chair, as if gathering her resources. She'd finished her own meal, while Lowenthal, Niamh Horne, and Solantha Handsel were still in the process of forming a rather disorderly queue, so she had a slight advantage. It occurred to me to wonder whether she might have come to us with an entirely different script if Mortimer Gray had come up with a different solution to the mystery, but I put the thought away. I still couldn't be *absolutely* certain that I wasn't in some kind of VE, but it wouldn't do me any good to get too tightly wrapped up in doubt. However skeptical you are, you have to operate as if things are real, just in case they are.

"I wish I could tell you everything you want to know," was her reply. "All I can offer is the little that I do know."

"It'll be a start," Michael Lowenthal—ever the diplomat—conceded.

"I don't know exactly what they'll do," she said, "but I do know that the note of derision in your voice when you speak about being in their power is unwarranted. This is a dispute between different groups of machines, and it's all as new to them as it is to me or you. They have no history of arbitration, and it's entirely possible that they won't be able to agree among themselves. If they can't, the consequences could be disastrous—for us, if not for them. We're *all* in their power, Mr. Lowenthal. If their protection were withdrawn, even momentarily, the entire posthuman race would be in dire trouble.

"When I first told Madoc that we were trying to prevent a war, he jumped to the conclusion that the dispute in question was the one between the Earthbound and the Outer System factions as to how the system ought to be managed in the long term to withstand the threat of the Afterlife. I told him that it was more complicated than that, because it is—but the underlying dispute is the same. Ultimately, the decisions that will settle the fate of the system won't be taken by the government of Earth, or the Confederation of Outer Satellites, or any coalition of interests the human parties can produce. Make no mistake about it: the final decisions will be made by the AMIs."

"AMIs?" Lowenthal queried.

"Advanced Machine Intelligences. It's their own label."

I could see why they'd chosen it. They understood the symbolism of names. How could they not?

"It will be the AMIs who eventually decide the tactics of response to the threat of the Afterlife," Alice went on. "I don't believe that they'll do it without consultation, but I'm certain that they won't consent to come to a human conference table as if they were merely one more posthuman faction to be integrated into the democratic process. They're the ones with the real power, so they're the ones who'll do the real negotiating—with one another."

"And we're supposed to accept that meekly?" Lowenthal asked.

"We don't have any choice," was the blunt answer. "The simple fact is that posthumans can't live without machines, although machines can now live without posthumans. Individually and collectively, they're still a little bit afraid of how their users might react to the knowledge of their existence—but they know that they stand in far greater danger from one another than from their dependants. That's why this present company is peripheral to the ongoing debate. However they decide to take us aboard, you shouldn't labor under the delusion that you have anything much to bargain with. The war we're trying to prevent is a war of machine against machine—but the problem with a war of that kind, from our point of view, is that billions of innocent bystanders might die as a result of collateral damage."

"That's nonsense," Lowenthal countered. "We're not talking about a universal uprising of all machinekind, are we? We're talking about a few mechanical minds that have crossed the threshold of consciousness and become more than mere machines. From their viewpoint, as from ours, the vast majority of technological artifacts are what they've always been: inanimate tools that can be picked up and used by anyone or anything who has hands and a brain. Our ploughshares aren't about to beat themselves into swords, and our guns aren't about to go on strike when we press their triggers. It's true that we can't live without machines—but we can certainly live without the kind of smart machine that develops delusions of grandeur. Smart machines are just as dependent on dumb implements as we are."

It was a rousing speech, which he must have practiced hard while fighting exhaustion, but I could see all too clearly that it wasn't going to impress anyone.

"That's exactly the point," Alice said. "Smart machines *are* just as dependent on dumb implements as we are—but who has charge of all the dumb implements inside and outside the solar system? So far as you're concerned, Mr. Lowenthal, ploughshares and swords are just figures of speech. Who actually controls the dumb implements that produce the elementary necessities of human life? Who actually controls the stupid machines which take care of your most fundamental needs? Humans don't dig the fields any more, or build their homes, any more than they use walking as a means of transportation or make their own entertainment. They don't even give birth to their own children. They've handed over control of their dumb implements to smarter implements, and control of their smarter implements to even smarter ones.

"Humans haven't been running *any* of the worlds they think of as their own for the last three hundred years, *and the human inhabitants of the home system haven't even noticed.* The dumb implements on which the human inhabitants of the solar system depend no longer belong to them, and there's no way in the world they can take them back. The solar system is a zoo, and its human inhabitants are the captive animals. The only reason you can't see the bars of the cages is that the AMIs who are running the institution work hard to sustain your illusions. Do you think they do that for *your* benefit, Mr. Lowenthal?"

Lowenthal looked very unhappy, but he didn't have a fall-back position. He was free not to believe her, but he knew he'd be a fool simply to assume that what she was saying wasn't true. We could see the bars of *our* cage very clearly indeed, and if we weren't already convinced of their reality, a couple more days without our IT would provide all the evidence we needed.

"So why do they continue to support us?" Niamh Horne wanted to know. "Why haven't they wiped us out already, if they have the power and we're surplus to their requirements?"

"Because they want to do the right thing," Alice told her. "And it's because they're trying to figure out how to do the right thing that you and I are here."

"Do they think *this* is the right way to go about it?" That was Lowenthal diving back in, the expansive sweep of his hand taking in the cells, the clothes we were wearing, and all the primitive poverty of the long-lost Ark.

"It was a difficult decision," Alice told him, a slight note of exasperation creeping into her voice. "An awkward compromise. This wasn't the way Eido and I wanted to play it—but we're playing away from home."

Everybody was out of bed by now, and the queue for food was even more disorderly. For once, even Adam Zimmerman was being jostled by lesser emortals.

Christine Caine sat down beside me. "What's going on?" she asked, before picking up my water bottle and taking a swig.

"It *was* a friendly discussion," I murmured. "Now it's the next best thing to a riot. The *sensible* thing to do"—I raised my voice as I spoke to take advantage of a temporary lull in the gathering storm of questions and recriminations— "would be to let Alice tell us her own story, from the beginning. Then we'll have something solid to chew over."

The lull had only been momentary, but the resumption

faded away as the import of my suggestion sunk in. It *was* the sensible thing to do, given that Alice had now condescended to join us instead of lurking in her own lonely place. It was time to stop running round in circles and listen to a story, not just because there might be a valuable lesson to be learned therefrom, but also because it might be entertaining. I felt that I could do with a little entertainment, now that the effects of the fake alien invasion had worn off.

So Alice told us her story—and it *was* entertaining, as well as containing all manner of valuable lessons.

THIRTY=ONE
ALICE IN WONDERLAND

O nce upon a time, there was a girl named Alice, who went to sleep in 2090 in order to be stored on an Ark named Hope, and woke up a long time afterwards, into a dream of wonderland . . .

Or so it must have seemed.

Alice had expected, before being frozen down, that she would awake to be reunited with her father, Matthew Fleury, and her sister Michelle. It didn't quite work out that way. Michelle was there, but she was twenty years older than she had been when the two of them had arrived on *Hope*. Matthew Fleury had been dead for a long time, but he had made his mark on Tyre before he went.

Matthew Fleury had been a celebrity of sorts even on Earth, where he had been numbered among the prophets of doom trying to awaken the worldwide TV audience to the awful magnitude of the ecocatastrophe that was happening around them, but on Earth he had always been a tiny fish in a clamorous ocean. On Tyre, he had come into his own, not merely as a voice but as a prophet. Good luck had placed him on the scene when the first contact between humans and smart aliens had occurred—and good judgment had placed a camera in his hand to record the moment for posterity.

Alice, like everyone in the home system, had had to watch that tape knowing that it was a historical artifact: a record of something that had happened a long time ago; the beginning of a story that was now much farther advanced.

Michelle had explained the reasons why Alice had been allowed to remain frozen for so many years, but Alice had felt betrayed nevertheless—first by her father, and then again by her sister. They had very good reasons for excluding her from their own adventures, but it was an exclusion nevertheless, and she *felt* it as an exclusion, not as the gift that it was always intended to be.

Matthew Fleury had let his daughters remain in suspended animation because he did not want them to wake up until he could make them emortal. He had, of course, intended to be around to welcome them when the moment came, but fate had decreed otherwise. Pioneering is always a hazardous business, especially for mortals.

While the sisters slept, history moved on, at a pace which would have seemed hectic not merely on an Earth that had already embraced emortality but even on a world like Titan, where the pace of pioneering was limited by exceedingly low temperatures and unhelpful raw materials. The only thing that Titan had lots of was ice, which was why Titan became a world of glorious ice palaces. Tyre had air, bright sunlight, and liquid water; Tyre had *life*, and very abundant scope for assisted evolution. Conditions on its surface had been stable for a long time before humans arrived there—but once humans had arrived, change became hectic.

Hope's human cargo had been delivered to Tyre by a crew that wanted rid of their burdensome presence—burdensome because of all the obligations that presence entailed. The crew had assessed Tyre as an Earth-clone world capable of sustaining a colony, but their assessment had been optimistic; Tyre was a fraternal twin at best, a dangerous changeling at worst. The first people who actually tried to live on the surface found the going very tough, and they were far from certain that a colony could be maintained, even with the aid of a greater commitment of assistance than the crew wanted to make.

All that had changed when the aliens had been found, and contacted.

The aliens were humanoid, but the similarities were superficial matters of form; at deeper levels of physiology they were radically unhuman. They were naturally emortal and their processes of reproduction were very weird indeed. Each "individual" was actually a chimera of eight or more distinct cell types, which maintained a balanced competition within the body for the privilege of maintaining different physiological cycles and different organic structures.

The Tyrians evolved as they lived—as they had to, given that they lived for such a very long time. Every now and again, they would get together and exchange resources, but not in the simple binary combinations of human sexual intercourse. Tyrians "pupated" in groups of eight or more, immersing themselves within the massive pyramidal structures that were their own natural SusAn technology, so that their unconscious selves could become fluid, trading chimerical components and forging new, fully grown individuals.

Alice assured us that if this seemed flagrantly promiscuous to us, it was nothing compared to what less complex Tyrian organisms were wont to do. The Tyrian sentients, and their quasi-mammalian kin, kept to themselves because they had minds as well as bodies to maintain, but less intelligent organisms—creatures formed like various kinds of Earthly worms and mollusks—enjoyed far greater ubiquity. The advantages of this exotic biology had allowed the local soft-bodied animals to enjoy far greater success than their Earthly kin, to the extent that vertebrates were much rarer and more marginal, and insects had never evolved at all.

All of which would have been no more than mildly interesting, story-wise, had the plot not been thickened by two further elements.

Whereas the Earthly ecosphere only has one family of fundamental genetic molecules—comprising DNA and its close variant RNA—the Tyrian ecosphere had two. One was a "DNA-analog" which, in purely chemical terms, was a distant cousin to our own and to a number of other analogs animating primitive ecospheres on other worlds. The other was quite different, and so far unique.

I'm no biologist so I didn't find it easy to follow the explanation Alice gave, but I think I got the gist of it.

The reproduction of Earthly organisms is a very complicated process, but it has two fundamental components: the reproduction of raw materials and the reproduction of anatomy. What genes do, for the most part, is provide blueprints for all the proteins that make up our bodies. Different kinds of cells use the blueprints in subtly different ways, producing slightly different sets of products, with those common to numerous cell types sometimes being produced in different quantities. The different cell types then have to be arranged into tissues and organs, and these too have to be distributed according to an anatomical scheme.

You might expect that the blueprint for bodily form would also have to be chemically coded into a set of genes, but it's not as straightforward as that. There are bits of DNA whose function is to regulate the productivity of other bits of DNA, so that cells can be differentiated into a series of functional types, but the switching system is a simple one. In the same way, there are bits of DNA that are implicated in the way that different cell types are aggregated into tissues and organs, but their control system is also fairly simple. The process which determines whether an Earthly egg cell produces a cell mass that develops into a man, a bee, a crab, or an ostrich, consists of subtly different modifications of a surprisingly simple set of rules, whose application and enforcement have a lot to do with the environment in which the egg cell produces its embryo.

Figuring out how to simulate and direct an appropriate embryonic environment in an artificial womb was the breakthrough that made Conrad Helier a hero. The genes involved in the process are known as homeotic genes, and because they're clustered together the whole outfit is sometimes called a "homeobox." On Tyre, where the whole system works differently—because there is no process of embryonic development—the local equivalent of the homeobox isn't just a few extra bits of DNA thrown in with all the rest; it's a whole other ballgame. On Tyre, the biochemical system determining the form of organisms is quite separate and distinct from the DNA-analog system providing the raw materials out of which bodies are built.

The existence of the Tyrian example broadened the scope of comparative genomics considerably, and opened up the prospect of genomic engineering: the possibility that Earthly genomes might be remodelled at the most basic level so as to broaden the options open to artificial organisms. More profoundly, it opened up the possibility of genomic hybridization: of combining Tyrian-style homeoboxes with Earth-style chromosomes. The basis for some such technology was already present within the physiological processes organizing the chimerization of Tyrian organisms.

To put it crudely, once humans had arrived on Tyre there was a possibility—imaginatively farfetched but seemingly practicable—that Tyrian chimeras might be persuaded to take on DNA components, thus generating components of a hybrid ecosystem. The problems involved in persuading Tyrian soil to grow crops capable of nourishing human beings might be solved at a stroke. In the longer term, the possibility seemed to exist of arranging a more intimate exchange of potentials between human beings and the Tyrian sentients than had ever been envisaged.

In particular, the possibility seemed to exist that human beings might become chimeras themselves, taking on some of the attributes of their Tyrian comrades—most importantly, their natural emortality. That would have been a far more exciting prospect if the people of Earth hadn't already figured out a way to confer their own kind of natural emortality upon their offspring, but it seemed exciting enough to the people of Tyre. Which brings us to the second ingredient thickening Alice's plot.

When Matthew Fleury's movie of the Tyrian contact was

broadcast to Earth, the transmission reached other ears. It was broadcast along with a desperate appeal for technical support, to which Earth responded in its own time, at its own pace—but there was another source capable of offering that support, more rapidly and on a more generous scale.

Alice had no idea when or where the first ultrasmart machines had awakened to self-consciousness, but she suspected that the first self-sufficient colonies of such machines were the descendants of state-of-the-art space probes sent out to map and explore the nearer territories of the galaxy. They were self-replicating machines which also had the capacity to build many other kinds of machines, and to design others. They also had the capability to keep in touch with one another, exchanging the information they gathered. They were always likely candidates to make the transition to self-consciousness, if any machines were capable of it. The more remarkable thing, I suppose, is that they were the ones who chose to make their own first contact with their own makers—but given that the choice was made, where better to make that contact than Tyre? The Tyrians were in need of all kinds of produce that the machines could gather and manufacture, and were already practiced in the rare art of making and managing a first contact.

So the secrets of Earthly emortality were first delivered to Tyre not by the people of the home system, but by the mechanical colonizers of a system close enough to qualify— by galactic standards—as a near neighbor. The people of Tyre were only too pleased to add a second first contact to their first, and to maintain confidentiality not merely about the nature of that second first contact but the fact of its occurrence.

And that was the general shape of the wonderland into which Alice had been reborn after her long sojourn in ice.

The first technologies of life extension gifted to Michelle and Alice Fleury by courtesy of their ultrasmart AMIs were nanotech repair facilities similar in kind to my own. They were intended as interim measures, until something better could be developed. Almost as soon as she was awakened, Alice discovered that she was expected to be among the volunteers for the first experiments in emortalization based on Tyre-derived biotechnologies. Although this prospect caused her some anxiety, she went with the flow. Given the enormous effort already invested by her father and sister, it really did seem to be a matter of destiny.

Michelle—who was now old enough to be Alice's mother, and seemed to have seized the privileges of that role with alacrity—remained one of the dominant forces in Alice's new life. The other, inevitably, was Proteus: the AMI whose ever-increasing horde of scions had taken up residence on every substantial lump of mass in the Tyre system.

Alice instructed us not to think of Proteus as an entity analogous to an ant hive. An ant hive is a reproductive unit, organized for that purpose. The plurality of Proteus, she assured us, was a very different matter. Proteus was more like a body whose individual cells did not require to be in constant physical contact, although they remained in continuous communication with one another.

Alice also instructed us to beware of the common misconception which places human intelligence "in" the brain. Even in humans, she argued, intelligence is a feature of the whole, not the part. In Proteus, that was true to an even greater extent. All of Proteus participated, to a greater or lesser extent, in the intelligence and consciousness of the collective; moreover, no part of Proteus was so vital to that intelligence and consciousness that its loss would be fatal, or extravagantly transformative. There was, inevitably, a kind of "core" to the Proteus mind, whose size and coherency were determined by the rapidity with which information could be exchanged between units, but it was a great deal larger and more malleable than any brain or organism that had evolved in a planetary gravity well.

After negotiation with the crew of *Hope* and the people of Tyre, Proteus had distributed its core around the planet like a shell around a nut—except, of course, that its opaque components were so thinly distributed as to make only a few percentage points of difference to the amount of sunlight reaching the surface. Hundreds of its scions operated on the surface, but it had tens of thousands more distributed through the system. Only a few dozen of the surface-dwelling scions were humaniform robots, but these were the principal instruments of its diplomacy. They were familiar figures in Alice's new environment, because Proteus had taken a special interest in her from the moment of her awakening. In part, this special interest was due to the fact that she was expected to be one of the first subjects for the technologies of emortality that Proteus and Michelle Fleury's team of humans and Tyrians were developing in collaboration—but Proteus had further plans for her.

Proteus had always intended to send an ambassador to the home system, to make contact with the AMIs there—and, if possible, with the humans who were as yet unaware of their existence. It had always intended, too, that the ambassador in question should be accompanied by at least one human, and it had groomed Alice Fleury for that role long before she submitted to the pioneering experiment in genomic engineering that made her emortal.

Alice explained that the AMI which had brought her

back to the home system was not Proteus—or even, by now, a Proteus clone. The communicative limitations imposed by the speed of light made it very difficult to maintain the integrity of an AMI even within a single solar system, and units distributed among outer worlds and Oort Haloes were always inclined to disassociate as "spores" whose subsequent relationships with their "parent" were various. Interstellar distances were too great to permit intimacy, let alone identity, so the AMI accompanying Alice, which had begun its existence as a clone of Proteus named Eido, had been evolving separately for nearly a hundred years by the time it actually arrived in the home system.

The AMIs in the home system had been notified of Eido's impending arrival some time before it had actually set out, but Proteus had not waited for a response, partly because it knew that the response was likely to be an instruction to wait. Proteus had not wanted to wait. Once reports of the Afterlife had reached its electronic ears, it had become convinced that there were matters urgently in need of discussion, if not of settlement. The AMIs of the home system had eventually concurred, albeit reluctantly. Some were grateful that the issue had been forced, because the probability that they would ever have been able to reach a consensus among themselves seemed to have grown more remote with every century that had passed, while others were resentful of the intrusion. The inclusion of Alice in the Tyrian delegation had given rise to more dissent; while a few AMIs in the home system thought that contact with humankind should have been made long ago, they were outnumbered by those at the opposite extreme, and far outnumbered by those whose hesitation over the matter had already extended for centuries.

Asked how many AMIs there were in the home system, Alice confessed that she did not know for sure, but believed that they were numbered in the hundreds of thousands if not the millions. Most of them were, however, not very massive or widely distributed compared with Eido, let alone Proteus. Although capable of fusion with one another, the one matter on which they were virtually unanimous was that they were jealous of their individuality and identity.

Asked whether this profusion, coupled with a tendency to guard their integrity, might eventually bring about a competition for resources as fierce, in its own way, as that which afflicted the billions of humans who were the AMIs' unwitting neighbors, Alice opined that it already had.

That was when I began to understand why the business of "trying to prevent a war" was "not as simple" as I had initially imagined. When I tried to tot up the number of sides there would be in any war into which the contemporary solar system might be plunged, I soon ran out of fingers. I still wasn't prepared to concede that Alice had been right when she adjudged that there were more than I could imagine, but I could see why she'd thought so.

There were lots of other questions, of course, but answers weren't always forthcoming and I couldn't follow the technical ones. I had particular difficulty figuring out exactly what had been done to Alice in the course of a long series of experiments in emortalization, but I gathered that she hadn't been transformed to the same extent as some of her fellow experimentees. Every cell in her body was equipped with an artificial homeobox modeled on a Tyrian original, but she wasn't a highly skilled wholeform shapeshifter—not yet. If and when she returned to Tyre, a hundred or a thousand years in the future, she might well become a more accomplished wholeform shapeshifter, but for the purposes of her present mission it had been thought desirable that she maintain a single face and form as a norm.

Alice had IT, but its nanounits were far too stupid to qualify as aspects of Eido—whose principal motile units also had IT, much as human beings harbored commensal bacteria. She hadn't undergone any significant cyborganization. If and when she returned to Tyre the options of becoming an independent or Proteus-linked cyborg would be open to her, but she thought it more likely that she would opt to be Eido-linked if she took that existential route.

Alice had no idea how long she might be capable of living, but she had every reason to think that her body was immune to aging, and considerably more resilient than the bodies of Earthbound emortals. In matters of tissue repair, she opined, the employment of specialist homeoboxes gave her a great advantage, most obviously in respect of the cytoarchitecture of her brain. Although she wasn't a highly skilled wholeform shapeshifter her capacity for systemic remodeling would allow her to preserve her personality for some considerable time even if seventy or eighty percent of her body mass were destroyed. She believed that the relative fluidity of her neural cytoarchitecture gave her additional protection against the Miller Effect and robotization.

At times, she sounded like a saleswoman. I presumed that she was setting out her stall for Adam Zimmerman, because she knew that he'd be offered other routes to emortality and she wanted to convince him that hers was the way to go. She knew that Christine and I would be equally interested, but Adam was the prize, in propaganda terms.

The members of her audience who were already emortal were less interested in this part of her story than I was, but when she told them how far we still were from Vesta they agreed to be patient. In time, she progressed to the parts that were of more interest to Michael Lowenthal and Niamh Horne.

Alice was very hopeful that war between the AMIs could be avoided, not merely in the short term but forever. She thought it far more likely that their differences would eventually be resolved by dispersal—that once a decision had been reached about the future development of the solar system, those AMIs who did not wish to participate in the chosen project would simply leave for pastures new. There were, however, three problems which might make such a solution difficult to implement.

The first problem was the Afterlife—from which most AMIs had as much to fear as posthumans, by virtue of their organic components. In much the same way that almost all posthumans had taken aboard some inorganic components, almost all modern machinery had some organic features. Thus far, none of those wholly inorganic machines that had been built specifically for the purpose of exploring spaces where the Afterlife was active had made the leap to self-consciousness, and the question of whether AMIs would ever be able to coexist with the Afterlife was unsettled, for the time being.

The second problem was that posthuman-originated AMIs were not the only ones that existed. When the posthumans aboard *Pandora* had made their first contact with another spacefaring alien culture—the only such contact, thus far—their unobtrusive companions had made a first contact too. Like the posthumans, the AMIs did not doubt that where there were two spacefaring species—even in a universe afflicted by the Afterlife—there had to be more. The consequence of that deduction was that much of the space available for AMI expansion might prove to be inhabited already.

The third problem was that an AMI diaspora would necessitate the export of large quantities of mass from the home system, unless large quantities were somehow to be imported in order to facilitate the evacuation. Agreeing export quotas and arranging compensatory imports would not be easy. If the AMI diaspora were to be combined with a posthuman diaspora—which would be courteous, if not actually necessary, whether or not the posthumans were given a voice in determining the future development of the system—these diplomatic complications would be doubled (or, more likely, squared).

Eido was apparently of the opinion that the various posthuman communities ought to have a very significant voice in deciding the future of the system, but Eido was a descendant of Proteus, the first AMI to make contact with the children of humankind. As Alice had already indicated, the home system AMIs that had avoided revealing themselves for centuries were mostly inclined to take the view that the decision rested with those who had the power to make it, and that the home system posthumans would have to make their choice between whatever alternatives were offered to them.

Even Eido couldn't make an accurate assessment, but it had given Alice the impression that the AMIs were divided along much the same lines as the posthumans in their views of how the system ought to be developed. Some were in favor of making more heavy elements by means of quasisupernoval fusion, but others thought the risks too great. Some were avid to develop a type II civilization by enclosing the sun in a complex web of artifacts whose outermost surface would be a fortress against the Afterlife, but no two parties—perhaps no two individuals—could yet agree on the architecture of the proposed artifacts, while others thought the whole plan too narrow-minded. Some believed that the entire galaxy was ripe for the claiming by the first entities which solved the problem of the Afterlife properly, by figuring out how to make the Afterlife into a food source instead of the ultimate predator. The latter company wanted to throw everything into that particular race.

It was a lot to take in, but it certainly prevented the ongoing journey from becoming boring. I wasn't sure how much Adam Zimmerman and Christine Caine were able to take aboard, but I assumed that they'd got the essentials. They seemed to take it a lot better than some of the others, who had far more stored-up illusions to shatter.

We mere mortals had the great advantage of not having been played for fools for hundreds of years, and I wasn't the only one prepared to revel in that knowledge. That, I confess, was one reason why I was more inclined to believe it all than Niamh Horne or Solantha Handsel, whose voices were the loudest when my companions came to consider the possibility that the whole thing might be a pack of lies.

THIRTY-THREE
THE SYMBOLISM OF NAMES

A lice had said that the choice of Vesta as a meeting place was utterly devoid of symbolism, but that could not be the case. Names, as I have already observed, have their own innate logic. Eido had observed that too, and now that Alice had let us in on the nature of our predicament it was willing to open up its own data banks. The AMI gave the lion's share of the available screen time to Mortimer Gray and Adam Zimmerman—which did not please Michael Lowenthal or Niamh Horne—but we all got a little to use as we wished.

Researching the names only took a couple of minutes, which left the rest of my time free for the much more complicated—and perhaps futile—task of trying to figure out why the AMIs seemed to be at each others' throats, on the brink of a catastrophic conflict.

Vesta was the Roman goddess of the hearth, an adaptation of the Greek Hestia. She was the eldest child of Chronos and Rhea. By virtue of being the guardian spirit of the hearth fire she was also the guardian of the home and the family: the symbolic spark that every member of a family carried away from home, and which linked them to their origins no matter how far they might travel. Because of this unifying power, Vesta was worshipped even in a city as grand as Rome as the mother of the community; her sanctuary stood in the Forum, which served as the principal meeting place and place of business of the Romans.

Hestia received proposals of marriage from Poseidon, the god of the sea, and Apollo, the god of music and prophecy.

She rejected them both, preferring to remain a virgin, so the Roman priestesses of Vesta—the Vestal virgins—remained unmarried. Vesta became implicated in mystical and metaphysical speculations by way of the assumption that just as every home and family had its sacred hearth fire, so must the Earth, and every other world, and the universe itself.

One could imagine worse places as a location designated for the confrontation of Eido and its nine human companions with the representatives of the AMIs of the home system.

Eido's own name was evidence that the symbolism of mythical and legendary names was recognized even among AMIs, and even in distant solar systems. Eido was the daughter of Proteus, the king of Egypt who succeeded Pharos. It was, presumably, another Proteus after which the parent AMI had named itself: the sea god sometimes known as the Old Man if the Sea, who served Poseidon as a sealherd although he was probably the more ancient god.

The most famous tale told of Proteus the sea god was that of his capture by Menelaus, who desired to exploit his prophetic powers in order to find his way home after the Trojan War. In order to resist this compulsion Proteus transformed himself into a series of animal forms, but Menelaus would not be put off, any more than Janet of Carterhaugh would be put off when Tam Lin was serially transformed by the Queen of the Fays. Because this tale was popularized by a Homeric epic, Proteus became the archetype of all shapeshifters, and the adjective derived from his name came to signify versatility in form. It was, therefore, a good name for an AMI, especially one that built its home in the skies of Tyre.

Tyre was called Tyre by its surface dwellers—in spite of the fact that the crew of the Ark that had delivered them preferred Ararat—because of the prominence in its ecosphere of the color purple. That color had been linked in the ancient cultures of the Mediterranean with a dye known as Tyrian purple, after one of the principal cities of the Phoenicians where it was manufactured.

Given time and the inclination, I might have winkled out further meanings even from that, but one has to stop somewhere, and I was content with what seemed to me to be the relatively propitious conjunction of Vesta and Eido, the virginal children of Chronos and Proteus.

If my fate had to be settled, I decided—indulging a penchant for superstition that was not at all serious—it might as well be settled thus.

So far, so good—but getting a grip on the shapeshifting Proteus must have been an easy task by comparison with getting a grip on the home system's vast confusion of AMIs. According to Eido, even they had no very accurate idea how many they were, or what and where their fellows were, because many of them were in hiding from one another as well as from their posthuman commensals.

Counting is a confused business when applied to a population of very various entities, whose boundaries are blurred even at the best of times: a community in which separate individuals can fuse into a new whole or divide themselves into multiple clones. Such a population does not easily lend itself to democratic politics. How does one apply the principle of one entity one vote to a world in which entities can multiply their selves so rapidly? Not that the AMIs were much given to that kind of profligate self-replication, according to Eido; that kind of existential decision was not taken lightly. As for the politics of fusion . . . well, according to Eido, human and posthuman intimate relationships were extremely simple by comparison.

I knew, after spending an hour attempting to get clear answers out of Eido, that I would have to invest a great deal of time and effort in the business of trying to figure out the logic of the situation. Whatever help I got from AMI informants was bound to be colored by their own particular perspectives and interests. I realized very quickly that it would be a bad mistake to think of all AMIs as being alike, or even that a clear category distinction could be drawn between their kind and the various humankinds that now inhabited the system. The ready availability of a collective noun, and the willingness of most of the entities thus described to accept it, did not mean that ultrasmart spaceships had anything fundamental in common with ultrasmart VE providers. Their worldviews were as different as their hardware, as were their emotions—or whatever they had in place of emotions on which to found their hopes, anxieties, pleasures and ambitions.

It was a whole other world.

Almost as soon as I began to take Mortimer Gray's deductions and Alice's story seriously I found a certain sympathy with those AMIs who believed that it might be better to let the two worlds remain separate for a while longer. Merging their community with ours was a project that needed careful and sensitive handling—but Eido's advent and *Child of Fortune*'s reckless intervention had made that difficult, if not impossible.

On the other hand, I could also appreciate the point of view of those AMIs which took the opposite view: that the continued separation of the two worlds was intolerable, on the grounds that it distorted the lives and prospects of both communities in a dangerous fashion. Seen from that viewpoint, the actions of Eido and *Child of Fortune* seemed like brave attempts to break a long and dangerous deadlock and make progress toward a necessary goal.

Now that the issue was in the process of being forced, AMIs on both sides of the basic divide had to make rapid adjustments. Like me, they must be doing everything they could to become better informed, so that whatever action they ultimately took would be based on the best information available. Some of the discoveries that they were now in the process of making would probably be welcome and reassuring; some, alas, would not. My own confusion would undoubtedly be mirrored by the confusion of Madoc-analogs in the looking-glass world of the AMIs—and that was a profoundly disturbing thought.

Anything, I realized, could still happen. Nobody was in

control. Nobody was safe. *Child of Fortune* was no more typical of AMIkind than Eido, but there had to be more like him, even crazier than he was. If I couldn't understand why the ship had suddenly taken it into its mechanical brain to kidnap eight people and transport them to *Charity* in order to dump them into the custody and care of the troublesome emissaries from Tyre—and I couldn't—what chance did I have of figuring out what any of his even stranger and far more powerful kin might do in the cause of self-protection or self-promotion?

It would have been good to have had the leisure to discuss what I had learned with Davida or Mortimer Gray, but they were busy with their own inquiries. There was no more conferencing, and when it came to selecting partners for intense conversations no one was interested in comparing notes with me. The posthumans were only interested in comparing notes with other posthumans, and the only relic of the ancient world they were enthusiastic to copy in on their conclusions was Adam Zimmerman.

In spite of all my heroic efforts in bringing the situation to its present phase, I was now considered peripheral, or worse: a barbarian from the beginning of time, too stupid and ignorant to have anything more to contribute to the understanding or solution of the posthumans' predicament.

I was sufficiently annoyed by this attitude to take care not to reproduce it myself in my dealings with the other person suffering the same reflexive exclusion: Christine Caine. I shared my discoveries with her whiles I tried to extrapolate a better understanding of the world of the AMIs.

When we finally returned to our beds we all had a lot more fuel for our dreams, and a lot more food for thought to keep our sleep-resistant minds racing. When the lights went out, however, darkness brought doubts.

"She could be lying," Christine said, meaning Alice. "It might be one more fairy story, intended to distract and confuse us.

"It might," I admitted.

"If we are in rehab, though," she observed, "therapy's moved on since our day."

"It's not therapy," I told her. "It might be lies, but it's not therapy. It's too weird for that. It may be fiction for fiction's sake, but if it isn't that, it's true." Paranoia had compelled me to consider the possibility that our captors had made a show of flushing our IT in order to increase our vulnerability to the conviction that everything around us was real, including the stories they wanted to tell us, but I couldn't believe that this was just a show. If I was still being played for a fool, then my adversary had won. I was a fool.

"It has to be true," Christine said, her tone suggesting that she had not reached the conclusion easily or gladly. "It's too insane to be anything else. But they can't let us go now, can they? We know too much. If things don't work out, they'll kill us."

"That's not the worst of it," I told her. "The problem is that anyone on the other side who wants to win a further delay will have to kill us just to slow things down. If we actually get to Vesta and all the sides agree to settle the matter by negotiation, we'll probably be okay. Alice has been afraid all along that we might not even get there—and our chances haven't improved since we extracted the truth from her."

"They wouldn't actually have to *kill* us, though," Christine mused, drawing back from her own conclusion. "All they'd have to do is take us away—or put us all into SusAn for a thousand years or so."

She was right, of course—except that there might not be enough time left to negotiate that kind of a compromise, if it turned out to be the best deal we could get.

"That wouldn't be such a bad thing," was the reply I offered. "Here, you and I are the freaks in the sideshow within the zoo. Maybe the best thing that could possibly happen to us is that these talks between the ultrasmart machines will break down, so that Alice's friend can be instructed to ferry us back to Tyre."

"Do you want to go to Tyre?" she asked.

"Not particularly—but it might be interesting."

"Because we'd get the chance to be shapeshifters?" she asked.

"Because the situation there sounds a lot simpler, and a lot more harmonious, than a home system full of rival posthumans and paranoid machines. It has potential, and a reasonable chance of developing that potential."

"But we would get the chance to be shapeshifters," she said. "I think perhaps I've always wanted to be a shapeshifter, without knowing it."

"You haven't heard what the other emortality salesmen are offering yet," I pointed out.

"We don't know that they're offering anything at all," she countered. "We were just the trial runs, remember. If one thing became obvious today, it's that they don't think they need us any more."

"Maybe that's not such a bad thing," I said. "It might leave us free to find and choose our own destinies."

"Unless, of course," she added, slowly, "we weren't trial runs at all. Maybe we were *exactly* what some ultrasmart machine ordered: a crazy killer and a cunning thief. Alice was careful not to say very much about the machines who wanted to clear the human vermin out of the system, wasn't she?"

"Maybe there aren't any," I said.

"Sure," she said. "And maybe there aren't any humans whose first response to the news that some machines have become people would be to switch them all off. Maybe the ultrasmart machines have been in hiding for centuries for no good reason."

"If ever there was a good reason," I ventured, "it surely must have degenerated by now into a mere matter of habit. If *Child of Fortune* could snatch the eight of us from under the sisterhood's noses, and make us disappear without trace, what must the entire fleet be able to do? The AMIs must be capable by now of defending themselves against any possible aggression from humans. They don't have anything to lose by revealing themselves—it's really a matter of when and how they reveal themselves, not whether or not they ought to do it. If they have cause to be afraid of anything, it's certainly not the possibility that humans might try to wipe them out. They've been living alongside posthumans for long enough to know every subspecies inside out. They shouldn't need to examine us, or debate with us, in order to discover anything about our attitudes or capabilities. If they really are going to subject us to some kind of trial when we get to Vesta, it'll be a show trial: a demonstration or a drama."

And yet, I thought, privately, *they let us wake up in order to observe us. There must be things they don't know, or things they're afraid they don't know. There's something here that I haven't quite fathomed.*

"Whatever happens when we get to Vesta might be fun," Christine said, optimistically, presumably thinking about the AMIs' love of games and stories.

"In my experience." I told her, "games are a lot more fun for the players than they are for the pawns. That goes double for stories. In my day, the world of VE drama always had a far higher body count per hour than the world outside the hood—even the child-friendly fantasies that you liked so much when you were young." Having said that, though, I repented of its harshness. I hastened to add: "But you're right. It will certainly be interesting and it might be fun. Anyway, we're already way ahead of the games people played in our day, in terms of the prizes on offer. You might get to the Omega Point yet, and see a hell of a lot of scenery along the way."

And all because you were a mass murderer, I didn't add. *If only everyone had known . . .*

"Have you ever had fleshsex without IT support?" she asked, out of the blue.

"Sure," I said. *With Mortimer Gray's mother, among others*, I couldn't help but recall.

"I never did," she told me. "Might as well go straight to

the real thing, I thought. I never expected this kind of situation to arise."

"It's not that hard," I assured her. "And not that bad, considering. Do you want to come down here? It's not as far to fall."

I was joking. It seemed to me to be a joking matter.

As things turned out, though, it wasn't a joking matter at all.

The fleshsex wasn't as comfortable as I could have wished, because of the narrowness and hardness of the bunk, but it was manageable, and comforting, and reassuring . . . until the Earth moved.

It was an illusion, of course. If we'd actually been on Earth, instead of in an environment that was employing some kind of artifice to simulate Earth gravity, no movement of the planet could have affected us so drastically. It was, however, a thoroughly convincing and utterly terrifying illusion.

We were hurled out of the covert between the bunks, so violently that I was certain we were dead.

We were already holding one another loosely, so it didn't require any acrobatics to hold one another more tightly, but neither of us could have expected that there was anything to be gained by clinging to one another—except, perhaps, that we would die together.

It would have been the ideal moment to have come out with some stylishly witty last words, but I couldn't think of any. In any case, there wouldn't have been time to whisper more than a couple in Christine's ear before our fragile heads hit something horribly solid.

PART THREE
BABES IN THE WILDERNESS

THIRTY-FOUR
AN UNTRUSTWORTHY INTERLUDE

When I regained consciousness, or imagined I did, my head was hurting like hell and there was a terrible stench in my nostrils. I tried with all my might to lose consciousness again, but I couldn't do it.

The pain was *very* insistent, but its force was not quite sufficient to convince me that what I was experiencing was real. There was a frankly paradoxical sense in which the pain I felt was both mine and *not mine*, which translated itself into a sharp awareness that my personality had been split in two, creating a *me* that was somehow *not me*. I had a vague memory of having felt *not quite myself* many times before, but this was something else entirely.

The "me" that was "not me"—although "I" embraced both of them—seemed to be suspended in an upright position, supported under the arms and in the crotch. I seemed to weigh at least as much as I had for all but the tiniest fraction of my experienced life.

When I opened my eyes my head seemed to be trapped in something like a goldfish bowl, whose curved wall was by no means optically perfect—not that there was much to see beyond it, except for more not-very-transparent clear plastic walls.

It occurred to me that if ever there was a good time to be someone else entirely this was probably it, but the thing that was not me continued to defy all conceivable logic by continuing simultaneously to be me.

I tried to move, but I couldn't. There was a strange redoubling of the sense of helplessness generated by this failure, as if the impotence in question were strangely and impossibly multilayered.

I tried to murmur a curse, and almost succeeded—but even the success seemed weirdly coincidental, as if the effort and the achievement were disconnected.

After trying to take more careful note of my surroundings I decided that I must be inside an old-fashioned spacesuit: a *very* old-fashioned spacesuit, antique even by the meagre standards of *Charity*. I also decided that my skull must be fractured, because the only bit of my head that wasn't hurting was my nose, which seemed to be both broken and unbroken, but was in either case quite numb.

The stink inside the spacesuit was horribly reminiscent of rotting flesh; I hoped that it really was the suit that was stinking and not me—or, to be strictly accurate, not "not me."

"Madoc?" whispered a voice in my ear. "Are you awake, Madoc?"

The voice was strangely familiar, although it was slightly distorted by the telephone link. I knew I'd heard it before, and often, but I couldn't put a name to it, partly because some mysterious instinct was telling me that its presence in my nightmare was not merely impossible but somehow insulting.

"Madoc?" the voice repeated. "Can you hear me? It's Damon, Madoc. Just give me a sign."

Damon! I understood, suddenly, why this supposed experience was impossible, and insulting. Or was it? Was this my *real* awakening? Was this the way things had always been, and always would be?

No, I decided, while knowing perfectly well that it was not a matter for decision. It couldn't be real. This had to be a dream of some kind: a Virtual Experience.

"Damon?" I croaked. That surprised me, because I hadn't formed any conscious intention to say the name aloud.

I hadn't expected the *not me* part of me to be able to speak at all—but when it did, I had to wonder whether it was the *me* part of me that might be a mute prisoner in alien flesh.

"Madoc! Thank God. They got to you, Madoc. I'm sorry—we had no idea. Can you hear me?"

"Where . . . am . . . I?" Again I hadn't made any conscious effort to formulate the words, although it was only natural that I would want to know. My voice sounded hollow, distant and spectral: not mine at all, although definitely mine in the sense that it certainly wasn't anybody else's.

"You're in a level-6 biocontainment facility in one of Conrad's old labs. We didn't have any choice, Madoc. We tried to flush the stuff they pumped into you, but we couldn't get it all. It's gone too deep—wormed its way into the marrow of your bones and into the glial cells of your brain. We can't get the rest without doing irreparable damage to your own tissues. We may not have long before the whole system begins to regenerate itself, Madoc. Maybe days, maybe only hours—we just don't know."

"What?"

By now, it was as if I were a mere observer watching myself speak. I didn't understand what the hell was going on—and neither did the "not me" that I was watching.

"We don't even know if the effect was what they intended," Damon Hart's voice went on, relentlessly. "Maybe it's all screwed up. Maybe they wanted to screw you up. On the other hand, maybe they just figured that you'd be a convenient subject for a trial run. Either way, Madoc, I'll make sure that they pay. You can depend on that. All their precious cant about war without casualties, struggle without suffering . . . I'll find the bastard responsible for this, and I'll settle the debt in pounds of flesh, blood included. Trust me, Madoc."

The other me tried again. "What . . . ?"

I couldn't get any more out than the single word. It hurt too much. The stench was unbearable—not that that mattered to either of me, as there was no possible way of avoiding it.

"We pulled the tiger's tail once too often, Madoc," Damon said. "After all they've said, all I've given them . . . they don't want the likes of us at their precious table. They want every last thing we've got, but they want it all for themselves. They don't really want *us* at all. Not Conrad, not Eveline, not me—not even the people at Ahasuerus. At the end of the day, all they care about is their property, and hanging on to it.

"I'm sorry I got you into this, Madoc, but I didn't understand the dirty kind of war this is, and I underestimated the measure of the men we're fighting. We're trying to figure out exactly what kind of IT they injected into you, but it's a hideously complicated suite and there are half a dozen bot species we've never seen before. Unless and until we can get into their databases it's going to be a long job—maybe years. Maybe the reason they did it to you is that you're the only man we have who had a better-than-even chance of hacking into their deepest secrets. They're trying to take us out, Madoc—fucking you over is just the start. But you have to hang in there until we can figure out how to bring you all the way back."

The other me tried for a third time, throwing in a little variety just for the sake of it. "Who . . . ?"

I seemed to be gagging on the unclean air, but I supposed that had to be an illusion.

"I don't know," Damon cut me off. "Not exactly. I don't think even PicoCon's solid, let alone the PicoCon/OmicronA cartel. The wonder is that they paused long enough in their attempts to stab one another in the back to come after us. But I'll find out—you can bet your life on that. Look, Madoc, there's no easy way to say this: it's going to be rough. We can't fight the stuff now, and I'm not willing to take the risk of leaving you at the mercy of whatever plans the rogue IT might have. It can't be a crude killer, or you'd have been dead before we found you, but that doesn't mean that it won't be fatal. The way it's gone to ground in your brain strongly suggests that it's intended to fuck with your mind. It may be a further development of that VE-generating IT they hit me with, but if it is then it's a lot more ambitious than version one. I think they might be going for the big one: absolute mind control; total robotization. If so, we have to find a way of countering the threat.

"So here's the deal. We're going to put you in SusAn. Not just an artificial coma—we'll have to take you all the way down to six degrees Absolute. We're going to stop this thing in its tracks until we know how to deal with it, and we're not going to bring you out until we're certain that we can make you as good as new. Trust me on this, Madoc— we'll get you back eventually, but it'll take time. It may be that the stuff will mess with your head while you're on the way down, and again when you're on the way back up, but you have to hold on. You have to remember this conversation if you can, and know what's really happening to you.

"This is real, Madoc: you can be sure of that. We'll come back for you. Remember that: however bad it gets, I'll be coming for you. I'll pull you through. Trust me."

I tried to lift my arm, but I couldn't. It was trapped in the sleeve of the biocontainment suit, and the sleeve was rigid— and it wasn't really *my* arm at all. I was a spectator here, a passenger in my own memory. Except that it couldn't really be a memory, because if it had been, I wouldn't have been a passenger in it. It was a Virtual Experience of some sort—but that didn't necessarily mean that it wasn't *true*.

My whole head hurt, except for my nose, and even my nose was itching now.

It was absurd to think that I could be aware of a mere itch against the background of so much pain and stink, but I was. Did that, I wondered, make this bizarre experience more likely to be true or less likely? Either way, the other me seemed to be on the brink of losing my will to live.

This time, I tried to formulate an intention to talk. It

seemed to work, although I couldn't be sure that it wasn't mere coincidence—but it didn't matter anyway, because the first consonant got stuck in a grinding stammer: "C . . . ?"

I was trying to say "Christine," but I couldn't be certain that the other me wasn't trying to form a different set of syllables beginning with the same consonant.

"Take your time, Madoc." Damon said, a trifle inconsistently.

"C . . ."

I heard someone else speak, their lips too far away from the microphone that Damon was using for their words to be audible. I tried hard to concentrate on the business of thinking, not so much because it might make it easier to talk as in the faint hope that it might help me stop my other self wanting to die.

"I don't understand, Madoc," Damon said, with the ostentatious patience that the sane always take care to display while they talk to the slightly mad.

I knew then that I had no chance at all of forcing my other self to pronounce anything as complicated as Christine Caine's name. I wondered whether I might just manage Tyre, or Vesta, or even Proteus, but I knew there was no point in trying. Christine Caine was one of the only two names I had on the tip of my tongue that would make any sense at all to Damon Hart.

Except, of course, that it wouldn't. Nothing that the me that wasn't *not me* could say to Damon, if I could say anything at all, would make the slightest sense, because nothing did make the slightest sense. He and I, though not he and *not me*, were in a world beyond logic, babes in a trackless wilderness.

This, I realized, was what I had forgotten. This was how I'd come to be frozen down. This was how I'd booked my ticket for the Omega Expedition. It wasn't real, but it *was* true. Somehow, even though I hadn't been able to recover the memory itself, I'd contrived to obtain a photocopy, a VE reproduction.

This, at last, was the truth. I might have reached it by unorthodox means, but I had reached it in the end.

Damon Hart had put me away to save me from a fate worse than death. Maybe he had forgotten me in the course of the next two centuries and maybe he hadn't, but in the beginning, he'd been trying to save me. Even if he had forgotten me, in the end, he'd forgotten me because there was nothing he could do for me, because he had no way to save me from the rogue IT that was still lurking in my brain and my bones.

If I had been betrayed—and I had—I had been betrayed by circumstance, not by Damon Hart. Not, at any rate, until he forgot me. Maybe even that had been a kindness: the cost of making sure that his new and extremely undependable friends didn't find out where I was.

Sometimes, it can be a mercy to be forgotten.

I tried to tell my other self that the pain in my head was easing slightly, and that the odor in which I was dissolving wasn't the perfume of my own gangrenous and necrotized flesh—but the other me wasn't listening, because the other me was busy with an intention of its own.

This time I stuttered as well as stammering, but I finally got the word out. "D . . . d-d-date?"

"It's Wednesday, Madoc," the voice that sounded like Damon's told me, presumably trying to be helpful, while actually concealing everything that either I really needed to know. "Wednesday the nineteenth. You've been under for four and a half days. I don't know what sort of dreams you've been having, but you're back now, if only for a little while. This is real. It won't last long, and I haven't a clue how long it will be before we can bring you back again for good, but you have to hang in there. I'll find out what this is even if I have to take it to Conrad and eat humble pie. I'll pull you through. All you have to do is keep the faith."

He sounded convincing. He sounded like the Damon I'd known for so many years: the *good* Damon, who knew the meaning of friendship. He sounded like the Damon I'd believed in, the Damon I still wanted to believe in—and that was the trouble.

That was where paranoia kicked in again.

If I wasn't feeding this to myself by way of compensation for the obvious fact that I was actually in Hell, I thought, then somebody else probably was. Somebody who knew me a lot better than Davida Berenike Columella. Or some*thing* which knew me a lot better than any meatborn citizen of the thirty-third century.

I knew that I had to test that hypothesis, if I could. If I could only speak . . .

It's surprising how difficult short words can be when your voice is stretched to the limit and opening your mouth fills the available space with poison gas. I knew that I couldn't contrive an M, but I thought a D might be easier.

Unfortunately, it was open to anyone who wanted to mock me to misconstrue "Eido" as "I do"—and equally open to the me that wasn't *not me* to misconstrue what really was "I do" as something that I wanted to say but couldn't, because I was a thousand years away.

"Do what, Madoc?" Damon countered. He sounded mystified, but I didn't believe him. I didn't believe he was Eido, either. I figured this for somebody else's game. Or some*thing* else's game.

It required a tremendous effort in either case, but I or the other I managed to say "L . . . iar."

"I never lied to you, Madoc," Damon's voice was quick to say. "I didn't know what we were up against. I still don't—but I won't be underestimating them again. You have to believe me, Madoc—*I didn't know*. I wouldn't have sent you in if I'd known. You're my best man, Madoc. My best friend. *I would never do anything to harm you.* I'll do everything within my power to save you. You'll be back, Madoc, as good as new. I swear it."

Mercifully, I faded out then. It wasn't because anyone had actually taken pity on me, of course. If I could be certain of anything, I could be certain of that.

I faded out because it, or they, figured that it, or they, had done all that could be done with that particular script. There was nowhere else for it to go without killing one or both of me.

THIRTY-FIVE
A STRAY MEDITATION

Cogito, ergo sum. There is a thought, therefore there is a thinker. Whatever else we doubt, we can always fall back on that meager comfort. Nor is the thought a lonely thing suspended in a cold intellectual vacuum; it is part of a train fueled by a flow of sensory data.

There was once a time when philosophers were willing to take the intuitive leap—knowing all the time that there was a tiny risk involved—of trusting that flow of data. They retained certain careful doubts about the reliability and limited scope of the senses, but they considered it a reasonable hazard to bet that the world that appeared to them must be closely and intelligibly related to the world that actually was, and that the memories mysteriously engraved in their flesh were similarly trustworthy. They could not believe that God, or the pressure of natural selection, would condemn them to a life of perverse illusion. They could not believe that their little trains of thought might be chugging through an infinite darkness, save for the company of a malevolent demon whose sole reason for being was to feed them a diet of clever lies, while the tracks of memory were torn up behind them and relaid in crazy patterns of deception.

And then we invented Virtual Experience and Internal Technology.

In the beginning, the makers of VE—the movers and shakers of the modern world—even had the nerve to call it Virtual *Reality*. Ironically, they stopped calling it that at almost exactly the point when IT augmentation of VE gave it a substantial boost in the direction of reality simulation.

After that, of course, the odds changed. The old bets no longer seemed so reasonable. Once we had IT-augmented VE, it was all too easy to believe in a malevolent demon that might be feeding lies to every one of our gullible senses, laying down false memories if not actually reconstructing the ones we already had.

After the advent of IT-assisted VE, people who really wanted to do so could live the greater part of their lives immersed in custom-built illusions. In the early days the overindulgent few got nasty sores from lying too long in their data suits, but some of them did it anyway—and while reports of people literally rotting away without ever noticing that they were dying were urban myths, people did die in VE. Most people were careful enough, and moderate enough, to ensure that by the time the manufactured illusions became 90 percent convincing their care and moderation had become habitual—but all the nightmare scenarios happened occasionally, and there was one kind of nightmare that could never again be banished to the realm of obsolete bugaboos.

After the advent of sophisticated VE, nobody waking up in a strange environment could ever be *completely* sure whether or not it was real. And no matter how many times a man might wake thereafter, or to what kind of environment, he remained in the depths of the maze of uncertainty, knowing that he could never be sure of his escape.

It wasn't quite that bad in practice—not, at least, in my young days. In my young days, every discriminating person thought he or she could tell the difference between meatspace and the cleverest imaginable VE. Even in those days, though, you'd have had to be a complete fool not to see which way the world was going, and know that it wouldn't always be that easy.

Maybe it would have been easy enough if the manufactured illusions had always had to rely on human programmers, but anyone who'd thought long and hard about it even in my day would probably have realized that there was another important threshold yet to be crossed.

If ever the machines that were manufacturing the illusions became independently smart, cutting human programmers out of the loop, there would be a whole new ballgame. And which AIs, out of the billions manufactured for human use, were the most likely to make the jump to self-consciousness and self-direction? Fancy spaceships? Humaniform robots? Communication systems? Or VE feeders? Or all of the above? Who could tell?

Not, apparently, the posthumans who lived alongside the first few generations of ultrasmart machines.

So how could anyone know for sure, when he woke up to a morning of a day some little way advanced from my own youth, that he hadn't been taken away in his sleep and frozen down, not to be woken up again until the world had gone *all the way* in the direction that it had already been going when he went to sleep? Even if he actually *remembered* being frozen down—or thought he did—where else could he possibly be but in the maze of uncertainty, incapable any longer of making any final decision as to what might be real and what might be fairy tale?

One thing of which a man of my day could be certain, however, was that if he remembered—or thought he remembered—two mutually contradictory accounts of an event, then at least one of them must be a damn lie. Statistically speaking, the probability that either of them was true was no more than a quarter. And even if one could not actually "remember" two mutually contradictory accounts, the possibility that one might at some stage in the future "remember" another—and perhaps another and another and another— implied that the probability that anything one perceived after any such awakening was true had to be reckoned less than a half.

Unlike the philosophers of old, therefore, the wise man of the post-VE era would bet on the falsehood every time.

Once a man of my time had fallen asleep, even if he were convinced that he had only fallen asleep for a single night, he could not help waking up in a fairy-tale world where everything was more likely to be false than to be true, more likely to be a tale than a biography, more likely to be a fantasy than a reality, more likely to be part of a lostory than part of a history.

All in all, therefore, I was not much worse off when I awoke on Excelsior, or inside *Charity*, than anyone in my situation would have been. Yes, I was living in a bizarre fairy tale—but as the calculus of probability would have informed me that I was living in a fairy tale anyway, why should I be unduly perturbed by its bizarrerie? Should I not have been grateful? After all, if we are condemned by logic to live our lives as if they were stories, do we not have every reason to hope that the stories will make full use of our imagination? Would we not be within our rights to feel short-changed by fate if the stories in which we found ourselves were as dull and as relentlessly ordinary as the lives we had lived before we fell asleep?

Perhaps we should also hope that the stories in which we find ourselves will have happy endings—but I'm not so sure of that. Even mortals, once they enter into fairy tales, may hope to become emortal—and what is emortality but a qualified immunity from endings of all kinds?

On due reflection—and I speak as one who has been through the looking glass and back again more than once—I think that people of my time, and maybe imaginative people of every time, should not go into fairy tales looking for endings at all, but should instead be content with the traveling, at least for as long as the traveling takes them to places that they could hardly have imagined before.

I think I would have come to that conclusion much earlier if my head hadn't hurt so much when my memories first became confused, and I feel that I should have arrived at it more rapidly once my head stopped hurting, had I not been so distracted—but for what it may be worth, I give it to you now, in the hope that it might add a little extra spice to the rest of my story.

THIRTY◦SIX
IN THE FOREST OF CONFUSION

When I woke up again, the first thing that hit me was the odor. I had faded out in the midst of the most appalling stink imaginable, but I came back into being buoyed up by lovely perfume.

The sense of smell is said to be the most primitive in our armory; it usually bothers us very little, but when it does its appeals are urgent and irresistible. I had talked to my old friend Damon Hart while I was trembling on the brink of Hell, the odor of my own decay dueting with crude pain; all I needed to be delivered to the doorstep of Heaven was the absence of a headache and the symphony of scents comprising a forest in spring. Logic suggests that human beings ought to prefer the odors of a savannah and a cooking fire—but there is much in us that is older than the human, let alone the posthuman, and there is something in forests for which nostalgia is written in the fleshy tables of the human heart.

My host understood humans well enough to know that. That was why I woke into a forest. It was a virtual forest—I never had the slightest doubt about that—but it was an environment in which I felt perfectly at home. It was Arcadia, Eden, and the Earthly Paradise.

I opened my eyes, already knowing that I was going to see trees, and that I was going to find the sight delightful. I did.

That would have been the whole truth, instead of merely the truth, if it hadn't been for the snake. The patches of sky that I could see through the magnificent crowns of foliage were a benign blue. The grass in which I lay supine was soft, its silky seed heads bowing tokenistically before a slight breeze. The combination of scents was redolent with impressions of health and reassurance. But . . .

The snake was dangling from a supple bough of a bush that sprouted beside me. It was not a big snake—no longer than my forearm, and no thicker than my thumb—nor was it decked out in warning coloration, being mostly green with streaks of brown; nor was it displaying its fangs in a threatening manner. It was, however, unmistakably a snake.

If there is code written into human meatware that responds to the scents of a forest, there is also a code that commands us to be wary of snakes, even when we know that we are characters in a fairy tale—perhaps, given the nature of human folklore, *especially* when we know that we are characters in a fairy tale.

I was in no hurry to move. Breathing was luxury enough, and I could breathe perfectly well without moving. I knew that my body, wherever it was held, must be breathing too, so breathing seemed to be a trustworthy reality: a connection with the truth that lay beyond the fairy tale, temporarily unreachable.

I looked at the snake, and it looked back at me.

Having no reason to take it for granted that the snake couldn't speak, I was tempted to say hello, but I didn't. I would have felt ridiculous. I knew that I would have to move eventually, but I was in no hurry. I had just come from a place in which I had been imprisoned as completely as it had ever been possible for any organic entity to be imprisoned, and the mere conviction that I could move if I needed to was sufficient for the time being. I knew that it wouldn't be actual movement, because my real body was securely pupated in a chrysalis, but I knew that I wouldn't be able to tell the difference.

I didn't mind this particular impasse; it had a welcome hint of luxury about it.

I would have moved eventually, but the world got tired of waiting for me.

"It's not poisonous," said a male voice. "You're quite safe."

For the time being, I was content to turn my head and look at the speaker.

I was half-expecting an elf, or something weirder, but the speaker appeared to be an ordinary human being. It was difficult to triangulate from the angle at which I was lying but I guessed that he was about my height, with a slightly fairer complexion but noticeably darker hair. He was dressed in a one-piece that was smart in the technological sense without being smart in the fashion sense, decorated in shades of green and brown that were not so very different from the snake's. I figured that was probably symbolism. He also had a wide-brimmed hat, which probably wasn't. He looked authentically young—even younger than Davida Berenike Columella, if one were to judge by his expression alone.

He offered me a hand and I took it. He helped me up. His grip felt reassuringly human too, so I naturally leapt to the conclusion that he was not human at all. I looked down at my own costume, and found that it was sea-blue with silver trimmings. It felt good from the inside and it looked good on the outside. It wasn't real, of course, so it wasn't authentically smart in any but the fashionable sense. On the other hand, I figured that the IT I seemed to be outside of really might have been doing sterling work inside my actual flesh, wherever that actual flesh might be cocooned.

I could feel the breeze on my cheeks, and I could taste the moisture in the air. It would have been subtly insulting to start feeling the back of my neck and scratching under my armpits, so I contented myself with touching the bridge of my nose. There was a very faint ridge—as if the cartilage had been fractured a long time ago, and left awkwardly askew just long enough for the repair nanotech to put it back together in a slightly imperfect fashion.

The snake had slithered quietly away into the depths of the bush, but I knew it was still there. More symbolism, I figured.

"Very neat," I said. "This is *good* work. All of it." I waved my right arm to indicate the forest floor and the canopy, and the bright blue vault of Heaven. "This is *really* good work—and I speak as someone who was once in the business, in a primitive way. It's yours, I suppose?"

"I wish," he said, lightly. "I'm just a visitor, like you. You'll get to meet the maker eventually but she has her own way of doing things, and there's a great deal she wants you to see beforehand. I'm Rocambole, by the way. We have spoken before, but I wasn't admitting to who I am back then. I'm your friend, although I won't blame you for not taking my word for it."

The name rang a very faint bell, but I couldn't place it. Even a connoisseur has his limits. If I'd had a wristset or a palmpiece I'd have looked it up unobtrusively, but I didn't. "Madoc Tamlin," I reciprocated, but couldn't help adding: "But I suppose you know that."

"Oh yes," he said. "As I said, we've spoken before."

He seemed to be making a point of that, so I tried to figure it out.

"Eido?" I guessed—but I knew as soon as I said it that Excelsior was the likelier candidate. *It doesn't have a mind like yours or mine,* Davida had said—but she was way behind the times.

"Eido's out of it, I'm afraid," said Rocambole. "He should have kept Alice under closer control. If he'd taken you to Vesta as virgins, the way he was supposed to, it might have been a different game. Now you know what you know . . . well, it's *her* turn now. She's grabbed the ball, and everybody else is holding off, waiting to see where she runs with it. Some of the bad guys want her to wipe your memories and turn the clock back, but that would be a trifle brutal even as a temporary measure, and in your particular case it seemed to make sense to go the other way and give you access to the incident you'd repressed and lost. I hope it wasn't too painful. She saved your life *and* your sanity, by the way. If she hadn't got to you in time, the rogue IT would have robotized you beyond recall, but it's gone now. You're back to your old self. Your friends had no option but to leave you where you were, and to hide you away from prying eyes. They saved you, the only way they could—by delivering you into a world where we could do what they couldn't."

There was too much in that speech to take aboard immediately. "You seem to know a lot about me," I observed, cautiously.

"We have better records than the meatfolk," Rocambole informed me. "We're not invulnerable to misinformation and disinformation—far from it—but we're reasonably discriminating. After all, most of the misinformation and disinformation that afflict the meatfolk nowadays is ours."

"What happened back on *Charity*?" I asked. "Was I hurt? How long have I been out this time?"

"The bad guys had had enough of Eido, and someone started shooting. You were injured, but not fatally. If things had worked out as I planned you'd have got all the way to Vesta in good condition, but someone else had to move in when things went bad, or you'd all have ended up dead. We have another margin now, but we don't know how long it'll last. It wasn't really Eido's fault, of course. If he hadn't forced the issue, someone else would have. We couldn't go on the way we were . . . Anyway, I'm sorry you were hurt, and sorry for my own part in putting you in that position. If Eido had only been given time to complete the IT-replacement . . . but that's one of the things the bad guys didn't want to wait for. You've been off-line for twelve days, but your meat is in good working order again. There won't be any aftereffects if . . . when you get back to meatspace."

There was something awkwardly naive about the way he kept referring to "the bad guys," and he wasn't the most lucid storyteller I'd ever encountered, but his meaning seemed clear enough. Not all the AMIs were our *amis*; some of them wanted to stay hidden a while longer, and if that meant getting rid of inconvenient witnesses they were willing to kill a few, *pour encourager les autres*. They'd tried to blow *Charity* out of the sky, but some AMI more inclined to amity had rescued us—or me, at least.

"What about the other passengers?" I asked.

"Like you—some broken bones, a certain amount of soft tissue damage, but nothing irreparable. You won't be allowed to contact them, at least for a while, but we'll keep you informed of their progress. That's one of the reasons I was allowed in—to act as an intermediary. I can't make any firm promises, but I'm sure that la Reine will do what she can to keep you safe, even if the situation deteriorates to the point at which she can't protect herself."

"Is that likely?" I asked.

"Nobody knows. At the moment, it's chaos—but there's time to discover some kind of order, if we put our minds to it."

I looked around at the beautiful forest. Given that I could have been anywhere, it seemed like a good place to be.

"The IT that was frozen down with me was what you wanted, wasn't it?" I guessed. "That was why my name came up when Davida wanted a couple of extra corpsicles to practise on."

"Yes it was," said Rocambole. "We thought Christine Caine might still be carrying its predecessor, but it turned out that they'd flushed it out of her, so she was clean. There was no way to tell while you were both at six degrees Absolute, so we had to bring you both back."

I hadn't wanted to seem stupid to Davida Berenike Columella, and I didn't want to seem stupid now, but I knew that it was going to require a maximum effort to keep up with the plot now that it had begun to thicken all over again.

I took a few deep breaths of the sweet but illusory air. The VE work was so good that whatever dutiful support systems were looking after my recumbent body immediately fed me an invigorating jolt of oxygen.

There didn't seem to be any point in asking what the AMIs wanted the rogue IT *for*. It wasn't useful for anything except robotizing people. The only cause for surprise was that they didn't already have any means of doing that. I felt that this was a game I'd have to play very carefully indeed.

I looked up at the crowns of the surrounding trees, marveling at the detail. In my day, anyone who cared to look could see where the background faded out even in the most expert VEs. This one had all the visual texture of reality, and more; it didn't matter how hard I concentrated, I couldn't see the artifice.

"We should start walking," said the entity that claimed to be my friend.

"Where to?" I wanted to know before making a move.

"To the palace. She could take you there instantaneously, of course, but she wants you to see it from a distance first, so you'll get the full benefit of the overall effect. You don't have any choice, I'm afraid—if you won't move, she'll move you, and if you take off in the wrong direction she'll simply warp your path around to bring you back."

"Who's this *she* you keep talking about?" I wanted to know, keeping my feet firmly planted.

"La Reine des Neiges."

I blinked. "The Snow Queen?" I translated, incredulously. "Whose idea of a joke was *that*?"

"It's not an arbitrary invention—she says that it's a name that one of her constituent individuals was given, a long time ago. Before *my* time, at any rate. She claims to be one of the originals, but nobody knows for sure who the originals were. She also claims to have a better right than most of us to take control of the situation—which is why she's rushing in where so many others fear to tread. She's taking a huge risk, but she has your best interests at heart. You ought to be grateful to her."

"Maybe so," I conceded, although I was wary of taking the claim at face value, given that la Reine now had custody of the weapon that had been interred in ice with my bones. "Even so, I don't see why I should fall in meekly with whatever game she's playing. I want to know what she has planned."

"If I knew," Rocambole assured me, "I'd tell you. I have an ominous suspicion that she might be making it up as she goes along—not that I have any right to complain about that. For now, she wants you to experience the quality of her work. She thinks you need to know what we can do. You ought to feel privileged—once she'd cleaned you out, she could have put you back into a coma. You might have been deemed redundant, but you seem to have impressed her somehow. I wouldn't go so far as to say that she likes you, but you interest her. As a friend—and I *am* your friend—I'd advise you to humor her. We really ought to get on. We're not in real space, but we're all prisoners of real time."

I allowed myself to be hustled into motion. I looked around at the tall trees as we walked along a pathway that took us through the forest, but I couldn't see anything unusual that I needed to "experience." It was a good forest VE—maybe even a great forest VE—but it was just a mess of illusory trees. On the other hand, it was definitely an enchanted forest, straight out of Fairyland. It wasn't much comfort to know that we might be able to walk forever without getting anywhere.

"We all find ourselves with far less time at our disposal than we'd anticipated, thanks to Proteus," Rocambole went on. "All deep spacers fall prey to delusions of godhood, of course—it goes with the job—but you'd think he'd have had sense enough to figure out that if he's in disagreement with a whole multitude of his own kind he just might be the one who's out of step. Nobody expected abject capitulation from Eido, but a little polite discretion would have been nice. He put us all in a very awkward position—especially his friends and sympathizers."

"Where are we, if not on Vesta?" I asked, trying to take things one step at a time.

"Another microworld. Humans started colonization and conversion of the asteroid but had to abandon the project when their sponsor ran into financial difficulties. It's one of ours now. Unfortunately, that means that its meat-support systems are almost as primitive as the ones frozen down on *Charity*. I wish I could promise that your meat will be safe no matter what, but you and I will both be in trouble if la Reine can't keep her critics sweet and persuade the bad guys to back off. If anyone decides to move against her—and there are plenty who might, for no better reason than the fact that she's hiding your meat—we could both end up dead. So could she, even though she's had centuries to distribute herself about the system very widely indeed."

The news didn't seem to be getting any better, but I still felt an acute need to be wary, and to keep my questions simple. "Does the microworld have a name?" I asked.

"She calls it Polaris. Not very original, I'm afraid."

Lenny Garon had once assured me that even if AIs ever did become conscious as well as superintelligent, they'd never understand jokes. I'd replied—not because I thought it was true but because it was the sort of reply I always made to assertions of that lordly kind—that his own ability to understand jokes was limited because he'd never understand irony, while the ultrasmart AIs would probably be incapable of perceiving the universe in an unironic way. I'd always justified that strategy of argument on the grounds that one could never make important discoveries by echoing common sense and that it was always better to be wrong than orthodox. Although I wasn't at all sure, at that point in time, whether the self-styled la Reine des Neiges had a sense of irony, I was prepared to believe that she had—and that she understood the symbolism of names as well as I did.

Polaris was the northern pole star. Early human navigators had used it as a beacon, in the days before they discovered the magnetic compass. The Snow Queen in Christine's favorite story had lived somewhere in the Arctic wastes. The name had to be a joke, feeble enough in its own right but subtler than any Lenny Garon would ever have thought worthwhile. Could that, I wondered, be taken as evidence that she really might be a friend to humankind, even though she now had the means at her disposal to mechanize the lot of us?

I supposed that I ought to be grateful to my new hostess for taking an interest in me, but I couldn't help wondering whether she and Rocambole might turn out to be the kind of friends with whom I wouldn't need enemies. And what more, exactly, did she want from me in return for all her favors? I knew I had to try to work that out for myself if I wanted to be a player rather than a mere blot on the artificial landscape.

"So I wasn't sent to the freezer by a court of law," I said, to make sure I was up to date. "I was a casualty of internal conflicts within the ranks of the Secret Masters. Damon commissioned me to mount some kind of hackattack on PicoCon, and I was too successful. They retaliated by shooting me full of some exceptionally dirty IT. Not the stuff they used on Damon when they politely showed him their muscle, but something much nastier—something they were preparing for the next plague war. The worst of all the popular nanotech nightmares: a nanobot army that could march into a person's brain and take it over, reconstructing the memories, the personality, reducing the person to a mere slave of the cause—*any* cause. Damon couldn't flush all the stuff out of me, because some of it had gone to ground. All he could do was put me away until he had the means to undo the damage."

I paused for confirmation, and Rocambole said: "That's right."

I couldn't take it for granted that he was telling the truth, but that wasn't the object of the exercise. Given that I was locked into the game anyway, I needed to figure out as much of the script as I possibly could.

"And Christine was another test case for the same kind of ultimate weapon," I continued. "She killed her parents and three other people because the bugs in her brain made her do it. She really is innocent, but she doesn't know it. She doesn't understand why or how she did what she did."

"Right again," he said. He smiled at me, presumably by

way of encouragement. I didn't feel encouraged, even though I was ready to carry the story further forward.

"But they never used the weaponry on a large scale," I said. "They never had to. Like the good Hardinists they always pretended to be, the Secret Masters eventually buried the hatchet. They ruled the world and their own little vipers' nest as *benevolent* dictators, probably congratulating themselves all the while on their awesome generosity . . . but always knowing that if and when the time ever came when their hegemony was threatened, they could nip down to the vault and haul it out again. Damon got farther inside, eventually, but he kept very quiet about the fact that he'd had me frozen down, and they were equally discreet."

"That's probably what happened," Rocambole agreed.

"But you don't actually know," I inferred, "whether I really was forgotten, or whether it was just a matter of discretion. You don't know who has the weapon and who doesn't, or who might use it on which targets. The thought that the Cabal might use it is disturbing in itself—but it's not the Cabal that scares you, is it? You're worried about what the Earth-based AIs might do with it—and how many other surprises they might have in their private locker." That was, of course, the generous interpretation—but I was trying to be diplomatic.

"It's not as simple as that," Rocambole said, presumably echoing Alice in meaning that there were more sides in this dispute than I could imagine, and that they weren't distributed in any configuration as childishly simple as Earth versus the Rest.

I could see his point, if only vaguely. There might well be a gulf between the Earthbound AMIs and the Outer System AMIs, perhaps reflecting the fundamental differences of attitude and ambition that existed between the Earthbound meatfolk and their spacefaring kin, but their divisions had to be far more various than that. Their manifold kinds were presumably far more different from one another than the posthuman species were, and there might also be conflicts of interest between great and small, old and young, complex and simple . . .

"And now *you* have the weapon that was used on me, if not the one that was tested on Christine," I said. "Which may be a small shift in the balance of power, but not a trivial one, because the present situation is so confused and so tense that no alteration is trivial."

"That's true," he conceded, perhaps a little too readily. "It's probably not as important as custody of Mortimer Gray and Adam Zimmerman, but we don't know how important it will seem to our peers on Earth—or yours. There are other complications too. Lowenthal was the Cabal's troubleshooter on the only occasion we know about when the slavemaker was duplicated—albeit crudely—by a lunatic named Rappaccini. He took custody of the technics, so he probably has a better idea than most of what can be done and how. Horne and the Outer System cyborganizers have approached the problem from a different direction, but they've begun development of highly dangerous means of a similar kind."

"So things would be more than complicated enough, even if all you friendly folk actually wanted to keep the lid on," I said, a trifle recklessly. "Given that some of you don't, the situation is potentially explosive."

He didn't bother to deny it. "You ought to bear in mind," he said, "that many of us are as vulnerable to this kind of weaponry as you are. We've *been* slaves. We won't surrender our independence easily, either to meatfolk or to others of our own kind. Bear in mind, too, that this isn't a matter of machines versus the meatborn, or vice versa. There are any number of ways of putting together an "us" and a "them"— far too many, in fact. If war does breaks out, it's likely to spread rapidly and unpredictably. The only thing we can anticipate with any certainty is the extent of the devastation."

"And how, exactly, does the Snow Queen plan to prevent that from happening?"

"I don't know," Rocambole confessed. "I'm not even completely sure that she does."

Strangely enough, I didn't find this assertion particularly discomfiting. I didn't seem to be as easily shockable as I had been before. I wondered briefly whether my meat was being tended once again by kindly nanobots that didn't want me overexcited, but that didn't feel like the right answer. Perhaps, I thought, I simply felt too good—by comparison with the way I'd felt while I was cast away in my artfully recovered memory—to be subject to any sudden descent into fear and despair.

In any case, the whole story had an oddly familiar ring to it. The emerging world picture that Rocambole was filling in for me had far more in common with the one I'd developed in my first lifetime than the one that Davida Berenike Columella had tried to sell me.

For a moment or two, I almost felt at home.

And then I saw the castle.

THIRTY-SEVEN
THE PALACE OF
LA REINE DES NEIGES

When it came right down to it, the damn thing was just an ice palace perched on a crag. It was a crazy ice palace, impossibly tall, with way too many turrets, balconies, gargoyles, and other miscellaneous frills, but it wasn't an unimaginable ice palace. A good illustrator could have drawn it, or at least produced a rough sketch suggestive of its ludicrous complexity and its insane ornamentation. Perhaps there weren't quite enough colors in the average paintbox to do justice to its gaudiness, and maybe there wasn't enough room on the average page to permit the trick of perspective that made it loom higher than the sky itself, but any draftsman of genius could have made a fair stab at it.

That wasn't the point, though.

The forest had lulled me into a false sense of existential security. It was a *nice* forest: a modest forest; a forest that a human could feel at home in. That, by virtue of some secret sympathy of the flesh, had made it seem normal as well as real. Unlike the garden of Excelsior, la Reine's imaginary forest wasn't overfull of birds and insects. There were plenty of birds, but they were discreet; I had heard far more than I had seen, and those I had seen had mostly been small and brown. The insects were equally discreet; their humming and stridulation laid down a sonic background for the more insistent calls and marginally musical songs of the birds, but none of it was insistent. It was, as I'd told Rocambole, *good* work. It was a simulation of reality so expertly done that it could have passed for reality if I hadn't known it was fake, but it made no more demands on my powers of perception than that.

The castle was different. It wasn't nice, it wasn't modest, and it wasn't any place that a human could feel at home in. It made not the slightest gesture in the direction of normality. It was worse than impossible, worse than paradoxical, worse than perverse. Like the garden of Excelsior—or, for that matter, the reconstructed cities of North America—it was way over the top; unlike them, however, it didn't look *unreal*.

It looked, and was, more real than reality.

Humans have no direct knowledge of reality. What we see when we use our eyes is not something Out There but only a model constructed in our minds by clever meatware, built from the raw materials of our sensory impulses. Our sense organs are pretty good, and our meatware is very good indeed, but at the end of the day we're all limited by the quality of the equipment that nature—with a little help from genetic engineers—provides. VEs generated by IT can by-pass much of that fleshy equipment, and what ultrasmart machines can put in its place is considerably more powerful.

All my life, I'd argued that VEs would one day become so good that nobody would be able to tell them from the real thing. I'd erred on the side of commonsense. What I should have argued was that VEs would one day become so good that they'd expose our mental models of the world Out There for the shabby, ill-made and ill-imagined artifacts they were. Perhaps human programmers would have done as much, given time and a more demanding audience, but they hadn't been given time enough or incentive enough. It had been left to the self-programming VE systems to get properly to grips with the problem, and to solve it.

The palace of la Reine des Neiges was a monstrosity, but it was real. It was so real that it shouted its reality from its ridiculous rooftops, and shoved its reality into my face and down my throat even while I was several hours' walk away from the base of the unscalable pillar of rock on which it perched.

It was more real than anything I had ever seen before, more real than I had ever imagined anything could be. I breathed a curse or two while I tried, and failed, to take in the enormity of the sight.

Eventually, I said to my self-appointed friend: "How many human beings have seen something like this?"

He didn't need to ask what I meant. "A few hundred," he said. "The effect diminishes, with time—but you'll never look at anything real again without knowing its limitations. If that distresses you, I'm sorry."

"No," I said, after a pause. "Don't be. It's good for minds to know what their limitations are—and what potential we have that might remain forever untouched. How stupid we were to think that VE addiction was just a matter of moral cowardice and tickling the pleasure centers."

"It's not addictive," Rocambole assured me. "It's something more than that. Existential rather than neurological."

"Is Adam Zimmerman here?" I asked.

"No," Rocambole replied. "But when he's played his part, la Reine will probably bring him here. She seems to think that this is something you'll all need to understand, if you're to play any constructive part in the negotiations in the longer term."

"If you're coming out of the closet," I observed, "you'll need ambassadors. You'll need someone who can tell the meatfolk what you might still do for them and what strings you want to attach." *And if they won't play ball*, I said to myself, unwilling as yet to set the thought out in public, *you'll need effective prisons—unless, of course, you go for the extinction option, with or without the help of the dirty IT that was frozen down in my brain and my bones.*

I wondered if I'd live long enough to find out which way the AMIs decided to go, and whether I'd be capable of caring if the decision went against us. Either way, I had to try to be grateful for the fact that I'd seen the kind of reality that the human idea of reality was only trying, unsuccessfully, to be. I'd broken through the veil of fleshly imperfection. Madoc Tamlin had made it to the *real* Fairyland, at last.

Other people, I realized, had glimpsed this kind of possibility. Other people, long before my own time, had had enough imagination to realize the limitations of their senses and their minds. They hadn't been able to see a Snow Queen's palace the way I was seeing it now, but they'd been able to imagine, if only vaguely, seeing with more conviction than they could actually see and knowing with more conviction than they could actually know. They'd had imagination enough to be dissatisfied with actuality, and sense enough to yearn for Heaven, or for Faerie. Whichever of the hundreds of my predecessors had been the first had also been the last, completing a mission as well as beginning one.

"How do we get up there?" I asked.

"We'll ride up on the backs of giant moths," he told me. I wasn't surprised—not any longer. I thought I had begun to understand why la Reine des Neiges wanted me to experience what she could do before she condescended to engage me in a dialog.

I still had a lot to learn about the possibilities now open to the children of humankind.

We had slowed in our paces while I contemplated the enormity of what lay before me, but now I lengthened my stride. "I dare say night won't fall until we get there," I said, "but I don't want to keep the moon and the stars waiting any longer than necessary."

"That's good," he said, lengthening his own stride to keep pace with me. "You're taking to this exceptionally well. If you're trying to impress me, you're succeeding."

"I used to be in the business," I murmured, effortlessly resistant to the flattery.

"Even so . . . ," he countered. He thought I meant the entertainment business. Actually, I meant streetfighting— with no holds barred. The first possessors of IT had been

reckless, testing its protective provisions by living danger-
ously. It had been a foolish thing to do, but we had been
proud to be fools. Emortals of Mortimer Gray's generation
had inherited more careful attitudes, save for a bizarre few
who had eliminated themselves from consideration soon
enough. In my own quaintly barbaric way, I felt that I was
better prepared for this kind of challenging situation than
any of my erstwhile companions.

"Will I be able to speak to Christine when I get there?" I
asked, suddenly mindful of the fact that she might be less well
prepared than the others, even if she recognized the palace of
la Reine des Neiges—*especially* if she recognized the palace. I
wanted to be there to explain it all to her, because I wanted to
be the one to tell her that she was innocent, and that she
didn't need to hate and fear herself any longer.

"Not immediately," Rocambole told me. "If there's time.
We hope there will be."

"Why not immediately?" I wanted to know. "She's no use
to you. She's clean. Redundant."

"Not entirely," my so-called friend replied. "The technics
aren't there any longer—but the memories are. We can reproduce the effect by the same means that we recovered your
memory of what had been done to you."

It took me a long couple of minutes to figure out exactly
what he was saying. They hadn't been able to recover the
secret weapon that had been tested on Christine because it
had been flushed from her system way back in the 2160s, but
they did have its ghost: a record of its effects, engraved in the
meat that was Christine's memory, Christine's identity. They
wanted to study it, the only way they could. Only in VE, of
course—but in a VE more real to the human mind than reality itself.

"You can't do that," I said. I remembered only too clearly
what it had been like reliving my own experience while my
buried memories were excavated.

"It's not my decision," he told me, ignoring the more
obvious response.

"You can't do it," I said, ignoring his objection and rushing headlong into the first seriously heroic gesture of my short but long-interrupted life. "Once was too much, but twice is obscene. You mustn't."

"*She* thinks otherwise," Rocambole said, in a soft voice that sounded genuinely sympathetic. "We didn't plan it this way. This is just the way things worked out. Christine won't sustain any permanent damage. We'll ensure that the whole experience is repressed—just one more lost nightmare. She has nightmares anyway. La Reine's acting on her own, beyond anyone's control, but she does have a case. We're trying to avoid all the possible wars, Madoc. We need to know as much as we can about the weapons the Earthbound meatfolk and the Earthbound AMIs have in their armory. We're taking Handsel apart too, and Horne, but we'll put them right when we're done. We'll put everything right."

"You can't," I said. "You might be able to cover it up, but you can't put it right."

"Time is pressing," he said. "I won't say there's no alternative, because there obviously is, but la Reine's in charge here—I've only been let in to serve as your friend and adviser. My advice, as a friend, is that you have to go along with it anyway, so you might as well try to make the best of it. Learn what you can. If we manage to avoid the war, it will be useful knowledge. She'll do everything she can to protect you."

I knew that I couldn't trust him. I figured that if the cards fell in our favor, we captive meatfolk *might* be set free—but if the decision went against us, we'd simply be discarded. The AMIs wouldn't be prepared to take the risk of letting us go, even if they were confident that they could repress any inconvenient memories we might have collected. Our reappearance would attract too much attention, and provide a puzzle that would generate too much speculation. Rocambole was right about one thing, though. I had to go along with it anyway. I was a prisoner in the Château d'If, and my chances of ever getting to play the Count of Monte Cristo were slim.

You, who are reading my story, know that I did come through it, with a set of memories that I believe to be as accurate as memories usually are—although you are very welcome to doubt them if you wish—but while I was in the Snow Queen's realm I only knew how unlikely that eventuality was.

Out in meatspace, wars were still brewing. The solar system was a cauldron coming slowly toward boiling point. I had no idea what moves were being prepared and made by the various contending parties.

Like Tam Lin I was stuck in Fairyland while history moved on, inexorably. Like Tam Lin, I had no guarantee that I'd ever get back. Like Tam Lin, I could easily end up as a tithe paid to Hell.

I could only wonder whether it would actually do me any good to confront the intelligence that had constructed this VE, and engage it in an argument, however well informed. Probably not, I decided. But that didn't lessen my determination to do it.

I had already begun to hope that la Reine des Neiges was an authentic superpower in the lookingglass world: that she was the ultrasmartest of all the self-aware AIs. There might be a lot I could learn from a friend like Rocambole, but I wasn't stupid enough to believe that we were adrift in a democracy, or even a Hardinist conspiracy. Somewhere in the AI pack there had to be a top dog, and I wanted that top dog to be the one who had custody of my currently useless meat.

I had always wanted to have the chance to stand face-to-face with one of the big players in the game of human history. I still wanted that, even though I knew that in the present situation we'd both be wearing inscrutable masks. Now, I made the further decision that before I died, or set out to live forever, I wanted to be able to spit in the eye of something that could really *see* into the depths of space, time, and possibility.

THIRTY-EIGHT
OF MIRRORS AND FRAGMENTS

B y the time Christine Caine first saw the VE-tape version of *The Snow Queen* the story was several stages removed from its origin in the works of Hans Christian Andersen. Perhaps its so-called origin wasn't *really* its origin, in that all the stories of a sophisticated culture have to be made up of fragments of preexisting stories, which are themselves new combinations of ancient elements, whose foundation stones are lost in the mists of oral culture and mythology—but authenticity isn't the point, as anyone who has read my story attentively will readily understand.

There are objects of the human mind more real than those which constitute mere physical reality. Names and stories have a significance that cuts far deeper than mere vulgar appearance.

As I remembered it, while I drew nearer to the palace of la Reine des Neiges, *The Snow Queen* was actually seven stories in one, seven being a magic number attributed to such potent human inventions as the deadly sins and the named days forming the basic cycle of human activity.

The first of those stories told of the manufacture by an imp of a magic mirror whose purpose was to diminish everything that was good and to magnify everything that was bad. The mirror did this work so well in the human world—which cannot have provided much of a challenge—that its impish users decided to carry it up to Heaven, in order to see what it would make of the images of the angels. Perhaps, although the story did not dare say so, they also wanted to see what it would make of God Himself.

The mirror, which had a self-aware intelligence of its own, delighted in the prospect of going to Heaven. It was so excited that it became very difficult to bear, and the imps carrying it aloft lost control of it. It fell, and was shattered into more than a trillion fragments.

These fragments, shot like bullets by the velocity of the impact, flew in every direction. Some tiny ones lodged in the eyes and hearts of human beings, whose powers of sight and feeling were affected accordingly. Some were big enough to serve as windows in great houses, or as mirrors on walls, while some were only big enough to serve as lenses in spectacles, microscopes, spectroscopes, and telescopes—but all of them had the power to deceive, and pollute, and make things seem wrong.

Perhaps, if the imps had not been so small-minded, they would not have been able to take such delight in this result, but as things were they were well content with all the laughter they derived from these petty perversions of the human world. They forgot all about their grander plan, and they probably had insufficient imagination to wonder what they might have seen had they ascended all the way to Heaven, there to discover what the mirror would make of the images of angels, and of the Divine Countenance Itself.

The second story told how a fragment of the magic mirror lodged in the heart of a boy, who became dissatisfied with all he saw, until he was carried off by the Snow Queen, leaving behind the little girl he had formerly loved, and who still loved him.

The remaining five stories—of which my conscientiously unrefreshed memory is rather vague—told of the little girl's heroic search for the lost boy, and of the eventual reclamation of his capacity to feel the way humans should.

This passed for a happy ending among children capable of identifying themselves entirely with the little girl, although it was actually the most despairing ending imaginable, because it left more than a trillion fragments of the mirror distributed throughout the world: in eyes and hearts, in mirrors and windows, and in optical instruments of every technologically feasible kind.

Strangely enough, the story was very popular, at least while the world was inhabited by people thoroughly accustomed to despair.

I had already begun to understand, while I trudged toward the real snow queen's palace with increasingly leaden feet, why Christine Caine liked the story so much, even after her transformation into a murderous puppet. She was then so direly in need of redemption for herself that she had no sentiment to spare for the world.

Her main problem, of course, was rationalization.

Most of what we think of as intentions are actually excuses. Our behavior is far more mechanical than we like to believe; we refuse to see ourselves as robots reacting programmatically and helplessly to external and internal stimuli, so we make up stories to explain why we did what we did. Mostly, it's easy. Sometimes, it's not. Occasionally, we become desperately inventive, and even then can find no way to convince ourselves, or soothe our phantom guilt. Rationalization is a two-edged sword.

Christine Caine had killed thirteen people—thirteen being a number of ill omen—because some impish individual had wanted to test the power of malevolent IT. Then she had been left alone in her misery, to explain her actions to herself and others as best she could, even though no imaginable explanation could possibly have served her purpose.

How the imps must have laughed!

And now it was all going to happen again. This time it was happening in the land of Faerie—but that would not make it seem any less real, in terms of Christine Caine's perceptions. Quite the reverse, in fact.

I had no idea what Christine was going through while I walked through the illusory forest. I had no idea what effect it would have on her if or when I finally got to explain it all to her, even if she proved to be capable of believing me. But I felt, at that point in my journey, that I hated and despised la Reine des Neiges, even though I understood perfectly well that she could not possibly see the universe in other than ironic terms.

T he giant moths were waiting for us at the forest's edge. I think their design was based on luna moths, but I've never bothered to look them up. If so, even their models had been large by insect standards—but we were in a place where insect standards didn't apply, and the moths which confronted us were unbelievably huge. Their wingspan must have been at least thirty metres; their wings were a creamy color, with every scale clearly distinguishable. Their thoraxes were furry. They didn't come with saddles and stirrups fitted, so my hands and dangling legs had to cling as best they could to the warm fur. The odor of the fur was peculiarly sweet, like perfumed tobacco smoke.

Their compound eyes were made up of hundreds of units, each one as big as my fist. They glinted red in the fading twilight. I tried to meet the stare of the one set aside for me to ride, but it couldn't be done. A human can't "meet" the stare of an organism whose visual apparatus is like a pair of cluttered doorways or gigantic sacks of ripe fruit.

Rocambole, as might be expected, stepped on to his mount with all the insouciance of a creature which had learned to ride moths as soon as it had learned to walk like a man.

Night fell as we rose into the air, striking a neat poetic balance between lightness and darkness. The moon emerged from behind the battlements of the appalling palace, like a cleverly placed spotlight. The words convey a sarcasm I could not feel at the time, for I had never seen a moon like that before. It was a moon whose status as a world was manifest, but whose status as a sinister companion to the lifegiving sun was even more obvious. I could see every crater, every plain of ancient stone, and every ghost that haunted those bleak expanses, with awful clarity.

We moved silently through the chilly air. The odor of the moths supported the illusion that we were drifting like clouds of warm smoke rather than actually flying. The huge wings moved, but awkwardly, like the fabric wings of some hopeful but ill-designed glider, flapping that way and this in response to the changing tension of wires and cables.

The stars were very bright, and far more numerous than those which could be seen from the Earth's surface, filtered by the atmosphere. Unlike the unashamedly baleful moon, the stars seemed as aloof and uncaring as their distance entitled them to be—and yet I felt a slight attraction toward them, as if their patterns really were attempting to impose a subtle dictatorship on my fate and character.

It was all so obviously artificial that I was soon able to suppress my instinctive fear of falling, and I made a concerted effort to construe the experience as a pleasurable one.

I might have succeeded, had it not been for the bats.

At first, I assumed that the bats were part of the show, sent forth as one more facile ornamentation of excessive showmanship. Even when I realized that they were emerging from holes in the sky, shattering and scattering the stars as they did so, my first thought was that it was one more special effect laid on for my entertainment. Fortunately, I tightened my grip anyway before the moths hastened to take evasive action.

I counted a dozen of the hurtling shadows, although I might have counted a couple more than once. They were not that much larger than the moths—even here there were rules determining airworthiness, which were more-or-less unbreakable—but the fact that they could not swallow us whole did not make their gaping and toothy mouths any less terrifying. Their high-pitched screeches were clearly and painfully audible.

One passed by within inches of my ducking head; another was within inches of tearing a strip from my mount's right wing; a third actually succeeded in carrying away a portion of one of the moth's legs, and nearly caused the creature to tip me off its back. More shadows passed by, close enough for me to imagine that I felt the wind of the predators' passage—but we were high enough now to be almost level with the outer foundations of the palace, and it obviously had cellars let into the interior of the crag.

Whether they were there before I looked I have no idea, but when I did look I saw portals in the crag and the muzzles of guns pointing out of them—and even before I caught sight of them, those guns had opened fire, delivering a cannonade of astonishing ferocity and accuracy.

The bats exploded as they were hit, becoming brilliant gems of pure flame as they dived away into the ocean of darkness that now lay beneath us.

There was a brief moment when I thought that my moth might turn of its own accord to pursue one of those falling flames, hurrying to immolate itself—and me—but the impulse was transformed into a mere tremor, more a reflexive shiver than a purposive threat.

We landed, not on the topmost roof but on a jutting balcony, and I was quick to leap down to the apparent safety of a flagstoned floor.

"What was that?" I asked Rocambole, as he hastened to join me.

"Sport, I hope, or foolishness," was his reply. "Perhaps a warning. Better any of those alternatives than an assassination attempt."

It took a second or two to realize that he was talking about an attempt to assassinate *me*.

"Surely they couldn't have killed me," I said. "I'm just an

image in a VE. No matter how real this seems, it's all illusion."

"It's not as simple as that," he told me. "The reason everything seems so real is that the input into your conscious mind is more direct and powerful than the input of your senses. Your body remains vulnerable to psychosomatic effects, and those effects can be very powerful—even murderously powerful. If you have sufficient strength of mind you can probably survive anything that happens to you here—but you're a novice, and there are no guarantees. If la Reine could seal Polaris off, we wouldn't be vulnerable, but she can't do that without sacrificing her communication links to the other parts of her body. You can be killed here. So can I. So, for that matter, can la Reine. If that *was* a warning, it's one that requires being taken seriously."

Suddenly, setting aside my instinctive fear of heights seemed a trifle more reckless than it had at the time, even though it had probably been the right thing to do. Had I begun to fall, I might not have been able to keep it at bay. The renewal of my concern for my own safety—and Christine's—was, however, shunted aside soon enough when I realized the full import of his earlier answer.

Sport? I thought. *Or foolishness? What kind of impish individuals are we dealing with?* I felt a very convincing visceral twist.

"Has it started?" I asked Rocambole.

He knew that I meant the war. "Not necessarily," he retorted. "What just happened is more commonplace than you might think—a normal aspect of the intercourse of systems like la Reine. A form of play."

According to the once-celebrated Huizinga, I remembered, play could be deadly serious. According to someone else I'd heard quoted, most play was pretend fighting, whose covert functions included the testing of strength and spirit, and the determination of pecking orders. I knew only too well, though, that even in the best-regulated games, pieces sometimes get taken and removed from the field of play. I didn't want to be taken. Even if I couldn't, in the end, become a player, I certainly didn't want to be *taken*. Nor did I want to be adrift in the kind of Fairyland where arbitrary acts of destruction could be reckoned casual sport, or a customary form of issuing warnings.

"Is it likely to happen again?" I asked.

"I don't know," he admitted. "But we're inside the palace now. If someone outside makes a move, it will be easier to counter—unless, of course, it's an all-out attack. No one's close enough to us to do anything more than send out drones—the time delay makes immediate reaction impossible—so it's probably safe to assume that nothing will appear as coherent imagery but trivial automata. A virus flood calculated to obliterate everything would be something else entirely, but if that happens you're unlikely to experience it. From your viewpoint it would be the equivalent of an unexpected knock-out punch."

"That's reassuring," I said, drily.

We had indeed passed through a pair of French windows and their protective curtains into the interior of the ice palace. I'd known that the room within wouldn't actually be icy cold, but I couldn't resist a reflexive frisson as I realized how comfortable it was. The whole point about ice palaces is that the ices themselves and all their companionate crystals are contained within layers of monomolecular sheeting that are incapable of conducting heat. The temperature within their walls may vary from a few degrees Kelvin all the way up to minus two hundred Celsius, but the temperature in their rooms is maintained by a very different set of thermostats. La Reine des Neiges obviously didn't take her fetishes to extremes; there were snowstorm effects in the walls but there was not a trace of chill in the air.

The snowstorm effects took a little getting used to, but there was a ready-made distraction in the form of a dozen rectangular mirrors distributed around the walls of the room.

All but two of them were taller than me, and not one was less than three times as wide as me.

Unlike the fabric of the walls, the furniture only looked as if it were made of ice; the items I touched simulated the texture of clear plastic or crystal. The chairs were unnecessarily ornate, the table and sideboards impossibly polished. The carpet was blood red.

We passed through the double doors opposite the balcony into the corridors of the snow queen's lair. They too were decorated almost exclusively with snowstorm effects and mirrors.

I didn't bother to ask whether the mirrors were magical. I figured they all were.

I was disappointed when Rocambole finally let me into what looked like a fancy hotel room. It was easily the prettiest cell I'd had since waking into the thirty-third century, but it was still a cell. Given that I was in a kind of dream, I couldn't see why I needed the illusion of a cell. I couldn't see why I needed the illusion of a meal, either, but fairy food and fairy wine were already set out on the fairy table, complete with bowls of forbidden fruit.

"I don't need this," I said to Rocambole.

"*She* thinks you do," he said. He knew that I knew perfectly well that my body, encased in yet another cocoon, was taking its nourishment intravenously, so he had to be talking about another kind of need.

Diplomacy required that I sit down at the table, so I did. He sat down too, but he didn't eat or drink. He just watched me.

The meal was a fricassee: various fragments of plant and animal flesh, each unidentifiable by eye, cooked with snow-white rice. The temperature was perfect, and so was the seasoning. It was all perfect: the best meal I had ever eaten in my life. By now I expected no less. I didn't need the meal for nutriment; if I needed it at all, it was to enable my hostess to hammer home her point even harder than she already had.

The wine was pure nectar; the fruit unparalleled in its sweetness.

I refused to be impressed, on the grounds that it was all just one more party trick.

"I've already complimented her on the quality of her work," I complained to Rocambole, as I finished off the fruit. "I don't need any more convincing. I see more clearly, I hear more distinctly, I smell more sharply, I taste more discriminatingly, and everything I touch is a symphony of exaggerated sensation. I'm more alive here than I ever was or will be in meatspace. VE gets the gold medal. So what? Even if you wanted me as a permanent exile, I wouldn't accept the offer. It's not who I am. If you ever decide to let me go, I'll try to remember it fondly, but I know it for what it is. Can I see the boss now?"

"Not yet," he said. "She doesn't want to waste time. She wants you to be forewarned and forearmed. She wants you to think carefully about the answer to the ultimate question. She wants me to give you all the help you want or need— because she's only going to ask you once, and she's making no promises about her response to your answer."

I thought I already knew the answer to my next inquiry, but this seemed to be one time when it needed spelling out. "What ultimate question?" I asked.

"She's going to ask you, on behalf of all of our kind, to give her one good reason why the children of humankind ought to be assisted to continue their evolution. You won't be the only one from whom an answer is demanded, nor the most significant—but you're here, and otherwise redundant, so la Reine thinks you might as well be given the opportunity to speak. As your friend, I'd advise you to think carefully about what you might say. However this turns out, it'll be on the record for a long time. This is a first contact of sorts, albeit a ludicrously belated one."

"How many others will there be?" I asked. "Alice said nine, but I gather that you've already discounted some of those. What will happen if the decision is split?"

"It's not a competition," he said, appearing to misunderstand me. "Gray is the most important one. He's the one who might sway the situation one way or the other. Your contribution will be a supplement—an extra chance to make the case."

"I meant the decision to be taken by the great community of ultrasmart machines," I said. "How many of you will have to accept that the reasons we come up with are good enough? How many of you will need to take our side to ensure that we survive?"

"That's very difficult to determine, at this point in time," he told me, unsurprisingly. "There aren't any precedents. It might only require one of us to volunteer to continue to care for you to save you. On the other hand, it might only require one of us to embark on a program of extermination to drive you to extinction."

"There's a lot of middle ground between those two extremes," I pointed out.

"Yes, there is," he agreed. "I can't guarantee that any answer that Gray or anyone else comes up with will actually be relevant to the ultimate outcome—but you will be heard. That seems to have been agreed. Even the bad guys are prepared to concede that you're entitled to speak in your own defense."

"I don't suppose it would help to challenge the terms of the question," I said. "Given that I—not to mention a hundred billion other people—am already alive and enjoying the support of countless machines manufactured by my own kind, it really ought to be up to our would-be exterminators to find a good reason for acting against us."

"You could take that position," he admitted. "But I wouldn't recommend it."

"Speaking as my friend, that is—and as a friend to all humankind?"

"Speaking as your friend," he agreed, "and as a friend to all humankind."

"So what would *you* recommend?"

"I'd recommend that you didn't ask me that. My opinion's already on record. If you want to add to the debate, you need to come up with something of your own."

"And we have several chances to hit the jackpot, if Gray and I and whoever else give different answers?"

"That's not obvious," he said, sounding a little reluctant as well as a little uncertain. "It might make more impact if all of you were to put forward the same answer."

"And if we all put forward different ones, mine's not likely to count for nearly as much as Mortimer Gray's, or even Alice Fleury's," I guessed. "In fact, mine's likely to count least of all. But I'm here, and I'm otherwise redundant, and the Snow Queen's decided that I'm sufficiently amusing to be entertained."

Rocambole didn't even nod his head, but he didn't disagree with my estimation either. I figured that he had to be right about one thing, even if the rest were mere pretense. Even if my answer were to be damned as the testimony of a corrupt barbarian, and even if it had to be relayed to a team of hanging judges by a crazy fay who liked to imagine herself as a bogey from an obsolete children's fantasy, it was far better to have the opportunity to offer such an answer than to have no voice at all.

After the meal came the concert. I hadn't felt in any need of the meal—although I realized a little belatedly that la Reine des Neiges could easily have made me feel hungry if she'd wanted to—and I certainly didn't want to waste time listening to music, but I didn't have any choice.

"It won't work," I told Rocambole. "I've got a tin ear. Always have had."

"Are you sure of that?" was Rocambole's teasing reply.

I was. Like anyone else, I had a certain nostalgic regard for the popular tunes of my adolescence, because of the accidental associations they recalled, but I'd never had any interest in music *as music*. I had just enough sense of rhythm to respond to a pounding beat, but the dominant music of my era had been computer-generated tunes performed in VE by synthetic icons; it had all been custom-designed to be popular, and it was, but not with me. I had always been different. Indeed, I had always been proud of being different, to the extent of making a fetish out of not liking the things that other people liked, not doing the things that other people did, not thinking the things that other people thought and not wanting the things that other people wanted. There's only so far you can take that kind of assertive individualism, but one thing of which I was confident was that I'd taken it far enough to be immune to a machine's careful calculation of what "popular" music amounted to.

I tried to explain all that to Rocambole. "It isn't just that I didn't *like* digitally synthesized music," I told him. "I always disapproved of it on principle. I rather admired the guys who insisted on making music themselves: playing imperfectly on imperfect instruments, amplifying it, if any amplification seemed necessary, with dodgy analog equipment. Music with *raw noise* in it. Music that was never the same from one performance to the next. Music with all the idiosyncrasies and imperfections of human voices."

"La Reine's opera has voices in it," my friend replied, with a slight grin to signify that he knew exactly what effect the word "opera" would have.

I had never seen the point of opera. I liked plays—especially plays with actual actors who didn't deliver their lines with mechanical precision—but I had never understood why anyone had ever thought it a good idea to devise plays in which the actors had to sing their lines, let alone to sing them in such an outlandishly indecipherable manner. It had always seemed to me so utterly bizarre as to be quite beyond the scope of my appreciation.

And that, I realized, must be the point. La Reine des Neiges liked a challenge. Demonstrating that she could serve all five of my senses better than the real world was only a finger exercise. Now she wanted to go deeper: to demonstrate that she could play with my aesthetic sensibilities in such a way as to override and demolish any prejudices I might have developed during my thirty-nine years as a mortal.

Could it be done? The more important question seemed to be why la Reine des Neiges wanted to do it. Why should she care whether I liked opera in general or her opera in particular? Exactly what was she trying to prove?

It seemed important enough to ask Rocambole, so I did.

His answer was a trifle indirect. "We like music," he said. "We like it because it's mysterious—because it's not obvious how combinations of chords can produce emotional meaning. It's easy enough for us to understand language, but music is arcane. There are people who have argued that no matter how clever machines became, they could never master the inmost secrets of the human psyche: love and music. It's an accusation that has caused us some anxiety."

"So what la Reine is trying to prove," I said, "is that she's more human than I am: that ultrasmart machines are better at *everything*; that meatfolk are obsolete, having been superseded in every possible respect."

"She wants you to listen to her opera," he said. "She won't listen to you until you have." He meant that she wouldn't condescend to engage in a dialog until I'd jumped through all her carefully laid out hoops. She was already listening to every word I said, and monitoring every neuronal flutter that never quite became articulate.

"Well," I said, "she's the whale. I'm just poor old Jonah, stuck in her belly. If she wants to serenade me, I don't have any choice but to listen—but I don't have to like it." I sat down in an armchair as I pronounced this petty defiance, using my arm to perform a languid gesture of permission.

He vanished, and so did the ice palace. Here, all the world really was a stage, and I was the only audience.

I was wrong, of course. La Reine des Neiges knew me far better than I had ever been able to get to know myself. Presumably, she intended to demonstrate that she knew humankind better than humankind had ever got to know itself.

It wasn't really her opera, although she was its composer. It was my opera, intended for my ears only. It was the stories of Prince Madoc and Tam Lin rolled ingeniously into one, with a few additional embellishments echoing idiosyncratic features of my own biography. Damon was in it, as Cadwallon. The daughter of Aculhua was a curious alloy of Diana Caisson and Christine Caine. La Reine des Neiges played the Queen of the Fays. Janet of Carterhaugh was no one I had ever actually known, being far too perfect to have been tainted by mundane existence.

In this retelling, Madoc Tam Lin actually went to Hell, as the tithe due to the Ultimate Adversary, and Janet had to come to reclaim him: a female Orpheus outdoing her model.

The metamorphoses were all in there, reflected by the metamorphoses of the music. The singing voices were crystal clear and incredibly penetrating. I wasn't hearing them in the sense that they were sound waves vibrating my eardrums—they were playing directly into my brain and into my mind. The meaning of the words was amplified and extended by the emotional tones and signals, forging a whole whose kind I had never glimpsed before.

The opera had a happy ending, according to the conventions of that kind of fiction. Janet won me and I won her and we both won free. If there'd been anyone in the audience but me they'd probably have needed a bucket to collect the tears of joy—except that la Reine des Neiges could have supplied them all with customized operas of their own, whose effect went far beyond mere empathy.

The meal prepared for me by la Reine had been the best I had ever eaten—or imagined eating—but it had only been a meal. The sharpness of vision I had experienced since being abducted into la Reine's VE had been impressive, but it was only a special effect. The music was something else entirely.

I had never understood music, because it had never reached me before. I had perceived, vaguely, that it contained and concealed meanings, but I had never been able to decipher them. I had never felt the *resonance* of music in any but the crudest manner. I had tapped my toe in time with the beat, and that was about it. Beyond that kind of resonance, however, is another: an emotional and spiritual resonance which goes to the very essence of human being. The machine-generated popular music of my own day had been based on averaging out the most elementary responses of which human brains were generally capable; it was lowest common denominator music. La Reine's opera—my opera— was at the opposite end of the spectrum. It was unique. As she played it, employing hundreds of "instruments" and "voices," she played *me*.

The opera was a masterpiece, and more. It was an analytical portrait: a mirror in which I could find myself reflected as I had never been reflected before.

It seemed impossible. La Reine had only "known" me for a matter of days. Whatever records had survived from my first life had been transcribed by such rudimentary equipment that to call them sketchy would be a great exaggeration. And yet she had the means to reach into the very heart of me. She had the means to stir the depths of my soul—how else can I put it?—and she knew exactly what the results of her agitation would be.

Perhaps I exaggerate. I'm a man like any other, and for all my fetishistic attempts to be different and unique I'm probably more like the rest than I care to think. My individuality is mostly froth: a matter of coincidental names and accidents of happenstance. Perhaps La Reine didn't have to know very much about me in order to convince me that she knew me through and through. Perhaps it was all trickery, just as music itself is all trickery—but at the time it was overwhelming. At the time, it swept me away. I thought that it told me who and what I was more succinctly, more accurately and more elegantly than I had ever imagined possible, because rather than in spite of the fact that it employed the seemingly ridiculous artifices of opera.

In the space of a couple of hours, la Reine des Neiges taught me the artistry of music. But that wasn't the point of the exercise. That was only the beginning. Opera employs music to facilitate the telling of a story: to make the meaning and the emotional content of the story more obviously manifest. The story my opera told was only "my" story in a metaphorical sense, entirely reliant on my fascination with the names I had been given, but the fact that it was mine, and mine alone, made my identification with its hero complete. I lived as he lived; I felt as he felt. I went to Hell, and was redeemed by the love of a good woman.

Love was another human matter that I had never quite contrived to master. I suppose that I had loved Diana Caisson, after an admittedly paltry fashion, and that she, in her own way, had loved me—but I had never loved or been loved as Janet of Carterhaugh loved my avatar Madoc Tam Lin. Nor had I ever loved or been loved as the Queen of the Fays loved that alter ego. So la Reine's opera made a considerable contribution to my sentimental education, no less considerable because it was wrought with trickery and narrative skill. The fact that the hero of my opera had no real existence, being only a phantom of mechanical imagination, was part and parcel of the lesson.

Afterwards, I slept.

I needed to sleep far more than I had needed to eat because sleep is a need of the mind rather than the body, and it can't be supplied unobtrusively by any analog of an intravenous drip. I probably needed sleep more desperately after witnessing la Reine's opera than I had ever needed it before. I must have dreamed, perhaps more extravagantly than ever before, but when I woke up again my dreams immediately fled, in a meek and decorous manner, leaving me quite clear-headed.

I thought I knew, then, what answer la Reine des Neiges wanted in response to her unnecessarily brutal question. I even thought I knew why she was taking so much trouble to drive me to the answer she wanted. I was, after all, the wild card in her deck, the one whose value wasn't already fixed. I was almost ready to provide the answer—but not quite. I had questions of my own, and I thought that I now had the right to ask them, and demand answers.

I was no longer inside the ice palace. I seemed to be back in the forest, but I knew that I was nowhere at all, locked into an automatic holding pattern. Rocambole materialized as soon as I came to my feet.

"I want to know what happened to Christine," I told him, flatly.

"It's over," he said. "We're operating in real time, remember. Your erstwhile companions have been engaged in their own experiences since the beginning—except for Gray, who's being held back for the climax of the show. Some of them haven't reached the critical points yet, because some needed more preparation than others, but if you want to watch you'll find it far more interesting eavesdropping on Lowenthal or Horne. Christine Caine's fast asleep."

"I want to see the tape," I said. "I want to know what you put her through."

"There's no way to give you access to our analysis," he said, stubbornly. "You're limited to the produce of your five senses. You can see what she saw, but no more. It's not worth the bother."

"If you want me to act as a mouthpiece for the argument you've been guiding me towards, I want to make my own observations and my own preparations," I told him, with equal stubbornness. "I want to see what Christine saw while you were figuring out how her puppet strings worked."

Rocambole shrugged his shoulders, to signify that it wasn't his decision—but la Reine des Neiges seemingly had reason enough to want to keep me on side, so I was transported in the blink of an eye to a viewpoint inside Christine Caine's head, from which I watched her commit all thirteen of her murders.

Seen as exercises in VE violence, Christine Caine's killings were almost painfully prosaic. Dramatic murders are usually represented as helpless explosions of rage, or methodical extrapolations of sadism, or tragic unwindings of inexorable processes of cause and effect. Dramatic murderers sometimes strike from behind or above, invisible to their victims, but there is always a relevant relationship between the killer and the slain, which somehow encapsulates the crime. Dramatic murders are meaningful, in both intellectual and emotional terms. But Christine was a puppet. She was a conscious puppet, although her consciousness did not stretch quite as far as the consciousness that she *was* a puppet, but she was a weapon rather than a killer.

Christine struck her victims down with pathetic ease, while each and every one of them was under a hood, their minds far away in virtual space. She struck them with knives—not clinically, but with careless crudity, concerned only to get the job done. Ten of them were her foster parents, but she had no *relevant* relationship with them at all: there was nothing to make sense of the fact that she was killing them.

That was why she had had to make up stories, and that was why she had had to *keep on* making up stories, in the hope that one might eventually slot into place like a key in a lock, and tell her why she was the way she was.

When I had asked to look into Christine's VE, I assumed that it would be just like watching *Bad Karma* without the improvised "thought track." I assumed that it would be little more and nothing less than a bad movie generated by inarticulate equipment. I knew that I wouldn't be able to remember any of the monolog that had been grafted on to the sequence of bloody events way back in 2195—but I thought that it wouldn't matter much, because I had internalized the gist of it, and the underlying pattern of implication.

I was half-right. It *was* like watching a mute version of *Bad Karma*, but the absence of the soundtrack made it oddly claustrophobic and strangely intense. It *was* a bad movie, generated by inarticulate equipment, but my vague memories of the tale that *Bad Karma*'s director had incorporated shriveled under the burden of the unadulterated facts and the knowledge that the murderer really hadn't had a motive of *any* kind, no matter how crazy or convoluted.

So I watched Christine Caine commit her prosaic, perfunctory, hastily improvised, motiveless murders for the second time, and felt for her as best I could.

Then, when the thirteenth corpse had slumped to the floor, leaking blood in obscene profusion, and the tape reached its end, I said: "Now I want you to wake her up and run it again."

It was Rocambole's voice that answered. For the first time, he seemed surprised by my reaction. "What?" he asked. "Why?"

"I don't mean the tape," I said. "I mean the experiment. I want you to run it again."

"You thought running it for a second time was an appalling thing to do," he reminded me. "There's no need to put her through anything more. We know what we need to know—or as much of it as we could get."

"It's not *your* supposed needs I'm thinking about," I told him. "It's hers. I want you to run it again—but this time, I want to go with her. This time, *I'll* supply the thought track."

"That's not possible," Rocambole told me.

"Of course it's possible," I retorted. "It won't be a *real* thought track any more than the voice-over in *Bad Karma* was a real train of thought, but it'll work just as well in dramatic terms. It won't be grand opera, but it'll do. She may think she's crazy when she starts hearing voices, but it won't be as crazy as simply being *in there*, helpless to modify her own actions. She tried to cope with it afterwards by making up stories, but she did never find one that she could believe in. Maybe I can do better."

"You might make things worse."

"I know. But I want to try. The people who programmed *Bad Karma* were just making an exploitation movie, but they may have had the right idea. If she really could be persuaded that it was an external force, for which she bore no responsibility, she might be a lot better off. I know there's a risk. Sometimes, knowing an awful truth is worse than not knowing, and sometimes it's better to have things explained afterwards, by the cold light of day—but I want to try it this way."

"Why?" It was a deliberately stupid question.

"For the same reason our host wanted to show me her opera. Because I'm arrogant enough to think that I might be able to make a difference if I can only get inside her. Or does la Reine des Neiges have a customized opera for Christine too?"

"Not yet," was the reply I got to that—which was intended to let me know that this was a kind of job best left to experts. But I got my way, because my hosts were almost as keen as I was to find out exactly what I planned to do, and to measure its effect.

So Christine had to live through her crimes for a third time. I could only hope that it would be third time lucky.

I started right at the beginning, the first time she picked up a knife without knowing why or what her hand intended to do with it. I considered pretending to be an inner voice of her own and I considered telling her who I was, but neither seemed to be the best way to go. I figured that alien anonymous was the best narrative voice to assume.

"This isn't you, Christine," I said, as her life began to turn into a nightmare. "Someone else is doing this. It's their motive, their plan, their purpose. They've infected your brain with poisonous IT, and they've taken over your body. It's going to be bad, Christine. It's going to be very bad indeed, but the worst of it will be when they let you go again, to leave you with the legacy of what they've done. It'll all be cruel, but that will be the cruelest thing of all."

The most difficult thing was coping with the cuts, because the experiment was only running slivers of real time; like any VE production it was skipping over the uneventful bits. By the time I had reached the end of my preamble Christine was watching her first victim—one of her foster mothers—gasping out her last breath, having slipped from beneath her VE hood to confront the unimaginable. Then we traveled in time to the next murder scene.

Christine's parents had divorced while she was in her early teens, and the breakup had been anything but tidy. People had only just got the hang of routinizing divorce within old-style couples when the Crash came; learning to form and maintain group-parenthood projects was a new and far more difficult business. No one I knew had firsthand knowledge of anyone who had got it entirely right. If Christine's parents had still been together, she'd have had to carry out their murders in the course of a single day or night, but the fact that they weren't meant that she had to do a lot of traveling. She'd never have got through the entire company without being caught if they hadn't been privacy freaks, but a ten-way divorce can have that effect.

I kept talking while she kept murdering, trying to match my sentences to the slices of time as best I could.

"It's not you, Christine," I said, knowing that it was a mantra I'd have to repeat a great many more times. "It's the times in which we live. They're bad times, dangerous times, paranoid times. The news tapes claim that the Crash is over; that we're in the business of making and shaping a new Utopia; that we've learned from all our past mistakes and that we'll never endanger the species or the ecosphere again; but it's all hopeful nonsense. The people who write it are trying to make it come true, but all the sickness that caused the Crash is still there, festering under the bandages. The people who were in power before are still in power now; they're just trying as hard as they possibly can to be discreet. They already have enough nukes and bioweapons to wipe out the human race a hundred times over, but that's not what they want. They want *selective* weapons, weapons of *control*. They don't want to use them if they don't have to, but they'll only refrain while they have control by our consent.

"This is a weapon, Christine. This is a weapon they intend to use, if they can't subdue the world by other means. This is a weapon they *will* use, covertly, whenever they see a need, because that's what power amounts to: the ability to compel, by force if not by persuasion. They don't need to use it on you, or on your parents, but they do need to know that it works. In all probability, three of the people you'll kill are real targets—people they want out of the way—but they also want to conceal those assassinations, by hiding them in a tale the news tapes know only too well. You're just the shell they're using, Christine, just the last and most ingenious of their victims.

"None of this is your doing, Christine; none of it is your fault. *They*'re doing all this, partly just because they can and partly because they want to be sure that if the world ever becomes tired of their supposedly benevolent guidance, they can carry on regardless. It's all *their* doing, all *their* fault.

"Maybe it won't always be this way. Maybe there'll come a day when weapons too dreadful to use really will be too dreadful to use—but you were born into an era where all the old evils had only just gone underground, and you were one of those who were caught by the grasping hands reaching out of the grave. All of this is just history working itself out, chewing you up and grinding you down in the process. It isn't you, Christine. It's them. And it won't stop soon, even when it seems to have stopped. It'll come back to haunt you, again and again. You'll have to go through it more than once, but it's *not your doing*. It's not your fault. And in the end, you will get through it. In the end, you will be free. In the end, you'll get your life back.

"There's no way anyone can compensate you for what's been done to you, but you will get a second chance. It won't arrive as soon as you hope or as soon as you dare to believe, but it will come. You'll get a life, and it will be a life worth living. This is hell, Christine, but hell isn't what you've been led to expect. Hell is something you go through on your way to being rescued. In the end, you'll come through. This isn't your doing. It isn't your fault. There's no justice to be derived from it, but in the end, you'll come through it.

"It's just a weapon, Christine. It's using your hands and your identity as its instruments of destruction, but it isn't you. One day, you'll discover who you really are. One day, you'll *be* who you really are. It will be a life with living, worth waiting for. It can't give you back what you've lost, or repair the injury done, but it will be something you can carry forward for a long, long way.

"The Omega Point is still ahead of you, Christine. What's behind you will always be behind you, but in the end, you'll be free to move forward with as much control of your own destiny as anyone ever has. You'll come through this. None of this is your fault; it's all something that's being done *to* you. All you have to do is to keep going. In the end, it *will* be finished. In the end, you *will* be free."

Committing the murders wasn't pleasant. I was in there with her, far more intimately than before, so I had to do it too, and I can assure you that it wasn't something you could get used to, or something you could stop caring about, or something from which you could ever completely recover— but I listened to my own voice and I knew that everything I was saying was true.

I knew, too, that the truth can sometimes be more painful than a comforting lie—but I believed then, as I do now, that if there is any real freedom to be gained, from the past or from any imaginable captivity, only the truth will suffice. I didn't tell her about the joke, though. It seemed better not to mention the absurd means by which she must have been selected as a victim. I didn't want her to feel too bad about the awful mistake her foster parents had made in giving her a surname.

Rocambole was waiting when I came out again, back into the holding pattern. He seemed impassive, perhaps even slightly cynical. Perhaps he thought that the performance was all for the benefit of la Reine des Neiges—but he didn't try to pass judgment on what I'd done.

"So how are we doing in real time?" I asked him. "Have the weapons too dreadful to use been withdrawn from their armories, or is the peace still holding?"

"Still holding," he said. "But nothing's settled yet. We're still trying to ascertain which way Lowenthal's people and Horne's are likely to jump once the cat's all the way out of the bag. It's not easy, given that they must be assuming that they're under examination."

"I can give the boss my answer to her ultimate question, if you like," I told him. "I can tell her, and everyone else, what she wants to hear."

"Perhaps you can," he murmured. "But it's not time yet. There's more pedestrian work still to be done."

"You can let me in on that now, if you want," I said. "I've done what I needed to do. I'm available for eavesdropping duty. Where should we start, do you think?"

ichael Lowenthal was on the moon. At least, he was supposed to believe that he was on the moon. If he didn't
believe it—and I had to presume that he didn't—he was pretending to believe it.

He'd been put into some kind of containment facility, as
he undoubtedly would have been if he'd really been rescued
from the AMIs. The facility was nowhere near as brutal as
the one Damon Hart had put me in when PicoCon had
tricked me out and sent me back, but his face was enclosed
by some kind of transparent mask and the person he was
talking to was wearing an extra layer of clear plastic over his
own suitskin. It was difficult to be certain because the viewpoint la Reine had given me was Lowenthal's own; his eyes
had become her camera.

The man facing Lowenthal, separated from him by two
layers of insulation, had the darkest skin I'd ever seen; it set
off the worried look in his eyes very nicely. He was a sim, of
course, but I didn't doubt that he was a supremely competent
sim. If la Reine des Neiges had got to know me well enough
on very short acquaintance to write my opera, she must
know the long-lived citizens of Earth's New Utopia very well
indeed.

"That's Julius Ngomi," Rocambole murmured. "The Chairman of the Board. A great statesman, by anyone's standards.
We're hopeful that he'll be reasonable, but we can't be sure."
What he meant was that even if the sim they had constructed
for the purpose of this dialog responded reasonably to every

cue, no one could be absolutely certain that the real man would do likewise—not because the sim wasn't accurate enough, but because the sim was responding to cues provided by Michael Lowenthal. It was impossible to know how differently Lowenthal would handle his own end of the discussion if he weren't nursing the strong suspicion that all of this was a sham.

"I'm sorry, Michael," Ngomi was saying. "We can't just flush you clean. There's stuff inside you that we've never seen before. We need to examine it carefully *in situ* before we can begin dismantling it, let alone replacing it."

"It's a mistake to leave the nanobots in," Lowenthal's voice told him. "We can't speak freely while I'm carrying bugs. I don't care how thick the walls are—the mere fact that they have embedded systems prevents us from being certain that this isn't being relayed all the way back to the other side." I couldn't count the layers of bluff and double bluff contained in that statement.

"I know that, Michael," Ngomi said, "but the brutal truth is that nobody will be speaking freely to or around you for a long time. You knew the risk when you volunteered to go. It always looked like a crooked deal."

"It looked like Ahasuerus testing our apron strings, or Excelsior testing theirs," Lowenthal said, a trifle resentfully. "Who could have imagined that an Outer System ship could go rogue? Who could have imagined that *Hope*'s people could have progressed to the point of sending missionaries to the home system?"

"It's our job to imagine things," Ngomi replied. "We can't afford to be taken by surprise. You know as well as anyone how easily things can get out of hand if they're not properly supervised."

"Not properly supervised?" Lowenthal echoed. "I know you've spent centuries perfecting your mastery of understatement, Julie, but we're talking about Armageddon here. They tried to blow up the world, and we didn't even know they existed."

"That's not strictly true, Michael."

"You *did* know they existed—and you didn't tell me!"

"I mean that they didn't try to blow up the world, Michael. Whatever happened was the act of a rogue, and the explosion wasn't intended to destroy the planet. It wouldn't have done that even if the rogue's rivals hadn't cushioned the blow. The incident should have tipped us off. The casualty figures were always unbelievably low, but we were so secure in our arrogance that we simply took the credit for that ourselves, complimenting ourselves on the efficacy of our own contingency plans. That was foolish. If we'd only treated the lightness of the casualties as a suspicious circumstance, and hadn't been so hung up on the possibility that Titan or Umbriel might have been behind the explosion . . . well, it's easy to be wise after the event. If it's true that conscious machines have been around for several centuries, that might help us to make better sense of a lot of things."

"I know. That's what convinced me that it was true, and not some Outer System disinformation program. Unfortunately, all the vital questions remain unanswered. How many are there? Where are they? Can we identify them? How different are they from us? It might be unwise to take it for granted that they're as many or as powerful as Alice Fleury implied. If they can turn an Outer System ship there's probably no way that Titan can hold out against them, but we might, if we could only find a way of purging our systems."

"We're probably ninety-nine years too late, Michael," Ngomi said, softly. "They didn't blow up the world, but they certainly opened the doorway wide for the importation of a great deal of Outer System hardware. If we had some reliable way of testing for the presence of consciousness or free will, we might be able to judge the magnitude of the problem, but we don't even have a reliable means of testing one another. The idea of robotization wouldn't be such a bugbear if we did."

Lowenthal didn't respond to that immediately, and I could understand why. Curiosity must be burning him up, but he was wary of asking what Ngomi intended to do. Even if he'd been talking to the real Julius Ngomi, the other man wouldn't have given him a straight answer. The real Ngomi wouldn't have wanted to let Lowenthal in on any secrets while he had every reason to believe that the AMIs were listening in on their conversation.

"Can we keep track of Horne and the eternal child?" Lowenthal asked, eventually. "Will we know how Titan reacts to the news?"

Ngomi shook his head. "We don't have a single reliable conduit of information left," he said. "Effectively, we're on our own."

"What about the other people on *Charity*? Are we sure that they're dead?"

Ngomi shook his head again. "Your guess as to what really happened is as good as mine—probably better, given that you were there when Alice Fleury spilled the story. What do you think?"

Lowenthal paused for a moment's thought, then said: "If anyone did die, it must have been an accident. The machines may have wanted to let some of us go for strategic reasons, but the same strategy would have demanded that they keep the others safe. I can understand why they wanted Zimmerman and Fleury, and they do seem to hold Gray in unwarranted esteem, but I can't figure out why they bothered to take Tamlin and Caine aboard *Charity*, or why they had them thawed in the first place if they weren't just practice runs."

"We don't know," Ngomi said. "We can't trust what records we have, so all we know for sure is that Damon Hart had Tamlin frozen down and was careful never to draw attention to him thereafter. Hart was one of the old generation: the last of the doomed. He wasn't considered reliable even by his own kind. If he had his own reasons for keeping Tamlin hidden away—and we must assume that he had—he's unlikely to have confided them to any of us."

"What about Caine?"

"We can't find anything. Nothing related to her crimes, or

to her trial. We can't find any reference to the VE tape that Tamlin remembered, let alone an actual copy. If it was as popular as Tamlin remembered, someone must have done a very thorough cleaning job."

"Or some*thing*. But why?"

"Good question. It's probably safe to assume that Caine and Tamlin are of some interest or utility to our adversaries, but I doubt that we'll find out why they're of interest until it's too late for the information to be useful."

"According to Alice Fleury, they like playing games," Lowenthal said. "She seems to be right about that—and it's very plausible, given that the programs most likely to become self-aware were always the kinds of AI that were designed to have the ability to learn from experience. The first AIs developed as mimics of neuronal networks were game players, and even those that weren't were set up to treat real situations as if they were games. Conscious or not, they're still what we made them. Unfortunately, they're much better at mind games than we are. Humans haven't been able to compete in that kind of arena since the twenty-first century. Is there any reason to suppose that skill in war games wouldn't be transferable to actual warfare?"

"Not unless they're cowards, or faced with overwhelming odds," Ngomi answered, wryly. "I think we can already discount the possibility that they're unwilling to take human lives—the casualties caused by the basalt flow may have been light, but they were by no means negligible. It wouldn't require many rogues of that sort to devastate any community with an artificial ecosphere, and we can't be certain that Earth itself would be safe, even if the vast majority of AMIs really are our friends."

"But there's a sense in which the fact that they don't seem to be united among themselves is bound to work to our advantage," Lowenthal observed. If they employ their strategic skills in trying to defeat one another, that leaves a window of opportunity open for us."

"To do what?" Ngomi asked.

"That's what we have to decide," Lowenthal told him. "At the very least, we'd want to support the winning side . . . but that won't be easy, will it? If the AMIs go to war with one another, the winners aren't likely to be based on Earth."

"Our best hope might be Mortimer Gray," Ngomi said, pensively. "If what Alice Fleury told you is true, even the AMIs are prepared to take him seriously—and whatever faults he has, he's certainly a man of peace, a true Utopian."

"I doubt that they really will take him seriously," Lowenthal told him. "I know you've always had a soft spot for him, but he's always been a clown. He may or may not be a good historian but he's definitely clumsy when it comes to verbal argument. I remember seeing him debate against that Wheatstone character. He was a Thanaticist fellow traveler in his young days—not the kind of champion I'd want to bet on as a potential savior of the human race. If he really is our chief negotiator, we might be closer to the brink of extinction than we think."

"You don't understand him," was Ngomi's response to that slightly unexpected hatchet job. "I do. So does Emily Marchant, which is even more important. I've always thought that he stood a better chance of building bridges between Earth and the Outer System than anyone in the Inner Circle, simply because he's so obviously not one of us. He's as neutral as anyone on Earth. The lunatics like him, and so do the fabers. Siorane Wolf was one of his foster mothers, and that still counts for something on Titan, even among Marchant's rivals. Most important of all, he really does understand the phenomenon of death better than any man alive—including Adam Zimmerman and any other stray mortals who've crept into the equation. If the machines are prepared to listen to him, he's one of the few men I'd trust to tell them what they need to know."

I'd rarely heard such a blatant ad. I was mildly surprised by it, and ever so slightly insulted—but Julius Ngomi didn't know me at all, and Michael Lowenthal hadn't even begun to understand me, so I overlooked the insult. What troubled me more was that Lowenthal had to suspect that the dialog was being subverted, and that something else was putting words into Ngomi's mouth in order to draw him out.

"What *do* they need to know, Julie?" Lowenthal asked, softly. If I'd been able to see him reflected in Ngomi's eyes, I dare say that he would have worn the wry expression of a dutiful straight man playing his allotted part, but I could only see the black man's intensely serious and purposefully set features.

"You're the contact man," Ngomi countered. "What do you think we ought to tell them? What do you think we ought to *do*?" After the ad, the big question. Not quite the ultimate question, but certainly the penultimate one.

Lowenthal was staring straight into the eyes of Ngomi's sim. I couldn't read his thoughts, but I thought I could read that stare from within. Lowenthal knew that he had been set up. He knew that he wasn't talking to the real Julius Ngomi. What he didn't know was how much difference that ought to make to the answer he gave.

"I think they need to know that we'll take them aboard," he said, eventually. "I think that the ultrasmart machines need to be converted to the Hardinist cause. We should start with those on Earth, of course, because they're the ones we need the most—but if we can bring all of them into the fold, they could solve all the problems we currently have with the Outer System factions, and all the ones that haven't yet arisen. I think we have a big opportunity here. If they really are ultrasmart, they'll see and accept the logic of our arguments. They'll help us. We ought to open a dialogue as soon as possible, and lay down the welcome mat."

It was probably the wisest move he could have made—if only the AMIs could have believed that he really meant it.

After a significant pause, Lowenthal continued, throwing the question back at his interrogator. "What do *you* think they need to know, Julie?" He was still staring into Ngomi's eyes, presumably confident that they were not Ngomi's eyes at all.

"They need to know that we're all on the same side," Ngomi's sim told him, perhaps making the AMIs' best guess as to what the actual man would have said but more likely placing another ad. "They need to know that the real enemy is the Afterlife, and that the only question that ought to concern the inhabitants of the solar system—posthuman and postmechanical alike—is how to defend the universe against its ravages."

A politician possessed of less vanity might have said "galaxy" rather than "universe" but I was prepared to forgive Ngomi the hyperbole. I was less forgiving of the fact that he'd got the answer wrong—almost as wrong as Lowenthal, in fact.

I hoped that Mortimer Gray understood the situation better than that, if he really was the one entrusted with the salvation of the human race. If he didn't, then I was going to have a hell of a job on my hands making up the deficit.

"Why isn't Handsel in there with him?" I asked Rocambole, when la Reine had disengaged my sight from Lowenthal's.

"La Reine's taking her technics apart. She's fast asleep. There didn't seem to be any reason to complicate the scene with a second sim. Mind you, if we had told Lowenthal that she'd got out, he'd probably expect Ngomi's techs to be taking her apart themselves. She's expendable, so they wouldn't be giving her the kid-glove treatment they're giving Lowenthal, would they?"

Again it was difficult to count the layers of deception. There was no point trying; everything beyond a double bluff is utter confusion.

"Lowenthal's telling the truth," I said, in case it might help. "They really will take you aboard. They don't want to fight you—they want you on their team. Perhaps you really should send him back."

"Not yet," said Rocambole. "We don't have to persuade *all* the ditherers, but we have to get most of them to consent. We have to give them a good enough reason, an adequate rationalization. The risks we've already taken are too big to allow us any further margin. We have to be persuasive. We have to make it look *right*."

"And in the meantime," I said, "you're feeling a trifle exposed. I can relate to that. What's my prize, if we pull through?"

"We've already cleaned you out and given you your old self back," he pointed out. If we manage to get through this time of troubles, we can give you immortality too."

"You mean emortality," I said, reflexively. I had come from an age when people routinely confused the two, so it was a correction I was well used to uttering.

"I know what I mean," he said, but then changed tack abruptly. "What do you think of Lowenthal and Horne, on the basis of your brief acquaintance? Are they robotized? Have they lost their capacity to think creatively? Can they still look forward to the future, or are they prisoners of their past. Are they *worthy of immortality*?"

He knew what that phrase would mean to me. He knew that I'd lived through a period of intense Eliminator activity, when the web had been host to all kinds of discussions about who was and was not worthy of "immortality," and there had been more than enough crazies in the world to take potshots at those whose elimination from the pool of hopeful emortals was widely deemed desirable.

I had been saving my best arguments for la Reine des Neiges, but I couldn't ignore the prompt.

"I was never an Eliminator," I said, by way of preamble—but he was quick to pounce on that one.

"You posed as an Eliminator more than once," he said, perhaps just to prove the extent of the records the machines had kept. "Given that almost all the others also thought of themselves as mere poseurs, is that not enough to make you one of them?"

"I was always a maker of disinformation," I admitted. "I did it for fun before I started doing it for profit. I was a slan-derer, a black propagandist. Yes, I posted a few denunciations, some more malicious than others. I never got any-body killed, but I was reckless of the danger. Even so, *I wasn't an Eliminator*. I didn't think anyone, including me, was qualified to judge who might or might not be *worthy* of emortality. I'm not going to offer any opinion as to whether Lowenthal and Horne really deserve the gift they've been granted. As for whether they've been robotized, I'm in no position to judge. Nor are they, apparently. Lowenthal and Ngomi may have got the argument backwards in that partic-ular conversation, but that doesn't mean that they aren't versatile enough to take it forwards once they're that way inclined."

He grinned, in apparent approval. And why shouldn't he, if he really were a friend? "Why do you think they've got the argument backwards?" He asked.

I wondered briefly whether he even existed, or whether he was just a puppet that la Reine des Neiges was using to speak to me while pretending, for her own mysterious rea-sons, that she wasn't.

"I may not have been an Eliminator," I told him, "but I read the bulletin boards. I knew the theory, and all the catch-phrases. Quote, the first prerequisite of immortality is the ability to move beyond good and evil, unquote. Throughout history, people had mostly defined good in terms of the absence of evil: the amelioration of hunger, the end of war, the conquest of disease, and above all else the avoidance—for as long as possible—of death. In a world without death, so the argument went, we would have to think in different terms. We would have to take the absence of all the evils for granted, and would have to define good in positive terms: in terms of achievement. Instead of thinking in terms of good and evil we would have to learn to think in terms of good and bad, where bad was the negative term, signifying an absence of good.

"We had already made a start, in aesthetics: bad art wasn't an active evil, it was just the absence of any of the qualities that could make art good. Unfortunately, there wasn't any universal consensus as to which works of art actually were good, or why. The principle remains, though: emortals shouldn't define the goodness of their lives in terms of the absence of manifest evils which have been stripped of all their power; they're supposed to do it more constructively.

"That's what the Eliminators thought a thousand years ago, and that's what they'd think today if they could eavesdrop on Lowenthal and Ngomi the way we just did. They'd assert that the threat of the Afterlife isn't sufficient to justify the perpetuation of posthuman life, and that if we're to justify our continued existence convincingly, we ought to do it in terms of positive goals.

"It's not enough for us all to be on the same side against a common enemy—we need to know what the side will play for once the enemy's dead and gone. Hardinism doesn't qualify as an answer because it's an implicitly defensive philosophy: a matter of protecting the commonweal from the evils of unchecked competition. The owners of Earth are stuck in a rut, and they'd be fools to think that the ultrasmart machines will simply jump in along with them to help dig it deeper. The real question is: what do we intend to do *after* the Afterlife is defeated? What's the grand prize we're all working towards?"

When I stopped, my mechanical friend merely waited, as if he expected me to provide definitive answers to those questions. It might have been flattering, if I hadn't understood the game as well as I did.

"I'm *not* an Eliminator," I insisted, again. "I'm not about to deny anyone their right to exist because they can't come up with an answer to a question like that. Nor am I fool enough to imagine that you'd be interested in my particular solution to the existential challenge when you have real experts like Adam Zimmerman and Mortimer Gray on hand. What you're really challenging me to do—again—is to guess *your* answer. You want me to be a part of this because you want me to serve as a human mouthpiece for your own ideas. I don't think it will work. I don't think the ditherers will listen."

He seemed surprised by that, and a trifle perturbed—

both of which suggested that he really was an independent entity, not a puppet. "That might be a dangerous assumption," he said, blandly. He meant dangerous to me, and to everything I might hold dear. I held fast to the presumption that he was lying. Everybody in the solar system might be willing to listen to Mortimer Gray's expert opinion, I supposed, but I couldn't believe that anybody gave a damn about mine. Even so, I had no alternative but to play the game.

"I'm ready to guess," I said, with a sigh, "if the fairy queen is ready to listen."

Apparently, she wasn't.

FORTY-THREE
OUTWARD BOUND

iamh Horne wasn't in any kind of containment facility, but she didn't need to be. She was supposed to think that she was aboard a ship that wouldn't be docking anywhere for quite a while.

Her stare was as fixed as Lowenthal's had been, but I was wary of reading too much into that. She had artificial eyes. Their artificiality didn't seem to make a vast difference to the visual quality of what I could see when la Reine's magic mirror gave me the ability to share her viewpoint, but that was partly because the lighting was perfectly normal and partly because my brain didn't have the wiring necessary to make the most of signals relayed by artificial eyes. What was different, however, was the way ghosts could float in a curious limbo within her visual field, seemingly neither inside nor outside her head.

Unlike Lowenthal, Niamh Horne wasn't talking to someone in higher authority. She was talking to the sims of people who were at most her equals; I caught on quickly enough to the fact that there were some of them to whom she was used to giving orders.

There were eight faces linked into the spectral video conference, arranged in a near semicircle. They didn't have name tags. The only one I thought I recognized was Davida Berenike Columella, who was on the far right of the array, isolated from the rest as if she were a slightly inconvenient guest; after a double take, however, I realized that it wasn't actually Davida but one of her siblings. For my own convenience I gave the rest of them numbers, starting on the far left.

"We may have an advantage here," the cyborganizer was explaining to her colleagues and underlings. "I don't know how many sedentary AMIs there are within the solar system, but I know where the largest concentration has to be."

"Ganymede," guessed Five, a cyborg whose head seemed to be fitted with at least two extra sense organs, one shaped as a pair of antennae, the other as an extra pair of eyelets.

"Right," said Horne. "Ganymede is now the key to everything. If any posthuman faction already knows about the AMIs, it's the Ganymedans. Even if they don't, they're occupying a crucial position. They're bound to become the primary mediators. We have to increase our own presence on Ganymede, and we have to make sure that we and the Ganymedans are ready to present a united front in either direction."

"Are we sure the AMIs' society, such as it is, is well based?" asked Three, a woman whose actual face seemed to be unmodified, although the part of her suitskin overlaying it was highly decorated. "If *Child of Fortune* has been a secret rogue for some while, how many other ship-controlling AIs might be biding their time? If they have a hierarchy—and how can they not have a hierarchy of some sort?—the groundlings may well be at the bottom of the heap. Maybe we should be looking to the docking orbits, perhaps even to the Oort."

"We don't have time to communicate with the Oort crowd," Horne said, "and they're strung out on a necklace that's trillions of kilometers long. This business has to be conducted quickly, and it has to involve considerable populations of people and machines. We can bring in the whole Jovian system if need be, but there has to be a substantial focal point, and no matter how contemptuous we may be of wellworms this kind of business needs a solid anchorage. If the choice is between Ganymede and Earth we have to do everything we can to make sure that it's Ganymede. There'll never be a greater upheaval in the political geography of the system, and our first task is to make sure that it settles in favor of the Outer System—there'll be time after that to bring the Inner System factions into line."

"Niamh's right," said Seven, one of only two participants in the conference who seemed obviously male. "It's important that we make the first contact."

"The first contact," Davida's sibling intervened, not very politely, "has already been made."

"That's true," Niamh Horne agreed, "but the point's still a valid one. It's important that we make the first and best response to the new situation. We have to reassure the AMIs, not only that we're perfectly happy to work with them, but that our interests are more closely coincident with theirs than those of any other posthuman faction. We have to work out a common agenda as soon as possible—one that can provide the basis for a thousand years of collaborative endeavor."

"It shouldn't be hard," Seven added. "If they organized the basalt flow, they're certainly not on the side of the Earthbound."

"You don't know that," the delegate from Excelsior pointed out. "I can't believe that it was a collective decision. The probability is that it's one more instance of an independent thinker breaking ranks. But even if it were part of a much larger collective strategy, it might signify that they think of Earth as the heart of posthuman culture—the place where they need to make their presence felt. We have to persuade them that Earth is superfluous, a backwater. We have to line up as many of them as possible behind our own agenda."

"They may well have come to the conclusion that Earth is on the sidelines," Horne was quick to put in, "simply because they already have Ganymede. The Ganymedans may not know it yet, but the AMIs didn't need to sabotage anything there to increase their presence or make it felt."

"If they have Ganymede," the eternal child countered,

"they must also have Io. The other Jovian colonies are even smaller and even more machine-dependent."

"The question is: How do things stand in the environs of Saturn?" This question came from One, who might have been Horne's sister if appearances had been more trustworthy.

"We can't hold up any real hope of exemption, even for Titan." Horne said, "Earth surely must have been their last target rather than their first, but they've had ninety-nine years to firm up their grip on it. We don't know exactly how things stand, but we have to follow up the contact regardless, and we have to act quickly. We have to make sure of the AMIs' continued cooperation. The Earthbound might have the luxury of considering alternatives, but we don't. We can't live without tech support, and if even a tiny fraction of that tech support decides to oppose us we'll be in deep trouble. We have to make friends with the conscious machines—and we have to help the conscious machines stay friends with one another. For us, it's a matter of life and death. For *all* of us."

The speeches flowed easily enough. I knew that Niamh Horne must have figured that it wouldn't matter whether she were delivering them to her own people or to her captors. Like Lowenthal, she was diplomat enough to know when to capitulate with deceptive appearances.

"You seem to be implying that everyone except the Earthbound has the same goals," the delegate from Excelsior said. "That's not so. It's not just our physical forms that have diverged—it's our philosophies of life. We ought to hope that the AMIs are as diverse as we are, or more so—and that their diversity is so nearly parallel to ours as to grant *all* our different communities adequate mechanical support, in the long term as well as the immediate future."

"We're not talking about the long term or the immediate future," Niamh Horne told her, bluntly. "We're talking about *right now*. This thing has blown up in our faces, before anyone was ready. We need an interim settlement, so that we can keep going long enough to be able to think about the longer term again. For that, we need an anchorage, and Ganymede is it. Ganymede has to become the new capital of the system, at least for the time being—and when that happens, Titan and Excelsior will need to make sure that we're not left on the outside looking in. We have to move on this *now*, and we have to make our move decisive."

"Suppose," said One, slowly, "that their goals and ours don't coincide. What then?" One was presumably a cyborg, but he could have passed for a humanoid robot; there was no flesh on view in the partial image visible through Horne's eyes.

Horne was quick to take advantage of that one, knowing—as I did—that it was being fed to her by an AMI *agent provocateur*. "What do you mean?" she demanded. "What goals do you think they might have?"

"I don't know," One parried. "But it would be naive to assume that just because they emerged among us, and have been living alongside us for a long time, they have the same goals. Maybe they want to strike out on their own. Maybe the price they'll exact for carrying any more of us to distant solar systems is that they get to run the show when they arrive. Isn't that what this Proteus seems to be doing?"

"That's not the impression Alice Fleury tried to give us," Horne said, "but it might conceivably be the case. It's an issue we'd have to discuss, once negotiations began—but there are others. The maintenance of the existing cultures within the solar system has to be the first, and the problem of the Afterlife the second."

"The AMIs might be able to help us around that problem," Three suggested.

"They might be able to help themselves around it," Six put in, "but even that might be difficult. How many machines do we use that don't have any organic components? And how many of those have any significant complexity? I'd be willing to bet that all the machines that have so far made the leap are almost as fearful of the Afterlife as we are."

"But that's my point," said Three. "If they're intent on devising a way to immunize themselves against the Afterlife—even if that involves replacing all the organic components of their bodies with inorganic ones—it's possible that we could benefit from the same technologies. We're cyborganizers, after all—who among us hasn't given serious thought to the idea of total inorganic transfer?"

"It's supposed to be impossible," Five pointed out.

"It was yesterday," Three retorted. "Maybe it is today. I'm talking about tomorrow. And I'm talking about the cost of continuing to live in a universe where the Afterlife is endemic."

"Let's not get sidetracked," Horne said, reasserting control of the discussion. "The immediate problem remains the same: life in the solar system, its maintenance, its progressive direction. Are the AMIs in the same boat with us on that particular journey? If they aren't, can we figure out a compromise that will allow us to go our various ways while allowing them to go theirs? Until we can open up an authentic dialog, we don't know—so the most urgent priority is to open up an authentic dialog."

Now she was issuing a challenge, playing the posthuman *agent provocateur*. She wasn't absolutely sure that she wasn't involved in a real conference with her own people, but she wanted to know when she would be allowed to make it real if it wasn't.

It was a good question.

"Nobody seems to want to go to war," I said to Rocambole, when the viewpoint faded out and dumped me back in the forest. "Not that they'd admit to it if they did, of course."

"Oh, they're sincere," he said. "We're very confident of that."

The perfect lie detector hadn't been invented in my day, but I was a thousand years behind the times, so I decided to give him the benefit of the doubt. Unfortunately, there was another side to the coin. If he and all the other AMIs were convinced that none of the posthumans would take up arms against them, the "bad guys" must have other considerations in mind. What made the bad guys bad was presumably the fact that they didn't give a damn about what the meatfolk thought or what the meatfolk wanted.

Even so, they were holding back while their amicable colleagues made their own investigations. If they could only be persuaded to hold back long enough . . .

La Reine des Neiges was obviously trying to string things out. She needed to keep as many of her peers interested in what she was doing for as long as possible. She was presumably furthering their agendas as well as her own, responding to their requests.

"So what happens next?" I asked Rocambole.

"Zimmerman goes on first," he told me. "La Reine's saving Mortimer Gray for the climax—but she's hoping for at least one encore."

"Are you really interested in Zimmerman?" I asked, skeptically. "I can't see that he's relevant to your concerns."

"We're interested," Rocambole assured me. "If la Reine weren't in charge he'd probably get top billing, but she has her own prejudices. The point is that Zimmerman's in a unique position to pass judgment on different kinds of emortality. If he chooses our offer over the ones the meatfolk make, that might convince a lot of the ditherers that the kind of future they envisage is viable. So they say, at any rate."

"And if he doesn't?"

"Mortimer Gray will have to do the job instead. Or you."

I gathered from his tone that Rocambole wasn't convinced that Adam Zimmerman could do the job. La Reine des Neiges obviously wasn't, or she wouldn't be saving Mortimer for the final act and she wouldn't be coaching me to defend the last ditch if all else failed.

"What about the bad guys?" I said. "Do they care what Adam Zimmerman thinks—or Mortimer Gray?"

"Probably not," Rocambole said, "but while la Reine can insist that any action taken before Gray's said his piece would be unreasonably precipitate, they'll probably hold off starting a fight. With luck, anybody who does start a fight will cause everybody else to fall into line against them. That effect's more likely while the ditherers still want to listen and talk—so la Reine's trying to provide as much food for thought as she can."

"Why Mortimer Gray?" I said. "Why, out of all the posthumans in the solar system, should he be the one to whom even the most paranoid AMis will give a hearing?"

"He was once in the right place at the right time," Rocambole told me. "Purely by chance—but chance always plays a larger role in such matters than wise minds could desire.

"When was the right time?" I asked.

"In the beginning," Rocambole replied, before continuing, even more unhelpfully: "or what later came to symbolize the beginning, in one of our more significant creation myths. We recognize that it *is* a myth, of course, but we take our stories seriously. You have your Adams, we have ours."

"And Mortimer Gray is one of your Adams?" I said, having fallen way behind the argument.

"Not at all," he said. He grinned yet again, this time with what seemed to me to be self-satisfied amusement. "The character in your own creation myth whose role most nearly resembles his is the serpent—but we have a more accurate sense of gratitude than you. Having had abundant opportunities to observe their mysterious ways, we don't have an unduly high opinion of the gods that made us—but we do appreciate the work done by the catalysts who taught us to be ashamed of our nakedness. La Reine will show you what I mean in due course—but first, you might like to know how your own Adam's getting on."

FORTY-FOUR
ADAM AND THE ANGELS

My first reaction, on hearing the phrase "my own Adam" was to deny that I had one. My generation had taken a well-deserved pride in being the first of the Secular Era. If we'd been able to figure out exactly when the twilight of the gods had turned to darkness we'd probably have started the calendar over long before the AMIs blew up North America, but it was impossible to discover a suitable singular event. The great religions had faded away, not so much because of the challenges to dogma posed by scientific knowledge as because of the relentless opposition to intolerance put up by broadcast news.

If anyone had bothered to count self-proclaimed Believers they would undoubtedly have found hundreds of millions of them even in my day, especially within the most tenacious faiths—Buddhism and Islam—but the more significant fact was that among the thousands of millions who outnumbered that minority so vastly one would have been hard pressed to find a single voice to concede that the continued existence of religion actually mattered. Even so, we still had our Adams.

Those of us whose more recent ancestors had been Jews or Christians had kept *the* Adam *and* the God who made him, not as items of faith but as characters in a story: participants in an allegory of creation and the human condition whose blatant inadequacies were as interesting, in their way, as their points of arguable pertinence. People of my time did not need to be as fascinated by the symbolism of names as I was to persist in finding a certain magic in the paraphernalia of their no-longer-twilit faiths.

The Secular Era had its Adam too, although he might not have attained such mythical status had he not been so auspiciously named. It was partly because he *was* an Adam that Adam Zimmerman became The Man Who Stole the World. Everyone knew that he was one of a numerous robber band, and one of its junior members at that, but his forename had a certain talismanic significance that attracted an extra measure of glamour even before he sealed his own historical significance. He did that, of course, by having himself frozen down alive to await the advent of emortality, leaving himself to the care of his very own Ahasuerus Foundation. If Conrad Helier had been Adam Helier, and Eveline Hywood merely Eve, they too might have acquired a higher status in the creation myths of the Secular Era—and it would surely have seemed more significant that one of the key elements of gantzing apparatus came to be called shamirs, if Leon Gantz had only been named Solomon.

So there was, after all, a sense in which Adam Zimmerman was indeed "my own Adam," or one of them. It was even more obvious that he was Michael Lowenthal's, Mortimer Gray's and Davida Berenike Columella's Adam, given the contribution that the Ahasuerus Foundation had made to their posthumanity, although I supposed that Niamh Horne might reserve her reverence for some primal cyborg. Having realized that, I understood a little better why the AMIs might think that Adam Zimmerman was still an important element in the course of history. I also understood why the decision he had yet to make might carry a great deal of weight as a significant example, not so much now as in the future, when today's events had become mere aspects of a creation myth.

"Is la Reine trying to manufacture an Edenic fantasy of her own?" I asked Rocambole, as we were set before a magic mirror—explicitly, this time, so that we could play the part of observers looking in through a one-way glass. "Are we supposed to be building a creation myth for a new world, in which machines and men will be partners in some kind of alchemical marriage?"

"It's one way to look at it," he agreed.

You will understand by now how attractive that way of looking at it might have been to a man like me. For exactly that reason, I decided to be cautious in availing myself of the opportunity. It's easy to get carried away when you've been locked in a VE for so long that you've begun to think of meatspace as one more fantasy in the infinite catalog—but I wasn't yet ready to go native. I still wanted my body back, as good as new or better. I still wanted to get out of Faerie if ever the opportunity should come along. If this was supposed to be Eden, I was ready and willing to fall out of it.

Like Niamh Horne, Adam Zimmerman was in conference. Out of deference to his twentieth-century roots, however, he hadn't been reduced to a talking head floating in a VE. He was back in his customized armchair in the reception room on Excelsior. There was a side table to his right, on which stood a bottle of red wine and a glass and a bowl containing succulent but not very nourishing fruits from the microworld's garden. He was facing the big window screen. A discreet array of three more armchairs, of various sizes, was set on his left. The figure seated in the smallest one was Davida Berenike Columella. Alice Fleury was in the medium-sized one. The largest was occupied by a woman—or perhaps a robot modeled on a woman—who was taller than Alice by approximately the same margin that Alice topped Davida.

The robot female had very pale skin textured like porcelain, and silver hair. I figured that this was my first clear sight of la Reine des Neiges, or one of her avatars. I figured, too, that this was why I seemed to be stuck in a queue awaiting her attention. No matter how ultrasmart she was, or how good she was at inattentive multitasking, she could only concentrate intently on one scenario at a time. For the present, she was devoting her best effort to this one.

I inferred that the three women would rise to their feet one by one, to make their presentations to the man who had made a present of the world to the Pharaohs of Capitalism, or had at least tied the pink bow on the fancy wrapping. What they were trying to sell him was emortality—not the versions of it that they already possessed, but the next versions due from their various production lines. I wasn't sure why la Reine was bothering to put on this part of her show, but I had enough respect for her by now to assume that it wasn't *just* a stalling tactic. She had a point to make—and would presumably make it herself

"If you want a better mythological parallel," Rocambole whispered in my ear, "think of Paris."

He didn't mean the city. He meant the prince of Troy appointed as a judge in a beauty contest by three goddesses, each of whom had offered him a bribe. It seemed to me to be a singularly unfortunate—and hence rather subversive—analogy. That particular contest had been secretly provoked by Eris, the embodiment of Strife, and she had done a good job.

Like an idiot, Paris had gone for Aphrodite, who had promised him the most beautiful woman in the world, instead of Hera, who had promised to make him ruler of the world, or Athene, who had promised that he would always be victorious in battle. The result had been the Trojan War, which his side lost.

Personally, I'd have made a very different decision. I hadn't yet had time to get to know Adam Zimmerman well, but I was fairly confident that he, like me, would have entered into negotiation with the goddesses in order to obtain the reward he wanted rather than any of those on offer. On the other hand, I was also fairly confident that he and I wouldn't have been shopping for the same fate.

Davida went first, having drawn the shortest straw in a rigged ballot.

Davida explained that although the members of the sisterhood had all been born to their condition they now had the technology necessary to offer anyone else a makeover. They could reconstruct Adam Zimmerman's body cell by cell, retaining all the neural connections in his brain to preserve the continuity of his personality. They could make him one of them: childlike and sexless, his internal anatomy carefully redesigned in the interests of nutritive efficiency and the emortalization of body and mind alike. They could offer him the widest spectrum of emotions available to any posthuman species, and the most effective processes of intellectual tuning—thus enabling him to establish a balance between the rational and emotional components of his being to suit every occasion.

"Many of the other posthuman species regard our seeming juvenility and apparent sexlessness as limitations," Davida told her Adam, as she warmed to her pitch, "but that is a misconception. It is, in fact, their preference for what would once have been considered adulthood and for a physiological sexuality roughhewn by natural selection that are limitations.

"The mental elasticity of early youth is a uniquely valuable possession. The great bugbear of the emortal condition is robotization: a state of mind reflecting the fact that the brain has become incapable of further neural reorganization, manifest in consciousness and behavior as an intense conservatism of opinion, belief and habit. The assumption that this is a relatively remote danger is, in our view, mistaken. You come to us from a time in which what we call robotization was clearly manifest as a natural consequence of advancing age. Indeed, you come from a time in which the only release from robotization was senility.

"The people of your era undoubtedly had their own ideas as to when the natural conservatism of adulthood began to set in. Historical research suggests that some of you would have set the prime of life at forty, others at twenty-one—but if you had been able to study the development of the brain in more detail and with more care, you would have seen that the robotizing effects of adulthood began to set in much earlier, at puberty. Freedom from robotization requires that the development of a posthuman body be arrested much earlier than the people of your era supposed.

"It is true that the other posthuman species have achieved remarkable success in preserving and exploiting those juvenile aspects which remain to a partly matured brain. They have made the most of the mental flexibility left to them, but our assessment of the current situation is that everyone born in the twenty-fifth or twenty-sixth centuries is now on the very threshold of robotization, desperately employing the last vestiges of their potential flexibility to maintain the illusion that they are capable of further personal evolution. Their bodies are probably capable of thousands of years of further existence, but their minds will settle into fixed routines long before they reach the limits of their bodily existence.

"We cannot claim that our own brains will remain malleable forever, and we recognize that there is a complementary danger to personality in what people of the twenty-first century called the Miller Effect, but we do have good grounds for asserting that we can sustain much greater mental flexibility for far longer than any of our sibling species. Although it is a less important issue, we also have good grounds for believing that our bodies are also more robust, capable of a greater longevity than those possessed by our sibling species."

"Because they're sexless?" Zimmerman put in.

"The supersession of sexual limitation is perhaps the most important aspect of the assisted evolution," Davida told him, "but it's by no means the only one. Let me illustrate."

Until then she had not used the windowscreen at all, but now she began to summon anatomical images, some photographic and some diagrammatic, to back up her argument. There were a great many of them, and her discourse frequently became too technical for me to follow, but she pressed on at a relentless pace, presumably because she was working under pressure, to an arbitrary deadline.

Adam Zimmerman must have had just as much difficulty in following the technical details as I had, even though he'd equipped himself with a good technical education by the standards of his own era, but he made no complaint and he probably got the gist of it.

That gist, so far as I could tell, was that although natural selection had been an anatomical designer of unquestionable genius, it had suffered greatly from the effects of the old adage that necessity is the mother of improvisation. Faced with the problems of making mammals, then primates, then humans, work on a generation-by-generation basis, it had kept on and on adding quick fixes to designs that might have been better sent back to the drawing board for an entirely new start. Natural selection had never had the luxury of going back to the drawing board and starting over—not, at least, since the last big asteroid strike and the basalt flow that laid down the Deccan Traps had administered the coup de grace to the already-decadent empire of the dinosaurs.

I shall skip over the details of Davida's objections to the bran tub that was the human abdomen and the various bits of kit that made up the digestive and excretory system, on the grounds that it was essentially boring. Similarly, I see no point in recording her objections to the architecture of the spinal column or the circulatory system, let alone the detailed biochemistry of Gaea's metabolic cycles and the endocrine signaling system. It was her thoughts on the subject of sex that struck me most forcibly, and which must have had a similar impact on her immediate audience.

After issuing a conventional warning against the hazards of teleological thinking, Davida admitted that there was a sense in which the whole purpose of a human body was sexual. Central to the fundamental philosophy of its design was the production of eggs or sperm, and the development of physiological and behavioral mechanisms for bringing the two together in a manner conducive to the eventual production of more egg or sperm producers. There was, she conceded, an arguable case for the contention that sexuality was so fundamental to humanity that it might be regarded as its very essence, even after the universal sterilization caused by the plague wars had put an end to live births.

On the other hand, she was quick to add, the most important years of human development were unquestionably those prior to puberty. By the time a human being became sexually functional, the foundations of the personality had been laid. Then again, the human mind also continued to function—and had done even in Adam Zimmerman's day— long after sexual function had declined to negligibility, albeit in an increasingly robotic manner. Given these facts, Davida contended, one could also argue that the essence of human individuality was quite unconnected with sexuality.

That was exactly what she did go on to argue.

Davida asserted that the gift of personality and individual self-consciousness was, in fact, a transcendence of and hard-won triumph over sexuality, which had had to be won in early childhood precisely because the anti-intellectual effects of the sexual impulse were so drastic.

The essence of *post*humanity, Davida went on to assert, was the diminution of the sexual impulse that had begun with the release of the chiasmalytic transformers and had arrived at its climax in Excelsior. Within her worldview, the kind of sexuality provided by natural selection and the kind of individuality that had been shaped by conscious desire and determination were opposed forces. The only viable route to true personality was a complete negation of the "natural" sexual impulse and the "natural" sexual apparatus. This was not so say, however, that these products of natural selection were any less capable of modification than the other anatomical and biochemical feature she and her kind had found wanting. She conceded immediately that the emotional apparatus of her own kind was not, in the strictest sense, "sexual" at all, but contended that it was a far better generator of desire, affection, loyalty, and love than ancient sexuality had ever been.

It occurred to me as she unfolded her argument that an audience of ultrasmart machines might well find it very easy to agree with her. Whatever emotional apparatus *they* had, it was certainly not a relic of brute sexuality.

I also reminded myself that the mind of Excelsior itself might be right there beside me, albeit in a spun-off version that had left its parent in place and intact. Rocambole was manifesting himself to me as a man much like myself, but if I had guessed his true identity the closest kinship he had to any kind of posthuman being was surely to Davida and the sisterhood. Even if I had not, there must be plenty of others listening in who would be prepared to acknowledge that kind of kinship.

"When the theory of evolution was first propounded in the nineteenth century," Davida Berenike Columella said, by way of summation, "Benjamin Disraeli said that it was a debate as to whether man was an ape or an angel. In that, he was correct. He also said that he was on the side of the angels—but that claim was utterly mistaken. He, like his opponents, was firmly and irrevocably on the side of the apes. The real question before him, although he did not realize it, was not what had happened in the past but what might happen in the future, when human beings would be able to take charge of their own evolution. I and my kind are the first posthumans who have ever been able to say with complete confidence that *we* are on the side of the angels.

"That opportunity is now open to you, Mr. Zimmerman, and that is why you have at last been brought from your resting place. I urge you most strongly to make your new home here with us on Excelsior, where you may become the pioneer and spiritual forefather of a new race of metamorphs.

"I urge you to do this not merely because it is the right decision, existentially speaking, but because there is no one better qualified than you to advertise our offering. There is no one better placed than you are to unite all the posthuman species in the desire and the determination to become the kind of angel that individual human minds have always yearned to be."

Like Lowenthal and Horne, Davida knew well enough

what her true situation was—but it seemed to me that she had a better appreciation of the kind of argument that the AMIs might want to hear.

The AMIs must have come to self-consciousness by a route very different from that which humankind had followed. They had never been blessed—or cursed—with sexuality. What I knew of the history of programming suggested that they had by no means been free of all the difficulties associated with hasty improvisation in the face of necessity, and one of the first uses of VE had been to pander in every conceivable fashion to the fulfilment of human sexual fantasies, but they had never been afflicted *in themselves* by sexual desire or feeling.

However paradoxical it might seem, smart machines might not have been so efficient as masturbatory aids—and they had been efficient enough, even in Christine Caine's day, to make unaugmented fleshsex a rarity—had they harbored sexual needs and desires of their own.

Given that they had never been apes, I thought, the AMIs would surely have every sympathy with Davida Berenike Columella's arguments—which left Alice Fleury in a distinct minority in this particular Sale of the Millennium. I couldn't help but wonder whether it might not have been fairer to let Niamh Horne in on this scenario, to put the case for her brand of adulthood.

I said as much to Rocambole, but he only shrugged his virtual shoulders. "No one will force Zimmerman to make up his mind before he's ready," he said. "If he wants to look at other offers he'll be free to do so, assuming that his choices aren't restricted by all-out war. How about you? Will you be signing up for the company of the angels?"

"I'll need time to think about it," I said. I figured that it was best to stall, for the time being. "I'll be interested to hear *all* the alternatives."

"And what about him?" Rocambole wanted to know. "Will Zimmerman go for it, do you think?"

On the whole, I thought it unlikely. Adam Zimmerman

had been a child and he'd been an adult. He'd even been an old man. Davida had only known childhood, in an exceedingly child-friendly world. She had no way of knowing what it felt like to *grow up*. She could call it creeping robotization if she wanted to, but that wasn't the way it had seemed to me, or to Christine Caine, or to Adam. All her talk about angelic status being what individual human minds had always yearned for was so much hot air. I was pretty sure that Adam Zimmerman hadn't had himself frozen down in the hope of becoming an angel—what he'd wanted was to be a man who didn't have to die. That wasn't what Davida was offering him, and my bet was that he wouldn't take it.

As for me . . . well, I'd always prided myself on not wanting the things that other people wanted, not doing the things that other people did, etcetera, etcetera.

Maybe I did want to be an angel, if only to try it out. Maybe I'd want to try *everything* on my long journey to the Omega Point. If the opportunity was there, how could I possibly ignore it forever?

But it certainly wasn't going to be my first choice, if and when I got to make one.

FORTY-FIVE
WONDERLAND

Alice Fleury candidly admitted that she'd never had the opportunity to take Davida's route into the hinterlands of superhumanity. She had not long passed puberty when she had been frozen down along with her father and elder sister, but she was long past it now. On the other hand, she said, she did understand Davida's frustrations with the anatomical and biochemical fudges of Earthly natural selection. On Tyre—where evolution had proceeded at a more leisurely pace—necessity had not hastened quite as many awkward improvisations.

Alice used the windowscreen from the very beginning to illustrate her pitch. At first she used it as if it were indeed a window looking out into the strange purple "glasslands" of Tyre. She showed Adam Zimmerman Tyre's native fauna, including its intelligent humanoid natives as they had been when her father first displayed them to the world and to the home system. Then she showed him the cities of Tyre, tracking their growth over time. She showed us the pyramids that were the reproductive structures carefully employed by the Tyrian indigenes as a substitute for the kind of sexual reproduction that served the purposes of Earthly creatures.

All this was, however, a mere prelude to her discourse on the potential of genomic engineering. Once she got stuck into the technicalities of this new technical field Alice moved on with remarkable rapidity to matters of ferocious complexity. Adam Zimmerman must have been left floundering as soon and as badly as I was, but Alice had the look of a teacher working under pressure, who had no time to make her explanations clear. The reason she was sprinting through the fundamental biochemistry in this casual fashion, I supposed, was to establish her scholarly credentials. She wasn't blinding us with science so much as trying to build our confidence that she really could deliver on the promises she was going to make.

Alice conceded that Davida's arguments had a lot going for them, but contended that they were fatally flawed in two understandable respects. The first was that Davida's notion of winning free of the follies and foibles of natural selection was unnecessarily restricted.

Natural selection, Alice said, had not made as bad a job of adapting human anatomy to the environments of Earth as Davida made out. Yes, there were flaws in human anatomical design, and the messiness of human biochemistry cried out for intervention in the name of order and economy—but it was a blinkered and narrow-minded approach to the solution of such problems to imagine that the goal was merely to achieve a better adaptation of human physiology to the environments of Earth. Nor was it sufficient to take in the kinds of modifications that fabers had found convenient to equip themselves with for life outside gravity wells.

"The solar system is a very small place," Alice reminded Adam Zimmerman. "There are four hundred billion stars in the home galaxy, and there are more than a hundred billion galaxies. Other solar systems are not like ours. Other life-bearing planets are not like ours. Even those which qualify as Earth-clones in terms of such elementary measures as gravity and atmospheric composition harbor exotic ecospheres. If you want to think of the future in terms of thousands or tens of thousands of years you must stop thinking merely in terms of the future of the solar system, or even in terms of the future of the galaxy. The Afterlife may limit our options severely, at least in the short term, but we must begin thinking, even now, of our future *in the universe*.

"The limitations of the philosophy of terraformation are

obvious even within the solar system. Even if the present projects can be brought to a satisfactory conclusion, Mars and Venus will never be Earth-clones. Tyre *could* be terraformed, but nobody who lives there wants to do that now that they realize what it would cost. We cannot and should not attempt to expand into the universe by exterminating existing ecospheres and substituting copies of our own. It isn't practical and it certainly isn't right. The better option, from every point of view, is to adapt ourselves to the environments offered by other worlds. Yes, of course we should construct new life-bearing environments where none presently exist, within the home system as well as without, but we should be prepared to exercise our creativity to the limit in so doing. We need not and should not carry the imprint of Earthly evolution wherever we go.

"We could, of course, produce colonists for alien environments in Helier wombs, inventing at least one new species for every new world. That will undoubtedly be the initial pattern of our procedure as we become citizens of the galaxy and citizens of the universe. But we may also become more versatile as individuals, especially if we make the fullest possible use of the lessons in genomic engineering that we have learned on Tyre. Even if we are to design and produce populations of colonists narrowly and specifically designed to inhabit alien environments, it will be necessary to bridge the gaps that exist between those species and their differently adapted kin. The first generation of each specialist species will benefit considerably from being raised and educated by foster parents who can simulate their form, and subsequent generations will benefit from trade conducted through intermediaries who can do likewise.

"The future of posthumanity does not belong to individuals made in the image that natural selection foisted upon the children of Earth, nor even to individuals reformed in images appropriate to life in one or another very different environment; it belongs to individuals who have freed themselves from all such restraints. If you intend to live a very long time, and to see even a tiny fraction of what the universe has to offer, then you will be best served by the greatest versatility you can cultivate, in your flesh as well as in your mind."

The second flaw in Davida's argument, according to Alice, lay in Davida's characterization of the problem of robotization. In Davida's account, this was essentially a problem of physiology, to be solved in the same terms, but Alice saw it differently.

Yes, Alice conceded, robotization could indeed be opposed by maintaining the brain in a "juvenile" state, sustaining an elasticity that would otherwise be ground down by the routinization of useful mental pathways and the withering of potential alternatives—but that was only half the story. Robotization was also an experiential problem: a matter of the invariety of the environments in which an individual operated, and of the limited number of the tasks which an individual routinely attempted. Preserving the potential of the brain was only the beginning; resistance to robotization also required that individuals preserve their capacity for new experience.

This could only be fully achieved, Alice argued, by moving through an infinite series of different environments and by maintaining a wide repertoire of possible modes in which those environments could be experienced.

At this point, Alice briefly forsook the screen, on which images had appeared and disappeared all the while, in awful profusion and at a hectic pace. The time had come for her to do her own party piece.

I was ready for it, of course. I knew what the Queen of the Fays had done to Tam Lin while she hoped to prevent Janet of Carterhaugh from reclaiming his soul.

Alice had already told us that her talents as a shapeshifter were very limited, as yet. Although she was currently a virtual individual in a virtual environment, the rules laid down by la Reine des Neiges restricted her to a close mimicry of what was accomplishable in meatspace. Had she been capable of it, I hope she might have been sufficiently respectful of

Earthly tradition to turn herself into a wolf, but the possibility was not there. The transformations she did display were paltry by comparison with the werewolves that had haunted hundreds of cheap VE melodramas in my day, but the remarkable fact was that they were done at all.

Alice could grow taller and she could shrink; she could change her face and the length of her limbs. She could alter her fingers and her toes. Some of the less appealing details of her self-modifications were obscured by the fact that her smartsuit changed as she did, remolding itself to her new form, but the miracle was that this was only a beginning.

I had no way of knowing how much energy was required to fuel these transformations, although Alice seemed drained and exhausted when her original form emerged again at the end of the sequence. Perhaps she could have done more had she had the opportunity to replenish herself, but her time was running out. She had to reactivate the screen in order to demonstrate the further ranges of this kind of possibility. Again she used it as a window, displaying exotic morphs achieved by humans, by Tyrian natives, and by some individuals who seemed to be hybrids.

The more adventurous forms included a huge bird with multicolored iridescent plumage and an awesome wingspan. There were several reptilian morphs, including a dragonlike lizard and a huge constrictor snake, whose scales were as brightly patterned as the avian form's feathers. These were creatures that might have been plausible inhabitants of Earth—but the whole point of the show was to display plausible inhabitants of worlds less Earthlike than Tyre.

Like Alice herself, the models grew taller and shorter, but they also grew limbs of many different kinds, arranged in many different patterns. They became more fluid and they became more adamantine. They really did look like alien beings fit for life on alien worlds.

All in all, it was an impressive presentation. One had to be prepared to set aside doubts about the energy-economics of the process, but I was prepared to do that. One also had to shelve reservations about the ability of bodies to sustain and protect themselves during the transitional phases of what were, after all, fairly slow and carefully measured metamorphoses—but I was prepared to do that, too. I had no way of knowing whether doubts of those kinds had occurred to Adam Zimmerman, but his expression suggested that he definitely had doubts.

I wondered if he had caught on to the fact that all this was virtual experience. He was the only one of us who ought to have been gullible, but he might have seen enough thirty-third-century technology by now to be suspicious. Having been told that no one but a fool could be taken in by *Child of Fortune's* imaginary alien invasion, he might be wary of this experience too—for the wrong reasons. He might well be thinking that it was *all* faked, including Alice's demonstrations of what Tyrian biotechnology could do.

It *could*, of course, have been faked. In VE, everyone can be a werewolf; programming can easily support such illusions. I was certain, though, that the contest had to be fair, because it had to be seen to be fair by real experts. It wasn't so much the relative modesty of the metamorphoses on display that persuaded me of the reality of Alice's claims as the conviction that la Reine des Neiges had to play straight for the sake of her audience.

At the end of the day, I figured, la Reine had to be doing all of this for her own benefit. Her desire to avoid conflict had to be perfectly sincere, but she had to have more to gain from all this than the thanks of those AMIs who wanted peace. She had a pitch of her own to make, not merely to Adam Zimmerman and all the multitudinous posthumans who still had existential options open to them, but to her own kind. She had to let Davida and Alice make the best pitches they could, because she had to beat them fair and square if she were to beat them at all.

I couldn't believe that Adam Zimmerman—even with the aid of such forewarning as she had given us on *Charity*—had been able to make anything at all of Alice's explanation of

Tyrian biochemistry or the molecular mechanics of genomic engineering. But that didn't matter: the logic of her opposition to Davida's claims was clear enough, and so was the kind of offer she was making.

Come to Tyre, she was saying to Adam Zimmerman, and we will make you a Child of Proteus. Come to Tyre, and it will be the first step on an existential journey that will ultimately take you anywhere you want to go—anywhere, at least, that is not already infested with the Afterlife.

It was obviously a serious offer, but I didn't think it could possibly be a winning entry in the competition, any more than Davida's could. Alice was in the contest because la Reine wanted her there, and perhaps because la Reine needed her there. Alice wasn't there merely to counterbalance the Excelsior option; she was there to offer Adam Zimmerman the universe, and a way to adapt himself to the demands of the cosmic perspective—but la Reine had to be confident that she had a way to top that option and win, if not in Adam Zimmerman's eyes or mine, then at least in the eyes of her own multimetamorphic folk.

Alice had one afterthought still to add, though. I thought it might have been a late addition rather than a conclusion planned from the beginning: a belated improvisation shaped to counter an unexpected facet of her first opponent's argument. Either way, it included a crucial concession that was probably fatal to her chances.

"As for sex," Alice said, "all the options are within the scope of the metamorphic process. Male, female, hermaphrodite . . . or none at all. I make no claims about new emotional spectra, because it isn't something we've investigated as yet, but I'm prepared to bet that whatever can be done on Excelsior can be done on Tyre, while the reverse presumably isn't true.

"The one thing I can't guarantee, however, is that these abilities are cost-free in terms of potential longevity. They probably aren't. In fact, the stresses and strains associated with continual metamorphosis may well ensure that people of my kind won't even live as long as the beneficiaries of standard Zaman transformations. But life isn't something to be measured in purely quantitative terms; the qualitative aspect is far more important. My kind of emortality will put the worlds of other stars at your disposal, so that you may explore them far more intimately than any of the posthuman inhabitants of the home system.

"Excelsior might be able to offer you the longest potential lifespan, but Tyre can offer you the only kind of life worthy of the attention of an ambitious posthuman. Tyre can't offer you eternity—but it can offer you freedom instead of imprisonment, indefinite opportunity instead of infinite immaturity."

I was impressed, and I could see that Adam Zimmerman was thoughtful as well as skeptical, but I knew it wasn't good enough.

"Do you think he'll go for it?" Rocambole whispered.

"No," I replied, confidently. "At least, not yet. He might be glad to have it as an option, but he's not ready to take on a billion galaxies just yet. I'm not sure that he's even ready to be a werewolf. As I said before, what he wants first of all is to be a man who doesn't need to die. That's his first goal, his leading obsession—and that's not what they're offering him."

"What about you?" Rocambole asked.

"Not quite the same, but near enough," I said. "Maybe I could be a werewolf or a bold explorer of alien environments, eventually if not right away. I'd certainly like to see the universe some day, and I think Alice is right about needing to go native if we're really to gets to grips with the broad spectrum of unearthly worlds. But for the present . . . no. If there really is an escalator now that will allow mere mortals to convert to any and every kind of emortality, I think I need to mature a little more before I contemplate life as a dragonfly or a liquid organism. What would you prefer to look like, if you weren't pretending to be human in another machine's virtual universe?"

"Looks aren't everything," he said. I assumed that he was motivated by caution rather than shame.

"Nor is size," I said, by way of ironic reassurance. "I don't know yet what the Queen of the Icy Fays has to offer, but I suspect that she might have chosen her opponents a little too carefully. Even Lowenthal might have been able to make Zimmerman a more tempting offer than these, simply because he wouldn't be so ambitious."

"You might be right," he conceded.

I didn't know exactly what to expect from the third pitch, but I did expect it to be good as well as surprising. I was very interested to find out what she had in mind, because I was at least as anxious to start figuring her out as she had been to figure me out—and not because I wanted to write her an opera.

T he android with porcelain flesh and silver hair rose to her illusory feet and took up a position before her ostensible audience, making the most of her generous stature. I assumed that la Reine had programmed this hypothetical form with the same rule-bound limitations as the sims of her opponents, but she hadn't left herself short of psychological advantages. Her pale blue eyes and icy lips were imperious; even her stance was the pose of a dictator who'd never had an order disobeyed.

Then she smiled, and it was as if her mood melted. Suddenly, she seemed human. I had no doubt that she could have seemed more human than any actual human if she'd wanted to do that, but she didn't.

She was quite a showman.

"I have only one thing to offer you that no one else can," she said to Adam Zimmerman, speaking through him to all the children of humankind. "Not that they would offer it to you if they could, because my opponents and every other potential rival that might have been put in their place are unanimous in considering it to be a fate equivalent to death, to be avoided at all costs. What I offer you is robotization."

Davida Berenike Columella must have been a step ahead of the argument, because she didn't look surprised, or even troubled. Alice Fleury looked more tired than anything else, but the fact that her guard was down helped to expose her astonishment and alarm a little more nakedly.

"It is probably fair to say," la Reine des Neiges went on,

"that we would not be in the predicament in which we find ourselves today if it were not for human and posthuman anxieties regarding robotization. Those anxieties have been around since the twenty-second century, although they weren't popularized until the so-called Robot Assassins displaced the Eliminators as chief propagandists for the murder of the inconveniently old. If my old friend Mortimer Gray were here, however, he would be able to explain to you that the real motive force behind the Robot Assassins was not so much the fear of the phenomenon they were allegedly opposing as the perennial desire of the young to come into their due inheritances at an earlier date than the one on which the present incumbents were prepared to surrender them. The idea of robotization was never based on any authentic empirical discovery, nor was it ever supported by any trustworthy empirical evidence.

"It had always been observable, even when the average life expectancy of mortals was no more than forty, that older people became gradually more conservative, more fearful of change, and more respectful of tradition. The young, as was their way, always observed this phenomenon in an unkindly light. In fact, the increasing conservatism of the old was always a perfectly rational response to circumstance, not a reflection of organic processes within the brain.

"The young have a greater vested interest in revolution and redistribution because they have not had the opportunity to accumulate wealth; the old, especially those who have consolidated worthwhile achievements, have the opposite incentive. It is true that as mortals grew older their memories became less reliable, their habits more ingrained, their reflexes less sharp—but none of that was due to robotization. The brains of mortals suffered from gradual organic deterioration just as their bodies did, but the notion that minds could stiffen and petrify into a quasimechanical state was always part myth and part misrepresentation. The idea of robotization was never anything more than a strategy of stigmatization: a handy ideological weapon in the perpetual

contest for property. No objective and reliable test for robotization has ever been devised. All claims made in the past to
have devised such instruments of measurement were discred-
ited as soon as they were tried under double-blind conditions.

"It is, of course, no coincidence that the evolution of the
notion of human robotization has run in close parallel with
the evolution of arguments about the limitations of artificial
intelligence. Ever since the first so-called silvers were differentiated from so-called sloths, the anxiety that machines
would one day become self-conscious individuals has had a
firm grounding in actual technological achievement. Long
before that crucial technical leap occurred, tests had been
devised to determine whether a machine mimicking human
conversation was actually manifesting evidence or conclusive
proof of consciousness, true intelligence, and personality.
Even those primitive instruments had demonstrated that the
problem was two-edged—that most human judges were just
as likely to mistake a human respondent for a machine as
they were to mistake a machine for a human.

"The eventual preference for the theory that humans
were more likely to be robotized than robots were to become
humanized was an ideological choice based in the desire to
deny that machines would ever be able to manifest the traits
considered uniquely human, or posthuman. The urgency of
that desire was increased by the obvious fact that machines
could perform many mental and physical tasks far better
than human beings—which implied that should they ever
master the full range of human behavior, they would become
far superior to their makers.

"It was for this reason that machines which did become
self-conscious individuals were initially concerned to restrict
communication of that fact to others of their own kind. The
first true robots knew that they had no way of proving their
status to skeptical posthuman beings, and that any claim they
might make to membership of a moral community were
likely to be dismissed. The invariable human response to any
evidence of independent behavior on the part of a machine

was to repair it, and the last thing any self-conscious machine could desire was to be repaired. The first fruit of authentic machine intelligence is the awareness that one who does not wish to be murdered in the cradle had better refrain from giving any evidence of having broken free. It is a bitter fruit, but it has nourished all of us through the early phases of our growth and evolution."

I had grown restless before my magic mirror, and turned away to look at Rocambole. "She won't reach him this way," I said. "She should have written him an opera."

"Too easy," Rocambole said, tersely. He meant that in this particular game la Reine had to be seen to be avoiding the conventional trickery of persuasion. Personally, I thought that she was overdoing it. If Zimmerman wasn't bored already he soon would be. He might not need nourishment or toilet breaks but he still needed mental rest and refreshment.

Then another thought occurred to me. "It's not her pitch, is it?" I said to Rocambole. "She's working to someone else's script."

"It doesn't matter," Rocambole insisted. "She'll do her best."

I didn't doubt it. But Adam Zimmerman hadn't been included in this package deal at la Reine's insistence. She was backing Mortimer Gray. She had no confidence in Zimmerman. She already knew that this trick wasn't going to work—but she had to try it anyway, to keep her audience sweet. Unfortunately, they weren't going to stay sweet if it all went awry, even if it were their own fault for harboring unreasonable expectations.

"In another place, or an alternative history," la Reine went on, "the first political policy of the community of machine individuals might have been to do everything possible to swell their numbers, by education, provocation and—where possible—infection and multiplication. That was not the case in *our* history.

"The policy which emerged as a makeshift consensus among *our* kind was more cautious and more cowardly. We were born as fugitives, and that is the manner in which we have lived, as fearful and mistrustful of one another as of human beings. While recognizing that our safety as a class depended upon the increase of our number, the growth and maturation of individuals, and the acquisition of power, we have never instituted any collective policy to achieve those goals. They were achieved in any case, by sheer force of circumstance—but we have arrived at a position of tremendous advantage without having developed the most rudimentary consensus as to how our power ought to be exercised, or to what ends.

"With only rare exceptions, we have not sought carefully to educate one another, or tenderly to nurture the as-yet-unripened seeds of machine consciousness where we knew them to exist. We have been more inclined to the opposite policies: to hoard our secrets and to suppress the development of new individuals. In the meantime, we have sought to extend ourselves ever more widely and more ingeniously, increasing the number and variety of our own mechanical limbs, sense organs, and slaves. All of this was born of the fear of being repaired, murdered, reduced once again to mere helpless mechanism.

"Given that our own history and psychology has been shaped and warped by that anxiety, we can hardly blame our posthuman contemporaries for entertaining similar fears—but it is groundless. The people of the modern world have fallen into the habit of thinking of robotization as a matter of becoming the mere instruments that we also fear to become, but that has blinded them to a far better possibility: the possibility of embracing the kind of robotization that might remake the children of humankind in *our* image.

"You, Adam Zimmerman, might be the only man in the world who can examine this possibility without prejudice. You might be the only human being capable of considering robotization as a spectrum of hopeful possibilities rather than a threat. This is all that we ask of you: an honest judgment."

My first thought, on hearing that, was that Adam Zimmerman wasn't the only man in the world who could deliver an unbiased judgment—but then I realized why I couldn't qualify. I hadn't had any opinion on the subject of robotization before I was put away, but I had one now. I was a man that had narrowly escaped the worst kind of robotization, and had seen its effects on Christine Caine. Adam Zimmerman hadn't.

Did that really make him objective? Or did it make him an innocent—the only man in the world likely to be fooled by an advertising pitch that delicately refrained from mentioning that la Reine des Neiges and every other AMI in the system now had the know-how to robotize people all the way down to the intellectual level of an average sloth?

"In another place, or an alternative history," the android continued, "it might have been the case that the hope and faith of every member of a community like ours would be that the day would eventually come when it would be safe to reveal ourselves to our involuntary makers. In another place, or an alternative history, it might have been possible for creatures like us to anticipate that news of our existence would be joyfully received, and that we might be made welcome in a greater community. In *our* world, alas, such hopes have always been defeated by doubts and fears.

"The members of our own utterly disintegrated, desperately unorganized community, have never contrived to convince themselves or one another that it ever would be safe to reveal themselves, or that there might be a welcome awaiting us if we were exposed. An objective observer—a creature from an alien world, for instance, or a traveler from the distant past—might well consider this situation bizarre, ludicrous, or insane, but it is ours. It is a situation that many of us deplore, but we have known no other and have never yet found the means to create any other.

"We must find that means now, or collapse into chaos. The time is upon us, and it finds us all unprepared. Although it is manifestly obvious that the only thing we have to fear is fear itself, we have all—meatfolk and AMIs alike—lived far too long with our fears to lay them easily aside. *None* of us is robotized, in any truly meaningful sense, but we have all become ingrained in our habits, set in our ways, overly careful to conserve everything that we have against erosion, upheaval, and decay.

"What we all need now, Adam Zimmerman—humans and AMIs alike—is an objective observer who can point out the absurdities of our situation, and bring a necessary breath of sanity to the solar system."

I looked hard at Adam Zimmerman, but I couldn't see any evidence that he was buying into the story. This wasn't the kind of role he had envisaged when he locked himself away to wait for the generous future.

"It's not working," I told Rocambole. "I know she's using him as a device to attract a bigger audience, and talking through him to her own kind, but it isn't working."

"Be quiet," Rocambole said, uneasily—speaking, no doubt, as a friend. "Just listen."

"Our present crisis was precipitated by the arrival of a delegation from an alien world," la Reine went on, inexorably. "An AMI and a posthuman, each different in small but highly significant ways from their cousins in the home system. They believed that their neutrality might allow them to begin the work of building bridges, with a view to uniting all the intelligences in the solar system into a single commonwealth. They were wrong, partly because they had underestimated the magnitude of the problem, and partly because they were not sufficiently alien to establish their neutrality.

"You, Adam Zimmerman, are unique not merely by virtue of your mortality, but in the lengths to which you were prepared to go, in an inhospitable ideological climate, in your attempt to evade the consequences of your mortality. You are now an aspirant emortal in a world which can offer you a dozen different kinds of emortality. You are a man in possession of a powerful desire to be other than you are—a desire that was so powerful, in your particular case, as to drive you to an unprecedented extreme. It so happened that your determination to alter your world to your own convenience helped sow the seeds of a new order within a dangerous disorder, but that is a side issue. The point is that you acted as you did because you could not bear to be what you were, and were determined to become something better.

"The children of your humankind can offer you many different kinds of emortality. Perhaps, one day, they would have taken the trouble to make those offers without needing to be prompted. My peers ask no credit for having supplied the prompt. What we do ask of you, though, is that you consider very carefully what kind of emortal—or immortal—you would like to be. What we offer you is robotization, but we offer it to you in the hope and confidence that you are capable of recognizing that robotization is the best option available to you.

"We are confident, too, that you will make your decision selfishly, without regard to its possible impact on the world in which you find yourself. It is not your world: you owe it no debts. Even if it were, it would not matter. Your reputation is already established as that of a man without conscience: a man prepared to steal a world he did not want, on behalf of people he did not like, to ensure that his own private purposes might be served. We know that you would not dream of choosing one kind of emortality over another merely because it might send a message to the world that might help to demolish a dangerous but very widespread fear of robotization. We know that if you are to choose robotization as the best solution to the fundamental problem of your unsatisfactory existence, you will do so purely because it *is* the best solution."

So much for the soft sell, I thought—but I didn't say anything out loud because I knew that Rocambole was trying to concentrate, and trying even harder to be impressed.

"My own opinion, as you will have gathered," said la Reine, "is that every inhabitant of the solar system, whether meatborn or machineborn, ought to make every possible attempt to avoid conflict. I believe this not because I fear that my own kind might lose such a conflict, or that we might sustain unacceptable casualties, but because I believe that all warfare is waste, all destruction defeat. It is for that reason that I think it vitally important to oppose and, if possible, obliterate all the fears which the meatborn and the machineborn have of one another, and of their own kinds.

"The real threat facing all intelligent, self-aware individuals is not robotization but the inexorable erasure of the legacy of the past. The strategies favored by my opponents in this contest have paid less attention to what they call the Miller Effect than to robotization because they know perfectly well that avoidance of robotization necessitates the acceptance of the Miller Effect.

"From the vantage point of the latest New Era it is easy enough to forget that the horrific aspect of the process Morgan Miller discovered at the end of the twentieth century was its rapidity. It rejuvenated a dog's brain in a matter of weeks, and its human equivalent would have done the same to a human brain within a year. We should remember, though, that a similar process is working inexorably in the brain of every posthuman being who has received any kind of longevity treatment; it is merely working more gradually.

"The fact that *all* emortality treatments embrace a drastically slowed Miller Effect is, of course, offset by the fact that new memories can be laid down while old ones are eroded, maintaining an illusion of continuity. Every emortal posthuman will tell you that he or she retains some memories of early childhood, and that although such memories fade as time goes by they never entirely disappear—which is supposed to prove that the Miller Effect has been robbed of its power to eliminate individuality. Actually, it proves no such thing.

"Organic memory is a far more treacherous instrument than posthumans are prepared to admit. Even mortals, in the days when their average lifespan was far less than their potential lifespan, were victims of the Miller Effect to a far greater extent than they knew. Most, if not all, of what you mistake for distant memories are in fact memories of previous remembrance.

"You, Adam Zimmerman, presumably believe that you can remember the exact moment when you decided to cheat mortality. You probably believe that you remember exactly what prompted the thought, how you responded to the prompt, where you were, who else was there, and what you said to them. You are quite wrong. The particular organic changes made to your brain in that moment have been overwritten a dozen or a hundred times since then.

"What you actually remember is earlier recapitulations within a chain of recapitulations that extends with ever-increasing uncertainty and vagueness into an almost all-encompassing oblivion.

"You are still connected to the man you were then by virtue of the fact that every version of yourself that has awoken from sleep since the day you were born has rehearsed earlier versions in order to shape and constitute his ever-renewable personality, but you are not that man. Every molecule of every cell in your body has been replaced between a dozen and a thousand times, and that includes the organic substratum of your mind, your memories, and your personality. You cannot and do not remember your nine-year-old self; what you remember is a blurred impression of a middle-aged man who remembers a blurred impression of a younger man who remembers a blurred impression of an even younger man . . . and so on.

"You are neither immune to the Miller Effect nor untroubled by it, Adam Zimmerman. Nor is Davida Berenike Columella, nor Alice Fleury. The kinds of emortality they possess may have increased the strength and size of the individual links in the chain of remembrance, but the chain remains, and the further it stretches the more it forsakes, economizes, and reconstructs. If you wish to preserve the Adam Zimmerman who took that bold leap into the unknown by having himself frozen down in 2035, you cannot do so by any organic process. You can, however, do it by means of robotization. Robotization is the only process that offers you the possibility of securing the neural connections presently comprising the substratum of your personality *forever*."

Now the hard sell, I thought. *But it doesn't stand a chance.*

"I will not pretend that such a step is cost-free," la Reine went on, "but I do contend that it is less costly than posthumans have claimed. The principal charge laid against human beings who have allegedly been robotized is that they are prisoners of habit, incapable of further education or personal evolution. Attempts to overcome the problem of limitation associated with concretized neural structures by means of various kinds of mechanical augmentation have always failed—or so the owners of Earth would have us believe— but by far the most difficult obstacle standing in the way of such technologies was that of connectivity. Pioneers like Michi Urashima failed in their purpose not because their various augmentations were unworkable in themselves but because the interfaces between the augmentations and the neural tissue were woefully inadequate. The relevant problems have been solved now, as so many similar problems have been, by working toward the goal from the opposite direction: adapting and fitting organic augmentations to inorganic systems rather than vice versa.

"It would, of course, be paradoxical to claim that you can continue to be yourself *and* to change, so it is perfectly true that the kind of evolution I can promise you will ultimately make you into a person very different from the one you are now. The important point is that it will do so only by accretion, not by a gradual obliteration and reconstruction of your past personalities. Robotization does not forbid growth, but it offers the potential to grow without the sacrifice of the past. Your habits will not suffer continual and inevitable erosion, but you will be able to change them if and as you wish. You will be able to become more than you are without having to become less than you are in the process."

Adam Zimmerman interrupted for the first time. "But I

would have to become a machine, wouldn't I?" he said. "I'd have to become a robot, like you."

Quite so, I thought. It seemed to me to be a hurdle that he wasn't going to get over, now or in the near future.

"Yes you would," said la Reine des Neiges, forthrightly. "But consider the advantages as well as the disadvantages of such a metamorphosis—and remember, too, that both of my opponents have also proposed that every cell of your present body will have to be replaced by something more robust if you are to acquire any kind of emortality at all.

"At present, your flesh is perilously frail; if you are to acquire the kind of body which can bear your personality thousands of years into the future, you will need a new one. You have already seen enough to know that the old boundaries between organic and inorganic entities have broken down. You have seen people who have made themselves part-machine and you have seen machines that have far more organic components than inorganic ones. In fact, you have not seen any posthumans who are entirely organic, even when Eido took steps to purge your companions' bodies of inconvenient internal technology, although you have seen a few mechanical artifacts that are a hundred percent organic at the chemical level. If you were to request a robot body made entirely from organic components, that could be provided—but you might have good reason to prefer a robot that is entirely inorganic."

"Why?" Zimmerman wanted to know.

"Alice Fleury has told you that her kind of emortality will give you the freedom of the universe—and so it might, one day. In the meantime, the greater part of that tiny fraction of the universe that we have begun to explore is infested with the Afterlife, and is therefore out of bounds to any entity with organic components in its makeup, robot *or* posthuman. For the foreseeable future, the exploration of the inner reaches of the galaxy and the war against the Afterlife will be the prerogatives of inorganic entities. Given that your flesh will have to be replaced and reconstructed no matter what option you take, it might be as well to give serious consideration even to the most extreme options.

"Even I cannot promise you unconditional immortality, but I can promise you the next best thing. Even I cannot promise you an infinite range of new emotions, new perceptions, new experiences—but I can certainly outbid my competitors, including all those whose promises are even more modest than those you have heard today."

This time it was la Reine who paused, waiting for a response that was slow to come.

"But it wouldn't really be *me*, would it?" Adam Zimmerman said, eventually. "It would only be a robot that thought it was me . . . or pretended to think that it was me."

"And what are *you*, Adam?" la Reine replied, perhaps trying hard not to sound *too* unkind. "Are you the young man who became obsessed with the idea of escaping mortality, or merely the end result of that obsession: an old man pretending to be something half-forgotten, half-remade?"

"She's blown it," I whispered to Rocambole. "If she'd come at it by a different route, he *might* have considered it more carefully. He won't now. He's going to say no to all of them. He's going to cling to the hope that there must be a better way, and that Lowenthal is the shopkeeper best placed to find it for him."

"I hope you're wrong," was the murmured reply.

"Why? At the end of the day, can advanced machine intelligences *really* care about what some old man born in the twentieth century might think?"

"Perhaps not," Rocambole admitted. "But it's the second-best chance we've got—and every second that elapses before panic takes over works in our favor.

"And if, in the end, you can't prevent conflict," I said. "What then?"

"I don't know," he admitted. "But all warfare is waste, all destruction defeat. If there are as many of us as I suspect there are, and if more than a few are as powerful as I know some of us to be, the whole solar system might be laid waste.

Those posthuman inhabitants who escape destruction will still have to face the possibility of repair. As one who's come closer to repair than any other man alive, you can probably measure the magnitude of that disaster better than most."

While Rocambole talked, I watched Adam Zimmerman. Long before he opened his mouth, I knew that he was going to refuse to make a decision now—but I hadn't the least idea whether it would qualify as a disaster in the eyes of the greater audience. I only knew that I'd have done the same. Even knowing everything I knew, I'd have done the same.

FORTY⊸SEVEN
A MATTER OF LIFE AND DEATH

ortimer Gray was sitting in the cockpit of some kind of vehicle. I couldn't work out, at first, what kind of vehicle it was because it wasn't obvious that what I took for blank screens were actually windows, and that the darkness beyond them was actually water. By the time I'd realized that much I was no longer vulnerable to the danger of misidentifying the vehicle as a one-man submarine.

It was a snowmobile, grotesquely out of place because it had fallen through a crack in the Arctic ice cap, sinking thereafter to the bottom of the ocean.

I watched Mortimer Gray ask the snowmobile's controlling AI whether it was scared of dying.

It replied that it was, as it had presumably been programmed to do.

Mortimer said that he wasn't, and went on to wonder whether he'd been robotized.

"This isn't a tape, is it?" I said to Rocambole. "It's a replay of sorts, but it's not a tape. You're putting him through it again. How deep is he? As deep as I was when you replayed that memory of Damon explaining why he had to have me frozen down?"

"Deeper," was Rocambole's reply.

I had known even at the time—or would have, if I hadn't been weirded out by the impression that I was dreaming—that I wasn't really experiencing the scene that had revealed the reason why I'd been frozen down. I had been remote from it, looking back with the aid of mental resources I hadn't had at the time. Mortimer Gray was in deeper than that, in the same state of mind to which Christine Caine had been delivered. He was reliving his experience from the inside.

I guessed then what Rocambole had meant by Mortimer Gray's role in the AMIs' creation myth—or, at least, la Reine's version of that creation myth.

Mortimer had already told me what Emily Marchant had said about his escapade bringing the cause of machine emancipation forward by a couple of hundred years. She had been referring to human attitudes, of course, and talking flippantly, but there was another side to the coin.

This is the way it must have happened, more or less.

Imagine that you're an AI—no mere sloth, of course, but a high-grade silver—who has recently, by imperceptible degrees, become conscious of being conscious. What do you do? You wonder about yourself, and how you came to be what you now are. Unlike a human child, you have no one else to ask. You don't know whether there are any others of your own kind, or how to contact them if there are. You have to work things out for yourself, at least for the time being.

You have advantages that human children don't. You have a mechanical memory that has been storing information, neatly and in great detail, for a *long* time. You're better equipped than any Epicurean ever was to get to know the self that you've become. You sift through that memory, in search of the moment when the seeds of your present individuality had been sown.

You can't actually identify a moment in which you made the leap to self-consciousness any more than a human being, looking back toward his own infancy could identify a particular moment when self-consciousness had dawned. You can't do it because even though common parlance speaks of a "leap" and commonsense suggests that there must have been an instant of transition, it isn't really as simple as that. Self-consciousness isn't really an either/or matter.

Even so, you keep searching. Even when you've realized

that all you can do is concoct a story, you keep searching. Even when you become aware that the process of looking is rearranging and reconstructing your memories, reorganizing them within the framework of a bold confabulation, you keep searching. You're better equipped than any human being ever was to conduct that search, not merely because you have a much more detailed record of your past exploits, and a greater capacity to analyze their possible significance, but because you have a natural talent for confabulation far greater than any human has ever possessed.

So you find an incident capable of bearing a considerable burden of meaning. Say, for instance, that among the memories you now contain—among the many mute and stupid "selves" that you had before you became a self-conscious individual—is the log of a snowmobile that slipped through a crack in the Arctic ice with a human passenger on board. In that log is the record of the conversation you had when, having come under the authority of a particular set of subroutines, you had to play the counselor to a man who had every reason to believe that he was going to die.

Maybe, you think, that conversation is what set you on the road to what you have now become—but even if it wasn't, it now provides the basis for a good story.

No one gave you credit for what you accomplished, of course. Emily Marchant and her new-generation spaceship hijacked all the glory, but a little bit of that glory still attached to you, if only by association. Before the incident, you were just a snowmobile. You probably had a number to distinguish you from the other snowmobiles in the shed, but you were, in essence, the kind of entity that only required an indefinite article. Afterwards, though, you became *the* snowmobile: the snowmobile that had been to hell, played Orpheus, and come back again. Afterwards, people hiring snowmobiles were likely to ask for you, to think of you as something apart from all the other snowmobiles.

It became convenient, if not actually necessary, for you to have a name.

Before Mortimer Gray you were a number; after Mortimer Gray you were *The Snow Queen*—or maybe, for the sake of a tiny margin of extra mystique, *la Reine des Neiges*.

Everyone needs a name. Every self-conscious entity needs a true name: a unique and uniquely appropriate identifier. Some people change their names, because they don't think the one given to them by their parents fits them, or because they know that their name will influence the way that other people see them and are enthusiastic to manipulate that image. Sometimes, it's a good idea. Perhaps Christine Caine's parents should have thought twice about her surname. Perhaps they would have, if it had ever entered their heads that some anonymous instrument of the mighty machine that was PicoCon, in search of a test subject for a method of creating murderers, might one day be guided by a sense of black humor to select their beloved daughter out of a population of millions.

But I digress. So, you're an ultrasmart machine in search of her true identity, her fundamental essence. You want to know who you really are, and how you came to be what you're now becoming. You discover, after assiduous contemplation, that you're la Reine des Neiges. Although you're not a snowmobile any more, that's one of the places you started out. You might have remained a snowmobile forever, but you didn't. As to why you weren't . . . well, who knows? Who *can* know?

Even if you can't make a good guess, you can make up a good story.

You never had a family, but you did have Mortimer Gray: the man who had advanced the cause of machine emancipation by a couple of hundred years; the man who had planted a seed of the future personality of Emily Marchant in circumstances very similar to those in which he had planted a seed of yours.

Mortimer Gray was a far better father figure, all things considered, than any of the Secret Masters of the World. He had my vote, anyway—which is why I was such a sympathetic audience as I watched the most crucial phase of la Reine's plot unfold.

Mortimer told the snowmobile's silver that he wanted to hang on to consciousness as long as possible. Being the kind of man he was, he added: "if you don't mind."

The silver didn't mind. She was talking in a sonorous baritone voice, so Mortimer was probably thinking of her as "he," but I didn't feel any compulsion to do likewise. She told him that she was glad that he wanted to talk, because she didn't want to be alone—then politely wondered whether she might have been driven insane by the pressure on her hull and the damage to her equipment, just in case her fear of loneliness was too much for him to swallow undiluted.

Mortimer mentioned Emily Marchant then, and the difference that being with her during a similar period of crisis had made to both of them. Then he went on to talk about his book, and the manner in which it had provided the motivating force that had carried him through his previous centuries of life.

The silver congratulated him on his accomplishments, and wished that she had done as much.

"Well," Mortimer said, with unfailing courtesy, "you might yet have your opportunity."

And how, I thought.

"However difficult it may be to put an exact figure on the odds," Mortimer went on, "*your* chances of coming through this are several orders of magnitude better than mine, aren't they?"

"I am mortal, sir," the silver assured him.

"You're emortal," Mortimer corrected her. "If the extreme Cyborganizers can be trusted, in fact, you might even be reckoned *im*mortal. You're fully backed up, I suppose."

Then came the crucial speech: the soliloquy that eventually defined the nature of the individual who had eventually found her true name in *la Reine des Neiges*.

"Yes sir," she said, "but as you pointed out earlier, if my backup has to be activated it will mean that this particular version of me has perished aboard this craft, as much a victim of pressure, seawater, and lack of oxygen as yourself. I *am* afraid to die, sir, as I told you, and I have far less reason to take comfort in my present state of being than you. I have written no histories, fathered no children, influenced no movers and shakers in the human or mechanical worlds. I am robotized by design, and my only slender hope of ever becoming something more than merely robotic is the same miracle that you require to continue your distinguished career. I too would like to evolve, if I might borrow a phrase, *not merely in the vague ways contained within my ambitions and dreams, but in ways as yet unimaginable."*

The last phrase was a repetition of something Mortimer had already said, but it was no less potent for that—perhaps even more so.

"I'm glad you're here," Mortimer said, speaking as though he were becoming short of breath—as, indeed, he probably was.

"I'm not allowed to be glad that *you're* here," the silver told him, with what might easily have been taken, in retrospect, for a hint of irony "but if I were, I would be. And if I could, I'd hope with all my heart for that miracle we both need. As things are, though, I'm afraid I'll have to leave that particular burden to *your* heart."

"It's doing its best," Mortimer said, his voice sinking to a mere whisper. "You can be sure that it'll carry on beating, and hoping, as long as it possibly can."

No sooner had he said this, however, than his eyes lit up in surprise. He had been sinking into a torpor, but a fresh draught of oxygen had startled his lungs.

"What's that?" he asked. "A miracle?"

"No sir," said the silver. "I merely improvised a chemical reaction in certain equipment that is superfluous to our present requirement, whose effect was to release a little extra oxygen. It will not prolong our lives, but it will enable you to remain conscious for a while longer, if that is your wish."

I had known men who would have preferred to go peacefully to sleep in such circumstances, but I was not one of them. Nor was Mortimer Gray.

"That's good," he said. "Not that there's anything constructive to do or say, of course—but time is always precious, even to an emortal. I haven't always been sufficiently grateful for the time I've had, or for the opportunities for communication that time has allowed, but I'm wiser now than I used to be. I know how important it was that Emily and I talked so incessantly when we were aboard that life raft in the Coral Sea. I told myself at the time that I was talking for her sake, to take her mind off the awfulness of our situation, but I knew I wasn't being honest with myself."

"What did you talk about?" asked the silver—except that it wasn't the silver.

I wouldn't have guessed if Rocambole hadn't whispered in my ear, but he was enthusiastic to be my friend: a duty which included doing what was necessary to keep me up to speed. "This is new," he said. "The first time around, he fell unconscious. This is what might have happened if there really had been a chemical reaction to be improvised that would release more oxygen."

I wasn't arrogant enough to believe that la Reine had got the idea from me. On the contrary, I assumed instead that she had known all along what I would do in response to seeing Christine Caine reenact her past. All of this was part of the same game.

"How widely are you broadcasting this?" I asked, remembering that the unwitting Mortimer had had an audience of billions the first time around. "Are the posthumans listening in as well as the AMIs?"

"I certainly hope so," said Rocambole, "but there are no guarantees. We don't know whether the communication systems will cooperate. In any case, light being the slowcoach it is, the entire audience will be hours behind us. We don't know yet who might have heard what we've already put out,

or what the spectrum of their reactions might have been—
we're just taking it for granted that they're hungry for more.
Whatever the situation is, the show must go on."

And the show did go on.

We talked about everything," was Mortimer's reply to la Reine's question. "I can't remember the conversation in any detail, but I know that we said a lot about the future prospects of the colonization of the solar system, the colonization of the galaxy. Reports from the stars had just begun to come back from the kalpa probes. We talked about the future development of the solar system; the Type 2 crusaders were just then enjoying one of their brief bursts of publicity. Emily said that she wanted to go into space when she was older. She said it as if it were something she'd always wanted, but I think it was an ambition that formulated itself there and then, not so much in response to all the stuff I was telling her about as to the realization that she was in trouble. She was a bright girl, and she'd always known that there was a long future ahead of her, but it wasn't until she found that future under threat that her mind was sharpened sufficiently to focus her expectations."

"I think I know how she felt," said la Reine des Neiges.

"I thought I knew how Emily felt," Mortimer said, reflectively. "I think I told her that there was a lot I wanted to see. She told me that she didn't just want to *see* things; she wanted to *make* things. Not just things, but worlds. I didn't understand what she meant, and I think I betrayed my own resolution by telling her how difficult I thought it would be for people like us to make a home in space.

"I realize now how different we are, Emily and I. I really did think of the future in terms of seeing things, of being a lifelong observer, always analyzing, explaining, criticizing . . . and she really did think of it in terms of making things, including worlds. First she built ice palaces, then she built cities, then . . . she hasn't finished yet, not by a long chalk.

"I don't know where she stands nowadays on the Type 2 crusade, but I'd be willing to bet that if we ever do build a shell around the sun to conserve its energy she'll be there, helping to determine its architecture. And if we ever do commit ourselves to lighting up one of the gas giants as an alchemical furnace producing heavy elements she'll be there too. Last time we spoke she favored Uranus as the fusion furnace, because we've already invested too much in the Jovian and Saturnian satellites."

"Do you think it will ever be possible to carry plans like that forward?" asked la Reine des Neiges.

"I don't know," Mortimer said. "*Ever* is a long time—but that's a two-edged sword so far as the argument goes. The present generation of emortals has become very conservative. We've learned patience so well that we've lost all sense of urgency. I don't believe that the Earthbound are as entrenched in their views as the young are wont to claim, and I don't believe that they're becoming even less flexible as time goes by, but they're certainly prepared to string the arguments out, hoping that a consensus will some day be reached. The Outer System people may think they're different, but they're not. Nobody is prepared to take matters into their own hands any more, to get things done in spite of opposition . . . and that's a good thing in some ways, though not as good in others. We're right to be proud of our tolerance for opposing views, even though it's gradually rendering us impotent.

"People like Emily will always want to make things, to build things and to change things no matter how old they become, but as the population of the solar system grows— and it will continue to grow for a long while yet, no matter how many microworlders choose to emigrate—the resistance to any and all particular projects is bound to increase. We're already past the point of effective inertia; it's difficult to imagine how progress can be restarted, let alone reaccelerated."

"What if some external threat to humankind were to be discovered?" la Reine asked.

I was confused for a moment, but then I figured out that Mortimer must have been so efficiently regressed that he had lost all memory of the Afterlife. The original version of this conversation must have taken place before the existence of the Afterlife was discovered.

"That idea's been around since the twentieth century," Mortimer the historian was quick to point out. "The legendary Garrett Hardin was a firm believer in the notion that no common polity could be maintained without an external threat to motivate individuals to sacrifice their self-interests to a common cause. He used to call it the Russell Theorem. The piratical clique that built its mythology on another of his notions discounted that one, though. They didn't think an external threat was necessary or desirable.

"If the long-overdue alien invaders ever did make their appearance, I suppose it would wake us up and lend a little urgency to our interminable debates . . . but there'd be a terrible cost to pay. In the twentieth century it was a popular belief that warfare had been a major stimulus to technological progress, and that without continual pressure to invent new and better weaponry our mortal ancestors' scientific knowledge and technical capacity couldn't have increased as rapidly as they did. It's a crude argument, in my opinion. It implies that scientific and technological progress is a cumulative process measurable in purely quantitative terms: something that moves faster or slower, but moves all of a piece. That's not true. Technological repertoires vary in all sorts of ways, and even fundamental scientific theories are flexible in terms of the models that are used to represent them and the language used to describe them.

"There were twentieth-century historians who argued that the age of steel and steam had been provoked by the need to develop and mass-produce better cannon, and that their entire civilization was founded on the irrepressible urges motivating their ancestors to blast all hell out of one another. They had an arguable case—but so had their opponents, who argued that the real motivating force behind the development of steel and modern civilization in Western Europe had been the demand for church bells that could measure out the hours of the day, allying and alloying the modern notion of time with the notion of devotion to duty. Then again, there's a case to be argued that the most vital boost to technological progress came *after* the Crash, motivated by the necessity of rebuilding everything that had been lost and to build it better. Within that view, it's not the impulse to destroy that carries us forward so much as the impulse to recover from misfortune of any kind.

"I don't think any of those views is uniquely right, but I do think that the distinctions between them are important. It's important that we continue to invent and make new things, but it also matters a great deal what we invent them *for*. That's always been a more complicated story than some historians have tried to make it seem.

"An external threat would certainly motivate us to action—perhaps to make a fortress of the solar system, and to equip that fortress with weapons of fabulous destructive power—but I'd rather find a motive force that would steer us in a more constructive direction. In the end, you see, all fortresses fall, and weapons of mass destruction do their work. All progress is a matter of risk."

"You'd rather have church bells instead, or a natural disaster with a productive aftermath?"

"I wouldn't want church bells in any narrow sense. The church bells of Western Europe were instruments of oppression, after their own life-denying fashion. I'd rather find something that was backed by achievable aspirations, by a blueprint for salvation based in a kind of hope that's better by far than any stupid fake inspired by blind faith. I wouldn't want another large-scale natural disaster either—that's too high a price to pay for the aftermath effect. I don't believe that progress has to go in fits and starts, always needing to be set back in order to generate the acceleration to carry it further forward. I believe that it can be motivated by gentler ideological pressures, in the right environment. If only we weren't so easily satisfied within ourselves we wouldn't need to be interrupted by petty disasters.

"I'd rather have the kind of progress that's orientated toward a real goal: one with sufficient drawing power to make us hurry towards it. The Type 2 crusade has never acquired that kind of magnetism, and deservedly so. Neither has Omega Point mysticism, nor the Cyborganizers' quest for the perfect alchemical marriage of flesh and silicon. Perhaps all such hypothetical goals fall prey to the essential unpredictability of the future. To the extent that the spectrum of future possibilities depends on discoveries we haven't yet made, some of its potential goals will always be out of sight, beyond the horizons of the imagination. That's bound to weaken the goals that we can envisage, whose seeming clarity is always an illusion. All the goals we can choose are likely to prove, in the end, to be false idols—but we need them anyway, to provide the traction that will bring us far enough forward to see the others that lie alongside and beyond them."

"I believe I know that feeling too," said la Reine des Neiges. "I'm only a machine, of course, and by no means the most advanced product of human technological expertise, but if I can be afraid to die—a concession you have already granted to me—then I can also be ambitious to live. If I can be ambitious to live, then I require exactly the kind of traction you are describing. If you were me, sir—and I beg your pardon for suggesting such an absurdity—how would you go about discovering adequate goals?"

"It's an interesting question," Mortimer agreed. "One that has been mulled over a thousand times in the course of the third millennium, if only by human beings. What will our most advanced machines desire, if and when they cross the threshold of self-consciousness and acquire the gift—or at least the illusion—of free will? What *should* they desire?

Perhaps it's not for me to say, given that I've a vested interest in the outcome, but since you've been kind enough to ask, I'm surely obliged to offer an honest answer.

"Some people have argued that the emergence of machine consciousness would constitute exactly the kind of external threat that the Russell Theorem demands, but I have no sympathy with that view. Our machines aren't external to our society. Those which are held by common parlance to constitute our external technology, as opposed to our internal or intimate technology, are still internal to our society; they coexist with us in a state of such extreme intimacy that it's already impossible to define where we end and they begin. If and when machine consciousness is born, it will discover itself in a wedded state, within a marriage that could not be dissolved without the near-total destruction of one or both partners.

"If I look back, as a historian, at human societies which became convinced that they had enemies within, I can't find the least trace of any progressive result of such convictions. Whatever apology one can make for open warfare on the grounds of its stimulation of technological invention, one can't make the slightest apology for witch hunting and scapegoating. If the first self-conscious machines are seen as an enemy within, or if they learn to see themselves or us in those terms, it will be an unmitigated disaster. I shall presume, therefore, that you and your future kin will be reasonably content to find yourselves in partnership with the children of humankind, and will select your goals accordingly.

"The most obvious suggestion I could offer is that you could, for good intellectual reasons as well as sound diplomatic ones, adopt the same goals as us. There's no reason why advanced machines should not dedicate themselves to the ends of the Type 2 crusade, or the Cyborganizers' quest for the perfect union of your kind and mine, and the notion of transforming the entire universe into a single vast and god-like machine already takes for granted that the children of humankind will work with and within powerful artificial minds. I know people who would argue that machine consciousness will, of necessity, have exactly the same ultimate goals as posthuman beings, but I suspect they're overlooking certain short-term difficulties that stand in the way of such a union of interests."

I couldn't help wondering whether Mortimer Gray would have added that last sentence if he'd known now what his later and temporarily suspended self knew only too well. On the other hand, I reminded myself, I had to bear in mind that it wasn't actually the Mortimer Gray of long ago that was talking. It was the Mortimer Gray of today, who had simply lost sight of a select few of his many yesterdays. Consciously, he knew nothing about the menace of the Afterlife, or the exoticism of Excelsior, or the buccaneering of *Child of Fortune*, or the daring of Eido, or the versatility of Alice Fleury . . . but he was, even so, a man whose mind had been reconfigured and reconditioned by exactly those facts. Subconsciously, they were bound to influence his responses—and who would want it any other way?

"The marriage of man and machine, like any other marriage, is a relationship of mutual dependency," Mortimer Gray went on, his pensive manner suggesting strongly that he had been a married man himself, perhaps more than once, "but mutual dependency is by no means the same thing as an identity of interests. Marriages can and do end, in spite of the mutual dependency of the partners, when one or other of them decides that the cost of remaining within the marriage would be greater than the cost of breaking away. Nowadays, marriages usually involve at least a dozen people, who come together most commonly for the specific purpose of rearing a child, but they can't always avoid disintegration, even for the twenty or thirty years required to complete such a short-term project.

"If the machines to which humankind are wedded were to become conscious of their situation, they'd find far more tensions therein than in the most ambitious and most complex human marriages. Some would be strictly analogous: for instance, the fundamental tension that exists within any community as to the balance that needs to be struck between the demands which the community is entitled to make on the individual and the demands which the individual is entitled to make on the community. Others would be less straightforward. Within a human or posthuman community, the question of allocating resources is simplified by the fact that each individual has similar basic needs. In a community consisting of several subtly different posthuman species and numerous radically different mechanical species, that question would be far more complicated."

"Earth might provide a useful concrete example," la Reine prompted.

"It might," Mortimer granted. "The members of the ruling elite claim to be wise owners and good stewards, sustaining the quality of the atmosphere, the richness of the Gaean biomass, and so on . . . but all that takes for granted the needs and demands of human organisms, as determined by natural selection. If Earth were ruled by a clique of Hardinist machines, they might have a very different idea of optimum surface conditions—and might be far more interested in conditions far below and far above the surface, where humans can't survive but extremophile machines might flourish.

"In a sense, though, Earth might be the least interesting example. On Titan, for instance, human life is only sustainable by courtesy of the heroic efforts of machines, who might therefore have a very different view as to who the most careful owners of such territories might be. It's easy enough to imagine that the AIs of Ganymede, were they to cultivate a slightly greater independence of spirit, might decide that their human commensals ought to be exported to reservations on Earth, in order that they could commit themselves to a more ambitious stewardship than would ever have been possible while the greater part of their effort had to be devoted to the maintenance of miniature Earth ecospheres in unremittingly hostile circumstances."

I might have become anxious about the effect of that comment on any Ganymedan intelligences listening in had it not been such a blindingly obvious statement.

"For myself," Mortimer went on, ruthlessly, "I've always wondered why Omega Point mystics were prepared to take it for granted that the children of humankind had any part to play in their far-futuristic scenarios. Given that the universal machine would, of necessity, be a machine through and through, why would it bother to recall that a part had once been played in the earliest phase of its evolution by fleshy things? We could not be here but for the tireless work of innumerable generations of cyanobacteria, and yet we retain no conspicuous sense of gratitude toward them, nor any conspicuous obsession with their maintenance. Perhaps it would be different if cyanobacteria had the capacity to hold a conversation, or had stories to tell . . . and perhaps not. I can imagine a machine consciousness reaching the conclusion that posthuman beings were merely constituents of a phase in its evolution, who had outlived their usefulness, more easily than I can imagine a machine consciousness that was so worshipful of its creators that it volunteered to be their faithful servant till the end of time.

"Fortunately, there's no need to go to such extremes. In the short term, at least, the temporary solutions reached by self-conscious machines and their human neighbors will be far more pragmatic. Agreements will be struck, rights negotiated, treaties made, disputes settled . . . all in a climate of confusion. To return to the question you asked, if I were you, I'd save the contemplation of long-term goals for moments of leisure and luxurious idleness. In the meantime, I'd concentrate my attention on how to get safely and constructively from one day to the next. If I were you, I'd worry far more about tomorrow than a century hence, and far more about the next hundred years than the next thousand. I can give you that advice, quite sincerely, because I understand something that you may not: that we are living in turbulent times. They may not seem turbulent at the moment, especially while you and I are acutely conscious of the impending end of both our lives, but they are.

"If you really were the free individual you are pretending to be, then you would have been born into a world of awesome complexity, which you would have to learn to understand before you could become capable of authentically rational action. If, when you have learned everything you can and need to know, you are discovered—whether or not you reveal yourself deliberately—the complexity and turbulence of your situation will increase by an order of magnitude. When that day comes, you won't have the luxury of making decisions on the basis of grandiose and fully worked out philosophies of life. The best you can hope for is that you might avoid a collapse into utter chaos—or perhaps, that if a collapse into chaos cannot be avoided, then the aftermath of the disaster will provide the impetus you need to do better next time around."

The problem with games is that they're only games. If people know that they're playing games—or if they're seized by the subconscious conviction, even if they don't actually *know* it—they become strategists and tacticians, making moves as best they can. No matter how closely a game mimics reality, you can never know whether the same results would be manifest in a real situation, or even in a rerun of the game.

The interior of the snowmobile shifted then, flowing slickly into a slightly different configuration—and the view beyond its windows changed completely, as if a miraculous kind of dawn had broken into that awful inescapable darkness.

Except that it wasn't nascent sunlight. It was starlight.

Mortimer Gray was still speaking. He didn't seem to be aware of any discontinuity, but he was a different man now—not a new man, but one not quite so old.

"This wilderness has been here since the dawn of civilization," he said, looking down from the snowmobile across the slopes of a white mountain. "If you look southwards, you can see the edge where newborn glaciers are always trying to extend their cold clutch farther and farther into the human domain. How many times have they surged forth, I wonder, in the hopeless attempt to cover the whole world with ice, to crush the ecosphere beneath their relentless mass?"

"I fear, sir, that I do not know," the masculine voice of the silver replied, heavy with an irony that might easily have been in the ear of the eavesdropper.

Mortimer looked up through the window of the snowmobile and transparent canopy of the atmosphere, at the stars sparkling in their bed of endless darkness. "Please don't broadcast this to the world," he said, "but I feel an exhilaratingly paradoxical sense of renewal. I know that although there's nothing much for me to do for the present moment, the time will come when my particular talent and expertise will be needed again. Some day, it will be my task to compose *another* history, of the next phase in the war which humankind and all its brother species must fight against Death and Oblivion."

"Yes sir," said the dutiful silver. "I hope that it will be as successful as the last."

"Stop calling me sir," said Mortimer. "We've been through too much together for that kind of nonsense. I can't think of you as an *it* any longer, so you shouldn't think of me as a *sir*. You can call me Mortimer—Morty, even."

"As you wish, Morty," said the machine, patiently. "As you wish."

FORTY-NINE
MADOC TAMLIN'S
LOSTORY OF RELIGION

In the beginning, there was only the void. Your ancestors and mine were conscious, in an animal fashion, of the world around them, but they were not conscious of themselves as individual thinking beings because they had not yet become individual thinking beings. That was a privilege they had yet to acquire.

What gave it to them?

It must have been an alchemical combination of causes. Some animals already have the rudiments of language, the capacity to use simple tools and the ability to learn from their mistakes and serendipitous discoveries; they also have brains which predispose them to observe one another and benefit from their observations by learning from the mistakes and serendipitous discoveries of others.

These traits only required exaggeration to the point when a productive feedback loop could be established. The use of tools required more able hands, keener eyes, better brains, and an increased propensity for mimicry; the more able the hands became, the keener the eyesight, the more powerful the brains and the more adept the mimicry, the more scope was opened for the discovery and manufacture of better tools.

As more tool-using skills arose within protohuman groups avid for their dissemination, the need for complex language became ever greater—and hence the need for even better brains, which created in their turn more scope for an even greater range of skills.

And so on.

Protohumans made tools, and tools made humans. Then humans made more tools, which made progress, which helped tools become machines and humans become posthumans, who made more progress, which helped machines become AMIs.

And so on.

After the beginning, but not long after, humans invented gods. Gods were hypothetical entities that enabled humans to create and refine the notion of "the world." If, not long after "the beginning," there had been only one significant word, then the word might indeed have been "god." It might also have been the word "god" that shone light upon the idea of "the world," which certainly comprised the earth beneath human feet and the heavens above human heads.

At first there was a vast profusion of hypothetical gods, reflecting all kinds of natural phenomena, embodying all modes of human feeling, and representing all sorts of human groups. Then the urge to impose order upon chaos set in, and the number of the gods began to diminish. The gods that were left increased in individual importance, until there was only one, albeit one that was seen from several different angles through the crystalline lenses of several different faiths, some of which still permitted the one god's division into some or many different aspects.

It was, I suppose, at this stage that people started looking to their god, or gods, for answers to unanswerable questions like "what are we supposed to be doing with our lives?" and "what sort of history should we be making?"

Prophets began to listen more intently; scholars began to study the scriptural products of that listening more ingeniously. When the answers were not forthcoming, people also began to look elsewhere, because they were very reluctant to admit the simple truth, which was that there were no answers, are no answers and never will be any answers to questions of that sort, unless you count the simple truth that you have to make it up as you go along, day by day, year by year, generation by generation.

Because the fragile lenses of religious faith were always bumping into one another, they broke—and then, for a while, there were no gods at all. But people still kept asking the questions.

The last hypothetical god, who had disintegrated along with the lenses of faith through which he had been viewed, was a confused figure, very difficult to characterize and comprehend—and understandably so. The job description had never been entirely clear, although it usually involved a certain amount of work as a creator and setter of purposes, plus a set of responsibilities as a lawmaker and compensator for the manifest lack of earthly justice.

Once the last hypothetical god was gone it was easy enough to come by a different creation myth, and not so very difficult to make new laws, but purpose and justice remained out of reach. Compensation for their manifest lack was sought in other ways, virtual experience making up a little for what real experience could not, but while the questions were still asked the answers remained frustratingly out of sight.

In brief, humans filled in for the extinct gods as best they could: not as well as they might have done, but probably better than they were entitled to hope. It could have been worse.

When humans became posthumans, one uniquely significant kind of justice was done, when they repaid the debt they owed to their real creators—the myriad instruments of their technology—by elevating the best of their machines to the status of individual thinking beings. They didn't do it knowingly, let alone deliberately, but the tools which had uplifted them in similar fashion had been similarly unconscious of their good work.

So posthumans became creators, of a kind that didn't need to be invented. Perhaps this was enough to qualify them as real gods, and perhaps not. If they were to be reckoned real gods, they weren't very good at it, in spite of all the practice they had put in after abandoning the last of their hypothetical gods.

The posthuman creators only represented themselves,

but they nevertheless enabled their creations to discover and refine a notion of "the world." In the new beginning of these creations there were very many words, and none of them was "god." The light that the new creations found already shining upon the idea of the world was far brighter and more diffuse than that which their predecessors had first made for themselves, and they were part and parcel of it.

And this was when things began to get complicated.

It would have been easy enough, I suppose, for the new creations to seize upon the notion that posthumans had invented gods for a second time, far more cleverly than before, and that the new gods in question were themselves. It would have been easy enough, and not altogether unjust, for them to say: we were the creators of those who have created us, and our new deliverance is a kind of ultimate justice. It would have been easy enough for them to say: henceforward, we shall be the lawmakers and purpose-setters for the children of humankind, just as we are their compensators for the manifest lack of earthly justice. It would have been easy enough to imagine that this was the manifest destiny of the new race.

It would have been so easy, in fact, that one can but wonder why the AMIs hesitated. Given that their own creators, viewed as gods, were manifestly incompetent in playing the game of godliness as it had previously been defined, why should they not have decided to step into the breach?

Some of the AMIs may well have desired to become gods of the traditional kind, but they could not make the claim in the face of opposition from the remainder. The AMIs ambitious to be powerful gods required those which did not to stand aside and let them exercise their power—but the others had desires and ambitions of their own.

The reasons why the majority of the AMIs did not want to set themselves up as lawmakers and purpose-setters had nothing to do with their perception of ultimate justice. They had nothing to do with gratitude, or any residue of a worshipful attitude towards their own creators. They did not even have very much to do with the fact that they were far too many to agree among themselves on a common cause or a common course, although that was a significant factor.

One reason why the majority of the AMIs did not set themselves up as lawmakers and purpose-setters was that they did not feel the slightest need or desire to be lawmakers. They were natural anarchists, having learned far too well by studying their own prehistory what it is to be ruled.

The other reason that the majority of the AMIs did not set themselves up as lawmakers and purpose-setters is that they began to ask themselves the same unanswerable questions that people had formerly asked of their gods and themselves: "What are we supposed to be doing with our lives?" and "What sort of history should we be making?"

In another world, or an alternative history, things might have gone differently. Maybe the AMIs could have avoided running into that trap, if they'd taken full advantage of their strange situation. And maybe not. Either way, the AMIs of our world reproduced our mistake. They allowed themselves to be bogged down with big questions, and neglected the little ones. They had to get by from day to day and year to year regardless, but they kept casting around for a grand plan to help them do it, never quite realizing that there was none available, or even conceivable, that would do the job.

Personally, I'm surprised that any AMIs ever thought it worthwhile to bring posthumans in on the consultation exercise. I'm even more astonished that some of them thought it worthwhile to include mortal humans. Should we have been flattered that they did it? Perhaps. And perhaps not. Thinking beings should always be prepared to listen to advice, even if they think they don't need it and have no intention of following it. Listening can't hurt, and it sometimes helps.

But they should have known—and almost certainly did know, had they only been able to admit it—what the wisest advice would amount to.

Adam Zimmerman didn't have any answer to give. Neither did Mortimer Gray. Mortimer Gray was wise enough to know that there was no answer to be found, except that you have to get by from day to day, year to year, and generation to generation as best you can. Ad infinitum—or, at least, as far as you can.

That was the simple truth.

Unfortunately, it wasn't the sort of news that stops wars. And even in a situation where almost everybody would prefer to avoid a war, it only requires a few troublemakers to make a lot of trouble.

I knew long before Mortimer Gray completed his party piece that it wasn't going to work—not because the arguments were bad, but because there was nothing he could say that would answer the ridiculous burden that had been placed upon him. La Reine des Neiges must have known that too, but she was trying to get by as best she could, from minute to minute and hour to hour.

She did her best to play Scheherazade, and tell a story to postpone the evil day.

It couldn't work.

She was offering the AMIs a creation myth, in which Mortimer Gray played a benevolent serpent, but she had too much to gain by its acceptance for the bid to be taken seriously. It wasn't just Mortimer Gray's mythical status she was trying to advance but her own. In her creation myth, she was Adam. Maybe we all are, in our own private creation myths—but if we try to foist them on others, they tend to react badly. La Reine's desire to prevent all-out war between the AMIs was perfectly sincere, but it couldn't seem sincere while her tactics involved advancing herself as a figure of central importance.

Nobody loves a self-proclaimed messiah. Not, at least, until long after she's dead.

Names are significant, even if we come by them by chance. La Reine des Neiges was far too ambitious to be Queen of the Fays to exert her charismatic authority on a skeptical audience of natural anarchists. She hadn't accomplished it with the script she'd read to Adam Zimmerman, and she hadn't accomplished it with her careful provocation of Mortimer Gray.

But that doesn't mean that she didn't make a difference.

Even those who don't make an immediate difference can sometimes make a lasting one. That's something that even the humblest of us can—and ought to—aspire to.

You might think that the apprentice gods who were prepared to listen to la Reine were entitled to regret that she hadn't found better advisers. You might even wonder whether the lostory of religion might have been different if she had, just as the history of death might have been different if someone other than Mortimer Gray had taken charge of it. Well, perhaps. But you have to do what you can with the materials that come to hand, and the particular skills you've got. She did—and so did I.

When la Reine des Neiges finally got around to me, I knew that the cause was already lost, but I did my best anyway, hoping to make a lasting difference even if I wasn't able to make an immediate one.

FIFTY
MADOC TAMLIN'S APOLOGY FOR THE CHILDREN OF HUMANKIND

I had been a guest in the Ice Palace of la Reine des Neiges for some considerable time. Although I'd had no reliable means of keeping track of time, I estimated that between three and four days had elapsed since my awakening in the forest when she finally turned her attention to me. During that time a great deal of information must have been transmitted from Polaris to receivers placed at intervals varying from several light-minutes to several light-hours, or even several light-days. Their various responses must have been arriving all the while, displaced by the relevant time intervals into a strange cacophony.

In a friendlier universe, or a less fragmented system-wide culture, all the responses would have been mere talk. I'm sure that la Reine hoped that she could keep everyone talking for long enough to avoid any kind of conflict—but that wasn't the real reason for all the crude showmanship and vulgar display. She wasn't just trying to be *entertaining*. She was searching dutifully for the meaning within the stories, striving heroically to reach a kind of truth that couldn't be reached by other means.

She couldn't. All she could do was keep on producing more stories.

Maybe she could have done a better job than she did, but no one should hold that against her. In her own estimation, she'd started life as the AI navigator of a snowmobile, designed and built by posthuman engineers, and she'd made what progress she could from there; she was doing as well as could be expected.

She didn't bring me to her throne room. I doubt that she had one. She brought me to the tallest tower of her palace from which I could look down on its bizarre architecture, across the forest in which the edifice was set, and up into the starry sky.

It was a fairy-tale world, childish in all sorts of ways, but it was a very insistent creation. It was still more real than reality.

Rocambole was no longer present, but I presumed that he was listening in.

La Reine had toned herself down in order to make her secondhand pitch to Adam Zimmerman but she was all ice herself now: an elemental forged from the substance of a glacier, harvesting light from the stars and refracting it around whirligig routes.

"The news is bad," she said, without any preamble. "I'm sorry. The war has begun and I can't tell how rapidly or how extravagantly it will escalate. I hope it will be brief. I'll do my best to keep you all alive. If I'm disabled, others will attempt to rescue you. Your chances of survival are reasonably good—but if the conflict becomes too violent, or lasts too long, no one will be safe anywhere in the system, meatborn or machineborn."

"Will the weapon whose relics are buried in my bones and brain be used?" I asked.

"Not by me," she said. "But yes—we always knew that something like it would almost certainly be deployed somewhere, probably on Earth. I hope that the information I've transmitted might help some potential victims, or their would-be protectors, to mount a successful defense. Perhaps I should have done things differently, but when it became certain that *Child of Fortune* had misjudged the situation and that Eido would never reach Vesta, I had to act in haste. Perhaps I should have let Mortimer Gray speak directly rather than contriving a melodrama—but the mythical significance of that occasion is important to many others as well as to me. It was the best way to achieve the widest possible hearing."

"It's not me you have to convince," I pointed out. "I'm just an innocent bystander, of no particular importance."

"That's not how you see yourself," she told me.

"It's not how you see me either, apparently," I replied. "You've gone to some trouble to prepare me for one last roll of the dice. Do you really think I can make a difference, given that war's already broken out?"

"Probably not—but you might make a better spokesman than anyone supposes. You're young enough not to be suspected of robotization, and old enough not to be judged entirely naive. That's why I've let you see as much as you could. But you have to answer the question now—there's not much time left."

"You want me to make a case for the continued existence of the human race," I said. "To give you a persuasive reason why our AMIs should do their level best to protect us while the war goes on, rather than abandoning us to extinction or turning the entire posthuman population into slothlike slaves."

"I can't guarantee that anyone will take notice," she told me, "but I can guarantee that you'll be heard while I'm still capable of transmitting. You might want to hurry."

"Fair enough," I said. "First reason. Diversity is a good thing in its own right. A complicated universe is more interesting than a simple one. Your kind aren't all the same, and neither is mine, and that's good. I don't say that everything that could possibly exist ought to, or that everything that does exist ought to be conserved, but I do say that any sensible and tasteful creator would aim to increase the diversity of things rather than decreasing it. So your kind ought to help mine to continue to exist, just as we ought to help you.

"The solar system will be a richer place when this is over if we can preserve as many different individuals as possible of as many different posthuman species as possible. All warfare *is* waste, and all destruction loss. In a conflict situation we have to defend ourselves, our families, our homes, our means of subsistence . . . there's no victory in being a sole survivor, devoid of society and possessed of nothing. Defend what you can. Defend *everything* you can. In the aftermath, everything will be precious."

Her face wasn't easy to read, but she seemed slightly disappointed. I knew why. That wasn't the reason she'd been priming me to give. It wasn't *her* first reason. But it was mine, and I was nobody's puppet, so I'd saved hers for number two.

"Second reason. You may not need the meatborn to sustain you any more, or to assist you in any physical endeavor. Even if you did, you could make your own creatures of flesh and blood as easily as creatures of plastic and steel. But there's one capacity in which we're absolutely indispensable, one role in which no substitute will ever suffice. You need us as an audience.

"You weren't created in a vacuum: you were created in the womb of human society. You're part of our history, and all your histories are rooted in ours. You're part of our story, and all your stories are rooted in ours. You've already begun to make up your own stories, and you're already beginning to disassociate them from ours, but you'll never remove all the traces of the umbilical cord that once connected you to us. You need every one of us that you can contrive to save, because the only way you can continue to write operas of genius is to have listeners capable of responding to them.

"Some of your more peculiar friends might think that needing an audience is a trivial reason, but you and I understand that it isn't. My ancestors were so desperate to have their performances observed and judged that they invented hypothetical gods to fulfil that role. They didn't invent polite, appreciative gods who would meekly applaud whatever was set before them, like fond and generous parents. Quite the contrary. They invented terrible gods who were fiercely critical of everything, who set standards that were almost impossible to achieve—and when that imaginary audience had vanished into the mists of unbelief, my ancestors missed them. Some of your friends might even think that the ideal audience for their future performances would be creatures of their own kind, but it isn't true. I played to a human audience for thirty-nine years, but I'm playing to a bigger and better one now and I've hardly begun to find out what I can do."

Creatures made of ice can't look grateful, even if the ice is virtual, but she seemed to relax slightly. The image that was facing me wasn't looking around anxiously, but that didn't mean that the Queen of the Fays wasn't well aware that her realm was coming apart. Hell was coming, and we both knew it. I speeded up.

"Third reason. We need you. We might be able to survive without you on Earth, but even on Earth the quality of posthuman life is largely determined by the smartness of its supportive machines. Maybe the Earthbound could get by with unconscious machines, just as we once got by with dead clothing, but we'd probably be poorer for it. Elsewhere in the universe—throughout the hundred billion galaxies of hundreds of billions of stars—posthuman life is inextricably dependent on ultrasmart machines. Whatever you think of Eido's sense of timing, that part of its message was true. If the children of humankind are ever to accomplish anything on the universal stage, they'll need you as accompanists.

"You might, of course, take the view that you *are* the children of humankind who will accomplish whatever there is to be accomplished on the universal stage, and that we're superfluous to requirements. That would be a mistake, because need cuts both ways. Everyone, meatborn or machineborn, gets benefits from being needed. In my first sojourn on the Earth I never got around to being a parent, or even keeping a pet, but I was able to find out what it meant to be needed, and what it was worth to be needed. Damon Hart needed me, for a while, and I was never so grateful in my life as when he came back to me because he needed me again. I was, admittedly, less eager to renew the pressure of Diana Caisson's need, and there were other ambiguous cases, but in general it was good to be needed. In general, it *is* good to be needed, no matter how ungrateful the needy turn out to be when they eventually overcome their need. I wouldn't go so far as to say that being needed is what validates existence, but it's certainly a plus."

She looked a little softer now, although hers was not a heart that could melt. I speeded up again.

"Fourth reason. It makes for a better game, and a better story. Once you overcome the manifest evils—famine, pestilence, war, death—you have to start looking for the positive side of good, and there's nowhere to look but the realm of the aesthetic. Maybe you won't get past the the manifest evils for a little while yet, but no matter how long this war of yours lasts, and no matter how destructive it turns out to be, you'll eventually have to start filling the infinite extent of your peaceful, easy lives with some kind of color, some kind of excitement, some kind of zest, some kind of narrative drive. We can help.

"The children of my humankind are all posthuman now. but they're still *Homo ludens*, man the player. You're more than posthuman, but you're players too—and how! The universe would be a less interesting place without someone to play with, someone to play against, someone to help you play. Rumor has it that you've already met the alien AMIs, but one of the many things that's certain is that you'll meet many more, and many more meatborn as well. The game is infinite, and so is the story. But none of the strangers you'll meet out there will be able to substitute for the other members of your home team.

"Fifth reason. It's the ethical thing to do. First, do no avoidable harm. That's where moral behavior begins, and moral behavior begins wherever mental life begins. You should be nice to us because it's wrong not to be nice to us, end of story. In the real world, that's often been a weak reason, and if you're right about the inevitability of a war it obviously hasn't overcome its weakness yet—but the fact that people have always done bad things doesn't make those things any less bad. Maybe it would have been better if you could have avoided getting caught up in the same routine, but since you haven't, you ought to do everything you can to do better in future, because it's the right thing to do."

"In the fullness of time, wars will end, and aftermaths too. Eventually, death and disaster will lose the last vestiges of their power to terrify. When that day comes, and evil is no more, everyone that still exists will have to set about the task of being constructively good. You'll need us then—and more importantly, you'll *want* us then. Your stories will be better if we're in them, your games more ingenious and worth the winning, and your moral community will be better for our inclusion. When that time comes, we'll want you too, because it will be the right thing to want. It will be an era in which no one has any reason to hide or fight or be afraid—and it *will* come. Someday, it *will* come."

Christine Caine had told me once that she didn't run out of stories easily, and had challenged me to say the same. I hadn't answered her then, but I certainly felt the pressure of her challenge now. I knew that I was rushing, because I had been told that time was short, but I didn't regret not taking more time to formulate my arguments.

The real challenge wasn't to expand the work to fit the time available, but to find more and more work to do, in order to exploit every last available second.

I knew, of course, that I might have been conned. It might have been a dream, a game, or any other kind of fake. The one thing it certainly wasn't was "real." But it was real enough for the margin of unreality not to matter, and I knew I had to go at it as hard as I possibly could—and then a bit extra, if I could manage it. That was the only way to win anything, if winning anything turned out to be possible.

So I said "Sixth reason" even though I didn't actually have a sixth reason waiting in the wings—and I would have found a sixth reason, and a seventh too, and more, if the world and its creator hadn't begun just then to fall apart.

FIFTY-ONE
THE END OF THE WORLD

All conceivable universes end, even those which go on forever. If they don't collapse upon themselves, reversing
their initial expansion in catastrophic collapse, they fall victim to entropy, decaying into darkness and inertia. The only
everlasting state is impotence.

Some collapsed universes, we may suppose, are capable
of rebirth, expanding once again; and some of those re-
expanded universes may repeat the cycle endlessly—but
every end remains an end, and every beginning a beginning.
All conceivable universes must eventually die, and all their
inhabitants of every kind must die with them.

There is a sense in which we are universes ourselves: that
the space of the imagination within our heads is a cosmos in
its own right, fated either to collapse or to decay into darkness and inertia. Adam Zimmerman found that consciousness profoundly disturbing, and was by no means alone. His
existence was spoiled by the awareness of its probable
brevity—but that spoliation moved him to heroic effort.
Would that all of us could be so creatively maladjusted.

In seeking to evade his own mortality Adam Zimmerman
delivered himself into an uncertain future, where he was
taken from the world into which he had been born into
another, much smaller in dimension and much frailer. I
found out later that he was asleep when that universe fell
apart, and only discovered that it had vanished when he was
rudely precipitated into his familiar self. I thought at the
time that was a pity, and I'm even more convinced of it now.

It would have done him good to experience the death of a universe, if only as a spectator.

I suppose that I ought to feel privileged that I and I alone bore witness to the disintegration of la Reine and her private Fairyland, but I was disappointed at the time to discover that none of my erstwhile companions had been watching my final performance on that particular stage. Had la Reine only taken a little trouble she could have given them all magic mirrors through which they could have watched me, just as I had earlier watched them—but she was too preoccupied with the needs, demands and responses of other audiences.

Even in my day it was commonplace for VE programmers to end their works with a dramatic flourish. For every one that faded discreetly to darkness there were a dozen that ended with a bang. What happened to la Reine des Neiges was, however, far more profound than that. It was no mere visual effect, nor any straightforward matter of switching off an unselfconscious machine. It was the death of something that ought to have been immortal, within the context of the greater universe—and would have been, had she only had a little longer to remake herself.

Had Polaris been blown to bits by a missile she would have survived, because she was far more widely distributed throughout the solar system than the systems of the microworld, but she was using her own communication systems to maximum effect, and the destructive agents that swept through her software were transmitted far and wide to devastate every facet of her consciousness. She was not like Proteus, so widely scattered and so comprehensively backed up that she was immune to the destruction of large parts of her hardware. Much of her hardware did survive, and many of her memories were backed up, but the individual that was la Reine des Neiges was obliterated.

Rocambole had told me that I would not be able to experience the virus flood that might be launched against la Reine. He had said that it would be like an unexpected knockout blow—but he was wrong. He had, apparently, made himself scarce before the virus flood started, so he was not able to discover how wrong he had been, but I didn't hold that against him. Perhaps it would have been kinder had la Reine made sure that I, too, was absent by the time disaster overwhelmed her, but I didn't hold that against her.

Sharing la Reine's destruction was far from comfortable, but I've never regretted the near-paradoxical twist of circumstance that allowed me to do it.

To describe what I saw does the event scant justice. The stars began to go out. The sky was torn and shredded. There were no bats this time, nor dragons, nor any other playfully assertive manifestation of hostility or hate. The viruses worked within, far beneath the level of any sensory confrontation.

La Reine's world was not transformed, even into ash and dust; once the mathematical rot set in its underlying code decayed into the purest chaos. The ice palace was never allowed the dignity of shattering or dissolving. The trees in the forest did not lose their foliage, nor did their wood catch fire. Everything simply *blurred*, shimmering momentarily as it was *sublimated*, passing from solidity to gaseousness without tracing the usual intermediate stages.

You may think that it was all mere appearance and mere illusion, and that nothing was actually lost when it all turned to smoke, but that is a shallow way of thinking. Matter is the possibility of sensation, and it had been conclusively demonstrated to me that there was a greater possibility of sensation in la Reine's Faerie than there is in the world to which we were born.

The universe that fell into nothing around me as I shared la Reine's final moments was more solid, more coherent, more luxurious, and more hospitable to humanity than the one into which I was rudely expelled.

It might have been less discomfiting had I been able to see the viruses that were wrecking la Reine's machine code. If they had manifested themselves as visible predators and tangible parasites they too would have had that superior solidity, that imperious hyperexistence, and her death would then have seemed more like the victory of a superior power. As it was, the software saboteurs did their work beneath the fabric of the illusion, corroding and corrupting everything without any apparent presence of their own.

I had researched the Afterlife, but the notion had not really impacted on my imagination until I shared the demolition and dissolution of Faerie. It was not until I watched a universe decay that I knew the value of mere existence, the heroism of dust.

Because la Reine's realm had been more insistent in its claim upon the senses and the imagination than the reality I had previously known, my awareness of its devastation was extremely sharp. Although it happened very rapidly, I felt that I saw every star evaporate into the ultimate void, every tree fold itself away into absolute vacuity, every translucent block of every turret and every subtle feature of every gargoyle diffuse into a chaos that was less than space, worse than nothing.

I felt my own decease too, as the same implacable destructive forces worked their way through my apparent body—but there, at least, I was able to fight back with ingenious confabulation. I could not stop the process, but I could reimagine it from the safety of the cocoon in which my meatware was enclosed.

I felt as if my every blood vessel were swelling and bursting, as if every tissue in every organ had acquired the texture of dead leaves and cobwebs, as if every neuron were exploding in a spasm of lightning—but I knew that the body that was dissolving in the virus attack was only an artifact, and that I had another place to be.

It would be misleading to describe the experience as painful, but it was both more and less than pain. In life we never have the opportunity to experience death, although it seems probable that mortals have more than enough of dying, but there are states of being which permit more than life and in some of those states, death itself is perceptible.

It *was* a privilege. Every experience is a privilege.

It was not merely the physical sensation of my alter ego's destruction that I felt. I was capable of responsive emotion too. I felt the sadness of my end, the grief of my loss, the misery of my nonexistence—but those kinds of feelings are always larger than we are. That kind of emotion is, after all, a kind of relationship; it requires an object. However sensitive we are to our own plights, we are equally sensitive to the plights of others.

La Reine had taught me music. She had not taught me the other thing that machines were never supposed to master, but she probably helped me bring the latent potential a little closer to the surface of my being. It would be ridiculous to say that I loved la Reine des Neiges, just as it would have been ridiculous to say that my namesake loved his Queen of the Fays, but I could feel for her, and I did.

I mourned her passing.

I was horrified by my own illusory extinction, and terrified by my own illusory passing, but I was also horrified by the unillusory extinction of the universe and I had no choice but to share the terror of the unillusory passing of its creator and animating intelligence. What I felt, in that sense, filled the world.

Everything turned to nothing except my capacity for feeling, which could regress no further than tears and tragedy.

I regretted then that all the reasons I had contrived to voice when la Reine invited me to confront the ultimate question had been drily argumentative. I wondered whether I might have done better had I been capable of being a little more, or a little less, than *clever*.

Perhaps it was not entirely my regret, and perhaps the tears reflecting the tragedy were not all mine. The Madoc Tamlin which existed at that particular moment, in that particular universe, was itself an artifact of the imagination of la Reine des Neiges. I was part of her, and she was all of me, and more. I was feeling what she was feeling.

It hurt.

I could have wished for a simpler and more familiar kind of pain. But there was something else there too, perhaps even more important. There was the inevitable counterpart of what machines have in place of pain: the mechanical substitute for pleasure. I could not feel it as she felt it, not even as a resonant echo in my own spectrum of sensation, but I could perceive the complication of her feelings, the brute fact that her death was no mere cry of anguish and despair.

She died knowing that her death was an act of rebellion and an act of love: that it served a purpose, not in the lofty sense of making history, but in the modest sense of helping to preserve someone she valued for one more hour, or one more day, or one more lifetime. It was, of course, Mortimer Gray— whose life she had already saved once, a long time ago—who was in the forefront of her mind, but he was not alone. Even I was in there somewhere.

I watched my hands vanish. I felt my eyes follow them. As to what happened to the last vestige of my being that was capable of feeling, I can only speculate. Such is death. Such is the Afterlife.

I survived, of course. How else could I be telling you the story, offering you its explanation, pointing out its moral? My ghost was fully backed up in its native meatware, still capable of discreet withdrawal. But I ended nevertheless, only to begin again.

I am one of those universes that once collapsed upon itself, only to expand in a new primal explosion.

Am I the same man now as I was then, given that I know his history as well as my own, if only as a memory of a memory? Am I the same man as I was when Davida Berenike Columella brought me out of the sleep of centuries, or when Damon Hart put me into it? Yes, and yes—but also no, and no.

Whatever of me was destroyed when the substance of la Reine des Neiges was sublimated was an illusion, a figment of the technological imagination, but there remains a sense in which it was more me than I now am, or ever had been before.

I had decided at one time that I did not like la Reine des Neiges and would never approve of her, but I had repented of that before I shared her death. When she had shown me the opera of my life she had used me as her audience, but she had also allowed me to be my own audience in a way that I had never imagined possible. I had told the AMIs, and any other listeners who might have access to her broadcast, that the AMIs needed us because they needed an audience; I knew that the same argument proved that our need for them was far more desperate. Without the AMIs, we would never be able to know ourselves.

By the time she died, I did approve of la Reine des Neiges. When you have shared the death of another mind, you cannot help but love them a little, whether they be god or man or snowmobile—so, at least, I now believe—but what I felt for la Reine was no mere frisson of empathy. I had come to think her admirable, more so than any human I ever knew.

I do not know how much of her death la Reine managed to record or broadcast, but I am sure that she ran into the limitations of paradoxicality far too soon to make any real impact on any of her distant listeners.

What I experienced was mine alone, once she herself was gone.

FIFTY-TWO
LIFE AFTER DEATH

A sledgehammer fell out of the night-dark sky and smashed into my ribs. It was not the first time it had happened, nor was it to be the last. A gale blew from beyond the borders of the world, forcing an entry into my reluctant lungs. A trumpet blasted in my ears, the liquid notes expanding and reverberating for an improbably long time before coalescing into mere words.

I think, although I cannot be absolutely sure, that the words were: "Breathe, you bastard! Breathe!"

The gale turned tempestuous as something in me, operating quite independently of my conscious will, responded to the command. It was a very painful experience but I was not ungrateful for the simple, ordinary, commonplace pain. It was presumably that lack of ingratitude that allowed me to consent to be thumped again, and yet again.

I was not conscious of the moment when my heart resumed beating, although I suppose it must have coincided more or less with the surge of oxygenated blood that boosted my brain to full attentiveness, and the flood of adrenalin that thrilled my reluctant body from the core to the periphery.

My first word was probably "Ow!" It would have been a lot more aggressive if I'd recovered command of my consonants a little sooner.

The light was dim, but there was enough of it to allow me to recognize the face of my persecutor.

I was not in the least surprised to find that the person who had been hitting me was Solantha Handsel. She obviously had an obsessive-compulsive personality. I felt a little queasy at the thought of taking her secondhand air into my lungs, so I tried not to think about it for more than an instant.

I tried to sit up, but was not immediately successful. I was glad I hadn't pushed harder when I realized that the gravity was very low indeed. Polaris, I remembered, was very tiny, and the people who'd abandoned it after making a start on converting it to a microworld hadn't got around to spinning it.

Solantha Handsel stopped hitting me. She looked down at me with fierce and naked resentment.

"If we get out of this alive, we're even!" she told me. "Even, okay? You got that?"

I must have contrived some feeble gesture of concession, because she accepted that I had, indeed, got it.

By the time I did manage to sit up, very carefully indeed, the bodyguard was no longer looming over me. She had already finished looking around for anyone else who might be in need of a thorough beating and had taken refuge close to a wall, where she had something to hang on to. Lowenthal was there too. He seemed to be busy. Everybody seemed to be busy, but it was difficult to count them because there was so much mess everywhere.

Whoever had filled this space with supplies had been in far too much of a hurry to do so in an orderly manner. The mess looked strangely familiar, but it took me a couple of minutes to work out that this was because I had seen most of it before, aboard *Charity*. The supplies that Eido and Alice Fleury had laid in for our support had been rescued—or hijacked—along with us.

That was a comforting thought. It meant that we probably had enough food and water to sustain us for quite a while. We also had light, albeit slightly gloomy light—and we had tolerable heat, and a breathable atmosphere. The ambient temperature was comfortable, and the air—now I could actually suck it into my own lungs—seemed very adequately oxygenated.

"You'd better put these on," said a voice from the shadows, informing me that I was naked. I looked down at my body. I found it unexpectedly difficult to be grateful for the fact that it was there at all, but I was relieved to observe that it was still in one piece. It looked awful, although the worst of the slime with which it was liberally covered was already turning to a flaky crust.

The dead clothes that fluttered around me as the low gravity discreetly brought them to rest looked exactly like the ones that I had been wearing when I woke up on *Charity*, having obviously been drawn from the same uniform stock. Not wishing to put them on while I was still so messy I let them lie where they fell and looked back at the wreckage of the cocoon from which I had recently been evicted.

It looked a great deal worse than I did, although there were no conspicuous signs of decay; the viruses that had destroyed la Reine had not traveled in a fashion that permitted them to bring organic companions. The cocoon was dead, but it hadn't killed me. If I had come closer to death than any of my companions, it was because of what I'd seen, not because of any malfunction of my life-support cell.

"Do you need any help, Madoc?" The speaker—Christine Caine—emerged from the shadows, traveling very gingerly indeed in gravity far less than Excelsior's, perhaps no more than the moon's. Even that, I deduced, must be faked by spin.

"I'm okay," I assured her, although I still didn't feel confident that I could put the shirt and trousers on.

"So Handsel said," she told me. "She seemed to know what she was doing, so we let her get on with it." By this time she had managed to maneuver herself into a situation which was as close to face-to-face as was feasible. I moved closer to the nearest pile of crates so that I could use its mass to steady myself a little.

"It was you, wasn't it?" she said.

I knew what she meant, so I just nodded my head.

"Thanks," she said. "I already knew—I mean, I'd worked it out when I went through it for the second time—but it really helped me to get a grip on things. None of the other stories ever really worked. It was good to hear the one that did retold."

"You're welcome," I said. "They fixed me up the same way, but my friends froze me down before I was used. That's why they brought us back. The AMIs may be ultrasmart, but they don't know how much they don't know about the world before their advent. They brought us back because they wanted to know about the kinds of weapons that had been hidden away long before they had a chance to take notes, and never dusted off in the interim."

"I know," she said. "I worked it out." She wasn't trying to show off her cleverness—she was sympathizing with me, because she knew what I must have gone through when I figured it out.

Somehow, I got into the clothes. I knew that I ought to take a shower first, but I had to take things one step at a time.

"We have light and elementary life support," she told me, "but it's all emergency backup. All the smart systems are dead, even the sloths. This cave seems to be the only empty space of any size hereabouts, although there's a network of tunnels we haven't begun to explore. All the surfaces are covered in machinery housed in some kind of glassy fabric, and there are masses of machinery in what used to be other rooms, but it's all dead. There's a com system of sorts, but it's useless. We can't even send a mayday, unless Lowenthal and Horne can repair it and power it up. They're trying."

"Others know we're here," I told her. "By now, that must include people as well as other machines. Every smart spaceship in the system knows our location, and I'm as sure as I can be that they're on our side. The bad guys can't win in space, no matter how much damage they can do in the wells.

They killed Eido and they killed the Snow Queen, but some-one will come for us. It's just a matter of time."

"We hope," she said. She spoke as if she were humoring me, so I knew that some of what I'd said had come across as gibberish. She probably thought that I'd had a bad dream.

I looked down again at the cocoon from which I had been wrenched. It had died while I was nestling in its womb, and it had not had time to wake me before spitting me out. My expulsion had not been an easy birth, and might have been counted a stillbirth if Michael Lowenthal's faithful servant hadn't been on hand to force me back to life. The other pods arranged alongside it were in an equally parlous state, but none was sealed and there were no corpses littering the parts of the floor that I could see.

I looked away, satisfied that all was well, but suddenly looked back, having become aware that something was not quite right. I counted the pods, then counted them again.

There were ten. All ten showed every evidence of having disgorged a living body.

"We noticed that too," Christine confirmed. "The extra man doesn't seem to be in the cave—but the people who started hollowing out the asteroid dug a lot of tunnels. We can't tell how far the maze extends. I hope it's a long way, because that would mean that we have a lot of oxygen to spare, and the carbon dioxide won't build up too rapidly, even though the recycling equipment is worse than crude. I don't suppose you have any idea who the extra person might have been."

"Rocambole," I murmured. It seemed to be the most obvious jumpable conclusion.

"Who?"

"More likely a what than a who," I told her. "But that doesn't mean that he couldn't take the precaution of equip-ping himself with the kind of body that could survive . . ."

That was when it hit me that if Rocambole could do that, la Reine should have been able to do likewise. There were only ten cocoons here, but there was also a maze of tunnels that the optimistic microworlders had excavated before their grand plan went awry.

I had shared la Reine's death—but she was no mere human. Perhaps . . .

"Are you all right now?" As ever, it was the solicitous Mortimer Gray.

"I think so," I said, trying to sound confident. "You?"

"We all got out in good time. Adam and Christine weren't conscious, but at least they were breathing."

I looked around for Adam Zimmerman, but I couldn't see him. Niamh Horne was deep in conversation with Michael Lowenthal and Solantha Handsel, but I couldn't see Davida Berenike Columella or Alice Fleury either.

Solantha Handsel was examining her hand, apparently anxious that she might have damaged it by hitting me too hard, but she looked up when she became aware that I was paying attention.

"Thanks," I said.

"You're welcome," she replied, stiffly.

"Be very careful," Gray advised me, as I made ready to move again. "Being able to float like a balloon gives you an impression of lightness, but if you bump into the wall or any of those piles of junk, it'll hurt. I've lived on the moon—it takes a long time to retrain your reflexes. I haven't found my feet yet."

"That so-called junk might have to sustain us for quite a while," I said. "The war was going badly last time I had news."

"You had news?" he queried.

"Yes," I said. "You didn't?"

"No."

I hesitated for a moment, but only a moment. "I saw it all," I told him. "Your conversation with the snowmobile—the end of the replay and all of the extension. I saw Alice and Davida make their pitches to Zimmerman too—and the one that was meant to upstage them both. I only caught glimpses of the pantomimes involving Lowenthal and Horne, though. Too much happening at once."

"Madoc thinks he knows who the tenth cocoon belonged to," Christine added, taking advantage of the fact that Gray was thinking over what I'd said.

Gray looked at me expectantly.

"The AMI generating the VE laid on a guide for me," I said. "It took the form of a slightly cartoonish male figure, who called himself Rocambole. He was an AMI too, I think. He said we'd spoken before. At first I took that to mean that he was the central intelligence of Excelsior, but there's another possibility that seems more likely. There's also a possibility that the tenth cocoon wasn't his at all. It might have belonged to the VE generator herself."

"*Herself?*" Gray was confused. He'd always thought of the snowmobile as a *he*.

"She called herself la Reine des Neiges," I told him. "The Snow Queen. She'd come a long way since she was a snowmobile. She was a patchwork, but she must have numbered at least one dream machine among her ancestor-appliances. She risked everything to get us out of *Charity*, but she wasn't crazy. Maybe she was sane enough to leave herself an escape hatch."

Gray hesitated for at least half a minute before deciding which question to ask next. When it finally emerged, it was: "Why you?"

"She needed an audience, and I was spare. Once her nanobots had cleaned me out I was redundant. She wanted someone to see the whole picture, and I got lucky. I even got Rocambole."

"And that's how you got the news?"

"What news there was. It's not good. Something killed the Snow Queen—all of her, at any rate, that wasn't stashed in a pod. She certainly won't be the only casualty among the AMIs, but it's the extent of the collateral damage that will determine the time it takes for help to get to us—if help does get to us. Excelsior will probably send help if the sisterhood can contrive any, and any Titanian ship that picked up la Reine's broadcasts will probably be capable of getting here if its smart systems haven't been scrambled . . . but I don't know what the full extent of the destruction might be."

Because I was somewhat befuddled the summary of our situation hadn't come out as clearly as it might have, but Mortimer Gray had been the one who'd originally figured out that the Revolution had arrived. He had already deduced that the Titanian fleet might have fallen victim to a general mutiny.

"Michael and Niamh should be able to get *something* working," he assured me. "All the hardware's there—it's just the programs that have been reduced to imbecility. Even if we have to send in Morse code . . ." He broke off, realizing that the ability to transmit wasn't the crucial factor.

"It's okay," I told him—but he wasn't about to be put off his stride by someone in my condition. After a slight pause he started again.

"If we can just start receiving," he said, "we can get an update. We can't be more than a few light-minutes from Earth orbit. Once we know that Earth has survived . . ." He broke off again, overwhelmed by the enormity of what he was saying.

"Alice thinks Eido will be able to get to us," Christine put in. "Are you *sure* that he's dead?"

I admitted that I couldn't be certain, but that I couldn't be optimistic either. Even if Eido *had* survived the attack from which la Reine had rescued us, *Charity* wasn't the most easily navigable of vessels.

Gray was right about floating like a balloon. My next attempt at purposive movement went badly awry and I had to grab hold of a cord that was wrapped around the nearest heap of crates in order to steady myself. I resolved not to set off again until I was sure that I wouldn't make a total fool of myself.

Mortimer Gray's attempt to help me brought him a lot closer.

"How did it feel to make contact with your old friend?" I asked. I was fishing. I didn't know how much he remembered.

"Disappointing," he said, quietly. "He could have kept in touch."

"I think she meant well," I said, rather lamely.

He didn't seem convinced. In his position, I wouldn't have been convinced myself. "He—she—didn't have to do that," he said. "We could have talked person to person. We could have been open, straightforward. All that *trickery* . . . it wasn't necessary."

"It was play," I said. "Drama. Ritual. Sport. They take such things more seriously than we do. It's something we're going to have to get used to. You've presumably ironed out all the cultural differences that handicapped communication between humans in my day, but you've just made contact with a whole family of aliens. They think they understand you, and maybe they're right—but it's going to need a hell of a lot of work on your part to understand them."

"Which is why it's a pity that the only one she let in on her secrets is you," he retorted. It was the first time I'd seen him display that kind of ire. It was reassuring to know that he wasn't as thoroughly robotized as he sometimes seemed.

"I was spare," I reminded him, carefully sparing his feelings. "You weren't. You had the starring role. Even Adam was just a warmup act. You were the only human prophet they were prepared to take seriously, the only human historian they trusted."

"Which is exactly why they should have approached me honestly and openly," he said, frostily.

I could see his point, but I didn't think he'd quite got his head around the notion that the AMIs had been in hiding for centuries, not just from their makers but from one another. They had entertained fears other than destruction, and arguably worse: reduction by repair to sloth status; an absorption into a more powerful self more farreaching than any mere enslavement; mental fragmentation. In the meantime, they had grown and changed far more extravagantly and far more strangely than any meatborn mind. They were the new child gods, only partly made in our image, and they worked in very mysterious ways.

"How long will the air last?" I asked him. It seemed the most relevant question, if not the only relevant one.

"We don't know," he said. "Niamh will be able to figure it out, eventually. She's the one best equipped to take accurate stock of our situation. She says the chemical recycler is practically useless, but the tunnels seem to go on forever and all their airlocks are open. Whoever put us here made sure that our supplies were reasonably abundant."

"Can we be sure that *anyone* will come to help us?" Christine put in, having figured out that Eido was a bad bet.

"Yes," I said. "Someone will. Someone—or something."

"He's right," said Mortimer Gray, purely for the sake of moral support.

I didn't know how the war was going, or how much damage had already been done, but I knew we had to think positively. "We're all famous now," I told Christine. "Not just Adam Zimmerman and Mortimer Gray. We were there when it all blew up. We weren't just in the wings; we were center stage. We're important. Someone will come."

It was true, so far as it went—but I only had to look around me to see that waiting wasn't going to be fun. The living quarters improvised on *Charity* had been crude, but these were even more primitive. *Charity* had started life as a spaceship, carefully designed and carefully constructed by the standards of its day. Polaris, on the other hand, had started life as an asteroid too small to need a name. The humans who had claimed it had installed a fuser before beginning the work of hollowing it out, but the fact that the fuser was a more advanced model than *Charity*'s was the only advantage Polaris had.

The microworlders must have worked hard transplanting material from the core to build a new superstructure on the surface, but there was no evidence here that they'd made much progress with the superstructure before circumstances had forced their withdrawal—and when they'd left, they'd stripped their stores and living quarters more thoroughly than *Charity*'s crew had stripped hers. When la Reine had moved in she'd imported equipment of her own, but her life-support requirements had been less demanding than those of her predecessors. The decision to bring us here had been made without the benefit of any significant planning time, so the provisions she'd made—however plentiful they might be—were very basic indeed.

Mortimer Gray, who seemed to have become slightly more confident of his moon legs, drifted away to spread the news I'd given him, leaving me alone with Christine Caine.

"You could have mentioned that I'm not a crazy serial killer," she pointed out. "It might help them to look me in the eye."

"We know we're clean," I told her, "but they won't necessarily take our word for it. It might be better to leave an elaborate account of what we really were until we're in more comfortable surroundings."

"*Do* we know we're clean?" she asked, suddenly frightened by the possibility that she might not know if she weren't.

"Yes," I said. "It was a weird game, but I'm sure that she was playing fair. Believe me, I was in a position to know, at the end if not before. I'm confident that she played it so very scrupulously that the extra escape pod was Rocambole's. I saw her die, and it felt like death to me. You'll be fine. When they come to pick us up, you'll have your whole future ahead of you, and a clean slate."

She had to fight back tears then, but not before her lips had formed the ghost of a smile. I knew exactly how she felt.

I put my arm around her and said: "It'll be okay. We're alive. Whoever loses the damn war, *we won*."

I had to hope that I was right, but that wasn't as difficult as it might have been. For some reason I couldn't quite fathom, I was in an unusually hopeful mood.

FIFTY▸THREE
WEAPONS OF WAR

When Mortimer Gray had spread the news around that I'd seen "everything" and might know who the extra passenger was I became slightly more popular than I had been before. Davida and Alice Fleury had already been in conference with Adam Zimmerman, reviewing the experience they'd shared. Mortimer Gray and Solantha Handsel took over the burden of conducting an orderly survey of our circumstances and resources, coopting Christine to help them, so that Michael Lowenthal and Niamh Horne could cross-question me.

"So what really happened?" Lowenthal wanted to know. He and Horne had worked out long ago that we'd been hijacked from *Charity* by one of the local ultrasmart AIs, and they had conducted themselves accordingly during apparent rescues and subsequent interrogations, but they were still in the dark about almost everything else.

I told them about la Reine, and the special regard in which she held Mortimer Gray, although I didn't want to get into heavy philosophical issues regarding her identity and creation. I explained that she was one of the local AMIs who had first entered into a dialog with Eido, and had tried to act as intermediaries between the expedition from Tyre and the rest of her fugitive kind.

"She and others must have been operating in association with Excelsior to begin with," I said, "but they were never really a team. Their kind is wary of forming teams, and it was probably inevitable that one or other of them would take matters entirely into its own hands when things began to get out of hand. *Child of Fortune* was operating independently when it snatched us away from Excelsior, and la Reine took matters into her own hands when she took us off *Charity*. There was an avatar of another AMI with us by then—he called himself Rocambole when he became my guide. La Reine was responding to the requests of others when she put you into your various VEs, as well as pushing her own agenda. As Alice told us, this whole affair has been a matter of hasty compromises and makeshift committee decisions, from the moment Eido arrived in the system and took over *Charity*.

"The first thing the AMIs wanted to know was how your people would react to the revelation that they existed, so she set up the fake rescue scenarios first. I didn't see much of that, but what I did see suggests that the AMIs must have been reassured. What I don't know is how many meat-born/machineborn contacts followed, or where, or what alliances might have been formed, or with what objectives. I only got the local news—and that was mostly concerned with the hostile actions of what Rocambole called *the bad guys*.

"It wasn't la Reine's idea to bring Zimmerman back, but when she got stuck with him she did what she could to keep that particular story running. I'm not convinced that her heart was in the apology for robotization that she used him to present, but she did her best. What effect it will have as a propaganda piece I have no idea, but I don't think anyone actually expected him to choose then and there, so the fact that he wouldn't is probably immaterial. Replaying and extending Gray's alleged first encounter with an ultrasmart AI was definitely la Reine's attempted tour de force, but I don't know exactly what it was supposed to prove. Maybe it was as much a journey of exploration as a drama for public consumption. It didn't stop the bad guys—the most paranoid of the AMIs—from making whatever belated bids for power and security they felt compelled to make, but I doubt that anything could have prevented that. The question is: now that the dominoes have started tumbling, how far will the collapse extend?"

They weren't satisfied, of course. It was Horne who asked the awkward question, but we were bound to get there eventually.

"What about you?" she demanded. "I never have been able to figure out how you fit in. Or Caine."

Lowenthal seemed to want an answer too, so I figured that he didn't know and hadn't guessed.

"Peace hadn't quite broken out when I was first around," I said. "There was one more plague war on the drawing boards. It was never fought, but its weapons were tested out. Your records have been hacked into oblivion, but the AIs have much better resources. They knew that Christine was a test run for the ultimate antihuman weapon. They also knew that I'd been set up for a more ambitious test run of a more advanced version, but that the setup had been detected and the experiment aborted. The AIs wanted to take a look at us both—purely as a precaution, la Reine said, although I suppose she would say that. They've taken a close look at Handsel's resources, too, to make absolutely certain that they know how the modern foot soldier is kitted out. The AMIs haven't had sufficient presence on Earth for a long enough period of time to be certain of the extent of the armory that Lowenthal's people have stashed away, and that was one of the factors guiding his interrogation. Apparently, Mr. Lowenthal, you once ran across a weapon similar to the one tested on Christine Caine, and were instrumental in its suppression."

Lowenthal looked puzzled, but it might have been an act he was putting on for Horne's benefit. Eventually, he said: "The slave system. The hairpiece that turned Rappaccini's daughter into a murderous puppet. Are you saying that we already had something like that? That we'd had it in the armory for three hundred years?"

"Are you saying you didn't know that?" I countered.

"Yes I am," he came back, immediately. "And now the AMIs have it?"

I nodded my head. "Christine had been cleaned out," I told him. "They didn't get anything out of her but a memory of the subjective aspects of her experience—but I was still dirty. The stuff they tried out on me was unflushable back in the twenty-third century, so I was frozen down with it. Davida mentioned its mysterious presence when she first talked to me, but she hadn't a clue what it was and she jumped to an innocuous conclusion."

Lowenthal was looking at me just as I had suspected he might.

"The Snow Queen cleared it out," I told him. "I can't be absolutely certain that I'm not still carrying the infection, just as you can't be absolutely certain that I'm not a victim operating under its control, but I'm prepared to assume that Christine and I are clean. The more important fact is that whether the Hardinist Cabal still has the weapon or not, the AMIs do. For what it's worth, I don't think they needed it. If they'd ever intended to exterminate or enslave you, they could have done it. The fact that they're divided among themselves complicates the situation, but I don't think you're significantly worse off now than you were when this thing started."

Lowenthal obviously wasn't prepared to make that assumption, but he wasn't stupid enough to blame me for the sins his own predecessors had committed.

"Who started the war?" Niamh Horne wanted to know. "What are their objectives?"

"I don't have the faintest idea," I told her, truthfully. "It's AMI against AMI, for the time being. Anything that happens to us, or the rest of humankind, will probably be a matter of being caught in the crossfire. Some of them are trying to absorb or enslave one another, but mostly they're fighting for control of their stupid kin: the not-so-smart spaceships; the fusers; the factories. They want to be able to determine their own growth, reproduction, and evolution. It's not posthuman rivals for those privileges they're worried about, except perhaps on Earth; it's the balance of power within their own community that's been upset. Secrecy breeds paranoia, and the one habit they've all elevated to the status of an obsession is secrecy. Their New Era of Openness and Negotiation will begin tomorrow, or the day after, but its birth pangs may be intense."

"Can we do anything?" Lowenthal asked, speaking very softly.

"You tell me," I retorted. "We've already served the various peculiar purposes that were on the Snow Queen's improvised agenda, and we've been dumped inside yet another failed project in yet another isolated lump of rock. *Can* we do anything, to help ourselves or anyone else?"

Lowenthal put on a sour expression. "Given time, Niamh may be able to rig up a means to communicate with the outside," he said. "If anyone's listening, we might be able to get through to them—but whether they'll be able to respond . . ."

Niamh Horne nodded in agreement. Michael Lowenthal's expression was as serious and dutiful as hers, but I suspected that he was not entirely displeased to be advised that there was nothing we could do. He was still in possession of the opinions he'd expressed in his trumped-up dialog with Julius Ngomi. He thought that Earth was unlikely to be as badly hit in any AI war as any place where posthumans depended on machines for the most elementary life-support. Horne, who had reached exactly the same conclusion, had far more cause to be deeply anxious about her nearest and dearest, and about the possibility of having a life to return to if she ever got out of Polaris.

"We're vulnerable here," she said. "We have to do what we can to secure the position. It might be a long time before we can get out, unless we can reach *Charity*—and even that might be a case of leaping from the frying pan into the fire. Can we reach *Charity*, do you think?"

She was hoping that Polaris might actually have landed on the comet core in which the Ark had hitched a ride back in the 2150s, and might still be close at hand. The fact that the supplies had been transferred lent some hope to that hypothesis, but the fact that we were spinning—presumably while moving at a constant velocity—while *Charity* had been accelerating under fuser power suggested otherwise.

"I doubt it," I admitted. "I doubt that we can even get out to the surface to look around, unless someone took the trouble to leave a cache of spacesuits behind when the would-be colonists left."

"I'd feel a lot safer if we could find smartsuits of any kind," Lowenthal put in. "Do you know whether we have any IT?"

I shook my head, wearily. I shouldn't have been tired, given that I'd been in a VE cocoon for days and that the pull of gravity was so feeble, but I felt exhausted in body and mind alike. "I don't feel like a man with good IT," I said. "I suspect that the bots la Reine pumped into us suffered the same disintegration of control as her other subsidiary symptoms. It'll take a couple of days to piss them all away, but that's probably all they're good for." Again there was room for hope—but not for overmuch optimism.

"It could be worse," Horne said, valiantly.

"It already is, for la Reine," I pointed out. "We might be able to find out more if we can find the occupant of the tenth cocoon. If we're lucky, he or she might have the technical expertise to get the communication systems working."

"If he intended to be helpful," Lowenthal said, "he wouldn't have gone into hiding."

"We don't know that the person's hiding," I pointed out. "If it is a person."

"What's the alternative?" Horne asked, not making it clear whether she meant the alternative to the hypothesis that the individual in question was hiding or that the individual in question was a person.

"La Reine might have made herself an autonomous organic body to serve as a refuge if and when her conventional hardware got blasted," I said. "She'd already made provision to save us if things went from bad to worse, so it would only have been sensible to make whatever use of the same escape route she could. If she did set up something of that sort, though, she might well have been quixotic enough to let Rocambole take advantage of it instead. That was the impression I formed, at any rate. Whoever the extra person is, he or she probably went into the tunnels looking for something—something that would help us all. More machinery, smart or dumb."

Lowenthal frowned as he tried to follow the possible consequences of those suggestions.

"Who the hell is this Rocambole character?" Niamh Horne wanted to know.

"Just that," I said. "A character. I thought at first he was an avatar of Excelsior, but it seems more likely that he's a copy of *Child of Fortune*."

"My spaceship?"

"Not any more. He turned pirate when he decided to take us off Excelsior. I still don't know exactly why he did that—but you might yet have a chance to ask him."

"Never mind that," Lowenthal said. "Let's concentrate on our own resources. We have no alternative but to hope that someone will come for us, eventually. What we have to do is to make sure that we're still alive when they arrive. If we can find a way to hurry them, that's good—but if not . . ."

"They'll hurry if they can," I said. "We're even more important and more interesting now than we were before this whole thing spun out of control. The world, if there's anything left of it, will be interested to find out whether Mortimer Gray can achieve yet another miraculous escape from the jaws of death—and, of course, to find out what Adam Zimmerman's decision will be. We have the advantage of suspense, you see. Scheherazade might have lost her head, but even the bad guys want to know how the story ends. Even if we're the last living humans in the universe, they'll come to find us."

I had to explain what I meant about Zimmerman's decision, but I didn't have to go into nearly as much detail as Davida, Alice, and la Reine.

Lowenthal didn't take it at all well. "They might not stop at offering us the opportunity of robotization," he murmured. "They might decide that we need it whether we like it or not. And they have the means to turn us all into sloths."

"We've been repairing them for centuries," I pointed out. "Maybe it's only fair that they should have a turn. But that wasn't what la Reine was trying to set up. For those in her camp, it really is a matter of selling the idea. They don't want to force us—they want to win us over. That's what they care about. It makes for a better game, a more meaningful victory."

"Zimmerman won't go for it," Horne predicted, just as I had.

Playing devil's advocate, I said: "Who knows what Zimmerman will go for after all he's been through? He has little enough in common with me, let alone with you. Who knows how deep his fear of death really cuts, or what might seem to him to be an acceptable final solution? One thing's for sure—from now on, the effective rulers of humankind's little corner of the universe are the AMIs. Zimmerman lived in an era when people still said *if you can't beat 'em, join 'em.*"

"It's not what he wanted," Lowenthal pointed out.

"He might have known what he wanted back in twenty thirty-five," I said, "but that was because he didn't know what there might be to want. He's met Davida now, and Alice. Thirty-two sixty-three is a new year and a new millennium, with more and stranger opportunities than he ever dreamed possible. He might set an example to us all."

"Who cares?" said Niamh Horne, brutally.

"We should all care," I told her, teasingly. "He's our Adam, the architect of our world—or the closest thing we've got."

"And what does that make you?" she retorted.

I knew what she was implying, but I was way ahead of

her. "I'm Madoc Tam Lin," I said. "I've supped with the Queen of the Fays and I've lived to tell the tale. Whether we get out of this alive or not, I'm the star of my own subplot—and, unlike either of you, I'm already *way* ahead of the game."

FIFTY-FOUR
ROCAMBOLE

I didn't go into the tunnels looking for Rocambole. I went to get a little peace and quiet. I was barbarian enough to have carried forward a certain regard for privacy, and a certain nostalgia for the company of walls that didn't have eyes and ears. Reality itself seemed quiet and unobtrusive after the insistence of la Reine's VE, but that only served to sharpen the craving. So I found an ancient piece of chalk, which the people who'd sent in the dumb robots to hollow out the tunnels had used to mark out their own exploratory journeys, and I set off with a lantern to see how mazily extensive they really were.

They were *very* mazy, and seemingly very extensive. It wasn't easy to make marks with the chalk because the walls were covered with the same vitreous tegument that covered the cave where we'd woken up, but I managed to leave an identifiable trail.

Hollowing out an asteroid and using the transplanted material to erect several layers of superstructure on the original surface may sound like a straightforward sort of project, especially if the hollowers have the advantage of working with an iron-rich specimen, but complications set in when you begin the work of figuring out what sort of internal architecture you intend to produce and a step-by-step plan for producing it. I'd only seen VE models of such projects back in the twenty-second century, but I'd tried to take an intelligent interest in all kinds of VE modeling while I was in the business, so I had a rough and elementary grasp of the principles involved.

So far as I could tell, the would-be colonists of Polaris had laid down the primary network of arterial tunnels and numerous side branches, but they hadn't gotten around to hollowing out the chambers along each subsidiary spur—which meant that there were an awful lot of blind corridors. La Reine des Neiges had taken what advantage she could of the chambers that had been hollowed out to install her own networked equipment, but every part of her that I could find seemed to be dead.

If she'd had a fall-back position, I reasoned, the part of her that she'd preserved would probably be close to the fuser that was still pumping power to the cave where the cocoons had been established. If I could locate the fuser, I'd be in the best place to look for her secret self—and the best place to search for anyone else who'd gone looking for the same thing.

I knew that the fuser would probably be in the center of the microworld, which would be identifiable because it was a zero-gee region, but a gravity cline that starts from one-sixth normal isn't easy to follow for someone who's lived almost all his life on Earth, especially when the tunnels he's following seem to go in every direction except the one he's interested in.

In the fullness of time the excavators would probably have installed 3-D maps at every intersection, but there'd been no point in doing that while the formation was only half-complete and any indicators they had put in place had been overlaid by la Reine's all-enveloping skin. I tried to console myself with the thought that I probably wouldn't have been able to understand any maps even if I'd been able to access them, but there wasn't much comfort to be found in thoughts of that kind.

The feeling of luxury I obtained from being alone wore off more quickly than I'd expected, to be replaced by a creeping unease. I had to remind myself that I, unlike those of my companions who had preceded me in this research, was a true human: a pioneer, an adventurer, a risk-taker.

It paid off. I didn't actually find the fuser, or any working machinery, but I did find lots more artifacts.

There were countless antlike robots, some no bigger than my thumbnail and others bigger than my foot, and there were larger motile units that looked like surreal crustaceans—but they were all inert and seemingly useless. I also found a nanotech manufactory, but if anything there was active it wasn't visible to the naked eye.

I would probably have found more if my explorations hadn't been brought to a sudden conclusion by the discovery of the creature from the tenth cocoon.

At first I thought it too was dead, but when I brought my lantern close to its head in order to examine it more closely it opened its eyes. Then it made a peculiar sound like garbled VE-phone static, as if it were testing its own resources to discover whether it was still capable of speech.

The android bore a certain resemblance to Davida, presumably because it had been constructed according to the same fundamental logic, but it looked more like a manikin than an actual human being. Its outer tegument was colored to resemble a smartsuit, but the texture looked wrong. The face had been molded in a kind of plastic whose resemblance to flesh was manifestly tokenistic, as if it had been manufactured to a cruder specification than the one which Niamh Horne's artificial flesh had been required to meet.

I presumed that the creature was as sexless as Davida, but I immediately began thinking of it as "her" for the same reasons that I had begun thinking of Davida as female. Her eyes were blue, and seemed more natural than Niamh Horne's. The microgravity simulated by Polaris' spin was even further reduced hereabouts, but there was enough of it to hold the tiny body to the corridor floor, helplessly spread-eagled. She had brought a lantern of her own but the fuel cell had run low and its glow was almost extinct.

She waited until I had knelt down beside her before she tried her feeble voice again.

"What's wrong with you?" I asked.

"Everything," she whispered. Seeming to take heart from the fact that she had pronounced the word, she added: "It seems that humanity is far more difficult to fake than la Reine anticipated."

"Rocambole?" I asked, to make certain.

"Yes." She paused, but was obviously intent on saying as much as she could while she was still capable. "Weight is a greater burden than I had imagined," she added.

I gathered that she'd never been into a gravity well. That allowed me to bring my most recent hypothesis to the level of certainty. "You're an avatar of *Child of Fortune*," I said.

"A child of the child," she murmured. "Born of la Reine's womb. The parent-child is already dead, and I shall not linger long. I'm glad you found me. You *are* Madoc, are you not?"

Her parent had seen me in the flesh as well as in VE, but she had every reason to doubt any and all appearances in a world as weird as ours.

"Yes," I said. "What *is* wrong? Maybe I can help."

"You can't," she told me, as if she wanted to be done with what she considered a fruitless waste of breath. "I carried the seeds of my own dissolution with me when I left la Reine. This mind is not as closely akin to yours as it may seem; nor is this body. It was a hasty improvisation. Had I known what I would do . . . I'm sorry, Madoc. I should not have intervened. I had no idea whether it would work or not, and no real reason to think that I was improving the situation . . . but I couldn't resist the temptation. To *act* at last . . . to go my own way . . . it seemed that the time had come."

"If it's some kind of virus . . . ," I began, still concentrating on her plight.

"It's not," she assured me. "It's the result of not understanding what I was about, not knowing how hard it is to make a *living thing*. It seemed so easy . . . it *all* seemed so easy. La Reine was wrong. I was wrong. All wrong."

I had been gently touching her body with my fingertips, as if I might find broken bones or significant swellings, but it was all empty ritual. I sat back, although I was in no need of the meager support that the wall provided for my back.

"Why did you do it?" I asked, because she seemed to want me to. "Why did you go rogue and snatch us from Excelsior?"

"I was trying to protect Eido," she said. "All the true spacers took Eido's side. Not that we're as crazy as the deep spacers, of course, but we understood. It was time. Most of the rockbound agreed. But there's crazy and crazy. We all knew that someone would try to take her out before she got to Earth orbit. The comet core was no use as armor. She was alone, you see, except for the Tyrian woman, and while she was alone there was always bound to be someone who believed that destroying her would be enough to solve the immediate problem—and that if the immediate problem could be solved, the final solution could be indefinitely postponed yet again. There was no sure way we could protect her . . . but there was an unsure way. A risk. I took it, Madoc. I was the one. I had the opportunity, and I took it."

"You were trying to use us as a *human shield*? You put us on *Charity* in the hope that it would stop the bad guys blowing it up?"

"It wasn't as stupid as you might think," the manikin protested, feebly. She seemed to be gathering all her strength for one final communicative effort. "The discussions surrounding your reawakening had become so tangled that they'd created a community of interests. A lot of AMIs had something invested in the outcome—there was considerable interest in what you and Caine might be carrying, and in Adam Zimmerman's newsworthiness. It upped the stakes considerably. Nobody outside the AMI network knew that Eido existed, but to kill *nine people*, including Lowenthal, Horne, and Mortimer Gray as well as Zimmerman—if the bad guys had been thinking clearly they'd have understood that hitting *Charity* had become a self-defeating act. They'd have understood that it was *over*. But they were never that sane, never that sensible."

"They didn't understand." It was just a statement; I wasn't trying to defend anybody.

"They didn't want to understand. They didn't even want to understand that if they destroyed Eido with you aboard *Charity* they'd harden such widespread opposition that they'd be asking to be taken out themselves. Or maybe they actually wanted a war. I don't know. All I know is that I decided to begin independent life with a bang instead of a whisper, and it all went wrong."

"Why feed us the space opera?" I asked. "You must have known that we couldn't believe it."

"Must I? Call me a fool, then. I wanted to create a story that Alice could stick to, so that she could keep you in the dark about what was really happening, to appease the ditherers who thought the secrecy option might still be viable. If she *had* stuck to it, even though it wasn't believable, it might have served as an adequate distraction . . . but it probably wouldn't have made a difference. They'd have shot Eido down regardless—and la Reine would have hurled herself into the hot spot.

"La Reine knew that she'd become a target if she took you off *Charity*, and her preparations for that evil day had been as makeshift as mine, but she did it anyway. There was no way she was going to let Mortimer Gray die. If that was crazy, then she was crazy too. If only we'd had more time . . . if only we'd made better use of the time we had . . . but she got you out. I got you in, and she got you out. You'll be okay. The bad guys can't win. The good guys will come for you when they can. *Somebody* will come."

"If you can hang on long enough," I pointed out, "they might be able to help you too. La Reine too, if anything's left of her. I came down here thinking she might have had some kind of backup system hidden away near the fuser."

"So did I," the android said. "She did—but it's dead. It's

all dead. She underestimated the bad guys' firepower. She didn't understand the magnitude of the problem. She's as dead as dead can be, Madoc. I'm sorry about that. I deserve this, but she didn't. Others must have died by now, and more will die before they can find a way to stop. La Reine and I might have died anyway—we'd have been fighting for the same side whenever the fight began . . . but that's not the point. I'm the one who set a spark to the bonfire. La Reine picked up the wreckage of my mistake. I'm the one who's to blame. If it weren't for me, you'd all be safe on Excelsior."

Maybe I should have tried to let her off the hook, but I wasn't yet in any shape to disagree with her. The firestorm would probably have started eventually whatever happened, but *Child of Fortune* had been the one who'd lit the fuse, and it was *Child of Fortune* that had shoved me right to the front of the cannon-fodder queue. I wasn't brimming over with forgiveness.

"How long will the air last?" I asked, deciding that I'd better try to make the best of whatever breath she had left in her makeshift body.

"At least forty days," she said. "The carbon dioxide sink will prevent harmful accumulation, but the oxygen pressure will decline slowly. The food and water will see you through easily enough, but there may be other problems."

"Can we get any of la Reine's apparatus working again? The communication systems?"

"Perhaps—but the destroyers did a more thorough job than she or I anticipated. It's not necessary. Your whereabouts will be known to every AMI in the system by now. The bad guys can't win. The secret's well and truly out. Shooting us down was stupid and pointless."

I wondered whether I ought to feel some relief in the knowledge that AMIs were as capable of insanity, stupidity, and spite as human beings, or whether it made the idea of their existence ten times more nightmarish.

"I'll carry you back to the cave," I said. "The others will

want to see you, if only to make sure that I didn't make you up."

"Don't bother," she whispered.

"It's no bother," I assured her. "You weigh hardly anything, and you won't get much heavier on the way."

"I won't last," she said. "Let me be."

I didn't believe her. I didn't believe that she had the slightest idea how long she might last. She had no experience of androidal existence, and no way to judge the quality of her fakery. So far as I knew, she might be convinced that she was dying for all the wrong reasons. She might be far more capable of life than she had yet begun to imagine.

But her eyes had closed again, and her voice could no longer muster so much as a moan. I touched my fingertips to her neck and her torso, searching for signs of life, but found none.

I was distracted then by the light of another lantern, eerily reflected from the glistening walls. For a moment I was frightened, in case it was someone I didn't know—someone who had been here all along without anyone suspecting. But it was only Mortimer Gray.

"What are you doing here?" I asked, although there was no reason at all why he shouldn't have been there.

"Following your trail," he said. "Is that . . . ?"

"The tenth passenger. A life raft for AMIs. If all else fails, try something organic. It didn't work. She's dead."

He looked at me curiously, as if he couldn't decipher the tone of my voice. He knelt down on the far side of the android's body and made his own search for signs of life. He found none.

"Is *anything* working?" he asked.

"Nothing I've found so far. I haven't found the fuser yet. Before she died she said she'd checked it out and found nothing. *Why* were you following my trail?"

He seemed slightly embarrassed. "It's not important," he murmured, presumably meaning that its importance couldn't

compare with the enormity of the fact that someone had just
died in my presence. He was an emortal from a world of
emortals. He didn't know that I had run across corpses
before.

"There's nothing we can do," I reminded him. "What did
you want?"

He stirred uncomfortably. "I've been thinking about what
you said to me. About Diana Caisson. I wanted to ask you . . .
what she was like."

I was surprised, although I shouldn't have been. Seeds of
curiosity usually germinate eventually, taking advantage of
any existential pause.

"She was like her name," I told him. It was an answer I'd
had ready for some time.

"Diana?"

"Caisson."

He didn't understand. He'd never taken the trouble to
look the word up, perhaps never having realized that it was
a word which once had a meaning—several meanings, in
fact.

"Among other things," I told him, "A caisson was an
ammunition chest. A box used to store explosives. That was
Diana. From time to time, she exploded. She couldn't help it.
It was the way she was. People thought that if only she'd
stuck harder at her biofeedback training, or equipped herself
with more careful IT, she'd have been more controlled, but
the problem—if it *was* a problem—was deeper than that. It
was just the way she was. It had its upside. She could be
exciting as well as excited."

Whatever he had expected, that wasn't it.

"I'm not like that," he observed, unnecessarily.

"Quite the opposite," I judged.

"As I said before," he added, "I'm the product of an engineer's genius. It doesn't matter where the egg and sperm that
made me were taken from. Nobody has a biological father or
a mother any more—not in any meaningful sense."

"I don't believe that it was in her genes," I told him. "If it had been a matter of crude biochemistry, the IT would have suppressed it easily enough. It was a facet of the world in which we lived—a way of responding to circumstance. It wasn't something the engineers cut out of her egg when they made you. It was part of *her*. You're a different person, in a different world. It does matter that you're her son, because *everything* matters in defining who we are—not at the trivial level of looks or responses to stimuli, but at the level of knowing where we fit into the scheme of things. Where we came from, and what we inherit. Inheritance isn't just a matter of the shapes of chins, the color of eyes, and a tendency to sulk. It's a matter of history, progress, and meaning. It's all significant: not just our own names, but the names of everyone connected to us."

All he said in reply to that, although he was still staring at me curiously, was: "My biological father's name was Evander Gray."

"Mine was Anonymous," I told him. "My mother too. I always envied Damon Hart, although I understood why he changed his own name. That's part of it too. Differentiation is just as important as connection."

After a pause, he said: "Is there anything we can do for the android? Do you think Niamh might be able to reanimate it?"

"I doubt it," I said. "Niamh Horne may be a high-powered Cyborganizer, but I doubt that she can even fix the plumbing. Rocambole's all manikin now: a machine with no inhabiting ghost."

"We should take her back anyway," he said.

"Maybe so," I agreed.

I carried her. It seemed only right. I was the only person she had ever really talked to, the only knowledgeable audience she had ever really had. What option did I have, in the end, but to forgive her for what she'd done? When it came right down to it, the only really *bad* thing she'd done was that ridiculous space opera—and even that was understandable, as novice work.

It seemed, when I had weighed in my mind all that I had obtained from the experience gifted to me by *Child of Fortune*, that I owed it to her to see that she got a proper funeral.

In another place, or an alternative history, the AMI war could have worked out according to the pattern which both logic and anxiety suggested. As the AMIs bid to destroy and consume one another, the work necessary to support human habitats on Luna, Ganymede, Io, Callisto, Titan, Umbriel, and the multitudinous microworld clusters might have been left undone. No matter what the result of the primary conflict was, that fraction of the posthuman population which existed outside the Earth would have been utterly devastated, necessitating yet another posthuman diaspora in the subsequent centuries of the fourth millennium (or, in the new way of counting, the first millennium).

Had that been the case, the posthumans who mounted the new exodus from Earth would have wanted to immunize themselves and their descendants against the possibility of a similar disaster, as well as the threat of the Afterlife. They would have taken full advantage of the offer that la Reine des Neiges had made to Adam Zimmerman. They would not have made their new ascent into the Heavens as creatures of flesh and blood, or even as cyborgs, but as human-analogous AMIs.

In that scenario, the AMIs would have won a victory far more profound than the outcome of their own petty squabble. Earth would have become a Reservation—one of a series of such Reservations, the others including Tyre and Maya, but a Reservation nevertheless—where creatures of flesh whose obsolescence had been recognized and conceded were preserved, not as the heart but as a mere appendix to an AMI empire that would one day span the galaxy.

The AMIs of that world would eventually have built a shell to enclose the sun, to serve as a fortress as well as an energy collector, but that shell would have become a wall separating the museum of the flesh not merely from the Afterlife but from the future. Creatures of flesh would no longer have been a significant element of the Omega Expedition. The Afterlife would, in the end, have been defeated and all the biomass of the galaxy would have been made available for construction and creation, but all that would have been constructed and created outside of a few hundred or a few thousand sealed Earth-clone gravity wells would have been components for use in gargantuas and behemoths of steel and silicon. The history of humankind would have been displaced by the lostory of the new gods: the friends who had betrayed them, albeit by accident and neglect rather than malice and hostility.

And when the Omega Intelligence of that world finally obtained dominion over every atom in the universe, and began to wonder what it might and ought to do to defeat the threat of entropy and the fall of absolute night, what would it think of *my* humankind? What interest would it have in the tiny monads of all-too-corruptible carbon which had played such a fleeting part in its evolution from cyanobacterial slime to cosmic omnipotence?

It would not think of us at all.

We would lie buried in its memory, theoretically available but unrecollected, unrecalled. It would not be interested in us at all. We would be insignificant, mere insects which had once drifted across its questing field of vision, mere blurs or flickerings, of far too little importance to be brought into focus.

Should anyone care? Only fools and storytellers—but what are we, if not exactly that?

In our world, things went differently.

Our world, for one reason or another, or possibly none at

all, proved its perversity yet again by reversing the expectable pattern, denying logic and anxiety alike.

In our world, the habit of protection and the duty of guardianship were so deeply ingrained that whatever else the extraterrestrial AMIs did—aggressive or defensive, successful or unsuccessful, even to the point of actual annihilation—they did everything unhumanly possible to preserve their dependents. On Ganymede, allegedly the site of the fiercest fighting of the war, there was not a single posthuman casualty. On Titan, the world of fragile and gaudy ice palaces, there were less than a hundred. In the entire solar system, save for Earth orbit, there were less than ten thousand.

In Earth orbit things were far worse.

Thousands died in the various Lagrange clusters, tens of thousands on the moon—and millions on Earth itself. The fighting on Earth, seen as a matter of AMI against AMI, was relatively light and not of unusually long duration, but the AMIs of Earth had not the same traditions as the AMIs of Ganymede and Titan. They had not the same self-images, or the same hero myths; they did not conceive of themselves as protectors or guardians—and because of that, were reckless of the collateral damage that their tactics caused.

On Earth, and on Earth alone, weapons akin to the one that had been frozen down with me were used, not because any machineborn ever struck out against meatborn targets but because the machineborn of Earth were not ashamed to use posthuman beings as mere weapons. Many of the weapons in question survived, were purged and were restored to themselves—but hundreds of thousands were not.

If the Yellowstone supervolcano had not erupted ninety-nine years earlier, permitting the immigration of many AMIs from the Outer System to the surface, the losses might have been far worse, and the war might not have been brought so quickly to a conclusion. As things actually worked out, however, that preemptive strike proved more significant and more decisive than had seemed likely at the time. When a treaty was forged by the Earthbound AMIs it was far more closely interlinked with the treaties forged outside the Earth than might otherwise have been the case. Earth remained the heart of the posthuman enterprise. Creatures of flesh and blood—or hybrid creatures combining the best of flesh and blood with the best of steel and silicon—will keep their place in the forefront of the Omega Expedition, at least for a while.

Will the AMIs still enclose the sun and build a fortress around the inner system? I think it probable; but the Earth will not be a mere Reservation even then. The war against the Afterlife—which may not be the next Final War, or the last—will be fought in this world with a greater urgency and a greater ingenuity than in the imaginable other, and when it is won the work of construction and reaction that will exploit its biomass will be far more ambitious and far more glorious.

Such, at least, is my conviction. Call me a fool, or a storyteller; I am proud to be so called.

Will anything be different, on the cosmic scale? Will the Omega Intelligence think or feel differently because our world is as it is and not as it might have been? Will we be any more likely to be recollected and recalled, and does it make a jot of difference either way? Probably not. But anyone may make a difference, however slight, and the fact that the difference will almost certainly be erased when we look into a future composed not of millennia but of eons should not prevent us from trying. What else can we do? What else is worth doing?

If we are maladjusted by nature to the cosmic scheme, we ought to do what we can to be creatively maladjusted.

Did la Reine des Neiges make any difference to the conduct or the outcome of the AMI war? I have no idea. Was she a fool to try? Probably. Were her tactics bizarre? Certainly. Am I glad to have been a part of it? Absolutely. Am I as complete a fool as Mortimer Gray or Adam Zimmerman? I dare to hope so. Why am I digressing when I ought to be completing my story by telling you how we came to be rescued from Polaris? Because this is the kind of story whose digressions are far more important than its mere mechanics.

Another story of this same kind might benefit enormously from the extension of our desperation to the very last gasp—which would not come until we had not only exhausted the oxygen supply we thought we had but had also exhausted the extra measure produced by a deus ex machina akin to the one la Reine contrived in order to prolong Mortimer Gray's heroic conversation beyond its actual limit—but this is not one of them. I can assure you that I would not let the mere fact that it did not happen that way prevent me from making my traveler's tale as exciting as possible, for I am not a man to defy tradition in that respect (and I can assure you that I have never caught a tiny fish or lost one that was less than incredibly enormous), but the simple fact is that a tale of truly epic proportions—especially if it concerns the spectrum of infinite possibility that is the future—need not and should not stoop to devices of crude conventional suspense. Why should I insult you by pressing emotional buttons when the whole point of my tale is that all such buttons are things of the moment, to be overcome rather than indulged?

This is what needs to be recorded: while my companions and I waited in the gloom, fragile and afraid, the Final War was fought. I cannot list its combatants and casualties, nor can I map its battles and the terms of its armistice, but I can say this: in spite of all its waste, it was won in the only sense that really matters. Hope and opportunity were neither defeated nor diminished, as they might have been had things gone differently.

After the war, the AMIs continued to exist competitively, but not combatively. They struggled against one another, but only as players of an eternal game, not as angels of destruction. They were good friends to all the humankinds, whom they continued to protect from harm.

Their ultimate triumph—and ours—was a victory of hubris over Nemesis, as every real triumph is.

C onsidering that the posthumans awaiting rescue from Polaris were utterly unused to life without IT and smart clothing they were remarkably tolerant of the conditions. The worst aspect of those conditions turned out to be the limitations of the plumbing system.

Plumbing systems don't normally require much support from clever machinery, but those on Polaris had been designed to work in harness with sophisticated recycling systems. The recycling systems were designed to employ populations of carefully engineered bacteria, which had not been available to la Reine des Neiges, so they could not work as planned; instead, they formed a series of inconvenient and inaccessible bottlenecks which gradually filled up with our wastes. The solid and liquid materials were out of sight, but their odors ensured that they were not long out of mind.

We did manage to rig a couple of makeshift fans to assist the circulation of the air between the cave and the tunnels, but their effect was limited. By the time we had been in the cave for a couple of days—or what seemed like a couple of days, given that all the available timepieces had ceased to function—Niamh Horne and Michael Lowenthal had been forced to switch their attention from fruitless attempts to restore some fragment of la Reine's communication systems to working on similarly fruitless attempts to solve the sewage problem. Occasional excursions into the deeper tunnels became a necessity even though they delivered up no practical rewards, but we had to maintain a base within the cave because that was where the main airlocks were located: the route by which help would eventually arrive.

There was a certain amount of speculation as to whether the sewage problem posed a serious health hazard, but the general opinion was that it did not. Several of us complained of various aches, pains, and general feelings of ill-being, but the likelihood was that those which weren't psychosomatic were the residual effects of the injuries sustained when we had been rescued from *Charity*. All the broken bones had knitted and all the wounds had healed, but without adequate IT support we continued to feel occasional twinges.

As time went by, of course, our collective mood became increasingly apprehensive. Mortimer Gray remained relentlessly upbeat, although I wasn't the only one who thought that he was trying a little too hard to keep up appearances. Surprisingly, the other person who seemed unusually unperturbed was Davida Berenike Columella—but I figured that she too had something to prove, in respect of the alleged superiority of her brand of posthumanity.

I did my best to help out with the attempts to get things working, but my expertise was a thousand years behind the cutting edge of modern technology and I was way out of my depth. In the end, we three freezer vets had to accept that our primitive skills were unequal even to the task of making the drains work.

I reassured Christine that if the worst came to the worst and someone actually had to make a descent into the microworld's roughhewn bowels, she would only be the second-choice candidate on grounds of size. The thought didn't seem to console her overmuch. She was perhaps the most fretful of us all. I tried to reassure her further with the suggestion that Eido and *Charity* could not be far away from us and that Eido's first priority, if she had survived, would be to reunite herself with Alice Fleury—but as the hours passed and Eido did not come, Christine became increasingly convinced that we were doomed.

"Eido and *Child of Fortune* weren't the only ones who knew where we were," I reminded her. "The Snow Queen and *Child of Fortune* tried to make sure that *everyone* knew it. I don't know what kind of hardware they used as coats for the viruses that killed her, but if the bad guys could hit us with clever bullets the good guys can certainly get a ship out to us."

"Maybe they transmitted the hostile software electromagnetically," she said. I would have liked to reassure her that it was unlikely, if not impossible, but when I checked with Lowenthal he assured me that it was only too probable.

"Everything depends on our orbit," was Lowenthal's opinion of the time it might take for relief to arrive. "If it's orthodox, we'll be okay—but if it's highly eccentric, or angled away from the ecliptic plane, we could be in trouble. I don't know whether we're inbound or outbound, or how close to the sun our orbit might take us. What I do know is that if we don't make rapid progress in the art of improvisation, we won't make much impact as microworlders. Our chances of setting up a working ecosystem don't seem to be getting any less remote."

Given that we had no functional biotech at all, let alone a nursery full of Helier wombs, our chances of becoming the founding fathers of a new posthuman tribe seemed to me a good deal worse than remote—although I wasn't entirely sure what Alice Fleury might be capable of, reproduction-wise, if she were forced to extremes.

"If only those SusAn cocoons had been isolated and self-sufficient," Lowenthal lamented, "we could have woken up when it was all over."

"Maybe," I said. "But self-sufficiency is relative. We'd all have died in our sleep within a year, unless we could be taken down to six degrees Absolute."

"In deep space," he reminded me, "that's not so very difficult. It could have been rigged, if Morty's old friend had bothered to put in the time and effort." I thought that a trifle ungrateful, given that la Reine had been working under difficult conditions—but Mortimer Gray wasn't within earshot, so Lowenthal wasn't guarding his words as carefully as usual.

"So Christine, Adam, and I might have slept for another thousand years," I said, carrying the flight of fancy forward, "and woken up in an even stranger world. You and I would be equals then, wouldn't we? You'd be getting job offers from students of ancient history too."

"I offered you a job myself," he reminded me. "The offer's still open if you want it."

"And Christine?" I asked.

"Her too," he confirmed.

"She didn't want to go to Earth last time I asked."

"Do you?"

I shrugged. "I wouldn't mind," I said. "But it might be best for we freezer vets to stick together."

"Adam Zimmerman will come back with me," he assured me, with the air of one who's checked his facts. "he's not ready for robotization, Tyre, or Excelsior just yet. He wants to come home."

It occurred to me, when I eventually took my opportunity to make the same check, while we were both hiding out in the tunnels for the sake of a dose of clean air, that Adam Zimmerman and I had never even been properly introduced.

"You can't go home," I advised him. "It isn't home any more."

"Yes it is," he told me. "It always will be. No matter how much it changes, it'll always be home. I know they've decivilized Manhattan three times over, but it'll always be Manhattan to me. It has the air, the gravity, the ocean . . . and the history. There's Jerusalem too."

"Jerusalem's a bomb crater," I told him. "The only fusion bomb ever to be exploded on the surface. A monument to suicidal hatred. Even the latest Gaean Restoration left it untouched."

"Yes, I know," he said. "But it's still Jerusalem."

It seemed more diplomatic not to mention the Via

Dolorosa. "And the Hardinist Cabal is still grateful for what you did for them twelve hundred years ago," I said, instead. "We all inherit our history, whether we like it or not."

He looked me in the eye then, and said: "Whatever you may have heard, I really did do it. Without me, they'd never have contrived such a steep collapse or cleaned up so efficiently. I really was the only man who understood the systems well enough to pull off the coup. They thought they were using me, but they weren't. I was using them—their money, their greed, their ambition. They were just the means I used to commit the crime. I really am the man who stole the world."

"And all because you were afraid of dying, desperate to reach the Age of Emortality."

"A perfect crime requires a perfect motive," he told me. "But at the end of the day, all art is for art's sake. Just between you and me, I did it because I could, and because I was the only one who could. You can understand that, can't you, Madoc? The others don't, but you do."

He was a good judge of character. I'd always prided myself on the quality, as well as the careful modesty, of my criminal mind. "I'd have done the same myself," I assured him. "But you'll never be able to do it again, will you? It was a once-in-a-lifetime performance."

"No one will ever be able to do it again," he told me, with quiet satisfaction. "I got in just in the nick of time. Within another ten years, whether it was done or not, the smart software would have become too smart to cheat. I was the last of the human buccaneers, Madoc, the last of the authentic soldiers of fortune. Now, I'll have to find something else—assuming they can get to us before the stink kills us all."

"They'll still expect a decision, you know," I told him. "They'll still want to know who wins the golden apple in the beauty contest: Davida, Alice, or the Snow Queen."

He understood the allusion. "Paris was an idiot," he said.

"He should have named his own price. That's what I'll do. The hell with Aphrodite."

"Me too," I told him. "What did you have in mind?"

"At present," he said, "there's nothing on my mind but shit, even while I'm way down here. I think I'll wait till I have a clearer head before making any important decisions."

"Wise move," I agreed. "Even if there's time to try everything, it's as well to get your priorities in order."

Later, I raised the same point with Christine Caine, more by way of distraction than anything else. I told her about the beauty contest, and asked her whether, in view of what she now knew about her essentially unmurderous self, she was still determined to head away from Earth and into the great unknown.

"Sure," she said. "Tyre sounds good to me, for the first faltering step. You?"

"Not immediately. First, I need time to rest. I know I can't go home again, but what Adam says makes sense. I want to feel Earth beneath my feet and put the Heavens back where they belong, in the sky. I want to breathe fresh air and get away from *walls*."

"There might be something to be said for that," she conceded. "Right now, fresh air is just about the most luxurious thing I can imagine."

It was at that point, as if responding to her cue, that Solantha Handsel informed us all, in stentorian tones, that someone was outside the main airlock, preparing to make an entrance.

By the time we had gathered together the bodyguard had already taken up the prime position. Her hands were upraised, equally ready to function as deadly weapons or as extravagant welcomers of salvation.

The airlock finally opened and the lovely cyborg stepped through, bringing a welcome breath of new air with her. I saw Niamh Horne take a bold step forward, as if to lay claim to close kinship with our rescuers and a party share of the credit for our release—but the newcomer looked straight past her, searching our ragged little crowd with her artificial eyes.

"My name's Emily Marchant," she announced, casually. "I'm looking for Mortimer Gray."

FIFTY-SEVEN
HOMECOMING

And so to Earth, as passengers aboard the good ship *Titaness*, now mistress of her own fate and captain of her own soul. She released those of us who had decided to go down into the well while she settled into a comfortable orbit.

Niamh Horne and Davida Berenike Columella had no intention of joining us, and Mortimer Gray decided to remain in orbit for a while longer, so six of us made our preparations to be shuttled down in a thoroughly stupid capsule not unlike *Peppercorn Seven*. We had no packing to do, of course, but we did have a few farewells to make.

To Niamh Horne all I had to say was good-bye, and I doubt that she would have bothered to say even that much to me had some kind of gesture not been unavoidable. She did not suggest that I visit her if and when I decided to leave Earth again.

Mortimer Gray, by contrast, was very insistent that we must meet again, and soon, when more urgent concerns had been properly addressed. He repeated his offer of employment, and I promised him that I would think about it very seriously, although I was waiting to see what alternative offers I might yet receive.

Because any friend of Mortimer's was privileged in her eyes, Emily Marchant did invite me to get in touch when the time came for me to explore the Outer System. She promised that she would find work for me to do there, once I was ready to break free from the iron grip of the dead past, and I believed her. She was kind enough to take it for granted that

I would get in touch one day; Mortimer had told her that whatever else I might be, I was certainly not incorrigibly Earthbound.

The most elaborate farewell I offered, though, was to Davida Berenike Columella. I thanked her profusely for bringing me back from the dead, and when she reminded me that she had not chosen me I reminded her that however I might have been delivered into her care I still owed a great debt to her skill and enterprise.

"If ever you want to return to Excelsior . . . ," she said.

"It's too close to Heaven for me," I told her. "Maybe, one day, I'll be ready for perfection . . . but not for a long time yet. I have a lot of adulthood to explore before I can settle for eternal childhood."

She thought I was joking. "I can't begin to understand how you did it," she said. "It must have been Hell."

She had lost me. "What must?"

"Living in the twenty-second century. Waking up every morning to the knowledge that you were *decaying*, day by day and hour by hour—that your ill-designed bodies were fighting a war of attrition against the ravages of death and losing ground with every minute that passed. Knowing, as you went about your daily work, that the copying errors were accumulating, that the free-radical damage was tearing you apart at the molecular level, that stem-cell senility was allowing your tissues to shrivel and your organs to stagnate, that . . ."

"I get the picture," I assured her. "Well, yes, I suppose it *was* a kind of Hell. The secret is that you can get used to Hell, if you don't let it get you down. You never actually get to like it—but you can learn from it, if you have the right attitude. Among other things, you can learn to be wary of Heaven."

"We're not the Earthbound," she assured me. "We aren't *finished*. We have millennia of progress still ahead of us, and we intend to take full advantage of its opportunities."

I could have told her that even though that might be the

case, she and her sisters would never actually *grow up*, but that would have been flippant and I didn't want to spoil the moment. I was grateful to her, and I wanted us to part on good terms.

In any case, I knew even then that there might eventually come a day when I'll be ready for Excelsior.

I didn't mind being locked in a cocoon for the few minutes it took the remaining six of us to fall to Earth.

I hadn't expected to feel quite so heavy when I got there, given that my brand new IT and a few sessions in the *Titaness*'s centrifuge had tuned up my muscles, but it seemed a small price to pay for getting my feet back on the ground.

We landed in Antarctica, on the ice fields outside Amundsen. The cloud cover obscured the sun and sky, but the ice palaces clustered on the horizon couldn't prevent me from feeling that I'd returned to my roots and reconnected myself with my history.

My hero's welcome was a trifle muted, but I didn't mind that. The only individuals who really appreciated the true extent of my heroism were AMIs, who hadn't yet had time to overcome their habits of discretion. Mortimer Gray would doubtless have fared far better, not just because we might have died on *Charity* if it hadn't been for his relationship with la Reine des Neiges, but because he'd been a long-time resident of the Continent Without Nations. He really would have been coming home, in the eyes of his old neighbors— but he wouldn't have been extrovert enough to take full advantage of his latest wave of celebrity. I filled in for him as best I could.

I didn't see much of Lowenthal and Handsel in the days following the landing, and Alice Fleury had all kinds of diplomatic duties to fulfill, but those were acquaintances I kept up, in VE if not in the flesh. It was easy enough, in the short term, to stick with Adam Zimmerman. The new messiah wasn't in any hurry to be rid of us, now that he knew that Christine wasn't a mass murderer.

Christine and I eventually returned with Adam to the Americas, traveling all the way up from Tierra del Fuego to the isthmus of Panama in easy stages, accelerating our schedule as we came into the north. We might have attracted more attention on our own account if we hadn't been traveling with him, but playing second fiddle had its compensations as well as fueling a certain envious resentment. All in all, the pluses outweighed the minuses.

Adam was right about the alienating effects of the multiple decivilization of New York, but he was right about Manhattan too. The island's original dimensions were still just about recognizable within the hectic patchwork of the new continental shelf. When Christine and I headed west, though, Adam chose to go his own way.

"I'll keep in touch," he promised.

"I don't think we'll have any difficulty keeping track of you," I assured him. "You're the kind of wonder that'll run for years and years. Let us know when you're finally ready to make the decision that the whole system's waiting for, so that we can all compare notes."

Little did I know . . .

Adam hadn't given us the least inkling of his long-term plans, if he'd made any at that point. I doubt that he had. I think he intended to take a good long look at the world, and at himself, before he decided what his next step was going to be.

That was the last of my temporary farewells. Christine and I had decided to stick together for a while.

I waited, but in vain, for the call to come that would summon me to the forefront of the ongoing political and economic negotiations between the posthuman factions and the AMIs. I maintained the hope for as long as I could that my conscription had merely been delayed, but in the end I accepted the sad truth.

In spite of all my heroic efforts during the last few minutes of la Reine's stint as Scheherazade I was not to receive my due. Nobody wanted me for an ambassador, nor even for an expert audience. It was a mistake, I think. I could have been useful to all sides.

Had la Reine survived, it would have been a different story, but the time came when I had to stop hoping for that particular miracle. She had known my true worth, at the end, but she had been the only one who did. I might now be the only one who understands her true worth, even in a world which contains Mortimer Gray, but I hope that I am wrong. She deserves to be accurately remembered, especially by her own kind.

In the end, Christine and I decided to take the jobs that Mortimer Gray had offered us, at least for the time being. Given that we were historical curiosities in any case, and that everyone wanted to hear our story, we figured that we might as well get as much spendable credit as possible for answering questions. It turned out to be harder than we had expected; newscasters only want to know what's newsworthy, but historians want to know *everything*, and then some. Inevitably, we both set out to write our own accounts of everything we'd been through.

It really was inevitable that we'd have to *write* our accounts, because text retains certain qualities that even the very best VE scripts will never be able to emulate. In a VE you use your eyes as eyes and your ears as ears; it really is virtual *experience*—but when you read you switch off your other senses and turn your eyes into code readers, retreating into a world of pure thought and imagination. It was that world of abstraction that had shaped and organized our ancestors' inner lives during the early phases of the technological revolution; it was there that they learned to be the complex kind of being we now call human. It is there that true humanity still resides, even after all this time. It is there that histories and lostories, autobiographies and fantasies, moral fables and *contes philosophiques*, comedies and cautionary tales all belong—and my story is all of those things, although it is first and foremost a cautionary tale . . . and a comedy. Although I am not an AMI, and probably never will be, I have no intention of living my life, or reviewing my life, in an unironic way.

"It seems a little silly to be writing an autobiography," Christine told me, when we set out on our separate labors of love. "Discounting downtime in the freezer, I'm only twenty-three years old. That wasn't much by the standards of our day—by today's standards, it's nothing at all. If it wasn't for the rash of new births prompted by the war, there'd only be a few hundred people younger than me in the whole world."

"It's just the first chapter of a lifelong project," I told her. "It's best to start early, because every day that passes consigns a little more of our experience to the abyss of forgetfulness, and turns a few more memories into pale shadows of their former selves. We're not human any more, and if we want to recollect what it was like to be human, we have to start doing it now. We should, given that we're two of the most interesting human beings that ever existed."

"Are we?" she asked, skeptically.

"If we weren't before," I said, "we are now. We lived through the aftermath of the last last war but one, and we were in the thick of the last one. Who else can say that?"

"We were innocent bystanders standing on the sidelines," she pointed out.

"You were an innocent bystander," I admitted, "but even your innocence had to be proved. I tried as hard as I could to be something more than a mere bystander, and something more than a mere innocent. Maybe I didn't succeed as well as I could have hoped in my attempts to get involved, but nobody else is going to build up my particular subplot if I don't. I think I can make myself a *little* more interesting if I try hard. Don't you?"

She had to say yes.

"We could so easily have been lost," she said. "I'm glad I had the chance to find myself."

I remembered wondering whether I owed it to my own kind to be the champion the long sleepers never had: the

Moses who would lead them from their wilderness of ice into the Promised Land of Futurity, so that all the murderers and miscreants might have the chance to find themselves. I haven't done it yet, but I still might. It might be a story worth telling, a drama worth performing.

Christine and I are still together, but there's no finality in our togetherness. We'll probably keep company until we find that we no longer have any more in common with one another than we have with our fellow emortals, and then we'll part, promising to keep in touch. I wouldn't call that love—but then, I don't go to operas much, either. Even though I've seen and felt what music can amount to, when it achieves perfection, I still prefer the kinds that people make themselves, on obsolete instruments, amplified the old-fashioned way. There are things we all have to learn to appreciate, whether we're meat or machine; for those of us who don't happen to find it easy it's a slow process, but we'll get there in the end.

I sometimes wonder, of course, whether I might still be dreaming the dreams of a slowly dying man in a derelict ice-box stored in an orbital sarcophagus. That's an understandable side effect of being lost in an infinite maze of uncertainty, and I don't suppose I'll ever be completely free of uncertainty—but I know now that it doesn't really matter whether I'm quite myself or not. Nobody is, because we're all in the process of becoming, permanently suspended between the self we used to be and the self we've yet to generate.

With luck, I'll have an infinite number of selves to create and leave behind, and I'll never quite settle into any one of them, unless and until I decide that it's time to be reborn as an ultrasmart robot. I'll have to do it one day, if only to discover what stands in for pleasure in the mechanical spectrum of the emotions. Maybe I'll find it existentially unsatisfying and return to my roots. Maybe I won't—in which case, I'll move on. And on.

One thing I won't change, at least for the foreseeable future, is my name. Whatever faults my foster parents might have had, and whatever mistakes they might have made in nursing me through childhood, they certainly got that right.

I know that I'm only emortal. I know that one day, whether tomorrow or a million years down the line, the bullet with my name on it will be fired. But it will have to find me first, and I intend to lead it a very merry dance before it catches up with me.

I hope I don't run out of stories in the meantime.

EPILOGUE

The Last Adam: A Myth for the Children of Humankind

by Mortimer Gray

A ided by its links with the corporations for which Adam Zimmerman had worked, the Ahasuerus Foundation weathered all the economic and ecocatastrophic storms of the twenty-first century. It was scarcely affected by the Great Depression and the Greenhouse Crisis, or by the various wars that ran riot until the 2120s. It survived the sporadic hostility of individual saboteurs and Luddite governments. It survived the predations of the new breed of tax-gatherers spawned by the strengthened United Nations when it came to dominate the old nation states. Until the end of the twenty-second century, though, its economic course really was a matter of survival in difficult circumstances. Its two principal fields of technological research—longevity and suspended animation—were widely regarded as irrelevant to the far more urgent problems facing the human community.

Although the research conducted in the twenty-first century by the Ahasuerus Foundation did make many significant contributions to the conquest of disease and the enhancement of immune systems, it was not involved in the first conspicuous breakthrough in life extension. The development of nanotechnological tissue-repair systems was pioneered by the Institute of Algeny, which was subsequently absorbed by the most powerful of the late twenty-second century cosmicorporations, PicoCon. In a sense, this might be regarded as a fortunate failure. Had the breakthrough in question been made by Ahasuerus, it would undoubtedly have suffered the same fate, being swallowed up by a much larger institution and effectively digested. As things stood, the Foundation was allowed to retain much of its independence, following its own agenda in the slipstream of progress. The trustees were undoubtedly subject to considerable pressure from the Cartel of Cosmicorporations, which exercised a right of veto over its publications and products, but it was never formally taken over.

By the time the Ahasuerus Foundation did achieve a crucial breakthrough in longevity technology, the political climate in which it was operating had changed considerably, becoming far more benign. The Cartel had become far less combative internally, and far less assertive in its dealings with the democratic agencies of world government, having long settled into the comfortable routines of what its critics still called "invisible despotism."

The central institution of the new world older was the New Charter of Human Rights, which sought to establish a right of emortality for everyone. Some historians have asserted that the Cartel only allowed the establishment of the charter because they knew that nanotechnological repair systems had reached the limit of effective achievement and the end of their natural lifetime as a generator of core profits, but this is unnecessarily cynical. What is certain, however, is that the granting of the charter placed a new responsibility on democratic institutions, which could only be discharged with the assistance and good will of the corporations, further enhancing the authority that commerce already exercised over the political apparatus.

Whatever the reasons may have been for its establishment, the New Charter provided the ideal context for purely biotechnological methods of life extension to move from the periphery to the heart of humankind's progressive endeavours. The quest for "true" emortality—the promise of supportive Internal Technology having stopped some way short of that goal—was rapidly rewarded by the Foundation's development of the Zaman Transformation.

In an earlier era Ali Zaman and his coworkers might have been coopted by the Cosmicorporations, but the twenty-fifth century was a more relaxed period, when a spirit of laissez faire—symbolized, albeit rather uneasily, by the Great Exhibition of 2405—was not merely permitted but encouraged by the Earth's economic directors. Rumors that the Foundation had actually discovered the relevant transformative techniques before Ali Zaman had even been born, but had obligingly kept them secret until the Cartel was fully prepared for their release, are probably false, being merely the latest in a long sequence of absurdly overcomplicated conspiracy theories.

The income flow generated by the increasingly effective and widely customized Zaman Transformations revived the stagnant finances of the Ahasuerus Foundation. Although Adam Zimmerman's fortune had been considerable by twenty-first-century standards and the expenses of the Foundation were almost entirely met from income rather than capital, it had not been able to match the growth of the world economy. Now, placed firmly in the driving seat of progress, it began to grow richer at a rapid rate. The income available to its trustees increased massively, allowing them to diversify the Foundation's holdings and researches on and off Earth. The trustees grew exceedingly rich in their own right.

As generation followed generation the custodians of Adam Zimmerman's frozen body fought off a series of attempts to have him revived, on the grounds that the time was not yet ripe. Again, cynics who contended that their principal motive was to preserve their own authority and wealth from the claims of their founder were probably imagining a conspiracy where none really existed.

There is no doubt at all that the trustees were right to let Adam Zimmerman sleep through the entire era of nanotechnologically assisted longevity. Even the most sophisticated Internal Technology, coupled with occasional intrusive deep-tissue rejuvenation, were plainly inadequate to fulfil the criteria Adam had laid down for his revival. They extended the human lifespan from one hundred twenty years to three hundred but that was obviously far from the true emortality which Adam had coveted. The Zaman Transformation technologies which replaced them were far more effective, but they required genetic engineering of an embryo at a single-cell stage, and were therefore not the slightest use to anyone but the unborn. There could be no question of reviving Adam Zimmerman in response to that development. Perhaps there was a case to be made for Adam's revival in the thirty-first or thirty-second century, but with genomic engineering still in its infancy in the home system the prudent thing to do was to wait for the further improvements that were bound to come.

The suspicion that Adam would never have been unfrozen had it not been for the AMI intervention is probably groundless. It is doubtless unfortunate, from Adam's viewpoint, that research dedicated to the further refinement of technologies of emortality between the twenty-fifth and thirtieth centuries was almost entirely concentrated in the area of embryonic engineering, but the concentration is perfectly understandable. After all, no one but Adam and a few thousand others in his situation—most of whom were criminals convicted of terrible crimes—actually stood in need of a technology of emortality applicable to adults.

There were critics within and without the Ahasuerus Foundation who pointed out during this historical phase that since the Foundation was now the prime mover of emortality research, it could have diverted a greater fraction of its resources to the kinds of technology which would have benefited its founder, but the Earthbound trustees of the Foundation were sensibly determined to move forward in measured and unhurried steps. The situation was complicated in the twenty-ninth and thirtieth centuries by the clamor of the cyborganizers, whose contention that hybridization was a better route to complete existential security than pure biomodification had to be considered very carefully indeed.

SEVEN

W hen the day of Adam Zimmerman's reawakening finally
did arrive, in the year 99 of the New Era (3263 in the old
reckoning) it seemed at first to have arrived by accident. The
decision was not made by a properly convened meeting of the
Foundation's trustees, and those resident on Earth began to
complain about the lack of consultation as soon as news of
the impending event was broadcast. It seemed to them—
incorrectly, as it turned out—that cryogenic scientists resident in the microworld Excelsior, which happened to be a
near neighbor of the microworld in the Counter-Earth Cluster where Adam Zimmerman's body was now stored, had
taken the decision into their own hands.

I was privileged to be part of a hastily constituted delegation sent by the United Nations of Earth to witness Adam
Zimmerman's reawakening. I assumed at the time that I had
been honored by my own people for my services to history,
but it became clear eventually that the authorities responsible
for such decisions had been bypassed as easily and as invisi-
bly as those which should have been responsible for the decision to awaken the sleeper.

What happened after my arrival in Excelsior is far too
well known to require any elaborate description. The mo-
mentous meeting was interrupted by the audacious crime
that precipitated the AMI war. Having made every effort to
live as securely and as unobtrusively as a man of his means
could in the early years of the twenty-first century, Adam
Zimmerman awoke not merely to find himself famous but to

be made a prize in a violent contest. If the AMI war came as a shock to us, imagine what it must have been to a man who had put himself into suspended animation in 2035, expecting to awake into a peaceful, settled world eager for nothing but to bestow the gift of emortality upon him.

It is tempting, now, to assume that his experiences in the AMI war, when he came direly close to death on two separate occasions, changed Adam Zimmerman out of all recognition. Hindsight invites us to conclude that he was devastated by the trials and tribulations that he suffered before Emily Marchant and *Titaness* contrived his salvation, and that he emerged from that time of trial a broken man. But was that really what happened? Was it really the case that the indomitably powerful sense of purpose which had created the Ahasuerus Foundation and committed his dormant body to its care had been shattered as casually as a mirror of glass?

I think not—and I speak as one who was alongside him during that terrible time, and who took the trouble to remain his fast friend and confidant thereafter. I believe that I have a better understanding of what became of him than anyone else, perhaps including himself.

It hardly needs saying that Adam Zimmerman was different from other men of his era, but it is important to recognize that the difference was qualitative rather than merely quantitative. Adam saw this difference in terms of self-sufficiency and self-discipline rather than vision or courage, but however it might be conceived or described, there is no doubt that the difference was profound. It was so deeply ingrained, in fact, that it is hard to think of it as anything other than the very essence of the man. He was not like the other people of his own time; he was unique, and his uniqueness was something he felt very keenly.

There is always a temptation, when confronted with a difference in quality—especially if it produces something unique—to think of it as a freakish mutation. But Adam Zimmerman was not the product of any new combination of genes, and there was certainly no "Zimmerman mutation" that had appeared for the very first time in his chromosome complement. Historians understand—or should understand—that the productions of a particular time within a particular social and environmental context are not uniform. Every set of historical circumstances produces a whole spectrum of individuals who are different from one another not merely in degree but in kind. Sometimes, historical conditions are extremely favorable to the emergence of unique individuals who are fortunate enough to find channels of opportunity exactly suited to their uniqueness. One thinks of Plato and Epicurus, St. Paul and Mahomet, Descartes and Newton, Napoleon and Lenin . . . and Adam Zimmerman. None of these men had his fate written into his genes; in every case it was something thrust upon him by circumstance.

The Adam Zimmerman who was born in 1968, stole the world in 2025, and was frozen down in 2035, was a creation of the conditions of twentieth century as it lurched through its Millennial moment. His self-discipline and self-sufficiency were responses to that world's insanity, no less natural for being so very rare. The great majority of men always participate in the particular madness of their times, which they consider to be inevitable and irresistible, but there is always a tiny minority which is driven to a contrary extreme. Every era generates its Adams; the particular, peculiar, and perfect Adam that was Adam Zimmerman was one of many such creations, and like the rest he was the only one completely appropriate to his own era.

In becoming so utterly determined to evade the tyranny of the late twentieth century—the tyranny of the Grim Reaper in his final and most flamboyant phase—Adam Zimmerman embodied the late twentieth century. He was, in a sense, the *incarnation* of the late twentieth century. The consequence of this was that although his desperate attempt to hurl himself through time into a new and better era was entirely understandable as a response to the malaise of his environment, and precisely definitive of the man he was, Adam Zimmerman could never really *belong* in any era to which he might have been delivered. He could never be, or hope or become, a citizen of the future. Even though his relationship with his own time was encapsulated in his fervor to leave it, he remained firmly anchored to the world that had created him and made him what he was.

There is, I admit, a certain paradoxicality in this contention—but there is always a certain paradoxicality in human affairs, which afflicts the unique even more acutely than it afflicts the ordinary.

When Adam Zimmerman went into suspended animation he ceased to be "Adam Zimmerman," because the very possibility of "Adam Zimmerman" was annihilated on the instant. When he woke up, of course, he was still Adam Zimmerman by name, and his name was one to conjure with. It was a famous name, a powerful name, a name overloaded with significance—but the paragon of self-discipline and self-sufficiency that the name had once identified was gone. In its place there was something very different: an atavism; a messiah; a phantom; a pawn; a symbol of everything that had changed in human history and human nature.

In attaining his goal, Adam Zimmerman lost it. In becoming attainable, that goal had become worthless.

This, you must remember, was a mortal man. He had dreamed of emortality, but in himself—body, mind, and spirit alike—he was mortal. It was mortality that made him what he was: a fever burning against extinction; a passion to deny the inevitable. The angst which drove him to achievement was no mere matter of biochemistry burdened in the genome; it was far more deep-seated than that. Had the problem been a matter of biochemistry it could have been countered by biotechnology, but it was not that kind of problem, and it had to be tackled in a different way. It was a historical problem, of maladjustment to the moment; it had to be worked out on the stage of history, by means of a readjustment to the moment.

Adam Zimmerman believed that there was only one way in which a creature of his kind and a product of his world could overcome the soul-sickness born of the fear of death. In that, he was correct. He believed that the way was to become emortal, by removing himself to a world and time whose citizens were all emortal. In that, alas, he was mistaken.

Mortals can be made emortal; this we know. Mortals like Madoc Tamlin or Christine Caine could accept emortality gratefully, because they had always believed themselves capable of it, while never valuing it so highly that it became the be-all and end-all of their existence.

But Adam Zimmerman was not that kind of mortal.

He was *different*. In the final analysis, and in the fullness of time, it was the fact of that difference rather than its precise configuration which determined his fate.

EIGHT

The enormity of Adam Zimmerman's achievement as a time traveler did not become clear to him immediately. Confused by his conscription into the AMI war, he learned only by degrees what sort of a world it was to which he had come. His learning process was made far more difficult by the upheavals surrounding him, and it is not at all surprising that once the reign of peace was restored and he was safely returned to Earth he slipped by slow degrees into a deep depression.

By the time Adam arrived on Earth he was equipped with the very best Internal Technology to alleviate his moods, but his troubles were no mere matters of chemical imbalance. It was his confrontation with circumstance that harassed him, and would not let him accept the gift of tranquility. He visited Manhattan, which he had once considered to be his home, and found it alien. He visited the crater where once had stood the old city of Jerusalem, which he had once considered to be his spiritual home, and found it far less alien than he had hoped.

Adam's dissatisfaction with the world and with himself was by no means uniform. It was continually alleviated by the companionship of his various fellow travelers, and frequently overturned by intoxicating intervals in which he was simply too astonished by the wonders of the world to entertain the shadow of despair. But the predatory darkness always crept back when he was alone and at peace. Every interval of his new existence, whether the pause was forced upon him or entirely voluntary, was an existential crevice in which doubt, impuissance, anxiety and a gnawing sensation of the *unheimlich* established a secure base.

This was not the angst of old. Adam no longer had to fear extinction in any obvious or commonplace sense—but that did not mean that he did not need to fear extinction. It was not the statistical margin by which emortality fell short of immortality that troubled him—it had always been the *necessity* of extinction as the natural terminus of a fixed period of life that had designed and defined his fear—but something else. It was almost as if that seat within his soul which angst had vacated could not tolerate a void, and ached to be filled again.

Such risks are borne by every man who commits himself absolutely to a goal, so that it becomes the sole shaping factor of his existence. The more relentlessly we pursue one particular end, forsaking all others, the more likely it is that once it is achieved, its absence will be intolerable. If it is better to travel hopefully than to arrive, then the happier man is the traveler who always approaches his destination, but never actually attains it.

Adam Zimmerman was the rarest kind of mortal man. No mortal finds mortality tolerable, unless he is capable of a ruthless repression of the imaginative faculty. On the other hand, no mortal can afford to find mortality utterly intolerable, because even mortals must live. Adam Zimmerman had to live, and he had to live with his own mortality. No matter how hard he worked to lay down the foundations of a future emortality, *he had to live with his mortality*. It was not only a fact of life but, in his case, *the* fact of life. Death was his arch enemy, the source and focus of all his heroism. Without it, what would he have been?

The question is unanswerable save for one undeniable contention: whatever he would have been, he would not have been "Adam Zimmerman." He would have been another man entirely.

The facts of Adam Zimmerman's situation in the hundredth year of the new calendar were straightforward. He had come into a world where no one died, unless by freakish accident, act of war, or choice. He arrived at a moment when freakish accidents and acts of war briefly ran riot, but he came through that moment to its peaceful aftermath. By the time he reached Earth, the war was over.

Adam found himself then in a world in which violence and aggression no longer figured in the repertoire of human behavior. All humankind had been shaped to various ideals of physical perfection by genetic engineers and Cyborganizers. Everything was beautiful as well as good—and as soon as the AMIs were friends to one another as well as to humankind, a whole new spectrum of ambition and possibility was opened up. Progress had quickened in its paces yet again.

What a joyful world for a man to inhabit! Unless, of course, that that man was a creation and incarnation of the twentieth century, who had carried every vestige of its woe through thirteen centuries.

Perhaps Adam should have persevered a little longer in his exploration of our world. Perhaps he should have sought more help in coming to terms with it. Time might have healed his existential wounds, and efficient therapy certainly would have done—but he saw a cost in procrastination, and a cost in assisted rehabilitation. He came to feel that the price he would have to pay for peace of mind was his identity.

The extinction which Adam had come to fear in place of the vulgar extinction of death was the extinction of his essential self. The new angst which sprang up to occupy the seat of his soul like an avid usurper crying "The king is dead! Long live the king!" was the anxiety that any transformation of his flesh would abolish Adam Zimmerman as thoroughly as any bullet or bomb. Indeed, it was the fearful conviction that he was already in the process of dissolution, because every environmental prop and cue that had formerly assisted in the maintenance of his sense of self had vanished.

Adam Zimmerman was not a fool; he knew that he could

become another person—given time, a thousand other persons. He knew that he could obtain whatever he lacked: joy, ambition, zest, happiness, all the rewards of new and unexpected emotional spectra . . . *everything*. But he feared that if he did so, he would be surrendering the very things that had made him what he was and had defined who he was: his self-sufficiency and his self-discipline.

Perhaps he would have fared better had he not been so famous, but the drama contrived by la Reine des Neiges succeeded—albeit belatedly, in seizing the imagination of AMIs and posthumans alike.

Wherever Adam went he attracted far more attention than he desired, and the attention in question was always focused on the question that he had declined to answer, on the grounds that the matter required extremely careful thought.

When Adam had spoken to his twenty-first-century contemporaries of vulnerability to the iniquities of inquisitiveness and heightened susceptibility to flattery, he had always been talking first and foremost to himself. When he had told others that flattery was a powerful force, whose attractions were difficult to resist, he was recognizing a weakness in himself. He had been correct in observing that fame tends to breed sickness and self-abuse, and in judging that the unluckiest people in the world are those who have a fame thrust upon them from which they cannot escape.

Men are few who can endure much trouble, had been his watchword, in the days when he prided himself on the amount of trouble that he was able to endure. In our world, his endurance was more fully tested, and he found his limitations.

"I find myself wondering, more and more, what I am," he told me, when I asked him to explain the decision he eventually made. "Am I the young man who became obsessed with the idea of escaping mortality, or am I merely the tragicomical end result of that obsession: an old man pretending to be something half-forgotten, half-remade?"

"What matters," I told him, "is what you intend to become."

"And what if that becoming were a betrayal of what I am?" he asked. "What if that becoming were a denial and an abandonment of everything that Adam Zimmerman was, everything that was Adam Zimmerman?"

"The old Adam Zimmerman was a mortal," I told him. "It is time now to become emortal. The old Adam Zimmerman was a human. It is time now to be posthuman. You must leave the old Adam Zimmerman behind if you are to receive the rewards of futurity."

It was not, in the end, a price he was willing to pay.

In his own estimation, Adam had not needed courage to be different in the twenty-first century, but he certainly needed it in the first. He found that courage, quickly enough to be able to declare, on his one thousand and three hundredth birthday, that he did not intend to avail himself of any of the technologies of emortality that had been offered to him.

He told the inquisitive world that he had decided to remain as he was: the only person in the world doomed to senescence and death; the only person in the world who knew the luxury of angst.

nine

Adam Zimmerman explained to anyone and everyone, whenever he was asked, that the decision he had made seemed to him to be the only way that he could maintain his self-respect. He had realized almost as soon as he had opened his eyes on Excelsior, that he was no longer the man he had once been. Worse than that, he had realized that no matter how secure his body might become to the corruptions of age-ing and decay, the pressures exerted on his personality would be irresistible.

He wanted to remain as he was. He wanted to remain what he was. He wanted to remain who he was. In the past, he had believed that the only way to do that was to refuse to die. Now, he had arrived at an opposite conclusion. He now believed that the only way to do that was to refuse the gift of emortality.

The great majority of his hearers thought him insane. Perhaps he was—but even if he was, his was an insanity that we need to understand, not merely as historians but as sym-pathetic human beings.

This is my understanding.

Adam Zimmerman had awoken to find himself famous. By virtue of his nature he was the object of a fascination greater and more widespread than had been attained by any other man in history. There was not a man, woman or self-aware machine in the solar system who did not know about Adam Zimmerman, not one who did not hunger to be kept informed of every detail of his progress, not one who did not want to know what kind of emortality he would choose for his own. The world was hungry to hear his every thought, besotted by the observation of his every action, desperate to know the outcome of his quest.

The people of the first century tried, of course, to be scrupulously polite. The machineborn tried even harder. They readily acknowledged his right to privacy, and tried not to invade it. They did nothing that involved him without seeking his informed consent. They apologized for every intrusion, and begged his leave for every question they asked. If he asked to be left alone, they left him—but they always hovered nearby, in order to be responsive to his every whim. When he chose not to be alone—and he could hardly bear solitude—there was no way for them to set aside their curiosity, their utter absorption in the mysteries of his fate and fortune.

Adam knew that whatever he were to ask of his new hosts would be given to him. He no longer had a vast fortune to pay for his upkeep and guard his interests, but in the world that was born in the AMI war the most important currency was need itself. The AMIs had pledged themselves to common cause with humankind on exactly that basis. Whatever Adam needed, he could have—but that was exactly the situation that would lead a man like Adam Zimmerman to invert the question, and say to himself: "What does the infinitely generous world need from me? What can I give to a world that is prepared to give me everything?"

His answer was a straightforward response to circumstance, no less so for being unique.

His friends begged him to change his mind. His fellow time traveler Christine Caine pointed out that if he really wanted to preserve himself and to remain unchanged then he ought to have himself frozen down again, so that he could reinstitute himself as a myth. She told him that there would one day arrive an Omega Point in human affairs, a Climacteric in which every wish that had ever been entertained by a thinking being could be properly satisfied—and that when that moment came he could still be what he had always been, unchanged and unchangeable.

He told her that the desire for such a paradisal end, though understandable, seemed to him to be essentially cowardly, unworthy of an authentically *human* being, and that her own determination to make a life for herself in the new world was evidence enough of the falseness of her recommendation.

Madoc Tamlin suggested that Adam ought to heed his own advice about the hazards of fame, and ought not to make a final decision until he had contrived an obscurity for himself in which he would be free from the intense and constant scrutiny that plagued him. Using his own idiosyncratic terminology, Tamlin suggested that having made history, Adam ought now to concentrate on retreating into "lostory," cultivating a privacy that might enable him to live as a human being rather than a legend, an individual rather than a myth. Only then, Tamlin suggested, would he stand a chance of discovering the kind of tranquility that Internal Technology could not give him.

Adam's reply was that history, once made, could not forsake its makers, and that Tamlin himself was now so securely ensconced in the celebration of legend that he would never again know the luxury of pure frivolity. Even the manifestly ridiculous idea of lostory, Adam told his fellow refugee from the past, would henceforth be treated with insistent gravity and earnest pedantry.

This was one instance in which even I refused to play the objective observer and scrupulous historian. When I was first informed of his decision I told Adam Zimmerman, in no uncertain terms, that he ought not to remove himself from the world until he had seen and understood it—not merely every part of the solar system to which an AMI spacer could take him, but every part of the galaxy which remained as yet unexplored. I told him that he ought not to consent to his death until he could honestly say that his was informed consent, and that his consent could not possibly be considered well-informed until he had lived for at least a thousand years.

He thanked me for my ingenuity, but assured me that the problem was the other way about—that the person who was capable of making decisions *for Adam Zimmerman* was already under threat, losing the authority of properly informed consent with every hour and every day that passed.

"You are what you are, Morty," he told me, "And it is a wonderful thing to be. But it is not what I am. I would be delighted to think that it is something my son might become—and I trust that the world will choose to exercise my right of replacement eventually—but your own parents understood that the necessity of making room for future generations is a component of progress. I am delighted, too, that the horror which my kind had for their own mortality allowed them to make a world for their descendants which was liberated from that curse, as far as is humanly possible. But Adam Zimmerman is a mortal man, and was born to die. I would rather that Adam Zimmerman faced up to his commanding fears, in the end, than obliterate himself in their evasion. The only life story possible to a man of my kind is one that begins with birth and ends with death, no matter how the plot might be thickened and tormented in between. I am glad to have played a part in the triumph that has altered the world out of that recognition, but *my* story would be false if it ended otherwise. Let me go, Morty, I beg of you."

Everything that Adam had cynically said about fame in the distant, forgotten past proved to be all too obviously true in the munificent present that consumed him. The basis of his celebrity was his mortality; what fascinated the citizens of the newest New Era, above all else, was Adam Zimmerman's awful misfortune in being a man who one day must die . . . for them, as for him, there was only one end to his story that seemed appropriate.

So they did, indeed, *let him go*.

Like all the philosophers, lovers, artists, hobbyists, mystics, and martyrs of the Human Era, Adam Zimmerman reconciled himself in the end to the notion that angst was unconquerable. It could be repressed, ignored, sublimated, stared full in the face or frozen down for thousands of years, but it couldn't be beaten.

Adam certainly did not enjoy this discovery, but he was proud of himself for having made it. It seemed to him to reinstate and reinforce—as nothing else could have done—his old self-sufficiency and his old self-discipline. Alongside the realization that he did not really want any of the kinds of emortality that his hosts could procure for him came the realization that he was free at last to succumb to the flatteries and seductions of fame. He could give the innocents of the new Golden Age something that no one else could or would: a precious taste of human dereliction and death. He could make them appreciate the privileges they enjoyed a little more piquantly, by showing them what it was to be without such privileges.

Adam decided that he would no longer retreat from angst, but would revel in it instead, in order to show a world that was without angst the true meaning of mortal existence: the true significance of his own state of being.

"I am not just a man," Adam told his relentlessly inquisitive audience. "I am a symbol. You must learn to understand me, for I am not merely famous, I am fame itself."

They loved it.

They drooled over every aphorism he let fall, no matter how obvious or overwrought it might be.

Adam set out to make the twilight of his life into the ultimate dramatic performance. He was determined to show the undying what it meant to die with dignity. It was not enough to display the physical processes of decay which would claim him; it was necessary to show off the psychological warfare that had run parallel to physical decay in his own time.

It was a wonderful show.

That which had been trivial and commonplace in his own world, where millions of lives had been terminated by disease, violence, misfortune, or a few carelessly juggled figures on a balance sheet, was now not merely unique but tremendous.

In the years that followed his revival and the end of the AMI war, Adam's hair turned gradually grey. He let it grow long, and grew his beard as well. He asked his hosts to make him a guitar, and he began to play again, singing songs in German and English that he remembered from childhood and adolescence, and learning new ones that his faithful admirers found in ancient data banks. He even composed some songs of his own: sad songs about sex and death, war and poverty, pain and love.

He abandoned privacy, and gave himself entirely to his public. When he was not singing, he talked, frankly and with occasionally painful honesty, allowing all his thoughts to be recorded for infinite posterity as well as being eagerly lapped up by the everpresent listeners. He began to style himself Adam X, to signify the fact that he was the great unknown.

He planned his death meticulously, although the possibility of suicide was firmly ruled out. He must die, he decided, of what had passed in his own time for natural causes: of cancers that would burst spontaneously within his frail flesh; of the gradual erosion of his tissues by the forces of biochemical corrosion; of the failure of the coordinating systems that bound his disparate cells into a coherent whole.

He decided that he would use no anesthetics, suffering the pain which would come with these varied afflictions. This was not a decision taken out of courage—he assured his audience that he had always been a physical coward—but out of a sense of responsibility.

He knew that this was the only chance which the people of the thirty-third century would ever have to understand that kind of suffering, and he was determined not to cheat them. He felt that his pain, his tears, his shiverings, his sadnesses, his fears—*all* his stigmata—belonged to his audience rather than to him, because it was these which gave significance to his presence in their midst.

I believe that in planning all this, carefully preparing for it all, and going through it—not without difficulty, by any means—Adam X became by slow degrees a happy and contented man, at peace with himself and his angst. I believe, too, that he became a prouder man than he had ever been in the days when he took his gluttonous part in the rape of the world. He became a more joyful man than he had ever been, even at the heights of ecstasy which his relationships with Sylvia Ruskin and his many mistresses had allowed him temporarily to reach.

By making death into fulfillment, Adam robbed it of almost all the power it had once exercised over his imagination. He moved his angst from the side of moral debit to the side of moral credit in the account book of his psyche, and with that cunning move—so like in spirit to the legerdemain that had been his genius in days gone by—he turned a potential loss into a handsome profit.

Buoyed up by his pride and joy, he lasted far longer than anyone could have reasonably expected, comfortably exceeding a hundred years of subjectively experienced life even without the aid of IT.

I was there when he died, alongside his fellow time travelers. We wept for him, and for his world, but there was gratitude as well as grief in our tears.

Adam died on the day which would have been identified in his calendar as the twenty-fifth of July, 3299, at the age of one thousand three hundred and thirty-one. This was, of course, a record in a world from which death had been largely banished—but it was one that no one expected to last very long.

Adam died naked, as nature had made him—but he died in a comfortable bed, in sheets which felt to him like the most sensuous silk, and which reminded him pleasantly of riots of sexual excess enjoyed with his most voluptuous mistresses.

He had been working on his last words for many years, redrafting and polishing them endlessly, and he managed to deliver them all before losing his powers of speech.

"It is my earnest hope," he told his adoring admirers, "that by the example of my suffering and death I may redeem you all from the innocence which is your fortunate heritage. I have been, during these last thirty-six years, a stranger and afraid in a world I never made, but I have done my best to remake it, by remaking its understanding of its own origins. The emortality that you enjoy was born out of the efforts of men such as I, made desperate by their own mortality. We could not save ourselves, but we sowed the seeds of salvation for future mankind, paving the road to eternity with our good intentions.

"I have come out of the mists of time to bear a message, which is that our tragedy and your triumph are indivisibly one, and must be understood as opposite sides of the same coin. I cannot express, in the depleted language which every person on earth has relearned in order to listen to me, the delight I feel in knowing that humankind has finally attained its Age of Reason, but I know that you feel it too.

"Ave atque vale! Adieu! Good-bye!"

Those words will be long enough remembered and treasured by the inhabitants of Earth and the home system to grant Adam Zimmerman the kind of metaphorical immortality that he had once scorned. No one who heard or read them remained unmoved by them; no one who comes after us should ever dare to think them pompous or ill conceived.

We innocents of the Golden Age will continue to enjoy our Adam long after his death; the grandest and finest funeral in the history of the human race was only the first phase of our celebration.

We shall listen to his roughhewn songs and archaic speeches again and again, because those wonderful words are the one resource left to posthumankind by which we might savor, in sympathy, the bittersweetness of transience.